LOW SEASON

DENNIS DRAYTON

DALENII DIGITAL

First Printing Paperback Edition: 2022

ISBN: 978-1-915239-00-6

Cover design by 100Covers

Published by Dalenii Digital

CHAPTER 1

08-12-2003 09:55 Atlantic Standard Time (AST)

"Piper Navajo Two Seven Delta, you are cleared to land on runway eight." Ferris acknowledged the control tower and lined up for the approach. When you landed at San Juan International you gave it your full attention. Tower blocks stood close to the runways, and lagoons surrounded the airport. Landing a heavy jet would be dicey but in a Piper Navajo it was a walk in the park.

Ferris dropped the flaps and concentrated on putting the Navajo down as gently as a feather.

One of the passengers was Carla, the camera-person for the movie crew who had chartered the flight. She was tomboyish and had not responded to Ferris's charm. But she wore tight white shorts as if she meant it, so he hadn't given up hope entirely. Maybe she knew less about flying than he did about f-stops, or maybe the way to a woman's heart was through a perfect landing.

There was an unusual amount of activity on one of the aprons near the runway, several vehicles driving around a taxiing Curtiss Commando. As the Navajo sank towards the ground the airport buildings obscured that apron.

Fixated on a three-pointer, he didn't ask the tower to double check before he was handed over. "Navajo Two Seven Delta, switch to Three Four Eight Point Six for ground control instructions."

Out of the corner of his eye, Ferris caught a flash of movement.

"Two Seven to control – traffic on runway, traffic on runway!" The other plane was flying ten feet off the ground, undercarriage still extended, right across their path. Ferris jammed on the brakes, cut both engines and cut off the fuel, all in one fluid movement. The other plane hit the Navajo, and the impact flung Ferris sideways in his seat and slammed his head against the port side window.

A white flash blotted out his vision. After a second he realised he was still alive, and his hands blurred as he cut all the other switches. He undid the lap harness and turned to his passengers. The cabin seemed undamaged, and the passengers shaken but unhurt.

He forced himself to stand up in an unhurried manner. The dread of fire made his blood pound in his ears but he said in a calm voice, "Okay people, we have an emergency. Everybody out!"

As he edged his way between the seats the dazed camera crew unbuckled their seat belts with maddening slowness. Ferris flung his weight against the door. The Airstair door folded open without resistance, and his momentum nearly carried him out.

He grabbed at the rim of the doorway to steady himself, and yelled at the camera crew again. "Out! Get out! For Christ's sake, get out!"

He ducked out and looked up at his plane. The collision had ripped the top off the tail fin and spun the Navajo onto the grass. Everything to his left was clear. Several police vehicles approached along the grass, lights flashing and sirens blaring. But no sign of rapid intervention vehicles.

Still trying to be reasonable, he stabbed his finger at a point well away from the plane. "Run that way, hurry now. The plane could burn."

Three of the four came to life and scrambled out of the plane and ran off in the direction he pointed. Carla hung back uncertainly on the steps. "My cameras," she said desperately, looking to the nose. Ferris strode out to the nose and unlocked the baggage compartment. His hands shook, but he handed her the aluminium reinforced boxes without dropping any.

"Take the most important ones," he said. "There isn't time to get everything. Now get out of here!"

"Aren't you coming?" she asked.

Ferris looked across the nose at the other plane. He looked back at the girl.

"I have to see why nobody got off that plane," he said.

A barely recognisable Curtiss C-46 Commando lay on its back ninety yards away, its nose buried in the dirt of the airfield perimeter. The Curtiss had cart-wheeled after the collision. The left wing had dug in and torn away in the crash, lying just beyond the

Navajo.

There was no fire, yet.

A shrill whine overhead made him look up to see a 747 climbing away. The control tower was already re-routing the planes behind him.

He could smell a hint of avgas at this distance.

Ferris heard the blare of police sirens, but he ignored them.

He took a deep breath, and started towards the wreck.

The air wavered as the fuel evaporated from ruptured tanks as he approached the Curtiss. The tang of avgas strong enough to taste when he passed the shorn wing.

Up close, the surfaces of the Curtiss looked badly corroded. The Pratt & Whitney Double Wasp engines and the fuel tanks were known for bursting into flames even on well-maintained aircraft. Ferris felt his skin crawl to the tick of the cooling engine metal. But the chances of fire lessened with every second as the engines cooled. The killer-whale snout of the Curtiss had ploughed up the grass at the edge of the field, crumpling the upside-down cockpit. Steeling himself for the inevitable, Ferris knelt and looked into the cockpit. Prepared though he was, his guts lurched at the sight of what had been the torsos of two human beings before the crash. He wanted to run, but still he made sure. He walked back along the twisted fuselage and looked in the windows of the passenger compartment, but there was no-one else aboard. All that he could see was an untidy bundle of plastic packages scattered along the upturned ceiling.

The howl of sirens behind him rose to a crescendo, and Ferris turned around to see the yellow rapid intervention trucks bowling down the runway. He walked back towards the Navajo.

Closer to, the field was teeming with police cars and officers wearing DEA and *Policia* flak vests, who were handcuffing his passengers. An unmarked Crown Victoria pulled up about ten yards from him, beacon flashing. The doors slammed open, and two stocky Latinos in dark blue DEA flak vests pointed assault rifles at him.

"*Manos atras,*" The two men shouted at him simultaneously. "*Abaco!* Hands behind your head, asshole! You deaf?"

Ferris held his hands up and tried to drag his mind back from the grisly sight of the two men in the wrecked Curtiss. "I'm the pilot of the Piper –" he began to say.

"*Abaco. Abaco.* Get on the ground!"

One of the cops stepped in so close Ferris could have caught the barrel of the rifle. "How many times you need to be told?"

"There are people on the other plane and I wanted to see if I could help –"

"Shut up! Lie on your face and lace your hands behind your neck." Ferris started to kneel, but the cop moved behind him and kicked the back of his knee and he went down with a grunt, cut off when his mouth hit the turf.

He twisted his head to spit dried grass and dirt and a foot landed between his shoulder blades and the cop wrenched back his arms painfully and snapped on handcuffs. Then they patted him down, went through his pockets and took his wallet.

"Hey you men, cool it," a voice said from above. "That's not one of our guys. Let him up." Arms under his elbows jerked Ferris to his feet.

The newcomer was a blond guy about thirty with a pink complexion. He was wearing a DEA jacket, but the holstered pistol said desk jockey.

"Who are you sir?"

"Tony Ferris. I'm the pilot of the Piper Navajo."

"Does he have ID on him?"

One of the other agents looked sullen and handed over Ferris's wallet.

The blond man flicked through the wallet. "Thank you. Mr Ferris, I apologise but you shouldn't have gone to the other plane, this is a charged and dangerous situation and my men can't take any chances."

He turned back to the two men. "Give me the keys to the cuffs and go check the plane. What did you see?" He asked Ferris.

"Two dead men in the cockpit," Ferris said. He looked nastily at the other two. "And there's a lot of fuel vapour so I wouldn't go shooting guns over there if I was you."

The two men scowled at him but went towards the Curtiss with their rifles lowered.

The emergency vehicles had stopped fifty yards away, waiting for the police to finish.

"I'm Assistant Special Agent in Charge Matthew Perez," the blond man said as he unlocked the handcuffs. "You're free to go, Mr Ferris. I expect the FAA will want to interview you but that's not a law-enforcement matter."

Ferris rubbed his wrists where the handcuffs had already cut welts into his skin.

The two agents finished making a circuit of the plane and nodded to Perez who in turn waved the fire-fighters forward.

Ferris tried to ignore the curious glances of the fire-fighters as they went past. He felt a little better as the immediate image of the dead men faded. An ambulance drew up nearby, a safe distance from the crash. Ferris wanted to get as far away from the crash as possible. Then the reaction hit him, and he started to shake violently, and before he could control himself he bent double and vomited. Seeing his condition, the ambulance crew came forward and helped him into the back of their vehicle.

Accident report facsimile page (redacted)

NATIONAL TRANSPORTATION SAFETY BOARD

WASHINGTON, D.C. 20594

AIRCRAFT ACCIDENT REPORT

RUNWAY COLLISION

CURTISS C-46 COMMANDO

AND HARVEY AIR PIPER NAVAJO

LUIS MUNOZ INTERNATIONAL AIRPORT

SAN JUAN, PUERTO RICO

AUGUST 12, 2003

PRELIMINARY REPORT

On August 12, 2003, at 1001 Atlantic Standard Time, Curtiss C-46 Commando N██████ collided with a Harvey Air Piper Navajo PA-31, N██████, flight 3428 at Luis Munoz International Airport, San Juan, Puerto Rico. Flight 3428 was completing its landing roll on runway 1, and the Curtiss was on its takeoff roll on the same runway. The collision occurred at the southern end of the runway. The two occupants of the Curtiss C-46 Commando were killed, and there were no injuries on Flight 3428. Flight 3428 was a chartered passenger flight operating under 14 Code of Federal Regulations Part 135. The flight was operated by Harvey Air Transport Inc. The Curtiss was operating under 14 Code of Federal Regulations Part 91.

The National Transportation Safety Board determines that the probable cause of this accident was the failure of the pilots of the Curtiss to effectively monitor the common traffic advisory frequency or to properly scan for traffic, resulting in their commencing an unauthorised takeoff roll when the Piper Navajo PA-31 (Harvey Air flight 3428) was landing on the same runway.

CHAPTER 2

09-02-2003 14:14 AST

"Transport safety my ass," Frank Harvey said, turning abruptly to Ferris. "Time for accident investigation guys to take a reality check. What the heck does 'failure to effectively monitor ground traffic advisory' mean? Those guys were on the run from the Feds for Chistsakes!"

They walked out of the building that housed the FAA offices, and the heat of the day hit them. The sweat started out in droplets on Harvey's face and Ferris felt his own shirt crumple in the humidity.

Sometimes Harvey really got on his nerves, and now, straight after the NTSB investigation meeting, was one of those times.

"You're taking it very calmly," Ferris said. "They almost made it sound like it was our fault. We've got reputations to uphold and a business to keep going."

"Take it easy Tony," Harvey said. "It was only a statement of fact report. I'm sure the final will be much clearer. Besides, there's no such thing as bad publicity."

Ferris barked a laugh. "Sometime next year maybe, but everyone will see the bloody preliminary with our company name on it. They even post the damn things on the internet."

Harvey shook his head. "Forget it kid, by the time tourist season comes around again it will have blown over. Nobody ever pays any attention. It's just regulators going through the motions. They don't mean it the way it sounds. It's not personal. At least they didn't say it was pilot error."

"That's no consolation to me," Ferris said. Nobody loved the NTSB findings, but this time they were particularly insensitive and off the point.

"I know," Harvey shook his head again. "And the fact remains that those cheap dope peddling punks smashed up two perfectly good aircraft. And screwed up part of our operation."

Harvey looked around, seeming to notice the humidity for the first time.

"Well, here we are," he said. "Plaza las Americas, for all your consumer needs and damn if the Postal Service ain't next door. If you want to catch up on your shoe shopping, this is the place. And the ball-park is down a block."

"I know Frank. And the National Guard armoury is a short walk away if I want to pick up any ordnance." Ferris wished Harvey would get to the point, if there was one. It was nearly three weeks since the crash and he hadn't flown. He could do his math as well as anyone else.

"Should have taken a taxi," Harvey said, looking around vaguely. "Damned if I'll find the car in this place."

He strode off to the entrance of the multi-storey car park, a furrowed look on his brow. Maybe he wasn't really a multi-tasking sort of guy. Ferris followed him doggedly.

"How is the Navajo?" said Ferris, he had to lengthen his stride to keep up.

"The Piper people say maybe three weeks to get to it on their service backlog, they expect the air-frame is bent out of shape so they are thinking of taking it apart spar by spar. Probably build a new one faster if they still made them, but at least they won't charge as much. I hope. Maybe it's a cunning plan to force me to buy a new Cheyenne. As if I had two million dollars lying around. Insurance will want to write it off instead. And leasing a replacement aircraft this late in the season is next to impossible. So, lucky you, you're the standby reserve for the foreseeable ..."

"I could spell Nilsson," Ferris said. Nilsson flew the company flag-ship, a Beech King Air 200.

Harvey shook his head. "You fighter jocks. Always competing. Nilsson is fine."

"Nilsson is getting old, near enough to retirement – if he had been flying the Navajo –" Even as he said this, Ferris saw a change in Harvey's expression and realised he'd said too much. Harvey kept his rating up to date for the King Air, although nobody could see why, as he never seemed to fly it. And he was older than Nilsson.

"Probably the same thing would have happened. You can't plan for these things Tony. Anyhow, let's face it, this is a shoe-string operation. This isn't Southwest. You see any chicks in hot-pants posing around my office? I don't get enough business to double up on pilots. So, I'm a plane short, one third pay is all I can offer you. You should welcome the chance for the break, relax on the beach, get some sun, have a medical check-up, maybe see a counsellor. That was real life out there, not some video game from Iraq where all you had to worry about was vaporising the odd mechanic when you fragged an airfield."

"I don't need a shrink," Ferris said angrily. "And when did you last see a crash?" Harvey shrugged his shoulders. "I saw a few in Vietnam," he said.

"That was thirty years ago, Frank. And this wasn't war, it was an accident."

"I've seen the plane," Harvey said. "And I've seen you. You were pretty badly shook up."

"Yes, what with the DEA making me eat runway," Ferris said. "But I'm alright now."

"Sure you are, Tony," said Harvey. "But, I think you need a rest."

"Like hell I do!" Ferris flared up. They were in the concrete parking bays now, and his voice echoed and several people looked around and Ferris realised he was shouting.

"Don't worry about it, Tony," Harvey said quietly. "You go see a doctor about a rest. Even if it wasn't for this, you deserve one anyway. You flew the ass off that Navajo this season."

He took Ferris by the arm and led him out into the deeper gloom. "Down one more level, I think. Also, I wanted to tell you about shifting operations to St Thomas."

Despite himself, and knowing that Harvey was changing the subject having won his point, Ferris responded. "What's wrong with St. Marc?"

"Nothing. But at St. Thomas we could keep an eye on the competition, and get better facilities."

"San Juan International has even better facilities," Ferris said sarcastically. "You'd be willing to give up all those nice concessions you wrung out of the Tourism Ministry in St. Marc?" Harvey let go his arm. "We might have a bit of trouble there. Shark Teeth insisted on a thirty percent cut. Now the new government are going over the books looking to make cuts and decided my public service contract is void and it seems the new government ethics commission has launched an investigation."

"Aw Jesus, Frank!"

"Tony, please. You're old enough to know how it works. I didn't go in there pushing money down their briefs like a divorcee at a go-go club. The goddamn minister asked me for the money, and said he'd look after me. I shouldn't have trusted the oily little turd. Anyway, damage done. And the new party, they are into law and order, the last lot were all about getting things done no questions asked with a lot of bribes along the way. Just as well they don't have an extradition treaty with anywhere I might be making an unscheduled stop-over."

"I live in St. Marc, Frank. What am I supposed to do, commute to St Thomas?" Harvey shrugged again. "We could work something out. I'm scaling back before anything happens. Service once every fortnight, the round-tripper will stop over on request. You're welcome to call on it anytime you like." Harvey rattled his keys. "Ah, here she is."

"Could be awkward to make that work – you will be on one island and we'll be on the other ... "

Harvey's voice got muffled as he got in the car. Ferris opened the passenger door just enough to put his head in the gap.

"I'm not going, Frank."

"Huh?" Harvey was trying to fit the key in the ignition and it didn't quite sink in as he fumbled. "Why not?"

"I'm not leaving St. Marc because you tried to bribe a minister –"

"Succeeded in bribing, boy."

"Whatever. Even if you pull out, I'm staying on, even if I have to use my own plane" Harvey laughed aloud. "That old birdcage!"

"She has a long life left in her." His Piper Super Cub was 30 years old and had been re-covered with red and yellow dacron. It had passed a recent airworthiness check despite several heavy-handed owners.

"How will you get charters without a broker?" Harvey challenged.

Ferris hadn't thought of that, but he shrugged. "I'll get by."

"Hmm. I doubt it. Need a ride to the hotel?"

"No thanks," Ferris said, "I have a date with the DEA deputy head." Harvey sighed and shook his head theatrically. "Holy shit Tony, two rutting sessions with the Feds in the one morning. You must be nuts. Look, these guys are politicians. Never go up against city hall. You want me to go with you?"

"Why? You think they will kick the shit out of me a second time in broad daylight? Don't worry Frank, I'm meeting the guy at police headquarters."

"Still taking on all comers eh, Tony? Comes a time, no matter how much of a hot-head you are, you learn to pick your battles. I was over fifty but everyone has to slow down eventually. Drop you off?"

"No thanks, I can walk." Ferris slammed the door and strode away. He heard the window wind down behind him. "What about the medical check, Tony?"

"Oh, get stuffed Frank," Ferris said, without looking back.

The DEA office was in a business park a mere four miles from the FBI regional office. Ferris wondered if it was federal allocation or if the different *Federales* got on so well they lived apart.

ASAC Matthew Perez looked more natural with no holster strapped on. He was the same blond, pink-complexioned guy from the crash, but he looked older and more assured in his air-conditioned open-plan office surrounded by the clatter of keyboards. Ferris still thought his subordinates could eat him for breakfast.

"I'd urge you to re-consider your complaint, Mr Ferris," Perez said. "These are good men. It takes a special sort of person to go out every day knowing you could get shot in the face by drug-crazed maniacs. A bit hasty maybe, but in a pressure situation, people do things by instinct and adrenalin."

"I don't buy it, I was a fighter pilot," Ferris said, sitting ramrod straight in his chair. "I know all about pressure situations. Are you saying your guys aren't trained properly and I should cut them some slack for being bad-ass?"

Perez blinked. "They made a mistake. We all make mistakes." His expression was so sincere, for a moment Ferris almost believed him. "Fine," he said, sitting back. "If that's the way it is, you would have had time to ask them to think it over and come apologise for the misunderstanding." Perez said nothing.

"No? I didn't think so. I might let it go if I thought it was a one-off but I don't think it was. I think your guys are like this all the time. I think they're out of control. I have heard the stories. I want to continue with the complaints procedure."

Perez sighed. "Well if that's what you want, it's your privilege."

"It's my duty," Ferris said. "But it is also my privilege to stand up for the little guy maybe just this once. Because I imagine there are a lot of ordinary people that these guys have pushed around who can't stand up for themselves. The strong have a duty to defend the weak. I'm sure you've heard that one."

CHAPTER 3

Ferris took a bus to the Sheraton. Without an income, he could no longer afford taxis on a whim.

Chad Schroeder was in the lobby talking on a cell phone. He waved to Ferris and said into the phone, "I'll call you back."

He folded the phone and smiled at Ferris. "Hi Tony, Vic is just finishing up. He said if you came in after 2 p.m. would you like to join him in the conference suites?"

Ferris nodded. Bad news travelled fast. He wended his way through the hotel to the conference suites and held the door for a couple of hotel staff carrying audio-visual equipment. Vic Schroeder was sitting at the end of a conference table fussing with a briefcase. He had the tanned and healthy look of a retired gym instructor or multi-millionaire and looked about fifty although Ferris guessed he was over sixty.

Schroeder looked up and smiled. "Hiya kid," he said. "Tough hearing?" Ferris grinned back. Here was the older brother he never had.

"Much as could be expected," he said. "It was Frank afterwards that ticked me off. He told me to take an unpaid break for the good of my nerves."

"Uh-oh," Schroeder said. He looked slightly uncomfortable. "And?"

"And I may have told him to take a hike."

"Well, it's been coming a long time, hasn't it. If the cell-phone contract comes through I'll be in the air-freight business myself. You have a couple of hundred hours on Beech 18s, right? I'm trying to lease one."

"Thanks Vic, but I was thinking of going out on my own." Schroeder looked dubious. "Have you thought that through? I know they're laid-back on St. Marc, but you will find you can't just wish yourself into business." Ferris felt a twinge of irritation but kept his voice level. "It was on the spur of the moment. But I think it's been on my mind for some time. It didn't come out of nowhere."

"Think about it. It takes time and money to set up a business, why not do a few jobs to get you up and running, ease into it."

"Frank said I won't be able to find a broker."

"There are ways around that," Schroeder said, and slapped him on the shoulder. "Cheer up Tony. Let me talk to some people."

"So in the meantime let me show you my amazing plan." Schroeder turned until he was facing a diorama taking up most of the conference table. Ferris recognised the layout of the harbour from the aerial view he had seen so many times. It was a model of the area of St. Marc around the town.

"Tony, do you remember the whole idea of the hydrofoil that the last government had?"

"Oh yes. De Hydro-folly, they call it."

"Yeah, that's the one." Schroeder smiled. "Somebody told the tourism minister about the hydrofoil from Kowloon and Macau. The idea was sound, the only trouble is, the glamour is there because the high-rollers use the hydrofoil to get to the casinos in Macau. You can rent a VIP cabin for a hundred dollars, eight people, much cheaper than a plane or a helicopter for a serious gambler on a budget. But ... "

"But it wouldn't work here," Ferris said.

"It wouldn't work here," Schroeder agreed, "because we don't have a casino. So ... " He grinned and gestured at the diorama. "Why not build our own casino?"

"Two words," Ferris said. "Cuba and Bahamas."

Schroeder grinned. "Give that man a cigar. Ask anyone, they'll say the competition is already in Florida, the Bahamas and Cuba. I think some of the competition is with Las Vegas, if you add it all up. So this is what my meeting was all about."

Schroeder paused and registered mild regret. "You just missed Arnaud and the people from Spearpoint Inc. I think I told you about him before, I met him at the melon growers conference in Tampa."

Ferris hid a smile. Schroeder's obsession with melon growing was a standing joke.

"He's a really amazing guy. Ex-French Army, Foreign Legion, I think. You know I'm developing a country club and extending it into luxury homes, and he's got an idea to set up a bodyguarding and security training school business on St. Marc, it's all part of building up the infrastructure to attract the big money, so I'm going to put him together with the St. Marc government."

Schroeder picked a laser pointer off the table and played the red dot over a part of the diorama with an unfamiliar kidney-shaped green area near the town.

"So here is phase one of the plan – the St. Marc Golf and Country Club. Full eighteen hole course, to be designed by the cheapest retired big name we can afford."

"So that's what the construction work is all about."

"Yeah. So, whaddya think?"

Ferris liked St. Marc as an unspoiled island and not as a 'destination'.

"Jeez Vic," he said lightly. "You won't get that model to fit inside your chopper." Schroeder pretended to cuff him on the ear. "Smart ass. I came on the Turbo-Goose. Besides, I got real architects to do this. It comes apart in sections. We can stow it on the plane no problem, show it off to the bigwigs in the new government."

"You got a pilot?" Ferris asked. The Turbo-Goose was a modernised nineteen-forties amphibious sea-plane and finding a qualified pilot was one of Schroeder's preoccupations.

"Yeah," Schroeder beamed. "I lucked out, Arnaud came across an amphibian pilot called Luis Garcia who just happened to be looking for a new gig. Cocky kid. I thought at first maybe too cocky. Had an expert sit in with him and he knows how to not let the Goose get away from him, which is good."

Ferris grinned. The Goose had a reputation of being tricky to fly.

"Anyway, he should be here any minute," Schroeder added. "Might as well introduce you." A tall guy with a Latin look swaggered in. He wore a leather jacket and jeans and cowboy boots and he had a shock of bleached hair.

"Luis, this is Tony Ferris, also a pilot. Tony – Luis Garcia."

"Pleased to meetcha Mr Ferris," Garcia said. He had a wide grin and firm handshake.

"You guys should get together for drinks at some stage," Schroeder said. "Right now, I want to get this stuff back onto the plane. See you later, Tony. Unless you want a ride back to St. Marc?"

"No thanks Vic, I need to unwind a bit first. No disrespect, but being a passenger on a flying boat isn't a relaxing way to start my break."

Ferris was still mad at Harvey. He resisted the temptation to go back to the airport and have words, instead he headed to the hotel bar.

On the way he checked his wallet. He had an American Express card and he never left home without it. But he was a cash guy and it was strictly for emergencies.

He had one hundred and fifty US dollars and about two hundred East Caribbean Dollars. It was enough to kick his heels up a little before figuring out how to get back to St. Marc.

It was too early for an indoor crowd, so he walked out to the beach-front bar. He enjoyed a margarita or four and the company of a well preserved if slightly stringy woman from Armonk, New York, who liked his jokes and wanted to show him the view from her room in the Marriott. By the time Ferris had admired the view the evening was wearing on and he felt mellow enough to face the future back in his own hotel.

When he got back, reception asked him to ring Chris Turner in St. Marc, reverse charges, or put it on Schroeder's bill. Chris was an old crop-duster who serviced a lot of the islands. Intrigued, Ferris made the call. St. Marc was behind the times so he had to ring the international telephone exchange who made the call, and eventually told him yes, the reverse charge call was being accepted by the callee.

"I have an Ag-Cat that needs collecting," said Chris. He sounded even more hoarse on the phone than in real life. "I got my leg smashed so I can't fly."

"Good God, what happened?" Ferris asked. "Did you crash?" Chris wheezed a chuckle. "No, a kid on a motor scooter knocked me down on market day. All those years in a crop duster without a scratch and then I step into the street without looking and I get my old bones broken. Anyhow, I'm stranded here and Schroeder tells me you're stranded there. Can I interest you in a working passage?" Ferris laughed in turn. "You mean like washing the dishes on a tramp steamer?"

"Exactly. I can only pay you a pittance, but if you can keep from bending the 'Cat into the ground, we have a deal."

CHAPTER 4

Ferris had a slight nagging pain over one eye when he went to the airport the following morning. After Chris's offer he celebrated with 'just a couple' of Bourbons in the hotel bar. Apart from the phrase "traffic on runway" repeating in his dreams he had a good night's rest.

As he walked across to Apron 5A, he couldn't stop himself looking towards the scene of the crash. He still did that every time, despite knowing that the police forensics people and crash investigators had done their thing in less than twelve hours. The wreckage had been cleared away, and runway 8 re-opened as if the crash had never happened.

He saw a boy called Paco peering into the canopy of a parked Cessna 172. Ferris walked over quietly and yanked the boy off the plane and held him aloft by the belt. It was easy, because Paco was a slight twelve-year-old.

"Paco," Ferris said sternly, taking Paco's right ear in his free hand, and twisting it painfully. Paco rolled his eyes and screwed up his face.

"*Si, Señor* Tony?" he said resignedly.

"You've been told about this, Paco," Ferris said sharply. I know you're into planes, but somehow I get the idea that you'd like to joy-ride one of these. Wait till you're older Paco, and stay away from the planes."

"But I have watched the planes so much señor Tony," Paco said excitedly. "I know all about them. It would be so easy –"

"Thirty hours instruction," Ferris cut across the rush of words. "When you're sixteen or seventeen, Paco. Come back then. Now get off the field and watch from the road."

Ferris released his grip on ear and belt, and the boy twisted lithely to land on his feet.

As he straightened, Ferris kicked him lightly in the seat to start him on his way. "Go!" he said with feigned anger. "*!Largo.*"

The boy darted off with an impish grin. Ferris shook his head ruefully. Paco was very like he had been twenty years before, a plane-mad nuisance pestering the local flying club. With the distinction that Paco had an unhealthy habit of trespassing in the light aircraft parks and tampering with the planes.

One of the airport policemen snatched ineffectually at Paco as he twisted past, and growled after him. He shoved his cap back and grinned sheepishly at Ferris.

"Falling down on the job again, Hector," Ferris said. "That kid could get a prop through the back of the head some day, and we'll all be very sad."

"Hell, I know that, Tony." Officer Hector DeJesus looked more like a country policeman from when Ferris was young than from a tough big city department. "Some containment operation if we can't keep kids out, never mind terrorists, but I'd need to be in four places at once to keep up with that little *delincuente*. His friends are hassling some plane-spotters at the perimeter and I was out there with my partner backing up the security guys and I started to suspect it was just a diversion so I came in here on the off-chance. It's just as well he don't break or lift anything or I'd be looking for another job. Anyway, speaking of security, how come you're here, with no plane and all?" He said this a little cautiously, looking Ferris over, taking in his security badge and airline bag.

"Chris Turner wants me to fly his Ag-Cat out to St. Marc for him. They told me it's parked over here."

"Oh yeah," the cop said, relaxing visibly. "The yellow bi-plane, right? Have a good flight."

"Thanks, Hector." Ferris went past the row of parked aircraft, marvelling as always at the number of older planes that he saw in the Caribbean. And yet the old Grumman Ag-Cat, a stubby tall biplane, stood out like an ugly duckling.

As he walked around the Grumman making the preflight safety checks, he wondered if he had been wise to put himself forward. When he first met Chris, talk had inevitably turned to flying.

"Surprised you haven't done crop dusting, but for an Ag-Cat you need hours on a biplane. You're a jet guy right?"

"I did my elementary training in a Tiger Moth."

"No kidding?" Chris's voice had risen in pitch to low baritone. "Surely it should have at least been a Chipmunk?"

"Our flying club was a bit old school."

"I'll say."

"I still have the log books on the yacht."

"I'll take your word for it. Hot damn, a Tiger Moth. You really are one of the old-timers," Chris said approvingly.

Nonetheless, Ferris had been needled enough to come back the next night with his log books, kept lovingly in biscuit tins on the boat.

Chris had peered at them in silence for a moment, then said, "One hundred hours on a Tiger Moth. Jeez you still keep your school lunch money too? Damn Tony, you look too young to be a biplane guy – keep using the Oil of Ulay!"

After that, Chris had challenged Ferris to fly an Ag-Cat, and allowed him to do a few circuits of the airfield, since they stood idle except early in the morning. Now, that half-joking instruction was paying off.

The cockpit of the Ag-Cat was encased in a frame of steel tubing so strong that the pilot could survive a crash that destroyed the rest of the aircraft. If he did crack up, Chris would have a canary and the NTSB would just love seeing him again so soon.

But a plane was a plane. Monoplane, biplane, jet, turbo-prop, piston-powered, you learned their quirks and if you were even half a pilot, away you went. And the Ag-Cat was a viceless aircraft, with a much better safety record than his beloved Super Cub.

His hands squeaked as he climbed into the cockpit, leaving greasy wet trails on the coaming. He wiped them away impatiently, and noticed a slight tremor in his hand.

He stowed the airline bag among the rollbars behind his seat and strapped himself in, checked the instruments, set the flaps and trim tabs, switched on the fuel, ran up the engine and asked the control for permission to take off. He received permission, and taxied out, praying that he hadn't confused the trim procedures.

He took her off gently, the flight to St. Marc was one hundred and eighty miles which was on the edge of the range of the Ag-Cat.

Because she was a biplane and lightly loaded, the Ag-Cat soared away from the runway after an incredibly short run. The thrill of the short take-off took Ferris back to the heady days when he had flown solo in a Tiger Moth.

He opened the canopy and let the wind stream past his face, ruffling his hair. He was flying again, and in a plane older than he was. At that thought, laughter bubbled out of him in the joy of the moment.

CHAPTER 5

Ferris stopped the Ag-Cat with a flourish outside the clubhouse of St. Marc Aero Club, blipping the engine showily.

The government wanted to rename the airfield to St. Marc International Airport. It had been built in World War Two as an emergency landing strip for USAAF planes on anti-submarine patrols. Nothing much had happened in the next sixty years.

The hangar had long since succumbed to the hurricanes and scavengers.

Grass and weeds grew out of the cracks in the runway and trees had encroached on both ends of the once five thousand foot runway. But there was still enough strip maintained for clearance of three thousand feet for the Beech King Air. Part of the old pilot's quarters survived as the clubhouse and an adjacent concrete blockhouse was now the customs shed. Ferris wondered if Walter Brunkard was around. Probably not, it was too early for him. Brunkard was the customs official, airfield and club-house manager and sometimes fuel pump attendant. The authorities didn't seem to worry about a conflict of interest.

As soon as the propeller stuttered to a stop, an old dog limped onto the paving, its tongue hanging out. It answered to Tuffy and was mangy and spent more time on the strip than anyone else.

It was good to be back.

Apart from that, the field was deserted, except for one man sprawled on a chair on the veranda of the club-house, puffing a cigar to judge by the cloud of smoke hanging in the air.

"Afternoon, Tony," Chris said from behind a cloud of cigar smoke. "Gotta hand it to you boy, Icarus reborn."

"Afternoon, Chris," Ferris answered. "Sorry to hear about your accident."

"Thanks." He tapped his stick on his outstretched leg with a hollow thump of plaster. "It seems I don't do hard landings without roll bars. Bones ain't as tough as they used to be." Ferris stepped up on the veranda and sat opposite Chris.

Chris was wearing a panama stetson. A scar ran up his right cheek bone and he wore a patch over his right eye socket. He looked like a cross between a pirate and an outlaw country singer. He was a legend in his own small way, and tall tales abounded. He had cheated death so often some people even joked about "Chris is my co-pilot". He had wizened, sunken cheeks, and looked about sixty. But it was hard to tell his true age, it might have been the effects of hard living or illness.

One story was that he had flown for Air America, and he had three ex-wives and seven children and did a lot of smuggling in the off-season.

Chris gave a wheezy, dry cough.

"Should you be smoking that?" Ferris asked.

"Dunno. Maybe. These are organic, you know? Counteracts the pesticides." He had one and a half lungs due to flying a crop-dusting plane without the proper safety precautions.

Chris swirled his glass of whiskey.

"Help yourself," he said, following Ferris's gaze. "Rufus the barman is cooling off down at police headquarters. Got too high on his own supply."

"We all drink too much," Ferris said. He went inside to the bar. He kept away from the spirits, and searched behind the counter for a bottle of Corona. After all, flying was over for the day, and it was bloody hot and thirsty weather.

Chris raised his voice and said, "I got a pretty garbled story from Schroeder about your outfit pulling out. Is that why you're up for flying ferry?"

Ferris put some ice in his drink as he chose his words. "Frank can be a bit of an ass. I needed breathing space to think things out, and he didn't give it to me so I decided to go out on my own."

"In your little red and yellow plane?"

"Yes. Why not?" Ferris looked up, beer poised under a bottle opener.

Chris toasted him, his single eye crinkling up. "Why not indeed, my friend. If you were thinking of taking up spraying, you should have got a crop duster model in the first place – with an air-tight cabin of course. The sprays kill more than the bugs, as I can attest. Or you could come in with me, for next season."

"I don't know," Ferris answered. "Maybe. I really enjoyed the flight across." Chris grimaced. "It's different flying a full hopper at tree top. I'm always open to taking new people on, but I wouldn't advise it. Not a fun job, my friend. So are you thinking of flying passengers?" Ferris sat down again opposite Chris. "That's the plan," he said. "Nothing illegal or chancy."

"I don't want to be discouraging," Chris said, "there's a lot of bureaucracy and the flying game isn't what it used to be. The high point for pilots was the late eighties. Then we got bigger, safer, cheaper airplanes. Anyway less planes, less pilots."

Ferris grimaced. "Now you sound like Frank."

"And he's a schmuck, but he's got a head for business and he's got a point. Doing more with less is our business now. And all the more so since 9/11."

"I'm listening," Ferris said.

"Take your Super Cub – it's a fun plane, but it's a pilot's plane. Not a passenger aircraft, no comfort. In Alaska or some place with no other planes for a thousand miles, sure. But here, you got competition. Better to lease something a bit more modern, Tony."

"What would you suggest?"

"A Bonanza maybe. I'm a bit out of the business, ask Matt Hollis. So there's irony for you, getting back at Frank by going to his competitor for advice. And Hollis is a shrewd business man too, wouldn't send you wrong."

Ferris opened his airline bag and took out a plain deal box.

Chris sighed. "Let me guess. Cigars. For Rolle?"

"Yeah, and a couple for Wally." Rolle always insisted on giving Wally Brunkard a couple of cigars to look the other way.

Chris shook his head. "Need to stay away from that kind of stuff man, it's a slippery slope."

"It's only ever small stuff like cigars." Ferris protested and pointed at Chris's own cigar.

"Yeah. Might be for him. But that's the way it starts. A bit of fun, bucking the system. The lack of big stuff smuggling on the island is because it's out of the way and a bit of a backwater, if it was somewhere like Bimini, you'd have tattooed crazy-men offering you a small fortune for a no-questions-asked night flight."

"I hadn't thought of it that way," Ferris admitted.

Chris snorted. "And are you going to put the box in the customs shed?" Ferris smiled. The Customs shed was a solidly built blockhouse, with an impressive customs seal padlock on the door, but a fault in the mechanism meant that the lock clicked open if you put pressure on the shackle at just the right place. Everyone knew, except Wally Brunkard.

"Well, whatever you do, Remember it pays to be a good dog. If you crap in your own house, the master will rub your nose in it. Between you, me and the wall, some of us have been known to run guns in our day and not even on principle, but times change. It's a smaller more vengeful world.

"Take it from an ignorant old man, I left school at sixteen having learnt nothing much and the only reasons I'm still around are advances in radical thoracic surgery and having the cunning of a hyena."

"Still, I suppose you need to do something. I know they're not big on regulations here but it's a good idea to have actual work to go with your work permit. With all the moaning about Haitian illegals they might decide to make an example out of somebody."

Ferris felt a slight jolt in his guts, it hadn't occurred to him that his work permit was in jeopardy.

CHAPTER 6

Two beers later, a very rusty Ford Sunliner convertible wheezed up the driveway to the clubhouse as they talked.

Wally Brunkard got out of the convertible.

He was known to all as Cousin Wally because he had blood ties to nearly everyone in the island and less kindly as Brunkard the Drunkard or just The Brunkard.

He dressed in a very crumpled, almost official linen suit. He was a roly-poly ball of a man with a bronze complexion and a sheen of sweat. He pulled a handkerchief from his pocket and mopped his face.

"Well speak of the devil," Chris said. "Your ears must be burning, Mr Wally."

"Afternoon gents," Brunkard said. "I do declare, it's a sad island for repairs. I'm some kind of kin to Bob Rolle and yet I can't get him to fix the aircon in this damn car."

Brunkard plumped himself down at the next table and from his jacket fished out a tiny electric portable fan and set it on the table. He turned it on and it whizzed like a tiny electric shaver. Brunkard watched it hopefully for a few moments and when it made no difference to the heat he mopped his neck again.

"Rufus won't be with us today, he got hisself in a brawl with the poe-leece and get his self chucked in chokey. People were saying he had too much of them Guinness Black Russians." He cleared his throat and continued in a slightly shamefaced and confidential tone. "And some of them were saying also that Aziz maybe provoked poor Rufus a little to lose his temper."

Sergeant Aziz was the scourge of the island, a police officer of Lebanese extraction, a stickler for the letter of the law. "All attitude and no latitude," the people said.

Brunkard's eyes lit up when he saw the plain box on the table. "Ah, Mr Tony. You brought some smokes."

Ferris slid the box across the table and Brunkard picked it up and opened the lid. He inhaled reverently over the box, selected a cigar and sniffed it and held it up to his ear and crinkled it, and picked out four more and put them in his pocket with a mournful sigh. By Ferris's reckoning that left about a hundred. "I am grateful Mr Tony, surely I am, but there are new regulations coming at the start of next month. An anti-corruption drive by the new government. Increased duties and audits of all ports of entry. It seems I ain't allowed to look the other way no more. Man, I'm going to miss these smokes. Couldn't afford the duty."

"I don't think Rolle could afford the duty either," said Chris unsympathetically.

"Ah Mr Chris, you're a hard man." Brunkard turned off the fan and mopped himself again.

Chris winked his one eye. "Not really, Mr Wally. Just pointing out the downside of all this new government honesty."

"I don't see why Rolle will be so upset," Ferris said.

Chris snorted.

Brunkard said, "Well that's why I want to tell you Mr Tony, I reckon Rolle might take the news better from you."

"Sure Mr Wally, I'll tell him the bad news," Ferris said. "but I don't see why you can't tell Rolle yourself."

Brunkard wriggled in his seat and his eyes shifted. "Well Mr Tony, you haven't been here that long and maybe you haven't seen it, but I'm sure you heard the stories about Bob Rolle. He got a bad temper you know – much worse than Rufus. Rufus is a hot-tempered man when he's drunk – but Rolle, he a cold man, that can turn hot like 'snap your fingers'."

"I haven't seen any sign of that," Ferris said sceptically.

"You know how Rolle, he set himself up as Angelique Gaillard's protector? One night two years ago, when she had recently caught his eye, two cane-cutters from one of the plantations came into town and got drunk and went looking for girls. They grabbed Angelique on her way home, and Rolle came in answer to her cries for help. He punched one of them and the fight went out of them, and he told them to go home."

Ferris nodded encouragingly, thinking the story was over. But Brunkard continued.

"Two days later, one of the two workers was found bobbing in the harbour minus his hands and his manly parts. The other nobody has seen again."

There was a silence for a moment. "Have you heard this before?" Ferris asked Chris.

Chris shrugged. "Yep. I must have missed the excitement. Doesn't mean it's not true."

Brunkard glowered at Chris. "Anyhow, that's how people tell it. Might be it's not true, but related or no I don't like to cross the man. Hell Mr Tony, you can talk to Rolle on your way to cricket. Get the bad news out of the way before he's had time to start drinking."

Ferris sat up straight in his chair. He had almost forgotten. Six months ago, in a fit of public spiriteness he had volunteered to help teach cricket to disaffected youths who had come to the attention of the authorities. It had been easy to begin with, because all the islanders were cricket-mad. But lately he had been saddled with a handful of the illegal migrant children, who were hard work. Particularly the French-speaking ones who didn't know or like cricket and wanted to play baseball instead.

Still, he had plenty of time to finish his third beer.

"Young Lincoln be doing a good job," Brunkard offered tentatively. "He may not be up to much at auto-repair, but he's a born athlete, I give him that."

"Yeah, young Linc is good," Ferris said, "but he wants to go on a sports scholarship to the States to be a baseball player, if I don't get there on time he'll have the kids playing rounders."

Chris laughed. "What good is a game if the bat can't be used as a weapon? I bet back in old England the bar-keps have a baseball bat behind the bar. I can't see them squaring up to a bottle-wielding drunk with a cricket bat."

"You may have a point there Chris," Ferris conceded.

Ferris felt a little light-headed when he left the clubhouse, and he walked carefully to check up on his little yellow and red Piper Super Cub.

"Beauty," he said, and patted the taut fabric of the wing, "You and me're gonna make lotsa money."

He slanted away to where he had left his bicycle. When he tried to cycle his balance was surprisingly off after one bottle.

He walked the bike half a mile, and he felt steady enough

to mount the bicycle. Soon he was rushing along with the wind whistling in his ears, like in a very slow open cockpit. The road dipped, and then turned onto a bridge. Ferris reacted too late and sprawled into the brush beside the road.

His shoulder hit the ground first and although he rolled, the impact drove the breath out of his body. He lay in a heap and coughed, and the cough turned into a laugh. He laughed uncontrollably until he ran out of breath again and coughed to a standstill.

"We all drink too much," he had said. It was true. Hazard of the trade.

The shadows lengthened as Ferris cycled on. The land around the airfield was mostly given over to coconut plantations producing copra, a flammable product not safe to transport by aircraft.

The shade of the trees made the temperature a little cooler, but the humidity sweated the alcohol out of him as he cycled slowly towards the town. The afternoon was closing in quickly and the air cooled as the heat of day rose away from the Earth.

There were a couple of small villages along the route as well but close to the edge of the town the shanties began. They were built mostly on government lands leased for farming to friends and supporters of the previous government. Who had instead built shacks which they rented to the most desperate and the most recent arrivals, illegal Haitian migrants.

The shanties were not safe after dark, but Ferris felt no immediate threat in daytime. True, lantern-jawed men and youths in worn t-shirts and shorts sat on the front steps of the shacks and regarded him blankly as he cycled past, but because he helped out with the cricket, he hoped there would be no trouble. The air was heavy with the stench of sewage and rap music from boom boxes powered by stolen electricity.

He had his mind on cricket training, when a police car came slowly the other way. After being on a US island Ferris felt a small tingle of alarm seeing a vehicle driving on the left. Like all the cars on the island, the steering wheel was on the right. Even the police were comfortable enough with the layout to not bother to pay for the conversion. A thickset constable whose name Ferris could never remember sat behind the wheel. On the passenger side was Sergeant Aziz, the terror of the island. Ferris waved a hand in acknowledgment. The patrol car stopped and Ferris swore under his breath.

The window came down and Aziz leaned out. "Mr Ferris, a moment please." Aziz got out of the car and glanced around at the huts before focusing on Ferris. He glanced at the airline bag tied to the back of the bicycle.

"I hope that's not undeclared goods just come through customs without duty being paid."

"Of course not."

Aziz raised an eyebrow. "Hmmm. I expect Brunkard told you about the new tax regulations," he said sourly. "I'd like to be a fly on the wall when Rolle finds out about our new policy of zero tolerance. But fortunately for you that's not the reason I stopped. The Superintendent wants to see you tomorrow at ten hundred hours, very sharp, concerning important matters."

"What important matters?"

Aziz glared at him. "Matters above my pay grade I would assume, as I have not been told. It must be nice to have friends in high places, Mr Ferris. Just remember the law is no respecter of position or influence."

"Thanks Sergeant," Ferris said. "I think," he added under his breath as the patrol car moved off with a clash of gears.

CHAPTER 7

Ferris braked his bicycle into the yard of Rolle Auto Services and hesitated. He didn't want to leave it outside where any passing tear-away could grab it, but he didn't want to wheel it between the gleaming black Dodge Ram and the ancient but gleaming black Peugeot 404 hearse.

And he felt a little apprehensive, remembering Wally's story about the cane-cutters.

The Ram had a "Chain Dogs" decal across the top of the windshield and a "Vote Independence Party" across the bottom. And all across the back of the cab was a painting of the torso of a naked woman, who looked very much like Angelique Gaillard. And over it another sticker: "Aids kills – use a condom man".

He propped his bicycle against a pillar in front of the hearse. He guessed if the bike fell and scratched the hearse there would be less trouble than chipping the pick-up.

A tall young man in denim shorts looked up from the engine he was tinkering with.

"Hey Mr Tony." A fleeting smile, just a flash of teeth and then it was gone. Lincoln wouldn't be seventeen for a couple of months. Recently he had started driving the hearse, but this was due to his serious demeanour, rather than the cause of it. He was also six feet one inch and had the muscles of a grown man to go with it. "Is it time?"

"Hey, it's the intrepid bird man!" A voice called from under the car. Bearings rattled on concrete and Bob Rolle slid into view, wiping his oily hands with an even filthier rag.

"Okay Linc, you go get cleaned up. Don't want to make the hot-shots wait for their favourite coaches, eh?"

Rolle was the typical mechanic in his sweat- and oil-stained singlet and shorts. And yet not only was he the owner of the garage but was also the silent partner in the general store across the street which doubled as an internet café with cheap phone booths, and he ran a funeral business where it was amazing to see him dressed in a sober suit with a bowler hat and looking grave. He was a natty man in his out-of-work hours.

Rolle waved at the bicycle and laughed. "Why do you use that thing, man?"

Ferris gestured grandly. "Hey, remember I saved up to buy an aeroplane."

"Sure, sure. And you live on a condemned boat that's so old, people take bets on how long before some storm sink it. Man, that's toney, Tony." Rolle creased up his eyes and shook with mirth. "Sorry, I gots to say it."

Rolle pointed to the bicycle. "Those the smokes? I should wash my hands first but bring 'em over, I can't wait. Gotta take a look. You hold the box."

Ferris obligingly unpacked the cigar box and held the lid open while Rolle inhaled theatrically.

"Ah," he said. "Well that's it then I suppose. Bet you and Wally get cold feet about the customs audit."

Ferris looked at him in surprise. "You know about that already? Wally only just told me."

"This really is a small island. So am I right? You out?"

Ferris shrugged. "I just got warned off a second time. I don't think Sergeant Aziz and I get along."

"Ha!" Rolle said. "You and the whole human race. What the body bag man say for hisself?"

"Body bag man?"

"You didn't know? He wasn't really in the Army, just battle-field burial detail. Made him a mean mother. Used to be quite human when he was young, but since he come back, he's a rule-loving machine with a bitter streak."

Ferris felt a chill. "Poor chap," he muttered.

"Oh don't feel too sorry for him, misery love company and he sure love to spread it around. Watch your ass now you're a celebrity and won't have me watching your back no more."

Ferris was puzzled. "What do you mean?"

Rolle smiled. "If you don't know, well then I don't want to spoil the surprise. Bet you worried about losing your work permit, but then again maybe you're going to be rewarded for past good deeds. Maybe all this cricket trainer nonsense trying to help juvenile delinquents counts for something with the highty folks in charge. Although the hell if I'd teach for free. Now if you paid me more than my time worth me in my other businesses, now we talking. Public spirit? Nuts to that and you can't eat gratitude."

Lincoln came out of the back, dressed in white trousers and golf shirt and carrying a cricket bag complete with two bats. "Ah he likes to dress for the part," Rolle said indulgently. Lincoln scowled for a moment then relaxed into seriousness again. "You say that every week," he said.

"That's cause I get a charge out of it every week. Well you two run along now, wouldn't do for the trainers to be late. Bad for discipline."

Rolle laughed uproariously at his own joke. "I crack myself up. Oh man." He walked back to his work shaking his head and chuckling.

The cricket pitch was on the old parade grounds on the edge of town.

Ferris took cricket training class at 5.30 pm on Tuesdays, and the adult teams trained and played on Saturday. The sun was low and the sting was gone out of the rays and Amos the grounds-keeper was only ten minutes late coming to open the shed to let them get out the nets and equipment.

While they waited, Ferris could hear some of the boys yelling as they played some sort of game of tag in the streets nearby. He sighed inwardly. As a way to keep the boys off the streets, it wasn't an entire success.

They started to trail in shortly after Amos arrived, and the more dutiful helped Ferris and Lincoln carry out the equipment. Amos seemed to have exhausted himself opening the locks and subsided into a deck-chair with his hat tipped over his face.

Ferris and Lincoln divided the boys into bowlers, batters and fielders, and as usual the Haitians were the last to turn up, herded by a police constable who scowled at them from the edge of the field.

All went well for a few overs, until the police constable sauntered off to resume his beat, then one of the fielders stepped forward.

"We always the fielders," he said. "When we get to bat and

bowl?" His name was Sonny Dubois, and he dominated the other Haitian boys despite not being the biggest. He was certainly the loudest and was backed by the reputation of his older brother, an up-and-coming kick-boxing champion and tear-away. His name and face were the only ones that stuck in Ferris's mind.

"Hey now Sonny," Lincoln said, towering over the skinny kid. "You're only learning the game. You can learn a lot from fielding. See where the other guys hit the ball, know the best place to stand. And later when you get to bat you will know not to hit the ball those places."

Sonny glowered. "You say that all the time. How we get to learn if we don't get to do it?" The murmurs of agreement from the others rose into calls of "yeah, why not?"

"Sonny, you behave now, you promised your brother," Lincoln said sharply. He sounded exasperated at having his will tested but he was unwilling to turn to Ferris to back him up.

"I not afraid of my brother. Maybe you are. Maybe you afraid he kick-box your ass good."

"Sonny." Ferris put some parade-ground lash into his voice without raising it much. It was a trick he had picked up from his old C.O. who had also been handy with his fists, but Ferris didn't see a drunken mess brawl in prospect here.

"You are always late arriving Sonny," Ferris continued. "If you come on time you can get a better position. As it is, you can bat in the nets in the after practice."

Sonny lowered his eyes and scowled, but the mutterings subsided. Being spoken to directly cut him off from the others and there were no more kick-boxing threats.

"You don't want to be giving in to his tantrums, Mr Tony," Lincoln said in a low voice as the game resumed.

"I know Linc, but I want to give these guys a chance."

"We *are* giving them a chance. My way is better."

"Maybe. When you retire you'll be one scary coach, Lincoln."

Lincoln smiled and then he looked back at the game and bellowed, "Marvin, catch with two hands, how many times I have to tell you?"

At the end of the cricket, the boys trailed off nonchalantly, herded by the scowling policeman who had returned around the correct time. Ferris said thanks and good night to Lincoln and headed for the yacht.

CHAPTER 8

When Ferris got to the yacht marina, he leaned his bicycle against the fence. It was so battered he didn't bother to lock it. It went missing a couple of times a year but always re-appeared after a few days.

The setting sun cast a red glow over the marina. It was the main tourist magnet for St. Marc, with yachts visiting from as far away as the UK and Portugal. It had electricity, fresh water and TV cables on every pontoon. The whole development backed up to the beach of the Grand Hotel de St. Marc, which made more money from the yachtsmen than all the other tourists combined.

With another pilot, Logan, he had bought a Bristol 39 yacht from a passing mariner sailing to the scrap-yard. They had re-named her *Trinidad*, and lived very reasonably aboard. Logan had moved to Miami, and so Ferris had inherited *Trinidad* for himself. Her old-fashioned cramped beam and peeling paint had a derelict look that displeased the marina owners. But she was cosy, if a bit large for one person. Ferris sometimes invited lady tourists on board.

The berthing facilities were expensive, but paradoxically, the onshore facilities were quite cheap, for Ferris cheaper than living in the hotel. He slipped a monthly bottle of whiskey and the occasional discreet envelope of twenties to Charles, the concierge to keep things smooth.

When he got on board, Ferris opened all the hatches to let the air circulate – the interior of the *Trinidad* tended to smell of mould and bilge.

It didn't help air circulation to have parts of the boat chock full of books on flying, aircraft maintenance and meteorology. He kept his log books in water-proof bags in the biscuit tins in a locker and had a huge collection of magazines that he kept meaning to tidy and cull, but he couldn't help himself.

He went ashore for a quick coin-operated shower, changed and headed out for the Bistro.

There weren't many nice bars in St. Marc. There were some low dives, such as a tough rap place called 'Ricks', usually thronged with rum-fuelled young men with grievances they were quick to share with a stranger and even quicker with their fists. The island grandees met in the Grand Hotel. And there was the Colonial Club, where a few ancient planters played bridge while they waited for the nineteen fifties to return.

Le Bistro was the unofficial neutral meeting place for all the island, which hit the sweet spot as the place to go. It was informal but stylish, it was mainly a restaurant but it was also a cafe and bar and some evenings a live band played calypso, *soca* and junkanoo. The chefs were Pierre and Celine, husband and wife owners of the bistro, trained in New York and Paris.

When he arrived at the bistro, the *maitre d'*, Angelique Gaillard approached him, stern and spectacular in a white satin blouse and black satin skirt.

"Table for two tonight, Ferris," she said. "Bob is lonely." Ferris read something in the neutral tone and felt a protective tingle in his stomach.

"He's not mis-treating you, Angie is he?" He asked.

She tightened her lips in a straight line and flashed him an angry look with her amazing green eyes.

"We been over all this many a time, Ferris," She said evenly, her French accent stronger than usual.

He raised his hands defensively. "Just asking."

"Well, don't, *buckrah*."

She turned and flounced angrily to the alcove where Rolle waved cheekily at Ferris.

Ferris admired her undulating hips as he followed her down the row of booths. Surely the men that came back a second night, even a second year, came to look at Angelique. "Easily the best piece of leg in the eastern Caribbean," Logan used to say. In the tourist season at least five men a night made a move on Angelique, but most of them backed off as soon as they found out about Rolle. Maybe they even got to hear the cane cutter murder story. Maybe they bought Wally a drink for the way he told it.

She could be very discouraging. He wondered if her rejection technique had evolved.

Angelique had come to work in the bistro after Ferris started going there. After some gallantry, Angelique declined his offer of a drink, but calmly sat down opposite him and told him that as much as his attentions flattered her, she was immune to his charm, as she preferred the society of other women. Ferris had been incredulous at first, and a little angry, but had seen the funny side.

"I like girls too," he said, "So we have something in common. There's no reason why we can't be friends."

She had laughed then, and ever since they sparred in a friendly way. Usually.

And in the meantime, Rolle. And the stories.

Ferris sighed as he sat down opposite Rolle. He had been hoping to tuck himself away in a booth after buying a rum, and stretch the drink out into the evening, when he chose from the early bird menu.

"Wassup Dog?" Rolle said with a beaming smile.

"Wally seemed very worried about how you'd take it. The end of cigars I mean."

Rolle waved a beefy arm dismissively. "Ah that Wally – afraid of his own shadow. Not so afraid that he didn't take his share I noticed. Bad conscience brought on by bad rum I expect. It will all blow over in a few weeks, Wally will get his mojo back and it will be business as usual."

Rolle looked around conspiratorially, and said, "I didn't want to say anything earlier, when Lincoln was there, case he take it the wrong way. I'm a bit worried 'bout the boy, you know? He's supposed to be studying for a sports scholarship for NFL right? But now since he take up kick-boxing and hang round with that Haitian rascal Rene Dubois, and the weight-training is off the scale, man. Ain't gonna hear me bad-mouthing the Haitian folks, they in need of a reasonably priced funeral director same as regular folks, but those Dubois boys are bad news.

"I be in the gym well early man, and Lincoln he was already there bench pressing two hundred fifty pounds man, with no one to spot him. I know he looks big but he's only a boy.

"Youth of today man, no talking to them, he that size, must be steroids – maybe you talk to him eh? I can't get no sense into some people except to beat it into them."

"It could be just creatine," Ferris said, bemused at the abrupt shift of subject. "And he didn't get it from me."

"Whatever it is, he ain't getting it from me neither," Rolle said surlily, "I smuggle cigars, not drugs for kids. I saw the way that goes down in New York City. I've seen that shit rip the heart out of a whole people. Brother against brother. And I don't mean just all black men against one another. I'm talking people blowing away their own kin for some of that damn rock. We gotta stop that kind of shit happening here."

He glowered into the distance and then he shook himself, and for the rest of the meal, talked about basketball.

With the table cleared, Ferris felt pleasantly relaxed except the presence of Rolle kept him watchful.

Rolle slapped Ferris on the shoulder. "Card time. Gotta go talk to the highty-tighty folks now, pretend I stoosh."

Ferris nursed his rum for a while and then followed. On his way into the lounge he saw Chris entertaining two older ladies who looked like they had got lost on their way to Palm Beach. Chris discreetly raised his glass as Ferris went by without breaking the flow of conversation.

As usual the guys had pushed together a set of tables to make a larger poker table.

Schroeder was banker, and in addition to Rolle, Ferris knew the others.

Doctor Hank Sanders, from the hospital, a young surgeon, dressed in a t-shirt and cargo shorts, looking like he came on a skate-board.

And Jimmy Chen, a journalist with the St. Marc Courier. It was a quiet night at the card club, sometimes there were far more players.

"Great news Tony," Schroeder said. "The minister of industry and tourism Mr Ransome has just signed a contract for a cell phone system. You know I love the island like a first wife but jeez I'm tired carrying that brick of a sat-phone around. We could have the first masts installed and ready to go in a couple of months tops."

"What Vic is not saying is that he's had sub-contractors signed up waiting for months," Jimmy Chen said.

"And why not," Schroeder said. "I build things. If I get to use them myself, all the better. You can be sure I'll do a good job."

"So are you telling people about your airline business yet, Tony?" Jimmy Chen said mischievously.

Ferris raised an eye-brow at Schroeder.

Schroeder shuffled the cards and said innocently: "I told you I'd talk to people and I did just that."

"He has been telling everyone who will listen and a lot of people who don't want to," Chen said. "I gotta tell you Tony, a journalist loves a good story but not one that follows him around. I resisted 'Local man escapes with life in air crash' so I might keep this one out of the paper too." Ferris smiled weakly. The plane crash was old news now.

Chips were a dime. Ferris lost half his chips in the first three hands and folded after that and just watched, not really following the game or the conversations but just letting his mind drift where the rum took it. He heard Rolle telling Doctor Hank, "One time people were envious of the Ram, you know? Can't see why, it belong to the bank mostly. But gave the high mucky-mucks a bad feel to see me riding high above them in their limousines maybe. Was talk for a while of a limiting of one car per family or an extra tax, can you imagine?"

Ferris noticed Schroeder looking at Rolle quizzically; he owned a Dodge Ram also.

And later Rolle gathering a pile of chips to him and laughing at his own interminable puns, "That's how we Rolle, baby."

The room snapped back into focus when Jimmy Chen said to Doctor Hank, "So would you think that in the last five years the people of Argentina got twice as many colds as in previous years?"

"I doubt it, it would be the featured article in The Lancet," Doc Hank said.

"Well that's what the figures for imports of pseudoephedrine might tell you, but since it is also the precursor of methamphetamine it might tell you that the Mexican cartels have got all the way to Buenos Aires. Where they think prying eyes might not see. But all governments keep statistics."

"How do you know all this?" Ferris asked, bemused.

"By keeping my eye in and watching the web. It's a new golden triangle, diamonds out of Africa to Latin America, cocaine, diamonds and emeralds from Latin America to the States, weapons the other way."

He flicked an apologetic glance at Ferris, who shrugged.

"And misery distributed in all directions," Rolle said grimly.

"Yes, well," Schroeder said. He obviously didn't like the trend of the conversation. "We don't have to worry about that sort of thing here. Intensive farming and a bit of tourism and you avoid all that sort of thing."

"Amen," Rolle said unexpectedly.

CHAPTER 9

*Out of the corner of his eye, Ferris caught a flash of movement. "Two
Seven to control – traffic on runway, traffic on runway!"*

Ferris woke with a hammering heart and a pounding headache.
The nightmare dispersed. It took him a moment to adjust to lying
in a bunk on the yacht, the hull rocking gently.

It didn't help that people had spoken about the incident tonight
sympathetically and put it into the top of his psyche.

A pity he didn't smoke. Right now a smoke would have calmed
the nerves and occupied the hands. And even though there is a
bottle of rum in the galley, it was too early.

Instead he turned on the light and dug out one of his flying
magazines and read that General Velasco of Colombian air force
had finally resigned. The Santo Domingo bombing scandal had
been going on for months. His mind wandered, and he thought
about getting the yacht painted. Buying the right water-proof paint
from the chandlers, and maybe save up money to pay a boat-yard
to do the painting.

The dawn came and he pulled on a t-shirt and chinos and
taking a towel, soap and a toilet bag, he sidled into the Grand
Hotel. It was one of his cost-cutting ploys. The showers on the
marina had coin slots to use, but in the Hotel, where even the
barest room cost a week's pay for a night, the shower rooms by
the swimming pool were free. Ferris rose early each day when he
wanted a shower, to beat the rush. As usual, there was no one
using the showers, and he was clean and feeling much better when
he left to buy breakfast.

At ten o'clock sharp, Ferris presented himself at the door of
police headquarters.

The police headquarters was at the edge of the old town, in a hundred-year-old colonial building.

The duty orderly ushered him into Superintendent Legett's office more quickly than usual, and Ferris was instantly alert, the relaxing effect of his breakfast forgotten. Superintendent Legett watched as Ferris sat carefully in front of his desk. He was a tall slim man, and he wore his outmoded white tunic with an air of complete comfort.

"Do take a seat, Mr Ferris," he said smoothly, half a beat too late.

"Don't mind if I do, Superintendent," Ferris retorted.

Superintendent Legett had been to a public school in England, and no matter what prejudice had affected his stay there, he had come back with a very British air of authority, and a carefully modulated voice. He was the kind of man who Ferris had learned to call 'sir' in the RAF.

Legett shuffled the papers on his desk, and suddenly his lazy brown eyes were very bright and sharp.

"The Drugs Enforcement Agency of the USA seem to have taken an undue interest in your activities, Mr Ferris. What have you done to annoy them? And Sergeant Aziz tells me that he suspected you of being intoxicated in charge of a bicycle again. Let me say this my patience is running out. Last night was the fifth time you rode that bicycle drunk. I'm delighted you don't drive a car. This island is developing fast. I won't have drunks giving it a bad name and causing a danger. I'll run you off the island if I have to." He smiled a little grimly.

"Which brings us to the second reason for this meeting. Now that Harvey Air Services no longer has a formal base in the island, you should know that in the normal course of events your work permit would automatically lapse and you'd be asked to leave the island. And currently we do not even have a normal course of events, we have a large influx of illegal immigrants and a great deal of political pressure to deport anyone with an imperfect legal standing. I'm sure you'll appreciate that some important people have the view that anyone even remotely connected with him is not really welcome in the island."

Ferris nodded silently. "So. As the associate of an undesirable person, who now says you are no longer in his employ, how can you possibly expect to be allowed stay on, when we have more than enough people to do all work in the island?"

Damn you, Harvey, Ferris thought savagely.

"I have enough money to get by," he said. "It hasn't all been parties and rum." Legett lifted an eyebrow. "Yes, but you are not a millionaire," he said. "There needs to be some public good in allowing you live here."

"I plan to use my own plane as an air taxi," Ferris said.

Legett nodded. "Apparently the Minister of Transport has powers of foresight. He rang me yesterday afternoon to wonder if you were planning to start an airline and had I any objection. I won't keep you in suspense. It's not a police matter. But you need to make a formal application. It seems you have influential friends who like you and would like to see you succeed. So do the right things. No more cigars. Do not even think of bribing any officials on this island, not even with a handful of cigars. I assure you, it is now an offence as well as a waste of time. That is all."

"Thank you, sir," Ferris said. He rose and went to the door. Legett's voice halted his hand on the door-knob. "Oh, and Ferris – if you don't want a car, at least try to buy a bicycle lamp and batteries. You really should spend more money in the island. It's made round to go round, as you British say."

"Yessir," Ferris said, resisting the impulse to stand to attention.

CHAPTER 10

The travel office was down the block and so Ferris stopped in there first.

Presiding over all was Martha Weaver, a large woman who could have passed for one of the Weather Girls.

"You can't do business without a permit, dumb-bell," Martha Weaver said insultingly. "Can't just come in here and flash your pretty boy smile like this is some nightclub."

"I'm on my way to the ministry now," Ferris said hurriedly.

"Humph," Martha said. "I don't see what your rush is. Harvey Air Services will still be flying in every second Thursday and OutAir will be flying in on the Tuesday and Saturday of every other week. And the rich folks charter their own. There is no gap in the market for you to fill. I've seen your plane, Ferris. And if you asked me, with all those nice airliners, nobody would want to fly in your noisy toy plane, but you didn't ask me, and to each their own."

"It's true, I didn't ask you," Ferris said with a grin and went on to the Transport ministry.

The desk at the Transport Ministry was manned by Reuben Bland, a fretful younger version of Wally Brunkard, but he knew his stuff.

"Here are the forms you will need to make an application, to be filled in triplicate. You will also need proof of commercial insurance. Also a guarantee deposit. I would recommend you engage a legal adviser to speed along the process as it can be very long and involved if there are any errors. That's just the way it is, you understand."

Bland pushed across a receipt book and Ferris leaned on the desk to sign it. He heard a door open behind him and looked up to see Bland registering dismay.

Ferris turned around to see the minister Mr Ransome standing behind him. "Oh hello. Mr Ferris, isn't it?"

The minister smiled benevolently. "I suppose you're here to apply for an air service permit. There will definitely be a large gap without the Harvey service, and I have no doubt that an application from a locally based operator would be viewed very favourably here."

Ferris heard Bland suck air through his teeth but said, "Thank you sir."

"Not at all," Mr Ransome waved his hand airily. "Mr Schroeder told me your plans. I suppose you will want to get started with telecoms contract as soon as possible." Ferris remembered what Legett said about the minister having foresight and felt uncomfortable.

"I'm afraid he hasn't said anything to me, Minister," Ferris said.

Mr Ransome's smile vanished. "Perhaps I misunderstood. I got the impression that Mr Schroeder would be the guarantor."

Ferris regretted not just nodding and smiling.

"Of course," Mr Ransome said, "It doesn't have to be Mr Schroeder. That was just an example, um, but a sponsor would be good, just a necessary formality. Well, I'll leave you to it, Mr Bland," he said, and went back into his office.

Reuben Bland looked outraged. "He never comes out of his office. It's most irregular."

"It has nothing to do with me," Ferris protested.

"Well we have procedures and due process here Mr Ferris, he should know better."

"I meant I had nothing to do with it," Ferris said. He felt the blood rushing to his face. "In any case I don't mean to imply that either you or the minister would do anything improper. What is the normal procedure for what happens next?" Bland pursed his lips. "Oh, as I said, once you or your legal adviser submit the application, normally there is a wait of three to five working days while the forms are processed and checks are made. And you will need to provide a surety to the value of fifteen thousand dollars, proof of insurance and as a new business you will need either a guarantor to the value of two hundred and fifty thousand dollars, or deposit the same amount in escrow."

The logical next step was to go to see Marlon Enright, the only real business lawyer in the island. Whose biggest customer was Vic Schroeder.

So from the Transport Ministry, Ferris went to the bistro. He thought a drink would settle his nerves and simmer him down. He ordered a rum and looked at the menu but the more he thought about it, the more annoyed he got.

Ferris hadn't paid maintenance since Jenny remarried a few years ago, and any money he used to sent to her he now saved but he was a pilot, not an investor and there wasn't much to show for the years since he had left the RAF. Apart from the *Trinidad* and the Super Cub it felt as if he spent most of his money on hotel rooms in San Juan, and on booze in those same hotels and nightclubs.

He had originally started 'living' on the boat as a joke but over time it became a genuine cost-saving exercise – he could only afford the Cub because the previous owner who had refurbished it had divorced shortly after and had to sell the plane in a hurry for a lot less than it was worth to pay *his* divorce settlement.

He drank the rum in fast sips but it didn't ease the knot in his stomach. He was good for the surety of fifteen thousand. And in an ideal world with a sympathetic bank manager, the guarantee of two hundred and fifty thousand would probably have been a difficult but not impossible proposition.

But with Mr Braynen, the manager of the First Bank of St. Marc, it had been hate at first sight. Braynen took money laundering requirements very seriously and no nit was too small to pick. After one fraught transfer to the UK, with maybe an early rum or two involved, Ferris and Mr Braynen had fallen out over a minor technicality, each accusing each other of being drug mules and hadn't spoken since.

The rum glass was empty. He put it down and tried to concentrate on the menu.

Which left him right back where Schroeder swooped in like a great white daddy and solved a problem that shouldn't have existed ... although his money was probably all tied up also.

It left a bitter taste. Some things just don't feel the same without the effort of winning them. Schroeder's help came with so many strings attached he might as well be a puppet. It would be worse than working for him.

He was still staring at the menu when Angelique came back.

"Have you decided what you'd like?" She asked. She was standing just a little too close.

"I feel like a piece of leg," Ferris said wolfishly. He ran his hand up the inside of her thigh as far as the hem of her skirt. Angelique stood stock still. In her rigidity he felt rejection and withdrew his hand.

"I don't see why you can't make an exception for me," he said sullenly.

Her eyes flashed. "What's wrong with you man, you think cos you got a nice smile, people going to let you do anything you want? Rolle would kill you for just looking at me, you know that. Anyway, you are supposed to be my friend, as you keep telling me."

"How come you put up with Rolle?"

"You know perfectly well. There is no place here for a girl like me. It's put up with Rolle or leave."

"I could protect you," Ferris said.

"I don't think so. You can't even look after yourself." Ferris stood and threw some dollars on the table. "You can keep the change if there is any." He walked in a stiff-legged fury back to the yacht. On the way, he passed Marlon Enright's office and the whole humiliating episode with the minister came flooding back.

CHAPTER 11

Where the street opened out onto the marina, he could see the sun glinting back off the villas up the hill where Schroeder lived. Schroeder had told him that he was welcome any time.

"To hell with it." He got out his bicycle and cycled up the hill.

He was bathed in sweat after two minutes and had to dismount and push the bicycle and after another five he just leaned it into the verge and walked the rest of the way.

As Ferris walked up the driveway he saw that in addition to Schroeder's cars, there were two pick-ups parked outside the house. Two muscular guys dressed only in shorts came out of the house and dumped a roll of carpet in the bed of one of the trucks and hoisted up a bundle of planks for the return trip.

Schroeder's Korean house-boy, Kun, held the door open. He was about sixty. His wife worked as the cook and house-keeper. Kun and Schroeder had worked together in a container shipping business going back to the Vietnam War. It wasn't clear whether they had a business or military relationship, then or now.

He took his eyes off the workmen and nodded to Ferris.

"Mr Vic is out at the pool," Kun said. He led Ferris out onto the patio. It had a swimming pool with a false horizon that merged with the sea. It was over the top but as the first of a series to be built in the golf and country club setting, Schroeder had to pull out all the stops.

Schroeder was sitting next to his swimming pool talking to a young man in a short-sleeved shirt who Ferris didn't recognise, but had the look of an architect rather than a workman.

He looked up and waved and said, "Kun will handle it," and stood up to greet Ferris.

"Hi Tony, I'm re-modelling the gun room." Schroeder collected guns. His gun room was a giant safe built into the basement. "You'll forgive me if I seem distracted. What can I do for you?"

"I've just been down to the Transport Ministry. The minister himself came and said hello and he seemed to think it was all sewn up, but his civil servant practically accused me of bribery and corruption. I just wanted to fill in some forms and now I have to get a lawyer as well? Look, Vic, I know you are just trying to help but I know how to take care of myself. I don't need people trying to help things along."

The two workmen again carrying a rolled carpet came up behind Ferris and Schroeder said, "Sit down Tony, and give the guys some room."

Ferris reluctantly sat on an aluminium deck chair. It was already hot from the sun.

"So what did the civil servant say exactly?" Schroeder asked.

Ferris told him.

"A lawyer makes good sense," Schroeder said. "I should have suggested that. I haven't heard of this Reuben Bland. Maybe he's just an over-enthusiastic young guy. I'm sure the minister will understand."

"But where am I to get two hundred and fifty thousand dollars?"

The two workmen shuffled past, carrying panels of wood.

"I told you it wouldn't be easy," Schroeder said. "But I can guarantee the money, until your insurance is running."

"I don't want to be beholden to you, Vic," Ferris said.

"Goddamn, just like Mikey," Schroeder said and swallowed. He looked away over the pool to the sea and shook his head.

After a long moment he looked back at Ferris. "Look, Tony it's a win-win." Schroeder said. "I figure you can earn the money back pretty fast, and just by trying to, you will increase the amount of business on the island which will be good for my other investments so I can't miss."

"It sounds too much like I would be working for you, Vic," Ferris said, and stood up.

"Now hold on, Tony," Schroeder said, and Ferris didn't realise that this was a warning and he turned and walked right into the path of the two workmen carrying another rolled carpet. The guy at the front tried to drop and jerk the carpet out of the way but ended up giving it more momentum. It hit Ferris in the chest and pitched him into the swimming pool. The water was body temperature but the shock of losing his balance jolted him. He sucked in water before realising what was happening and floundered before adjusting to what had happened.

"Oh hot damn," Schroeder said, and bent double, slapping his knees with mirth.

Ferris spat out water. "I don't find it that funny," he said and waded to the ladder.

The two workmen had lowered the carpet and stood poised between concern and mirth.

"Sorry man," the front guy said. "You moved too fast."

"Don't worry about it," Ferris said.

Kun appeared at the top of the ladder and offered him a hand. He was impassive, but Ferris suspected a glint in his eye. He could hear Schroeder chuckling.

"Would you like a towel, Mr Ferris?" Kun said.

"Sure," Ferris said. "But I'm sure I'll dry off fast enough." Schroeder was still shaking. "Nothing hurt but your dignity … Come on Tony, lighten up." The laughter was infectious and Ferris couldn't keep a grin off his face.

"Okay," he said, "there's nothing like falling on your ass to make you forget your dignity. If I ever had any. You were saying?"

"Just trying to help, Tony, sorry if it worked out the other way. Really, no strings attached. Usually the islanders stick together and try to help each other and they don't mind outsiders doing the same."

"Yes, they like to stick together," Ferris said, "but they don't particularly like outsiders, look at the way they talk about the Haitians."

Kun handed Ferris a towel.

Schroeder looked uncomfortable. "Maybe the Haitians are a special case."

"It's a sign of the way things are," Ferris said.

"Look Tony, you've had a rough few weeks. But tomorrow is the start of the rest of your life. It's trite, but true. Think it over, and then go see Marlon Enright, Huh?"

Ferris finished rubbing his hair and handed the towel back to Kun.

"I show Mr Ferris out," Kun said, his English mysteriously worsening. He stayed silent as he led Ferris back through the house, and Ferris felt like he was being hustled out. Kun paused as he opened the door and looked at Ferris.

"Goodbye, Mr Ferris. Mr Vic is a very patient man. You lucky he like you so much." And with that Ferris found himself out in the sun again.

CHAPTER 12

Ferris felt he had been sent away with his tail between his legs. But by the time he got back to the yacht he realised he wanted to fly more than he wanted to be right. He also realised that he was not right.

He changed his clothes and went back to the bistro.

When he came through the door, Pierre looked up with a tight expression. Ferris spread his hands in a placatory gesture. "It's okay Pierre, I've come to apologise."

Pierre looked him up and down. "I don't know what happened Ferris, but I'm not sure you're welcome here any more. I'll see what the girl says, but me and Celine will have the final decision. Wait here."

He disappeared into the back and came back out with both Celine and Angelique.

"Well?" Celine said.

With an audience of three, Ferris felt his throat going dry. "Angie –" his voice faltered. "I don't know what came over me. I'm ashamed and I'm not sure how to make it up to you. I have no excuse and I apologise."

A silence stretched out and then Angelique sighed and looked away. "Okay Ferris, we all make mistakes."

Pierre didn't look convinced. "Thanks Angie, you can go back to work now." He waited until the door closed behind her, looking at his wife. Celine nodded, and Pierre strode forward and stuck out his chin.

"You so much as look at her funny again Ferris, I won't bother going to that pain in the ass Aziz. I'll just break your hand with a meat mallet. Do we understand each other?"

Ferris nodded.

"Fine," Celine said. "We're not so desperate for business. Perhaps you should try somewhere else for a few days."

***

Marlon Enright was the best business lawyer in the island. He was the only business lawyer in the island, but he brought expertise to this monopoly. He also did pro-bono work as a public defender.

He asked Ferris some pointed questions, jotted notes to the answers, and pursed his lips at the mention of the fifteen thousand dollar surety and said, "I'll phone Mr Schroeder and get an agreement written up. Drop back in a couple of days and there should be some papers to sign. If you could drop in your aircraft documents today we can get the application in progress."

***

Over the next two days, Ferris made good use of his bicycle, cycling out to the airfield. Mindful of what Superintendent Legett had said, he even bought and attached an expensive lamp.

He lovingly polished the fabric of the Cub, until all the oil specks were gone, and she gleamed.

On the third day he went back to Enright's office. Where the lawyer sat and watched him read through a long legal document. It was full of parties of the first and second part. But in it Victor G. Schroeder agreed to be guarantor in Ferris's new airline business.

At the end of the week an official Transport Ministry letter arrived, asking him to come reclaim his documents.

Reuben Bland looked sweaty. "You'll be glad to know everything is in order, Mr Ferris." For a moment Ferris thought he looked disappointed, but then Bland smiled. "The minister would like a word. It should be alright now that everything is signed correctly."

"I'm delighted," Ferris said, keeping all trace of irony out of his voice.

Bland knocked on the door of the office of the minister and ushered Ferris in.

"I understand your aircraft is only a small two-seater Mr Ferris?" Mr Ransome said, uncorking his official fountain pen.

"That's true minister," Ferris said cautiously. "But I have to start somewhere. It would take me twenty years to save for the one I used to fly here."

"Oh, something of a bush operation." Mr Ransome looked crestfallen but he perked up as he signed and handed back the documents. "But I am sure with more business it would happen sooner, yes?"

The minister added slyly, "As the only aircraft based here, you will be something of the national flag carrier. Maybe a case could be made for a business development loan? A community sustains itself and prospers through the encouragement of local industry and enterprise. Perhaps we could talk to Mr Davern?"

Ferris decided this was a good time to just smile and nod.

"So are you ready to be a bush pilot, Mr Ferris?" Mr Ransome said, re-corking his pen. His eyes twinkled. He was back in a good mood.

"Without passengers, I'm afraid, Minister."

"That all changes immediately, Mr Ferris," the minister said delightedly. "There will be Airmail for the post office and other urgent deliveries. And as to your Air Taxi service, we have your first customer awaiting you in Puerto Rico. Mr Davern from the IMF is coming on one of his visits to us, and it seems neither of your competitors have a schedule that coincides with his itinerary. So you might say the field is open to the flag carrier. Mr Davern expressed the wish to fly in as soon as possible, in any plane available, so we will take him at his word. Good-bye and good luck, Mr Ferris."

CHAPTER 13

At San Juan International, Ferris felt slightly ridiculous landing the little Piper among all the big aircraft. He was relieved when he parked the plane without incident, locked the Cub in case Paco was lurking, and went in search of Davern.

William Armstrong Davern III, was reputedly a roving economic adviser associated with the International Monetary Fund, who travelled the Caribbean telling the island governments how to run their economic policies in a manner that kept their loans performing.

Ferris spotted him in one of the departure lounges, dapper in a blue linen suit, with a calf-skin briefcase and a single slim overnight bag, and a slight frown puckering the ageless skin of his forehead.

His face cleared when he recognised Ferris.

"Ah, Tony old chap. They said you were coming. I didn't quite know if I'd understood the message or not. Have you gone out on your own?"

"That's right," Ferris said and led him back out towards the plane.

"If I might be so prying," Davern said. "When you say you are gone out on your own, are you completely self-sufficient or do you have backers?"

"Vic Schroeder volunteered to be my guarantor. Heck, he practically demanded to be."

"Ah. How is my poker nemesis?" Davern visited St. Marc often enough to be a regular guest player at the poker club.

"Still planning to redevelop the island's melon industry. Or cantaloupes. And casinos."

"Is a casino a breed of melon? Dear Lord, if I never hear about melon farming again it won't be soon enough. The man has an obsession. Everyone should have a hobby but seriously. Cash crops are no good for developing an economy."

Davern stopped dead when he saw the plane. "My God, is that a Piper Cub?"

"Super Cub," Ferris corrected him.

"They still make those?"

"Not since 1994."

"Well. Hum. I did give the prime minister a good talking to about cutting his cloth to suit the measure but I didn't think they would take it so much to heart. I usually arrange the flights myself and add to expenses. Is it safe? It's only cloth isn't it?"

"Dacron. And it's only dangerous if you crash."

"Well don't crash it then," Davern said with a sigh. "My assistant wouldn't be happy. I need to travel with him sometimes, you're going to have to get something with more than one passenger seat."

"I'm looking to lease a Cessna or Beech Bonanza, this is what I had at short notice."

"Beech Bonanza, isn't that the one they call 'the Doctor Killer'? Jesus," Davern said. "It just gets better and better. Still, mustn't complain –if the client is following advice then progress is being made, even if there might be an ulterior motive."

The Cub didn't stretch to an intercom system but Ferris had installed a battery operated set. The plane was a bit noisy, but it allowed the pilot and passenger communicate without bellowing.

When they were safely on their way, Ferris noticed Davern had a white-knuckle grip on his briefcase and decided to take the man's mind off flying. He casually mentioned the news about the government cut-backs in St. Marc.

"They don't have social welfare here, the food subsidy is the only thing that helps people make ends meet," Ferris said.

"Don't talk to me, I'm just the messenger boy," Davern said irritably. "I only play banker at the poker table. I'm a taxation consultant, I advise governments working with the IMF. I don't work for the IMF. The governments are my clients but they are free to ignore my advice. I get to sit on my tail in planes and in conferences for too long and all I get out of that part is haemorrhoids and a bad liver."

"Oh, I don't know if they ignore you," Ferris said. "The minister of Transport gave me a pep-talk about national self-sufficiency and sustainability."

"Did he now?" said Davern with a laugh, "We gave the old boy a couple of those presentations but he didn't seem to be paying attention."

"He also said he'd be asking you about an air taxi business development subsidy," Ferris added with a grin.

Davern grinned back, his hands relaxed on the briefcase.

"My esteem for the minister goes up and up. That makes a lot more sense than Schroeder and his hydrofoils and melon farms – and the minister is also putting the arm on me with this flight. Best blackmail ever."

"You don't like the Super Cub," Ferris said. A statement rather than a question.

"I can't stand flying. I know, I know," Davern said irritably at Ferris's raised eyebrows, "I have to fly to do my work. But on heavy jets, it's like being on a train. I know you love small planes and to each their own. Some people love Harley-Davidsons. Strange people."

"I'm all for customer feedback," Ferris said gamely.

"Seriously, Tony. Even a doctor killer looks good in comparison. I'd love to show support but I'm a nervous wreck – I'll be taking the Harvey Air Beechcraft on my next leg. It's pricey, but for the time saved and the stress reduction, I'd pay double again. I'd love to see you make a go of this Tony but you need the proper equipment. Here's the card of a leasing company. Talk to the guy, for the love of Mike."

They landed back on St. Marc in the early afternoon, and without the cooling effect of the slipstream the humidity hit like a wet blanket and Davern wilted in his suit, looking the way Ferris felt. An air-conditioned government Mercedes was waiting to whisk Davern away from the airfield.

Ferris couldn't face the heat or the prospect of an early drink so he borrowed the club-house phone and placed a call to Matt Hollis in San Juan.

"Mr Ferris, how can I help you?" He could tell from the polite but cautious tone that Hollis couldn't quite place him.

"We did some drunken wing-walking on Chris Turner's biplane once." A second's pause then Hollis guffawed so loudly Ferris had to hold the phone away from his ear.

"Shoot, *that* Tony Ferris! And how is that old vulture, the Birdman of Ag-Cat-raz? I swear he was a Spad jock back in the day and crop-dusting is his way of keeping his hand in."

Ferris told him about his need for a bigger plane. "The Navajo is out of my budget," he added.

"I should say," Hollis said. "I'd suggest leasing a fast single? A second hand 260 hp Beech Bonanza can carry four to six people. It's 35 miles per hour slower than the Navajo and the range is only two hundred fifty miles instead of a thousand. But on the short hops here neither the speed nor the range will matter too much. And on the other hand it's a lot faster and roomier than your own plane, and one hell of a lot cheaper to run than a Navajo or any other twin. With me so far?"

"Makes sense," Ferris said. He felt a spike of excitement. The discussion made the business seem more real.

"Not a lot of bigger singles going around," Hollis added. "Very small market. Yep, your best bet would be Olympiakos Leasing. Darius is a good kid. Straight shooter."

Ferris smiled, wondering what age Darius would be.

CHAPTER 14

He met Schroeder on the way in to the card club in the evening. "So how did Bill like the ride in your flivver?"

"He wasn't best pleased. Practically demanded I get a newer plane."

"Let me see – four seater, two hundred fifty horse-power, two hundred fifty miles range? Much more economical than the big boys." Ferris had to laugh. "You certainly get on top of your facts when you want to, Vic."

"I asked Garcia to look up figures," Schroeder said. "He's under-employed. Anyway, it makes sense. I'd advise talking to Marlon to get it all straight." Schroeder paused. "Speaking of Garcia, he's flying in Mr Arnaud and the team from Spearpoint tomorrow. I'm throwing a party tomorrow night and the great and good are all invited. I'd like you to come too."

"Gee golly," Ferris said. "Will the Governor be there?"

"He's invited," Schroeder said uncertainly.

"Seriously, I'd be honoured." Ferris said.

The lounge had the usual poker players, Jimmy Chen and Doc Hank, and Davern bringing up their numbers but also at another table sat a party in business suits, including George "Pappy" O'Dowd. O'Dowd had been the Transport Minister in the last government, and rumour had it, the only person who dared tell Rolle what to do.

"Don't mind us, people," O'Dowd said jovially. "I might even join you later if the game isn't too hot for my taste." He chuckled at this, and Schroeder smiled weakly back.

"Thanks, uh, Mr O'Dowd."

"It's George and Vic, remember?" O'Dowd flashed his famous mega-watt smile and turned back to his guests.

Jimmy Chen said, "So Vic, what's this I hear about a yacht party?"

"Small island," Schroeder said, showing his teeth. "No secrets."

"What yacht party?" Rolle said. He had come in late, his eyes glassy as he slid into a vacant chair.

"Rumour has it," Chen said, and paused significantly, "Which Vic will neither confirm nor deny, that tomorrow night he will be holding a launch party on a sixty-nine metre Italian super-yacht which has just arrived in the harbour."

Schroeder looked displeased. "We're both off the clock here, Jimmy. No business at the card table, remember?"

"Fair enough," Jimmy Chen said, but he looked disappointed.

"It's just a small gathering." Schroeder relented. "With some government ministers and other good folks, announcing the golf course and country club."

Rolle's eyes narrowed. "Country club? Don't we already have a Colonial Club?"

"The golf course is hardly new news," Schroeder said uncomfortably.

"Country club. Now, that doesn't sound so bad," Rolle said, his voice rising. "Is it going to have a nice high fence to keep the natives outside? You may not have noticed that we have a doctor here but no nurses or porters. Surprised you be slumming it here Schroeder, when you could be up having cocktails with the High Yeller Feller."

The High Yeller Feller was the Governor, the Honourable Philip Chandros, who was very nearly white, a fact made much of in the island when feelings ran high.

"Hey now Bob, there's no need to talk like that," Schroeder said quietly, with only the mildest reproof in his voice. "We're all here because we want to be and enjoy the company. There's no black and white or rich and poor at this table, just friends. I don't do this to feel superior or to be one of the boys. Like you said, the Colonial Club is there for that sort of person."

"Hear hear," said Davern.

Rolle looked around slowly, then rubbed his hand over his face. The motion smoothed out the tight lines of anger. "Man, you're right. I apologise. Sorry you guys, I'm way out of line."

His gaze seemed to be drawn to Angelique who was passing the room and then he looked away quickly. "The black mechanic makes a speech. Oh Man."

O'Dowd had come across the room and now he stood behind Rolle.

"Rolle, you should guard your tongue," he said.

"Yes Pappy, I'll go to my room now." Rolle said. He threw money on the table. "That should cover it." He held up a five dollar bill to O'Dowd. "I'll get my own car, but keep the change, my good man."

For a moment it looked like O'Dowd would step forward and strike him.

"Rolle, go home," he said.

"Way ahead aya," Rolle said, and walked out.

Ferris hesitated, then excused himself and followed Rolle out through the restaurant.

"Bob, are you okay?" he asked as he caught up.

Rolle turned and smiled. "Had a skinful, baby." He swayed slightly. "That Shark-tooth mofo. Had it up to here with that bastard. Day will come when I whip some hunks out of his ass. Mark my words. Only so much a body can take."

"Do you want a lift?" Ferris asked, mystified. But he knew one of the nicknames for Pappy O'Dowd was 'Shark Teeth'.

"Thanks but no. It's okay. I'm probably not going to drive. Maybe a walk home to clear my head."

He started to turn away then stopped. "All just friends, he said. Do you believe that?"

"Yes," Ferris said.

"Ah, you white guys, always willing to believe in lies. Now lookee here, *in vino veritas* – you know how the drink talk and it tell truth. I'm not really your friend. But I don't mean you no harm. Let me ask you – do you really want to be your own boss? Or do you just want a change of boss?"

Ferris opened his mouth and paused. "I don't know," he said honestly.

"You try to be a good man, Tony. Respect. But that guy is not your friend neither. I don't like him, and not just for that club. Maybe by his own lights, he try to do the right thing but you should watch out for yourself."

"I don't know what you mean, Bob," Ferris said.

"Can't make it no clearer," Rolle said and laughed. "It's all about how to make friends and influence people. Be seeing ya, big

guy."
He waved and walked out into the night.

CHAPTER 15

When he got back to the lounge, O'Dowd and his guests were gone.

"That was a bit tense," Doc Hank said with a wince.

"The rum and the heat," Schroeder said absently.

"You sitting this one out, Tony?"

"No, deal me in," Ferris said. Chen caught a winning streak, and the others were too distracted to turn the run of play and Ferris didn't much enjoy losing.

After about thirty minutes Schroeder threw in his cards and pushed his seat back.

"Sorry guys, my mind is elsewhere. We can pick it up another night." With that they broke up.

"Cheer up, Tony," Jimmy Chen said as he gathered in his pile of chips. "I have a way for you to earn back my winnings."

"I think that's it for the cards this week," Ferris said glumly.

"Nope, I mean paying work," Chen said. "I got a gig from the tourist board people, aerial photography of St. Marc, hasn't been done for a dog's age."

"You're a photographer too?" Ferris asked.

"Freelance reporting doesn't entirely pay the bills in an island with one daily paper," Jimmy said ruefully. "Besides, with photography I let the pictures do the talking and I don't need an editor to correct my spelling."

"You do realise some people, rude people, call my plane a bird cage?" Chen grinned wryly. "I'm a big boy. Also on a tight budget, so I couldn't afford a helicopter or a bigger plane. Also you are local, and I can only pay half until my wages."

Ferris walked out to the car park with Schroeder.

"Tony, I know you find Bob Rolle amusing, and don't get me

wrong, he's a fun guy to have around – but he's a loose cannon. Look at the scene just now with Mr O'Dowd – talk about biting the hand that feeds you."

"Biting which hand?" Ferris asked.

Schroeder gestured vaguely at the car park. "He's a Mr Fixit for O'Dowd's political machine. Something must be wrong if they nearly came to blows. But it would be better for you not to side openly with Rolle. O'Dowd is out of favour but he's part of the establishment, and Rolle is … just some dirty tricks mechanic with a shady past."

The lights didn't reach to the back of the parking lot, where Schroeder had left his car.

"Bob is alright," Ferris started to say.

Three masked men stepped out of the shadows. They were carrying iron bars and knives.

One of them stepped ahead of the others. He had dreadlocks and looked vaguely familiar.

"Give me your wallet, old man," he shouted at Schroeder, in a strong Afro-French accent.

"What if I don't want to?" Schroeder said evenly.

Dreadlocks shuffled into a crouch and waved at his friends to fan out. "Then I teach you to behave," he said, and swung the iron bar. Schroeder flowed under it, and his straight right connected with the man's jaw. And knocked him flying.

The two others circled Ferris. One went into a boxing stance like Danmyé, the capoeira of Martinique, and let fly a flurry of punches and kicks. Ferris blocked and side-stepped, instinctively. From the speed of the attackers he guessed they were in their late teens. Gravel crunched as the second youth shifted his weight. Ferris ducked and a foot whizzed over his head. Ferris lunged into a counter-punch with his shoulder behind it. His knuckles hit the young man's crotch and the youth shrieked and dropped to the ground. The second youth stepped back and pulled a knife. Ferris shuffled back to widen the distance and brought his fists up into a defensive boxing position.

"Stay back, Vic," Ferris panted. But Schroeder's blood was up and he closed with the youth from the side and grabbed for the knife. The youth jerked back and swiped, and the blade caught Schroeder on the palm. He cursed but Ferris moved in fast with the youth off balance, and landed a kick on the shin.

The young man grunted and lunged, but Ferris stepped back and again kicked at his assailant's weighted leg. His heel thudded on bone and the youth swore and stumbled back.

The guy Ferris had nutted still rolled on the ground, retching and moaning. The one Schroeder had punched was trying to sit up, shaking his head.

"Go get help, Vic," Ferris said.

A huge voice bellowed "Hey!" and the car-park lit up in the glare of spot-lights.

The masked leader shouted: "*Nu devon ee partee, lay jandams sonn arrivay!*" He sprang up, and with the help of the knife man, dragged the third youth to his feet and supported him under the arms as they ran off into the night.

A truck roared up next to Ferris and stopped in a squeal of tyres. Ferris was surprised to see it was Rolle's pick-up and not the police. Rolle stepped out into the glare of the lights carrying a baseball bat.

"Stupid sons of bitches," he said. "I was asleep in the cab, they coulda had me cold. You alright?"

They both looked at Schroeder, who shrugged and then looked down at his hand. "That stings," Schroeder said. He fished a handkerchief out of his pocket and wrapped it around his hand.

"Maybe you're right after all Rolle, maybe just trying to help people with work doesn't solve anything."

"You need to get that seen to, Vic," Ferris said. His heart still hadn't slowed to normal speed.

A stain spread ominously across Schroeder's handkerchief.

"I'll explain to Pierre," Rolle said. "Ferris, I think maybe you need to bring Schroeder to the Emergency room."

"Just a scratch," Schroeder said, "But you drive." He was still on an adrenaline high. But he handed Ferris the keys and got in the passenger seat. Ferris got into the driver's seat and started the engine.

The Michael Schroeder Memorial hospital was only a three minute drive but within the first block Ferris was wondering if checking the bistro's first aid box might have been a better idea.

Schroeder was wired.

"Bam-bam, one-two – combinations Tony, none these natural fighters understand them, some life in the old dog yet eh?" He jogged in his seat and tapped on the dashboard.

"Vic, try and sit still, we're nearly there."

Then he was quiet for a moment before saying, "Shit, it won't stop bleeding." Ferris pulled up outside the hospital and switched on the overhead light. Schroeder's handkerchief was almost completely red. And spots of blood had splashed all over the console between the seats and on the dashboard. "Vic, you need stitches."

Doc Hank had arrived at the emergency room ahead of them. "Fancy seeing you again so soon," he started to say with a smile, then saw the blood-soaked handkerchief and whisked Schroeder off.

The reception area of the emergency room was deserted and Ferris tried to read an old copy of Fortune magazine but he was still keyed up after the fight and restless. He kept looking at his watch and it felt like forever but it was only fifteen minutes later that they came out.

Schroeder's hand and wrist were wrapped in a large padded bandage. "It's not as bad as it looks," Doc Hank said. "Twelve stitches, it was a deep gash but clean. And you're lucky no tendons got cut but I wanted to immobilise it."

Sergeant Aziz walked into the reception and glowered. "I hope you were planning to report this? Luckily Pierre thought to inform us. A statement can wait till the morning, but did either of you notice anything specific?"

Ferris mentioned that the attackers looked in their late teens, and spoke heavily accented French.

"Haitians or Jamaicans I'd guess," Schroeder grunted. "You can take the man out of the yard but you can't take the yard out of the man eh?"

"It's a problem," Aziz said. "But we're on it. I had Constable Gombs out there, supposedly on patrol."

"We didn't see any sign of him," Schroeder said. "But no great harm done."

"Really," said Aziz icily. "Men with knives and iron bars, security lights broken and Gombs asleep in his car some place. The Superintendent will have my hide."

Ferris drove Schroeder home.

Schroeder was silent most of the way. "Thanks, Tony," he said at last. "Hey, they need to get up to speed on the security around the country club eh? And who the hell is Constable Gombs?"

CHAPTER 16

In the morning Ferris went down to police HQ and made a full statement about the mugging. After that, he went to see Marlon Enright to ask about the aircraft leasing contract. "Sure Tony, Mr Schroeder has your back on this one. You can either bring back the contract, or run it past Flores." Ricardo Flores was Schroeder's attorney in San Juan.

As he headed back to the marina, he saw Jimmy Chen sitting outside the gate on a moped. "I was going to cycle," Ferris said. He eyed the pillion of the moped dubiously. The gap between Jimmy and his crush-proof camera box on the rear rack looked child-sized.

Jimmy handed him a helmet. "Time is money, Ferris. You weren't seriously going to cycle to the airfield at this hour? 'Mad dogs and Englishmen' is right."

Jimmy always had a slightly mad glint in his eye, which Ferris assumed was due to the way light fell on his spectacles. But on the ride out to the airfield he got to see the true wildness. Despite being the pillion passenger, Ferris was taller than Jimmy, and could see over his head. He got to see the road whizzing past at appalling speed.

He was relieved when they arrived at the airfield in one piece.

Schroeder's red Dodge Ram stood outside the club-house, and Schroeder sat on the veranda.

"Hi Vic. How's the hand?"

Schroeder held up his bandaged hand. "Hardly a tickle. Doc Hank gave me such strong pain-killers I probably shouldn't be driving. Don't print that," he said to Jimmy ruefully.

Jimmy held up his camera case. "I'm Jimmy the tourism photographer right now Vic, don't worry. Chen the crime reporter will be by later. You waiting for the King Air?"

"Yep," Schroeder said unhappily. "My guests had to switch planes. Garcia hit an underwater obstruction on take-off this morning. There's a three-foot long gash in the Turbo-Goose. He's staying in San Juan to see if it can be patched up. Getting it repaired will be a nightmare. I'm not even sure the people who reconditioned it are still in business."

The whistle of turbo-props interrupted him.

"Here they come. Looks like I get to throw my party after all. Speaking of which, Jimmy, did your editor tell you that you're invited?"

Jimmy looked taken aback. "I'm sure the Courier will want to cover it but the society page is hardly my thing, Vic."

Schroeder grinned. "Pierre and Celine are the caterers." Jimmy sighed. "Food bribes? Okay then, I'm in." They watched in silence as the King Air landed as if rolling down a ramp.

With a pang of envy Ferris recognised Nilsson's shock of white hair in the cockpit.

The plane slid to a halt fifty yards from the end of the runway and idled while four people climbed down the stairs, three men and a woman.

"Come on," Schroeder said impulsively. "I'll introduce you quickly. Put names to the faces. You can talk to them later at the party."

He strode forward and Jimmy Chen shrugged at Ferris and followed.

A stocky bow-legged man with an oiled black ponytail walked briskly ahead of the others. He had a drooping moustache and wore a loose beach shirt and docker shorts. A valise swung from his left hand. He tensed as Schroeder approached and only relaxed when he recognised him, but stayed very alert looking at Ferris and Chen. Ferris knew the type. Trained killer or bodyguard. Or both.

The rest of the party came up, and the obvious leader stepped forward. He could have been anywhere between forty-five and sixty, bald on top, white hair at the side cut back very severely, with the lean muscular body of an Olympic swimmer or a soldier who never let age get in the way of his training.

"Vic," the bald soldier said with a wide smile. But his eyes, also, stayed watchful.

"Robert," Schroeder said. He pronounced the name in the French way, confirming that this was the notorious Colonel Arnaud. "Excuse the hand. I'm sure you guys are looking forward to freshening up after flying all the way from Florida."

"Yes," Arnaud said. "It was an early start and I am not so young now."

"I hear you," Schroeder said. "I want to introduce a couple of my acquaintances. You'll meet them again later, but as they happen to be here, this is Tony Ferris, a local pilot, and Jimmy Chen, from our newspaper. Guys, this is Robert Arnaud, CEO of Spearpoint, and fellow melon nerd."

"Enchanted," Arnaud said, and shook hands with them both. The skin around his eyes crinkled in a charming manner when he smiled, and Ferris mistrusted him immediately.

"And in turn, allow me to introduce my associates: Juanita Cardénas, and Erik Braun." Juanita Cardénas wore a fashionable pants-suit. It looked tailored, but a woman might have said it was just a little too tight. Ferris realised he had been looking at her and holding her hand a beat too long.

Braun was probably in his late thirties, he had greying hair, cut short but not in a military style, he also looked very fit and hard.

Arnaud gestured at the ponytail, who still watched carefully, balanced on the balls of his feet. "And this is my bodyguard Oscar Quintero. No doubt Vic has told you I am in the security consultancy business but I found out in Mexico that there is no irony in having my own security consultant."

"Captain," Quintero said and almost clicked his heels. Something like a polite smile tugged at his moustache.

As they shook hands Ferris noticed tattoos on Quintero's muscular arms.

"I hope to see you later guys," Schroeder said, and led his guests to the Ram.

"Well mother's sick," Chen said mysteriously. He watched the party getting into the Ram and then followed Ferris over to the parked Cub.

They watched the King Air taxi back to the end of the runway.

"What did you think of the heavies?" Chen said.

"The bodyguard school people? Scary," Ferris said.

"Bodyguard school my ass. Did you see those tattoos?"

"I didn't get a good look."

"Winged swords, stuff like that. Either special forces or gang markings. I don't know which is worse. As for his boss, that man is a mercenary, he wants to train more mercenaries, the island will be over-run by gunmen. When I recognised the name, I volunteered to write an exposé for the Courier. But the editor got cold feet, it looks like the halo of the Michael Schroeder Memorial Hospital touches Arnaud. And so, never a disparaging word. But you should look him up on the internet."

Ferris felt bewildered. "But at the moment it's all about casinos and mobile phone masts isn't it? Where do mercenaries fit in? Aren't you putting two and two together to get five?"

"Could be," Chen said. "Then again reporter's nose maybe, I know bodyguard schools and mobile phone transmitters don't add up to mercenaries."

Nilsson had the King Air turned around at the end of the runway and the air wavered with turbine noise and jet fumes as he wound it up with the brakes on.

"I don't get it," Ferris said.

Chen sighed. "And maybe there is nothing to get. Look, I can't confirm it and you would need to get into a good newspaper archive service to see where I'm coming from. Back in the day, Arnaud was one of Bob Denard's crew when they tried to take over the Comoros islands. They made three coup attempts – last one was only two years ago."

Ferris held his breath as the turbines of the King Air blared and the plane came down the runway. Fourteen seconds and the wheels came off the ground and Nilsson had the gear stowed smoothly and banked away. The noise of the turbines faded.

"Wasn't that Mad Mike Hoare?"

"No, he tried to take over the Seychelles. That's ancient history. Hoare's out of jail and retired now. But the same idea, tough white guys take over some backward island. Makes you think doesn't it?"

Chen opened the passenger door, and put his camera bag inside.

"Oh come on," Ferris said. "They'll hardly start a coup here, will they?"

"It doesn't seem likely but I doubt if they are here for a holiday either. Or for melon farming. Anyway, like I said you can look it up. Let's get flying, your time is my money."

"How slow can you fly this thing?"

"Above fifty is safe. I can drop it to forty-five with full flaps but it will seem like standing still even at sixty unless you want to go really low."

"Sounds good," Jimmy said. He spread his map out on the ground, and traced a rough route across the bay. "Most of the photos of the harbour are about twenty five years old. I figure one pass each way should be enough. Maybe a couple of circuits, and we'll avoid wasting film on the empty places Schroeder is going to dig up."

"You don't approve of the Golf and Country Club?" Ferris asked.

"Do you? I'm not hating on it like Rolle but I'm not crazy about it either. But stuff happens. Could be jobs, and the island could do with more jobs. Maybe that's the big announcement at the party tonight."

"Still looking for a reason to be there?"

Chen scowled. "I bet he rang up and told the editor himself. Still if I get paid and Pierre's canapés are as good as they say I can't say no."

He bundled up the map, and Ferris pulled open the door of the Cub.

He cut inland over the town, and circled it, taking in the shabby sprawl of the shanties, and the bold sweep of the Corniche road. He decided to follow the road to see how far it had progressed. It wasn't something he thought about on the ground, and when he flew passengers or freight, taking the shortest route safely took his mind off sight-seeing.

He flew along above the Corniche, and marvelled at how far it had stretched, the finished section was almost ten miles long, at a guess, and the track being cut through the brush was perhaps fifteen miles further on. He reached the end of the finished stretch, and banked the plane to look down on the construction work below. The trucks and mechanical diggers were like toys as they moved about slowly.

As he circled, he noticed a spur road leading off the highway, and followed its direction with his eye. It seemed to lead towards the airfield, so he turned the plane and lined the nose up with the minor road, and followed it. It ran straight as an arrow to within a mile of the airfield, and Ferris decided to ask about it when he got back.

CHAPTER 17

When they landed Jimmy said, "Thanks Tony, that was just the ticket." He dug out his wallet. "Like I said, I can pay you half now, the rest at the weekend." Ferris hesitated. "Aren't you going to check the photos first?" Jimmy smiled. "I'd say most of them are perfect, you get a feel for these things. I burned through some rolls. I will develop the contact prints after work and if I need to re-do any, we can go up again tomorrow if you're game."

"Sure," Ferris said, "You can let me know tonight at the party." Jimmy wrinkled his nose. "I'd almost forgotten. God, it feels like being kept back after school." Jimmy stowed away his camera and lenses. Ferris spotted the St. Marc Courier stickers on the side of the crush-proof aluminium box, and smiled. Lenses were expensive.

Another hair-raising moped ride and Jimmy dropped him off at Rolle's internet cafe. Ferris bought some time on a terminal. It was cheaper than at the hotel. He tried all the big search websites. As Chen said, he could see articles about Robert Denard, but all he could find about Arnaud was a possible match in a long-ago French UN mission in West Africa and one mention at the website of melon growers festival in Tampa. He did searches to see if there were any pictures of former members of the French 2nd Marine Infantry Parachute Regiment and the French Foreign Legion, but nobody resembled Arnaud or any of his crew.

The session timed out so he closed down the browser and logged out. Rolle had come in and sauntered over. "Yo Tone, you clear the cache?"

"No," Ferris said, nettled. "What's that mean?"

"Jeez, don't they got no computers in your fighter planes?"

"Those were different computers, and we trained for years."

"Yeah, this sheet is worse than filling out government forms. The young uns take to it like fish to water but anyone over twenty five is a baby. I was hoping Linc would take an interest but no chance since he went sports-mad. But lemme show you a cool trick even an old-school mechanic can pick up." Before he could move, Rolle leaned over and relaunched the browser.

The search page came up, and Rolle tutted "See? Noo privacy man. Bet you were researching your soon-to-be new best friends. But no harm done, right?"

Ferris stared at him. "Ive no idea what you're talking about."

Rolle laughed delightedly and tapped his nose. "There is none so blind as them what don't want to see, eh?"

He was silent for a moment and clicked through some settings. "Lookee here – clear cache. For future reference. Still, you're showing some survival skills. Don't trust the builder-man."

Ferris stood up. "Last time you said it was the rum talking, but I still don't get you."

"None of my business but could be he's blowing smoke up your ass man, you ever wonder where he got his money? You wouldn't really trust me, right? So why you trust the S-man?"

Ferris shrugged impatiently. "He was in the container business in Vietnam right when the war took off is how I understand he made his money."

"Riiight, you keep thinking that," Rolle said and patted him on the shoulder. "You going to his shindig later?"

"I suppose so," Ferris said.

"You'll notice I wasn't invited. But aye man you've arrived at last. You ain't be talking to riff-raff no more Tony, you be in company with the high mucky-mucks now, governor and all."

"Oh very witty," Ferris said irritably. "Why do you talk like that? You're an educated man."

"Man should remember where he came from," Rolle said. "I'm from the fisher-folk, and my old man still go out in all weathers. Talking like them reminds me who I am. I'm not white on the inside like some. And being able to talk like a New Yorker sometimes make me forget that."

Ferris went back through the hotel and deliberately passed by the weekly social of the charitable committee, which was just breaking up. All the island matriarchy were there to see and be seen, Mrs O'Dowd, Mrs Legett, Mrs Merriweather and among others, Mrs Braynen the wife of the bank manager. Mrs Legett was an elegant lady who was always dressed in a twin set any time Ferris saw her and today she was in canary yellow.

Superintendent Legett sat sipping an iced tea at a side table waiting for his wife to finish air-kissing the other ladies who lunched. He looked younger and less imposing in a short-sleeved casual shirt and civilian trousers.

Ferris stopped in front of Legett's table.

"Might I speak to you for a moment, sir?"

"Of course," Legett said warily. He waved to his wife who smiled back although she did glance at Ferris dubiously.

A waitress of about fifteen rattled a fresh pot of tea onto the table nervously. She looked vaguely familiar.

"Thank you, Shareen," Legett said, "And how is your mum?" Shareen lowered her eyes but smiled slightly.

"She's fine thanks, Mr Legett."

She looked up at Ferris and he finally recognised her as the daughter of one of the chambermaids. "Hi, Mr Ferris. Can I get you anything?"

"Nothing right now, thanks," Ferris said, as he sat down.

"Miz Wilson's daughter," Legett confirmed. Ferris kept a neutral expression, he wasn't sure how far knowledge of his one time friendship with Mavis Wilson was spread. "Nice kid. No need to look surprised Ferris, I actually look for the good in people. When I'm off duty." He sighed. "Although I think you want to talk work. Well?"

Ferris summarised what Chen had said.

Legett sighed. "Thank you for your concern, Mr Ferris. We know perfectly well who Arnaud is." He sipped his tea absently. "I know some people like to think it's charming and backward here, but we do have a T1 cable and we also have links with Interpol and foreign intelligence agencies. And I do take seriously the double role of our police as a national security force." Legett nodded and smiled across at his wife, without missing a beat.

"But the last time I checked, we still had a free country and Arnaud appears to be what he says, a retired soldier who has become a businessman. Not a particularly successful one, but with Mr Schroeder's help perhaps he can turn that around. He has all sorts of impressive letters of credit the ministers liked and I had Aziz go through their luggage and apart from a couple of pistols for which they have permits, there was nothing suspicious. We will be watching Mr Arnaud closely if that sets your mind at rest and if he does anything out of the way we will come down on him like a ton of bricks."

Ferris opened his mouth and not wanting to look like a goldfish he said, "I apologise if it sounded like I was trying to tell you how to do your job."

Legett waved tiredly, and rose. "No harm done. Don't let Jimmy worry you, he means well but he hasn't had his big scoop yet. If they still use that phrase. Now, if you'll excuse me, I must rescue my wife."

He strode languidly across the room and Ferris wished as usual that he had kept his mouth shut and not got carried away with Jimmy Chen's talk. He was still baffled because surely Schroeder would also know about Arnaud's dubious past and why would he want to do business with him?

Going back to the marina, Ferris saw that the sixty-nine metre Italian super-yacht had moved to moor on the most desirable jetty, right up against the hotel. It looked impressive and had three decks, but from living on a yacht himself he knew that the inside would be maybe eighty feet long by fifteen wide and if Schroeder invited more than sixty people it could get cosy. He checked his post box and there was an embossed invitation signed by Schroeder.

Going out on the pontoon he saw a new boat berthed opposite the *Trinidad*, a gleaming navy-blue hulled, forty foot, cutter-rigged ocean yacht. Even from the pontoon it looked more spacious and modern than the *Trinidad*. The stern said *Grainuaile, Pensacola*.

As he approached, a red-haired woman stepped down onto the pontoon.

She smiled and put out her hand.

"Hi, I'm Marcie Clark." She was nearly as tall as Ferris, and between thirty five and forty perhaps. She obviously didn't give a damn about cosmetics because she had freckles and her face was lined and dried out by the sun and wind. She had the lean physique of an athlete but her t-shirt and shorts had curves in all the right places.

"Tony Ferris, of the *Trinidad*." She looked so commiseratingly at the *Trinidad* that Ferris felt a stab of embarrassment about the peeling hull. Then she looked back at him.

"I'm having a house-warming tonight to get to know all the neighbours," She said. "Would you like to come? Deck barbecue, Bring your own beer."

"I'd love to," Ferris said regretfully. "But I've already promised to go to another party and I can't duck out."

"Why not?" Marcie said directly.

Ferris nodded at the giant Italian cruiser.

"Oh," she said. "Some other time then."

CHAPTER 18

Ferris dug out his best smart casual, and headed out at 7.30 pm. He cut through the hotel on his way and checked his appearance in one of the full-length banks of mirrors in the hallway. In his lightweight poplin suit he looked like a seedy limousine driver.

In the bar he met Chris Turner talking to Davern.

"Hey Tony," Chris said. "We were just talking about this reception." He held up an invitation. "Slightly to my surprise I got invited, although I'm sure I'll stick out like a sore thumb. I have a black eye-patch but no tie, black or any other sort. So, I left my straw hat home."

Davern laughed. He had changed only his tie but looked formal. "I think it's an informal gathering, only the government and I will be dressed up."

"So how is Vic after the mugging," Chris asked. "I heard he got his hand slashed?"

"He seemed fine after," Ferris said. "Doc Hank said the nerves and tendons weren't damaged."

"Glad to hear it. And Rolle scared the muggers off? Wonders never cease." Davern looked at his watch. "We better be on time, no such thing as fashionably late with VIPs on a schedule." As they walked out to the jetty, Davern said,

"I'm glad this is so close. The government limousine is embarrassing. Next time I'll just rent a car."

"Will the Legetts be there?" Ferris asked.

"Probably, why?" Davern said.

"I made a fool of myself earlier today telling Superintendent Legett all about Jimmy Chen's conspiracy theory."

"That's very interesting Tony, I didn't know there was a conspiracy theory." Ferris told them the story.

"Could be a coincidence," Chris said. "Not exactly free of the taint of fortune soldiering myself. Kind of bummed Jimmy didn't have me in the frame."

Davern smiled weakly. "Could be. Well talk of the devil, you can tell him yourself." He indicated Jimmy Chen at the head of the gang-plank just ducking onto the deck of the super-yacht.

A white-gloved steward stood in the doorway, the effect somewhat spoiled by the moustached Quintero standing behind him watchfully. He had changed into a pale linen suit and looked like what he probably had been, an undercover Latin cop. "Captain," he nodded to Ferris. His expression didn't change as Davern and Chris came up but Chris said "Oho," out of the side of his mouth as they passed through the door.

The lounge on the super-yacht was about six hundred square feet. Very expensive white leather benches against the walls and a huge conference table in the middle took up a large chunk of the space. Schroeder's harbour diorama sat in the middle of the table, looking small. To the side stood a catering table with Celine and Pierre setting up while Angelique distributed glasses of champagne.

The lounge was still sparsely populated with Schroeder, his pilot, his nephew, the French party and Jimmy Chen.

Schroeder came forward.

"Bill and Tony, you've met everybody. Chris, you know Pierre, Celine and Angelique, and that was Oscar Quintero outside with the steward."

He drew Chris forward and made introductions.

Arnaud and Braun were dressed in ordinary dark suits that should have been badly fitting and too hot but in an annoying Continental manner they looked relaxed and comfortable. Ferris caught Braun's eye for a moment and he inclined his head politely. Braun was already holding himself aloof from the party, discreetly reverting to a bodyguarding role.

Ferris was paying more attention to Juanita. She was wearing a clinging low-cut silver-grey mini-dress. Angelique glided forward and offered him a drinks tray.

"Hey, Ferris," Angelique said. "You must be happy, your kind of woman, eh, the obvious type." Ferris took a champagne glass and felt heat rising in his cheeks. "I don't think she's interested."

"Oh, don't worry, I think she is. Anything in trousers is the phrase, yes?" She gave him an icy smile and sashayed back to the side-table.

Ferris looked after her briefly and got a distant nod from Pierre and Celine.

He found himself shaking hands with Arnaud.

"Captain Ferris, I was asking Vic about the aspects of scuba diving tourism. Sadly he is not a diver. Are you, Tony?"

"Not really," Ferris was bemused. He was trying not to look at Juanita, who seemed to be paying rapt attention to Chad Schroeder. He wondered why Arnaud seemed oblivious to her, the dress alone was drawing the attention of everyone else in the lounge.

"Do you know of any interesting wrecks?" Arnaud asked. "Spanish galleons perhaps."

"Well," Ferris dragged his attention back. "There are wrecks around every island in the Caribbean. Lots of reefs mean lots or wrecks."

"Quite so," Arnaud said. "Nothing special then in one way. Perhaps you should invent some lost treasure ships as a tourist attraction."

"Isn't this guy something," Schroeder said, re-joining the conversation.

"How do you say, always one must search for the angle." Arnaud said modestly, but his eyes danced. "I am an unsuccessful business-man, everything I essay turns to failure. A little bit of this, a little bit of that – Vic, as your president said, we French have no word for entrepreneur."

Schroeder laughed so loudly that everybody looked around and smiled.

"You slay me Arnaud, really you do," he said. Superintendent and Mrs Legett arrived as they spoke, shortly followed by Prime Minister Merriweather, Tourism Minister Ransome, then his rival and predecessor Pappy O'Dowd, and all their wives, who pretended to be very delighted to see each other again. Schroeder darted away to greet them, and Jimmy Chen wandered over, a strange intent smile on his face. Ferris re-introduced him to Arnaud.

"So, you know Vic from a melon conference?" Chen said.

"But of course, but it is a crowded field and the government here are not enthused, if that is the word. A romantic hobby I think was what the minister said. I think even Vic knew it was a polite way of saying no. What can one do? So to show that I have steadiness, it seems I have inadvertently entered the telecommunications business with Vic."

Chen snuck a sideways glance at Ferris. "It seems to be happening to everyone. You ran a security business in Mexico?"

"Yes, but again not very successfully," Arnaud said. "We French had an unfortunate start in Mexico. You know, *Cinco de Mayo* and all that. How do you say in English, persisting historical and cultural difficulties due to that imbecile Napoleon the Third."

Arnaud turned back to Ferris.

"And so Vic has been telling me about the French influence on St. Marc, it is more benevolent yes? So I expect to be more welcome there. Do the people here speak French?"

Jimmy looked at Ferris with a grin.

"Well," Ferris said, taken aback to be nominated as St. Marc's cultural expert. "There are a lot of French names but I haven't heard it spoken in the street and people only ever speak in English to me. Perhaps they speak French at home."

"It is good to find somebody to speak French with," Arnaud said, with genuine longing. "Braun was in the Legion but he prefers English."

Angelique hovered with a freshly restocked tray, and Ferris gestured her over.

"Angelique is from Martinique," he said.

"*Est-ce vrai?*" Arnaud said.

"*Oui, je suis de St Pierre,*" Angelique said brightly.

And after that Ferris couldn't keep up. He was both pleased and annoyed to see Angelique come alive to Arnaud's gallantry and genuine home-sickness.

"Well," Jimmy Chen said. "We're out of that particular conversation."

"Yep," Ferris said. "What do you think now?"

Chen shrugged. "It might be the champers, but he's growing on me. Plausible old devil. I can see how Schroeder might be taken in."

"It's their shared love of melon farming," Ferris said, watching as Arnaud gesticulated and spoke even faster.

"Big-time business romance," Chen agreed. "A bit sickening to watch but alcohol helps. Seriously though, I still don't believe in this whole security and bodyguard thing. And I really can't see them in the mobile phone business. You see that baboon outside?"

If he's security then the cure is worse than the disease. I'd rather take my chances with Vic's muggers."

"I didn't realise you cared so much," Ferris said.

"The snarky attitude is only skin deep," Chen said. "Anyway the photographs look good, except for around the marina. I want to do something a bit different if you can take me up again tomorrow morning."

"Sure," Ferris said, making a half-hearted mental note to not drink too much for the evening. "Here comes the governor."

CHAPTER 19

The music stopped and the volume of conversation dropped and all eyes turned to watch the entrance of the governor, the Honourable Philip Chandros.

Schroeder was in his element going over to be introduced by the prime minister and there was a great deal of bowing and hand shakes before the conversation returned to normal levels.

Ferris again looked over at Juanita talking to Chad. Chad flinched like he had been slapped and then laughed. Juanita walked off to rejoin Arnaud.

Ferris grinned. "I'm going to say hi to Chad," he said.

Chen grinned back. "That's one of the social stories I don't cover," he said.

"What's up Tony," Chad said. "I just got my ass handed to me by Miss Ice Cool in Bogotá."

"You think she's Colombian?" Ferris asked.

"I'm no expert, sounds like a South American accent, definitely not Mexican or Puerto Rican. Although when you've just been told 'You speak Spanish like a field hand', *hablas español como un campesino* ... At least I think that was it. My Spanish, she isn't very good-looking, unlike the lady."

Chad heaved a sigh. "Latina women have such big asses and yet they carry it off. I wonder if the dress is glued on. I would be so tempted if I wasn't a respectably married man."

No 'if' about it, Ferris thought.

Chad looked over at Vic, who had just finished introducing the serving staff to the governor and was now enthusiastically explaining his diorama to the governor, who nodded politely.

"Vic's arrived, anyway. The man from Shakopee entertains a Governor."

"Shakopee?" Ferris said absently. Vic looked unhealthily pale in the artificial light. Maybe the contrast from the dark blazer he wore but his fresh bandage looked discreet and Ferris wondered if his sore hand was bothering him.

"Shakopee, Minnesota. Where we're from. It's a dump. I think part of the reason he likes it here is that it reminds him of home back before Saint Paul swallowed it up."

"Does anything about this bodyguard and casino business bother you?" Ferris asked.

Chad wrinkled his nose. "I could care less about melon farming or eco-tourism, or whatever Arnaud is selling to Vic. But don't worry, Tony. I'm the CFO of the Schroeder group, but Vic is the CEO and CFO of Vic's life and money, and he is able to look after himself. He's shaken hands with the devil more than once, as he says."

"Yeah, he's used that one on me."

"It's a family favourite, once a week like roast beef. Don't sweat the bro-mance thing – that's the Schroeder charm in action. Vic does shovel it on, but we're famous for our charisma – except in my case, it skipped a generation."

Luis Garcia wandered over. "Hey Mr Ferris, Mr Chad."

"Call me Tony," Ferris said. "I heard what happened to the Turbo-Goose. Tough luck." Garcia spread his hands. "That's just it, helluva thing. I can make the big ugly old lady sit up and beg. Never let her get away from me the way these old flying boats do, and I'm just getting her unstuck and *pow*. It's like I hit a goddamn island. Just as well there was no one else on board, I thought I was a goner. I did a circuit but there was nothing in the water I could see. But at over eighty knots a small branch would do that damage. I'm afraid to land it on water now, even patched up."

"Well, here's to happy landings," Garcia toasted them. He drained the glass, and beckoned, and Shareen Wilson appeared with a fresh tray.

"Hey, Mr Ferris," Shareen said.

"Hi Shareen," Ferris said. "I didn't know you were here."

"Just helping out for a couple of hours. Wanted to see the governor. He even said hello." Shareen had big green eyes, and Ferris wondered vaguely if that came from her father and who he might be.

"How's your mum, Shareen?"

Shareen giggled, "Oh she fine, Mr Tony. But she say to watch out for you."

"Not a bit of it, girl. Too old, but I'd still give your momma a chase." Shareen simpered at Luis Garcia, who had already drained his glass.

"Can I get you another drink, Mr Garcia?"

"Mr Garcia is my father, honey child. But surely yes, another *cerveza* would be nice ..." Shareen giggled and nearly tripped as she went away.

Garcia flashed a smile at Ferris. "Sweet little thing."

"She's very young," Ferris said sourly.

Garcia assumed a look of injured innocence. "Hey, I hear you. Mr Schroeder set me straight on the local customs. No gay stuff, no local married women, no speedos or short-shorts in town, no public humping on the beach ... and no under-age kids. I miss any more no-nos?"

"That's about it," Ferris said. "You strike out with the silver dress?"

"I might have blown my chances by talking to her chest. But even before that, I got a heavy bitch-shield vibe. On top of which, it's a kind of square party," Garcia offered. "I appreciate Mr Vic inviting me but what's a younger guy to do around here?" He had a point. The Governor had left unobtrusively but with the ministers in their suits and Legett in his dress uniform it was very staid.

"It might pick up when the government ministers leave," Ferris said. "They look restless. They're stand-up guys but not what you could call party animals."

"I hope so." Garcia looked down at the neck of his cerveza. "Otherwise I'll try my luck at this crazy Rick's place that everyone warns me about."

"Yeah, not everybody goes to Rick's," Ferris smiled. Maybe Garcia had some fighter pilot blood in his veins after all.

"Well, I'm out to the deck for a smoke," Garcia said. "I'm sure Shareen will be able to find me."

"God, how I hate that damned machine he flies," Chad said. "It's like being in a mini-bus with engine trouble, and it lands on water? No thanks. And the cost of the damn thing. Amortizing once-a-month flights in the company accounts is a nightmare. Vic always says, if it flies, floats or fornicates, you should rent it. At least he rented the yacht for tonight. He could have rented a banquet hall at the hotel for a fraction. But the yacht has more glamour and it's coming out of his own money."

A disturbance rippled through the crowd and instinctively Ferris headed towards the commotion.

In a corner, Quintero had Garcia on his knees in a wrist lock. "What's going on?"

"Mr Garcia has forgotten his manners," Quintero said through his teeth.

"Quintero, that's enough," Braun said, appearing beside Ferris. He repeated it in Spanish. "Let him go."

Quintero unwound his muscular arms and Garcia straightened, shaking his wrist. "Jesus, man. You got some grip."

But Braun had hustled Quintero outside.

Garcia shook his head ruefully.

"What was all that about?" Ferris asked.

"Beats me," Garcia said. "I think he took exception to me talking to Shareen."

"Talking, that's all?"

"Far as I know. Like I said, I'm cool with the rules." Ferris wended his way to the bar grimly. Shareen was collecting a fresh tray of drinks. "Shareen, has anybody been bothering you?" She looked at him with big startled eyes "Why, no, Mr Tony." Ferris couldn't tell if she spoke the truth. "Well, tell Celine if there is. There's nothing to be afraid of." He noticed Superintendent Legett hovering nearby. "Anything the matter, Mr Ferris?" the superintendent asked. "Not that I can find, sir," Ferris replied.

"Cheer up then," Legett said. "You're scaring the children." Ferris made his way back to Chad who raised his eyebrows in inquiry.

Before Ferris could say anything the lights dimmed except for a single spot on the diorama. "Aaand here we go," Chad murmured.

Schroeder stepped into the spot beam. "Your Excellency, ladies and gentlemen, welcome and thank you for coming. I will be brief … I want to get the official part over so that you can enjoy the hospitality. As you know I love an excuse for a party."

Mild laughter greeted this. "That's true at least," Chad said to Ferris.

"Many of you have already seen the architect's model and plans for the new St. Marc golf and country club. I really believe that attracting high-net-worth individuals to the island is the path to prosperity for all and I hope it meets with your approval. And now his excellency the governor."

The governor waited for the polite applause to subside and made a witty and short speech in which he covered all the usual points about islander self sufficiency and community values and made it all sound fresh and new. Ferris stole a look at Davern who had a polite smile fixed to his face.

"And after this, the big-wigs will start to slip away," Chad murmured, "And the party might take off."

"Well Luis will be relieved," Ferris said.

"What was the scuffle about?"

"Seems Quintero thought Luis was hassling Shareen."

"And was he?"

"He says not and so did she."

"Huh. Like I said, Vic is the buyer. He better beware."

As they talked, the crowd slowly and subtly sorted itself, the ministers gravitating towards the governor and the business people arranging themselves around the ministers.

Ferris wanted to get to talk to Schroeder alone but as the host, he never seemed to have a minute to himself.

Now he was talking to Mr and Mrs Ransome and Juanita. Juanita was making a splash among the elegant ministerial wives. It was clear Mrs Ransome admired the daring dress. She was talking to Juanita with real engagement and Ferris realised that this was both her and Juanita's job and also the purpose at the party. Charm offensive, or networking was the new jargon. The RAF had tried to train him in this as well as piloting but in the social sphere, he remained a farm boy at heart.

Vic said something to Juanita, and they both turned and looked over and Vic raised his glass. Juanita held eye contact way too long, daring him.

"Looks like that girl has her sights on you," Chad said. "Maybe she's found out you're an ex-fighter pilot. Vic tends to talk too much."

"I don't know why," Ferris said. "I'm just a broken down old beach bum who happens to own an airplane, nothing else to distinguish me from the other rummies."

"Take any edge on an island," Chad said. Davern appeared and drew the minister aside.

"I better go say hello to Vic," Ferris said.

"We both better, but don't be the first to talk business. Can't do that even in the family, and much as he likes to play the father figure, he's not your father, Tony."

Ferris flushed. "I never said he was."

Chad smiled sadly. "Remember he never said so either. Been there, Tony."

CHAPTER 20

When they crossed the room, Mr Ransome intercepted Ferris and pumped his hand enthusiastically.

"I'm very glad to see you Mr Ferris," he said. "We need modernity more than ever. I was just telling Mr Davern that my officials have explained to me and Mr Schroeder that the geology of the island doesn't really support intensive farming and that his fine hobby is not a feasible business proposition here, or many other of the smaller islands in the Caribbean. We don't really have soil here. It is a pity as Mr Schroeder is so enthusiastic."

"Thanks be to Keynes," Davern said. "The subject might be closed forever." He smiled at Ferris and steered the minister to one side.

"Hi guys," Schroeder said. Juanita had moved away to take a champagne glass from Angelique. Schroeder followed Ferris's gaze.

"Great combination," Schroeder said absently. "I wouldn't mind seeing some girl-on-girl action, there."

"For God's sake, Vic," Chad said.

"Hey, come on you guys. Have you seen that dress up close? Made me forget I'm an old guy. Anyway, I didn't mean to talk tail. Where was I ... "

Chad moved away, hearing his uncle talk like him made him uncomfortable. "Puritan. Hypocrite," Schroeder said absently.

Schroeder got a far-away look in his eyes and looked around to see Juanita talking animatedly to Mrs Braynen, the bank manager's wife. Mr Braynen was beside her and Ferris glared across at him coldly.

"Goddamn that dress is a wonder of engineering," Schroeder said. "And Tony, smile at Mr Braynen, otherwise folks might think you want to punch out the poor man. He is the local source of money, after all."

"That's the sort of thing Frank would say," Ferris said, smiling despite himself.

Davern rejoined them. "Ah, I heard mention of Frank," he said. "I hope you don't mind Tony, I and Vic were discussing his business. The belt and suspenders business plan."

Ferris raised his eyebrows.

"Yes," Schroeder said, "Bill is on the high-powered side for me to be consulting him, but he does some private consulting to keep his hand in."

"Also, government work isn't as high-paying as you might think," Davern said. "It helps to have a second iron in the fire. Which is where you come in ... "

"Now whoa there Bill," Schroeder said jocularly. "Last time I tried to explain my business philosophy to Tony he jumped in my swimming pool to escape. I'd back up."

"Okay," Davern said. "Vic told me you didn't like the idea of doing work for him."

"They say you shouldn't do business with your friends," Ferris said.

"People say a lot of things, Tony," Davern said. "And mostly it's BS. When you start a business, it takes time to build it up, and the more income you have the more options it gives you. For instance, even in a couple of weeks things in San Juan will have cooled down and if this doesn't work out, you might bury the hatchet with Frank and get back your old job."

"I don't see that happening," Ferris said.

"It's one example of a choice," Davern said. "I congratulate you on getting recognised by the government here, but the contracts from them will be very small. They will want you to lease a bigger plane and yet the business they send your way will barely pay for the fuel in your own plane, so you need to diversify."

"Bill, I'm no business man. On current evidence I can't run a business and it's true, the Super Cub is no airliner."

Schroeder waved encouragingly. "Minor details, bub. You can learn as go. You've got a natural head for figures – you've been a jet fighter jock for Chrissakes. I did it and I started in construction."

"And look where it's gotten you," Davern said.

"Ow, got me there," Schroeder said. "Look Tony, I got myself between a rock and a hard place.

When this cellphone mast tender came up, my love for the island got the better of me and I jumped in feet first. My stateside lawyers were mad at me for getting carried away and signing up. Even Marlon was dismayed I didn't run it past him first. Mr Merriweather is a shark in Uncle Remus clothing, The penalty clauses and dead-lines are amazing. The telco equipment must be on the island in ten days or pay a daily fine *and also* the contract gets thrown open to competition again. It wouldn't be the end of the world but it's prudent to spend a little extra time and money."

"State the problems," Davern said drily.

Schroeder looked hunted. "The trouble is I over-committed and I have other demands on my own time so I need people to step in. I don't have telecoms experience nor do any of my people. It turns out Arnaud does, of a sort. It might only have been riding shotgun for the execs but he has contacts.

The melon growing was a coincidence.

As a bonus, Mizz Cardénas, as well as filling a dress distract-ingly, has been an executive in Telefónica México."

"Bill, how much do you really know about Arnaud?" Ferris said.

"He comes highly recommended by my colleagues in Mexico City. Great anti-kidnapping advice."

"I meant his background after leaving the army." Davern in-stantly looked very watchful. "Oh, I know he's had his troubles if that's what you mean. Awkward moments where he strayed into politics."

"I'll say," Ferris said.

Davern shook his head. "Tony, not everybody gets to be a gentleman once they stop being an officer. I'm sure you could think of some of your own comrades where it didn't work out."

"True," Ferris said. He was hardly in a position to call the kettle black.

"Look Tony it's a try-out," Schroeder said earnestly. You do business with people, see how reliable they are, if they do business the same way as you do. Sometimes it works out and sometimes it doesn't. Usually, there's no hard feelings either way. In my experi-ence you do business with saints, losers, conmen and murderers. The trouble is, you often don't know which until afterwards."

"I suppose," Ferris said, unconvinced.

"State the second problem," Davern prompted Schroeder.

Schroeder took a deep breath. "Oh what the hell. I thought the lead-time was sufficient so I saved some cash by arranging the telco equipment go by surface on a tramp steamer, which was a mistake as the nearest port they visit is Philipsburg, St Martin. In three days time.

I thought I had that taped with the Turbo Goose. And now Garcia breaks the Goose. There are no charters available for love nor money. But belt and suspenders like Bill said. I talked to Matt Hollis and I have a Beech 18 in reserve. Although it's a melon, according to Hollis. It's another tricky plane isn't it?"

"If you're not used to older style radials yes," Ferris agreed.

"Well, right now Luis is off my Christmas card list. He has no certification on any piston driven twins. If I need to use the Beech he can't fly it, even if I trusted him to. And what do you know, there are no certified pilots available at short notice."

Both Schroeder and Davern looked at him expectantly. "Except me," Ferris said.

Schroeder looked hopeful. "You do have certification on the Beech 18?"

"Thanks Vic, but I'm afraid to say I don't like the looks of Arnaud's crew. And this job sounds like I'd be ferrying them around a lot. I would not turn my back on the Quintero character."

Schroeder relaxed slightly. "That might not be a problem. Keep an open mind, it might never happen. It's a backup. It's only a couple of flights and Quintero would not be involved."

"Never say never," Davern said with a smile.

"I'll think it over," Ferris said.

"Do," Schroeder said. "And I'll respect your decision. A fella has to make up his own mind and like I said, win-win is the way I like things."

Schroeder excused himself and went to talk to the governor, and Ferris went for another drink.

When he turned around the governor had discreetly left. It was a signal for the other worthies. Shortly after, the prime minister had left, and the other ministers trickled away politely.

As the crowd thinned, half of the catering equipment was whisked away and replaced by an audio system and a DJ.

Ferris was glad to set that Shareen had left. There was no sign of Garcia, perhaps he had gone to Ricks after all.

Junkanoo replaced the muted elevator music that had been playing.

Jaunita sashayed over and had an earnest chat with the DJ. There was much nodding and the music switched to a fast Latin beat and Juanita whooped, "*!Cumbia!*"

She strode across the floor and dragged a startled Arnaud away from his conversation with Jimmy Chen. Arnaud smiled apologetically and paused to pick up the beat and started to dance with her.

Ferris walked over to join Chen. "Don't you dance, Jimmy?"

"No, I'm a writer not a lover," Chen said. "With apologies to Michael Jackson. You?"

"The RAF cured me of my two left feet in the cockpit but not in the ballroom." Chen grunted unenthusiastically. "Well, the champagne has worn off and my journalistic duty is done. See you in the day-light and away from the whiff of the brimstone," he said nodding toward Arnaud, who was executing the mambo with such agility that Ferris revised his age estimate down ten years.

The crowd thinned further, all the VIPs had made their excuses and left and the DJ was pumping up the volume. Some younger women who were the partners or escorts of Schroeder's associates joined in the dancing.

"Time for the old guys to get some shut-eye," Chris said with a twinkle, as he passed, accompanied by Davern.

"Speak for yourself," Davern said. "I have an early conference, but for that I'd be strutting my Travolta stuff."

Ferris went for another drink and spotted Juanita slipping out onto the rear deck.

He grabbed a second drink and headed the same way. Effacing himself from the crowd, near the door, Braun was reclining on one of the white leather benches, looking relaxed but alert.

"Hey Braun," Ferris said. "Not getting to enjoy the party?"

"Absurd as it may seem, Captain, I am on duty. I leave the sociability to the commander. Even on a sleepy island, threat assessment to the principal is a good way to keep on your toes."

"The only threat I can see is your plug-ugly friend," Ferris said truculently.

"Quintero?" Braun smiled. "He's very good at his job, you needn't worry, Captain."

"But I do worry because I can't figure out if he's a soldier or a gangster. And either way, we're not at war."

"Business is war by other means, don't you think? Especially in these latitudes. After all these years you're still thinking like a European, Captain. The Hague convention doesn't count for much down here. Quintero is a good fighter and that's what matters."

"Cocktail?" Ferris gestured with the second glass.

"No thank you, Captain. One to be sociable, then mineral water. You know how it is, one cerveza too many and your edge goes."

Braun rose, nodded pleasantly and headed for the other door. Arnaud was right, he had a great grasp of English.

Going out on the deck, Ferris felt hot blood tingling his ears. Maybe he was imagining it, but possibly he had just been called out about a jet that skidded off a runway. If they cared enough to look, the NTSB report of the incident would be publicly available.

CHAPTER 21

Juanita was leaning over the stern rail, smoking a cigarette.

She turned. "Hello, Captain Ferris."

"Call me Tony," he said automatically. He held out the spare cocktail glass.

"Thank you, most kind. And you must call me Juanita." She took the glass and smiled. "You are not enjoying the party?" She arched her eyebrows and also her back, ever so subtly. Up close, the effect was electrifying and Ferris had to remember to keep his hands to himself.

"I don't dance and I am bored of business talk," he said.

"So." She blew a smoke ring, pouting her lips around the 'o'. "You don't want to ask me about the cell phone tender. I wonder, how should I feel about that?"

"Are you enjoying the party?" Ferris asked, more to make a reply than anything else.

She sipped at her drink. "Yes Tony, I am enjoying the party. I am relaxed. I have had some drinks and people are kind and friendly. Now I am a little hot from dancing so I come out to enjoy the sea breeze and a cigarette."

She leaned back against the guard rail and the light of the deck spot lamps and the pier flood beams rippled across the silver grey dress. The dress clung to her from collarbone to thigh and showed off all her curves.

"But you have come out from the party. Why is that? I am a woman, so I am curious."

"I wanted to talk to you, I was curious after talking to Mr Arnaud."

"Oh?" She arched her back again, unmistakably. "Did you also wish to talk to Braun and Quintero?" Ferris grinned sheepishly.

"Braun is polite. But I might have punched Quintero."

"And why is that?" She asked.

"Perhaps I don't like his face or maybe I just don't like his sort of tough guy." Juanita sipped the cocktail again and her moist lip gloss sparkled in the indirect light.

"Phttt. He is not a tough guy so much as a savage. His sort don't have much time for women and we don't have much time for them. Are you a tough guy, Tony?"

Ferris laughed. "Once, perhaps. Now I'm just a guy with a small plane and romantic notions about living on a yacht."

She straightened gracefully. "You own a ship?"

Ferris laughed again. "A boat. Not like this. A little one."

"Even so. It must be exciting to have such freedom, not to be tied down to one place, to take your home with you, no?"

"I suppose so," Ferris was charmed. He could feel the heat of the alcohol and the attention going to his head and other places.

"I would like to see your little yacht," Juanita announced, draining the glass.

"But the dancing?"

"I can dance another time, It is not far?"

"Only two hundred metres. You can almost see it from here." Ferris pointed absently into the clutter of masts.

"Very well," she said. "You will bring me?"

She swept out through the lounge and down the gang-plank without a glance, past Braun and Quintero. Ferris strode after her, trying to look casual. He tried not to trip over the cross pieces of the gangway as Juanita strode ahead of him. Her buttocks swayed under the dress, moving up and down with each step around the unyielding line of a thong, like beach balls in a school science experiment.

"Well," she said challengingly, pausing on the quay. "Which way? I am not a mind reader." But oh yes you are, Ferris thought. "Come on," he said, aloud.

Her high heels made a clopping on the wooden decking of the floating pontoons and she walked unsteadily from alcohol and a lack of familiarity with high heels. Ferris offered his arm and she ignored it, but after stumbling over one of the cross-pieces, she relented and linked arms.

"No rush," Ferris said, "It's not far."

The dance music on the Italian cruiser faded into the hubbub of pop music and shouted conversation from the *Grainuaile*.

"Sounds like we went to the wrong party," Ferris said ruefully.

There was a throng on the next boat to match the noise level.

"Oh, it's a real boat."Juanita said. She pronounced it "butt".

As Ferris handed Juanita over the rail onto the *Trinidad*, a couple of the revellers yelled a cheery greeting. Ferris waved and thought he saw Marcie in the crowd wave back before he turned away.

"You know these people?" Juanita asked.

"No, the brotherhood of the sea. Or parties. I've never sailed my yacht but the other yacht people assume I am a sailor. Would you like to visit their party?"

"Not really, I want to see your butt first."

"Rightio," Ferris said, not bothering to correct her.

The *Trinidad* shifted slightly under their weight and Juanita staggered and giggled. Her heels made sharp thocking noises on the deck.

"Strictly speaking you shouldn't walk in heels on the deck of a yacht. It's bad for the timber. But then this isn't a yacht any more. Strictly speaking." Ferris could feel himself starting to babble as his hands twitched. Juanita looked very fetching in her silver dress, breasts jutting out the front and buttocks behind.

He unlocked the cockpit hatchway and led her below deck.

"Oh I'm sorry. Are you always very strict?" She teetered on one leg as she slipped off one shoe and almost unbalanced against him as she kicked off the other.

"Oops I think I have enough to drink no?"

She looked up and her lips were parted in a glistening pout and Ferris couldn't help himself and he kissed her. She giggled and swayed back and overbalanced as the edge of the bunk caught the back of her thighs.

Her lips were soft and inviting and his hands clawed her skirt up over her hips.

"You got a rubber, Tony? Now would be a good time to get it." She sighed into his ear as he kissed her throat and as if by an outside force his hands unfastened the eye-hooks of her dress. Her shoulders shrugged away the straps of the dress. Ferris pushed her back onto the bunk and she squirmed and they pawed mindlessly at each other.

"You like this?" she panted. "You're gonna like working with me a lot." It was like a punch in the guts. Ferris felt the haze clear and the lust wilt out of him.

"Is that what this is about?" Ferris said hoarsely. "You screw me so that I work for you? That's how real this is to you?"

"What is wrong?"

"Nothing. I'm no longer interested," Ferris said coldly, pushing away from her.

"What you say?" Puzzlement wrinkled her brow.

"I suddenly realised you're just a fat farm girl."

Her eyes narrowed and she swung her fist but Ferris even drunk had fighter pilot reflexes and he caught her wrist long before it connected.

"I think you should go," he said through gritted teeth when he released her wrist.

She shook her hand. "I think so too. I think something is wrong with you."

"I'll walk you back to the party."

"I can find my own way," she said, scrambling out of the bunk.

"I insist," he said. They ignored the party on the other boat on the way back, and when they got to the hotel entrance, she walked straight ahead without another word or a look back.

CHAPTER 22

"Two Seven to control – traffic on runway, traffic on runway!"

The alarm clock woke Ferris. Coming out into the sun, he had a throbbing behind his left eye, but it didn't bother him. The party next door had petered out around midnight so he hadn't been kept awake by that. And his annoyance with Juanita had passed after a couple of swigs of rum. Apart from just before he woke up, mostly he'd had a full night's sleep. Just not restful.

He sighed when he saw Jimmy Chen on his moped at the gate. Ferris climbed on and pulled the chin straps of the crash helmet extra tight. Strangely he had no fear in the Super Cub despite it being far more dangerous than the moped.

Chen wanted some high angle photos from five hundred feet directly over the yacht marina. Photos from a height and angle impossible to achieve from the hotel, which he could visit any time.

Ferris dawdled the Piper across the marina, flaps fully down and engine throttled back to forty-five miles per hour. The water was as still and blue as a swimming pool and it almost felt like they were hovering.

Chen was happy after two sweeps. "That should do it."

Back on the ground, he said, "I'll pay you the same as yesterday."

"That's not necessary Jimmy, fuel and time were about half of yesterday, not counting the ride out."

"Are you sure you're not undercharging?"

"It's an opening week offer, interest-free credit. The compensation is for the wild moped driving, not for the flying."

Jimmy smirked. "Maybe I need to throttle back at that. Your plane scares me too, no offence."

Wally Brunkard's convertible pulled up as they talked. Chris got out and hobbled around.

"Hullo, the island's two most up and coming young business-men in the one place? What an honour."

"You're walking better, Chris," Chen observed.

"Yep. I persuaded the docs to give me a light sports cast, the sort athletes get. It amused them.

I wouldn't care to say if I've flown with one good leg before, but time is money and with a deadline to get my insecticide dusting done before the storms so I can't mess about enjoying the break."

"Why so early," Ferris asked.

Wally Brunkard rolled his eyes. "Mr Chris is an early bird. The turbulence, I understand."

"Well then, let's get to the refuelling." Chris said.

"Where's Rufus?"

"Rufus done disappeared," Brunkard said. "He's laid low since he got out of the cells." Ferris looked at the pair, Chris on his walking stick and Brunkard looking as unfit as ever. The slightest exertion would reduce Brunkard to a puddle of sweat. Neither of them was up to wrangling the airfield's antique hand-pumps.

"I'll give you a hand," he offered.

"I'd rather watch paint dry," Chen said. "Or in this case emul-sion. If they don't like the photos I can always enter a contest. I'll see you tomorrow, Tony."

Brunkard, relieved, provided Ferris with a very soiled overall which nevertheless kept the grime of the fuel lines off him. Chris went to taxi over the new Ag-Cat and Brunkard produced his keyring and unlocked the fuel pump. Ferris was amused to see that the padlock was in perfect working order.

Unlike the motley contents of the customs shed, the aviation spirit was a coveted commodity and no temptation was left out for anyone trying their chances in the dead of night.

Chris supervised, graciously accepting Ferris's assistance. Brunk-ard fussed around, managing to seem very busy while Ferris worked the pump. In the heavy overall he sweated a lot, but the even though the pump was feeble, the Ag-Cat's tank was small.

"And you, Mr Tony?" Brunkard asked hopefully, when forty US gallons had gone aboard the Ag-Cat. "Your plane is not running low?"

"Thanks Mr Wally, I have about two hours worth on board."

Also he could get it considerably cheaper in San Juan.

"Much obliged, Tony," Chris said. "Like I said before, if you want to have a go at crop-dusting, let me know. Things might be a little hectic right now but in a week maybe."

Brunkard dropped Ferris at Marlon Enright's office. Enright wasn't in, but his assistant told Ferris the leasing agreement was quite detailed and Enright's associate office in San Juan were doing the bulk of the work on the contract, and it would be ready in about a week.

Ferris felt good after his work for the day and he felt like he was on a roll so he visited the chandlers above the marina and bought a can of paint, a can of primer, and a batch of sanding paper.

There was no sign of life on the *Grainuaile* when he got back. Perhaps the party had been wilder than he thought. The marina was very quiet, apart from the crockery washing noise of rigging lines tapping against masts, and the sleepy cry of a few birds, all the noise seemed to come from the direction of the hotel.

Ferris found an old yachting cap in the cabin and dug out a tiny folding stool and the last of bottle rum. He set down the stool next to the worst of the peeling paint and set himself to work sanding.

Marcie, wearing sunglasses, emerged from the cabin sometime after one. She walked hunched up like someone who expects the worst and wants to get over it. Ferris grinned. It was an amateur mistake by Marcie, she obviously wasn't a hardened drinker. The first beach cocktails of the season had that effect on the clean-living, they forgot that in among the refreshing fruit juice lurked high-proof alcohol that didn't get diluted.

An hour later or so, she hurried back down the pontoon carrying two bottles of water and vanished below decks without even looking around. The quietness of the marina continued, an occasional sound of hammering came from the boat-yard up the slip and from time to time somebody boarded a yacht or walked up to shore, but mostly it felt deserted.

The repetitive circular motion of sanding became calming and hypnotic and Ferris found if he rubbed gently he didn't sweat too much and his hands didn't cramp up too often. He felt like he could go on for hours.

When he was happy he had got at the peeled patch, he went below for the primer and found a box of dried out brushes in the galley. They were so stiff he thought they were useless, but when he dipped one in to stir the paint it softened enough to dab paint onto the bare patches. When he was finished the shore side was mottled with grey circles almost as if it had been machine-gunned by the coast guard. He found to his surprise that he had enjoyed himself.

In the evening he went along the shore to a shack that bought fresh from the fishermen straight off the boats, and bought fried conch and peppers.

He went back on board and considered going up to the bistro.

He was still a little sore about the Juanita incident and he wasn't sure how he'd react if he was asked about it. The pleasant rum-tinged buzz of his day of painting felt fragile. Besides, it wasn't a card game night, and he wanted to think things through. He opened another bottle of rum and fell asleep after a couple of swigs.

The following morning, Ferris was stirring himself and touching up the paint on the *Trinidad* when Sergeant Aziz came down the jetty, a manilla folder under his arm. His tunic was pressed and his cap peak, belt and shoes gleamed in the sunshine. Only a bulge in his pocket spoiled the perfectly fitted uniform. Ferris idly wondered did he have a wife or did he sit alone on a police bunk at night, ironing and shining shoes and thinking how to make the world miserable on the morrow.

"Permission to come aboard?"

"Safe enough, the new paint is on the hull below the deck line." Ferris wiped his hands on a cloth. Somehow the paint had got everywhere.

"Can we go below?" Aziz asked.

"It's cooler up here," Ferris pointed out.

"Also more public," Aziz said.

Ferris sighed. "As you like," he said, and led the way below. When they were safely in the galley, he turned and raised an eyebrow.

"I have to ask," Aziz said. "Where were you after the party, two nights back?"

"What's wrong?" Ferris felt alarm at the flatness of Aziz's tone.

"Please don't answer with a question."

"Alright, I came back here, with a woman. Juanita Cardénas. We had a disagreement and she went back to the party. I stayed here."

"Any witnesses?"

"The people on the next yacht were having a party and should be able to confirm. What is this about?"

"Shareen Wilson was missing for two days. She turned up. She'd been raped. With a broken bottle, or a machete. The doctors may be able to determine which."

"Good God," Ferris said and sat down. "I had no idea she was missing. Will she be alright?"

"She'll never be alright again," Aziz said. "You see, the conch fishermen pulled her out of the bay about three hours ago. Whoever it was didn't bother to weigh down the body."

"How dreadful," Ferris said, still not taking it in. "The poor kid. Who could do such a thing?" Aziz sat down opposite Ferris and opened the folder.

"I'm sorry but I have to do this," Aziz said, and fanned 9-inch full colour photos across the galley table.

Ferris didn't have time to prepare himself. He knew vaguely that postmortem decay was very swift in the tropics but this was much, much worse than he had imagined. He felt his gorge rising and the cabin got too small and close and he ran up the steps into the air. It took about ten breaths before he was sure he wasn't going to vomit. Better to not think of the object in the photos as Shareen. He blinked and the tears ran down his cheeks.

He flinched when he realised Aziz had followed him and stood beside him.

"It's good you can still cry. In Iraq they told us only women cried," Aziz said absently.

Ferris finally let go of the hand rail. "Are you happy now?" He asked bitterly.

"No," Aziz said, quite gently for him, "But it needs to be done. I expect a lot of tears when I show those pictures. Some will be crocodile tears, of course. You see, the person who did this will either be indifferent or over-react. The Frenchmen are combat vets and will have seen worse, so their reactions will tell me nothing."

"I don't understand you," Ferris said. "Please tell me you didn't ask Mavis to identify the body."

"No, that won't be necessary. It will be a closed casket funeral. We're not monsters. Except for whoever did this."

"I can't accept this," Ferris said.

"I know," Aziz said. "You are going to say that this should not happen, not in the island. But there are bad people everywhere and we got a real bad one out there now that needs to be stopped. Would you come in and give a saliva swab? We don't have a DNA facility here, we shall have to send to Florida, but we could eliminate many people."

"Yes," Ferris said, finding a focus for his anger. "I'd like to help, in any way I can."

"In that case, the first thing is to tell me everything you can remember about the evening," Aziz said, and pulled a tiny tape recorder out of his pocket.

***

When Aziz had gone, Ferris mechanically tidied away his painting gear. He had the presence of mind to wipe the brushes on an old rag. Then he went back into the cockpit and sat and stared out over the bay. He was still there when Jimmy Chen hailed the boat.

"Hi Tony, I brought the cash. But you don't look so good. What's up?"

"You just missed Sergeant Aziz. He might have a scoop for you. Shareen Wilson was murdered."

"Oh God." Jimmy's eyes were huge behind his glasses. "I knew she was missing. But this is shocking. Did he say much?"

"Not an awful lot but he showed me some gruesome crime scene photos and after questioning me he wanted me to make a statement and submit a DNA sample."

Jimmy shook his head. "You shouldn't really make a statement to the police Tony," he said. "Not even to the straight arrows like Legett and especially not to a barracuda like Aziz. And I wouldn't trust them not to buck up a DNA test."

"Very likely," Ferris said grimly. "He rattled me with his nasty pictures."

"It's a dirty trick," Jimmy said. "Well, forewarned is forearmed. But you should go talk to Marlon just the same."

CHAPTER 23

When Jimmy Chen was gone, Ferris sat in a blank daze. His stomach rebelled against the idea of alcohol and the pleasure in painting was gone.

Two police officers with clipboards came onto the marina and started to visit the berthed yachts. Ferris recognised one, last seen driving Aziz's car. He was a tall man running to fat who never seemed to hurry anywhere, which was a good idea in the heat.

Ferris guessed they were canvassing witnesses and watching their slow progress made him restless.

He wondered if he should visit Mavis Wilson, the mother of the murdered girl. It had been a long time since he had direct contact and maybe now was not the time.

She lived in the old town. It was a step up from the shanties but still a place an outsider hesitated to visit. He could ask Charles.

He got up and went into the hotel.

Charles the concierge was his usual professional self, but his smile was barely a flicker, and his eyes were haunted.

"Yes we're all devastated. Poor Mizz Wilson took it very badly. The doctor had to give her a sedative." He lowered his voice and leaned forward. "The police took her home and said not to talk about the matter and for the manager to refer any questions on to them, but since you know Mav- Mizz Wilson and poor Shareen I see no harm."

"Thanks, Charles," Ferris said. "Any messages for me?" There was a phone message from Reuben Bland at the Transport Ministry that he could collect the duplicate documentation. Half-heartedly Ferris went and collected the papers and lodged them at Marlon Enright's for safe-keeping. There was no news on the leasing contracts.

When he arrived back at the marina, the tall fat constable sat outside the gate enjoying the last sun. He got up and sauntered over when he saw Ferris.

He had eyes set too close together and Ferris wondered if he was as slow in the wits as he was on his feet.

Maybe somebody at headquarters had decided that the shoulder badges were too impersonal because he wore a name plate that said "CST Gombs"

"Hey Mr Ferris," he said jovially, "Sergeant Aziz wanted me to tell you that your statement will be typed up tomorrow morning and you can come by to read and sign it anytime you like."

"Have you made any progress?" Ferris asked and instantly regretted it, from the way Cst. Gombs grinned at him.

"You mean, are you in the clear? 'Fraid not. Miss Cardénas doesn't back up your alibi, she said you were not a person to trust."

"Surely my neighbours saw us?"

Gombs ceremoniously pulled out his notebook and licked his finger before opening it. Ferris wondered again how Gombs had passed the police exam.

He seemed to be enjoying himself and Ferris decided he didn't like the man. Aziz at least had the decency to maintain a facade of serious professionalism.

"Mizz Marcie Clark and her guests confirmed they saw you and Mizz Cardénas going onto your yacht but most of them didn't see her leave, and based on that level of observation, they didn't see you and they didn't *not* see you so there's no alibi ah-tall, if you catch my drift." He looked very pleased with his turn of phrase.

"That's great," Ferris said flatly. "And what am I expected to do about it?"

"Nothing, just keeping you up to date with the investigation." The constable chuckled and walked off shaking his head.

Often Vic Schroeder put his business associates up on his own estate but because of the refurbishments, Arnaud and his group were staying in the hotel. Without conscious decision, Ferris found himself in the air-conditioned glass "Atrium Cafe" that looked out over the marina.

"What did you say to the police?" Ferris said, trying to keep his voice level.

"Mr Ferris." Juanita Cardénas put down her glass of iced tea. "Nice to see you too." She looked as cool as the conditioned air.

Juanita was wearing a loose fitting linen suit that did her no favours and instead did indeed make her look like an overweight peasant girl.

"Well?" Ferris said.

"If you are staying, you might as well sit," she said.

He did, but on the front edge of the chair. "Why did you tell lies to the police?"

"Did the police tell you not to discuss your statement with anyone? They did me." Now that he thought about it, Ferris remembered that Aziz had told him just that. And the invitation to sign his statement was the only official news. Maybe the fat constable was stirring things up.

But a child had been murdered and Ferris didn't see why he should be a vehicle for wasting police time.

"They did. But then they came back and said you didn't back up my statement."

"Why should I help you when you don't want to help me?"

"This goes beyond not helping me. You are deliberately trying to get me into trouble."

Juanita sipped her iced tea. "Such a shocking and terrible crime," she said. "Without an alibi, suspicion could attach to you, no? Rumours could harm your business." She put down her glass on the table. "Perhaps even a risk of vigilantes, if the police seem slow in their investigation."

Ferris felt disgust. "I don't believe this, are you trying to blackmail me? What do you want from me?"

"Just that you agree to fly for Mr Schroeder. Then I will tell the unpleasant sergeant whatever you want."

"What's that to you?"

"Now that I am working with Mr Schroeder, part of my job is to see that he succeeds and one thing holding back his plans is your reluctance to fly for him."

Ferris flushed. "Does the death of the girl mean nothing to you?"

"I didn't know the girl."

"You can sit there and say that, in the same hotel that you took drinks from her!" Juanita shrugged. "I remember her from the party. But the world is an ugly place."

Ferris stared. He wanted to slap her. "Okay," he said. "If that's the way you want it. But you're being childish as well as illegal.

There is such an offence as 'wasting police time', they also have 'perverting the course of justice'."

He stood. "You might want to have a long think about both of those before you talk about doing me favours or not."

"I don't think you and me are going to like each other," Ferris said to Juanita.

She stared back at him, unblinking "That is entirely up to you, Captain."

Striding back through the hotel, Ferris met Schroeder coming from the business suites.

"Oh, hi Tony," Schroeder said listlessly. His cheeks were drawn. "You've heard the terrible news?"

Ferris nodded. He didn't trust himself to speak.

"Everyone is in shock," Schroeder said. "I don't think they know how to handle the situation. Luis was in police custody. He turned up yesterday with bruises and scratches. He said he tangled with the fishermen down at Rick's but the police weren't happy with his alibi."

Schroeder looked around and lowered his voice. "Everyone is under suspicion. God help me, but I'm glad I have an alibi."

"I thought I had one too," Ferris said tightly. "But it seems Senorita Cardénas thinks holding back my alibi will encourage me to reconsider your offer of work."

"She what? The interfering little bitch." Red dots appeared on Schroeder's cheekbones. His lips worked. "Why would she do that? That's just disgusting. Some people have no sense of decency."

"That's what I think," Ferris said.

"God dammit. I'll talk to Arnaud. I've got this Tony. I will make this go away. And maybe have Mizz Cardénas go away too."

Schroeder turned away and then hesitated. "I won't be at the bistro tonight, but you can reach me at home if anything comes up."

A sense of gloom and dread held the town. People were slower to smile than usual, their normally jolly and loud street conversations subdued, so that away from traffic noise, the town was quiet.

On his way to the bistro Ferris noticed more police officers on patrol than usual.

The atmosphere in the bistro was also muted. The members of

the card club were at their usual table but made no move to open the packs of cards. There was no sign of Schroeder nor Davern.

"Hi Tony," Doctor Sanders greeted him. "Do you want to drop into hospital administration tomorrow? They have a round trip courier job. I won't bore you with it now."

"Sure doc," Ferris said. "Thanks for letting me know." Rolle offered around cigars and when the others declined, smoked with no sign of pleasure.

"I don't understand it," Rolle said finally. "What are the cops doing?"

"Can't blame them for being careful," Jimmy Chen said. "At least they've given up on the DNA sample nonsense. They needed to fly in a specialist CSI team and it would take weeks to process the DNA. And only one chance in a million."

"Who knows," Hank Sanders said, "There are a lot less than a million people here and they were trying to do something. As it is, they may have no firm suspects, nothing to build a case on."

"Well, they need to get a move on with their science," Rolle said. "Or people will be taking the law into their own hands."

"Why is that?" Ferris asked.

"People are saying maybe the same people that mugged you and Schroeder murder Shareen."

"That's a big jump," Ferris said.

"Rumours start," Chen said. "Next thing somebody will want to teach the Haitians a lesson."

"Yes. People aren't talking about much else except poor Shareen," Rolle said.

Hank Sanders smiled sadly. "Maybe we should try, though."

"Maybe we should," Chen said. "Unless you have any insights you want to share Doc?"

"Come on Jimmy," Doc Hank said wanly. "Give it a rest. We're all off the clock now, aren't we?"

"No harm no foul doc," Jimmy said, holding up his hands. "Sorry, you're right, I have to switch off." They tried discussing the long range forecast for the hurricane season. Chen said the new five day forecasts might be useful but nobody would ever be able to predict a better or worse year for storms, except fortune tellers.

"Computers are no match for chaos theory," Hank Sanders said. He drained his glass and stood up. "Well fellas, I'm going to have an early night if you guys don't mind. My heart isn't in it."

When he was gone, Chen said, "He probably did the autopsy."

"For God's sake Jimmy," Ferris said. "Have a heart." Rolle put away his cigar case with a sigh. "Doc's not the only one bummed out, I'm heading as well. See you fellas around." Jimmy grinned crookedly at Ferris. "And then there were two."

"You didn't say who you thought the murderer is," Ferris said.

"I'm not a fan of whodunnits," Jimmy said, "You're a clever fella Tony, but better to leave it to the professionals. Some really dangerous suspects. Although the police don't seem to think so. Braun, Quintero and Garcia flew out to San Juan this morning, did you know that?"

Ferris remembered Shareen talking to Luis Garcia. He reached for the card decks and said, "I better give the cards back to Pierre."

CHAPTER 24

The other plane was flying ten feet off the ground, undercarriage still extended, right across their path.

When Ferris finally woke up, he felt as if he had just fallen asleep, and not in a good way. He had re-learned the hard way that rum could put you out but it didn't keep you out for long.

For a few confused seconds he teetered on the edge of sleep again. Then he levered himself out of his bunk. There was no use pretending the nightmares wouldn't come back if he didn't get up.

The marina was quiet again. He dragged himself to the showers and used the cold for as long as he could bear. It pulled him together enough to get shaved and dressed and then he checked in with the concierge desk.

Charles had two messages: a reminder from Doctor Sanders to phone the hospital administration and ask for Doctor Widdowfield, and that Sergeant Aziz wanted to see him down at the police headquarters.

Ferris was hung over enough to resent the police summons even though he had expected it. So he rang the hospital first and arranged to call on Doctor Widdowfield at noon. He let off some steam by walking the long way round to police headquarters.

In the quiet station foyer, old Sergeant Colbert sat at the desk like the ageing black sergeant in any movie. He smiled at Ferris in recognition.

"I expect you're here to sign your statement. I'll ring Aziz down." While he was waiting, Colbert chatted away as he worked. He reminded Ferris of a kindly old uncle and he felt his blood pressure returning to normal.

Marcie Clark came out of the offices and saw Ferris as she paused to put on her sunglasses. She nodded to him, and smiled at Colbert.

"Thank you and good day, ma'am." Colbert said. "Be seeing you."

"But not too soon," Marcie said with a wan smile and stepped out into the glare of the sun.

"Another statement?" Ferris asked.

"I couldn't say," Colbert said carefully.

Ferris felt sure Marcie had just seen Aziz and he got annoyed again. He waited for another five minutes until Aziz appeared and led him into an interview room.

"Did you send your fat side-kick to see me?" Ferris asked.

Aziz looked slightly surprised at the question. "You mean Gombs?"

"Was he supposed to tell me about Juanita Cardénas not backing up my story?"

"I might have suggested that he mention it. We have to stir things up in this case, and even a blunt instrument like Gombs comes in handy."

"I don't know what your game is Aziz, but I don't like it."

"Relax Ferris, if I was looking to frame somebody I could just snatch a couple of dock boys or Haitians off the street and beat them till they confessed to the Kennedy assassination." He held up a stapled sheaf of pages. "If you want to read through that and make sure it's a true record of what you said first, we can discuss other matters. Unless you want to alter your statement?"

"No," Ferris said. "I stand by my statement."

"You forgot to mention that you were friendly with Mavis Wilson," Aziz said. Ferris looked at him sharply but could see no sneer. Aziz kept a neutral expression.

"That's not relevant," Ferris said grimly.

"Very well," Aziz said, and slid the printed statement across. He sat unmoving until Ferris looked down and started to read the statement.

Ferris was fuming, but there was nothing he could fault in the statement, the type was smudged slightly but the spelling was perfect. He paused and signed.

Aziz nodded when he looked up. "Your copy," he said and handed across a second stapled sheaf.

"I just wanted to let you know that your current jetty neighbour Mizz Clark has confirmed your story, and also Mizz Cardénas has

retracted her statement, she says she got annoyed because you made a move on her and then turned her down. She went back to the party and didn't see Shareen again. And so, your statement is corroborated. For now."

Ferris felt himself going red.

"Should you be telling me any of this?"

Aziz took back the signed statement and pen before answering.

"Probably not, but I wanted to see how you took it. Relieved but still annoyed is my guess, which is good. Angry is usually not guilty."

"Well that's very ... educational." Ferris managed, and stood up.

Aziz also stood up and went with him to the door.

"It's a pity we adhere to due process here. There's a lot to be said for a little third degree when you have a weak case and a lack of time, it would lance the boil before things go bad."

"So you *do* have a suspect."

Aziz showed his teeth. "See, that's where the loose talk ends. We always say we are following a definite line of inquiry. Have a nice day, Mr Ferris."

CHAPTER 25

At noon exactly Ferris sat down opposite the medical administrator, Dr Widdowfield.

"I won't over-burden you with the details Mr Ferris, but the situation is urgent. We will run out of DtaP vaccine in days. The scheduled delivery was due six weeks ago. It didn't happen, so we had to ask San Jorge Hospital in San Juan if they could spare us a batch. I'm just off the phone. They will put together an emergency pack for us, to be collected tomorrow.

"At the same time we have a batch of blood samples that should have gone on the Harvey flight yesterday but there was a mix-up. It's a bit awkward, we want to get the bloods analysed statim so they need to go today. If you could combine the two deliveries it would be most gratifying."

"Are the vaccines fragile?"

"Don't worry they will be in a special crush-proof packing in a sealed, cooler style container. The only thing apart from safe, secure delivery is a chain of custody, make sure you get sign off for everything individually."

"Don't worry doctor, I had military training, I can do that much."

"What are your rates for San Juan, including your overnight stay?" Ferris gave him the number and instantly regretted it. Schroeder's tip was to triple actual cost. Dr Widdowfield thumped on a desktop calculator.

"Oh, that's very reasonable Mr Ferris. I take it you have kept the rate down because of the return trip?"

"Yes," Ferris said. Still, it was a medical mercy mission for the community and the rate was fair and he was delighted to be doing his courier air taxi thing.

The hospital had even more paperwork than the Ministry of Transport, but when he finished, he rang Wally Brunkard to arrange customs clearance and filed a flight plan with San Juan.

He picked up the cooler box from the hospital analytics lab, took a taxi out to the airport, signed the customs declarations for Brunkard and flew without incident to San Juan International.

The traffic was chaotic in San Juan and it took the taxi well over an hour to get him to the children's hospital and he got the signed receipt for the blood samples and handed over the letter of authorisation for the vaccines, and after another twenty minutes the lab desk checked his identification and told him all was in order and if he could come back in the morning at 10?

With time on his hands, Ferris decided to go back to the airport and seek Matt Hollis and maybe even find out from him where Olympiakos Leasing was and meet them.

It took an hour to get back out to the airport.

It was less tiring than walking outside in the sun and humidity but the walk through the terminal was endless. The contrast with the orderly chaos on the runways was stark. People stood in long queues, in huge clumps, sometimes for no apparent reason, many shouting at the tops of their voices. Children screamed and got underfoot. Ferris loved it. The lively bustle of the crowds of travellers relieved him of the oppressive feeling of the last few days.

Out of the corner of his eye he saw a bow-legged man and looked around abruptly.

He saw no one he knew. Ferris stood and watched for a minute but there was no further sign of the man. The only bow-legged man he'd met recently was Quintero, Arnaud's bodyguard.

The incident made him uneasy, and after a moment of uncertainty, he went to check on the Super Cub. The care given to the blood samples had distracted him and he couldn't remember if he had locked the plane. His log books and other documents were still aboard.

He picked up the pace and cadged a lift from a man driving a fuel bowser to the small aircraft park.

Ferris stepped down off the tanker in time to see an overalled figure dart out from among the planes. An engine blipped and roared, and a yellow and red Piper Super Cub bumped out towards the runway, and he felt a rush of horror as he recognised his own plane. Ferris broke into a run, trying to cut off the plane as it turned clumsily onto one of the taxiways. The man in overalls was almost level with the tail-planes of the Cub, and he grabbed an elevator and pulled himself forward until his hands curled over the leading edge of the tail-plane. Ferris supposed he was trying to weigh down the Cub and prevent it from taking off. The engine roared raggedly as the throttle opened abruptly, and the Cub swayed as it lined up on the taxiway, the wings jolting wildly as the wheels skidded, and the man hanging from the tail-planes was nearly shaken loose.

Ferris was now running on a converging course with the Cub, and he could see into the cockpit, and he saw that the pilot's head barely showed above the dashboard cowling.

"Paco," Ferris shouted uselessly, in sudden realisation. "Don't do it, you stupid little bastard, you don't know how to fly."

But his voice was lost in the blare of the engine. He was still twenty yards from the taxiway when the Cub crossed ahead of him, and he almost slowed to a jog. The engine faltered and nearly stalled, and Ferris sprinted again. But the Super Cub's engine caught and roared on strongly as ever. The elevators of the Cub waggled up and down energetically, trying to dislodge the man on the tail-plane, but he hung on grimly. Ferris fell further behind as the Cub lurched out onto the runway in another dangerous wheeling turn which tipped the plane onto one wheel and almost scraped a wing-tip on the strip.

The impact as the plane regained two wheels finally bumped the man on the tail-planes enough to jolt him off. The Cub accelerated away quickly, and Ferris ducked involuntarily as a Beech King Air pulled out of its landing approach with a jarring blast of turbo-props, barely missing the wing of the Cub with its undercarriage. Ferris turned to watch the Beech make a very bumpy landing two hundred yards on, then he looked back at the Cub. Her tail was up and she was running on the barest tip of the main wheels, and then she surged up and away from the runway, climbing at an almost suicidal angle, the little engine screaming with the near stall strain. Ferris reached the man in overalls. "Thanks for trying to stop her," he said.

The man grinned at him. "Never again buddy. But at the time it seemed worth it." Ferris looked back at the Cub as she tottered away towards the runway boundary.

There was a sudden puff of smoke from the engine, then a sharp report reached back to Ferris, and the Cub seemed to drop like a stone. "Oh God no," Ferris said, and he ran again.

The Cub plummeted and crashed on the zebra-striped section at the end of the runway. The crack and twang of the breaking aeroplane sickened Ferris, as he watched the nose telescope and the wings snap off, while the tail folded slowly and drooped over the ruined nose.

Then there was silence except for the drumming of running feet on the tarmac, and Ferris wondered, will it always be like this, endlessly running to the scene of different crashes?

Across his numbed mind, came the inconsequential thought that Paco had considerately crashed at the far end of the runway, so that even the 747's could land and take off uninterrupted, as normal.

As he got closer to the wreckage, he could see that the engine had pushed back into the cockpit, and suddenly he didn't want to go any nearer, because he had enough people in his nightmares, without the broken body of Paco added to them.

But he forced himself to go on, and the mechanic and he arrived almost together and stepped around the shattered wing to get to the cockpit. Paco was pinned between the engine firewall and the pilot's seat, his face a mask of blood. The engine cooled with the familiar ticking noise, and the warm machine smell mingled with a scent of fuel, but not as if the fuel tank had ruptured. The mechanic studied the wreck for an instant, then seized the door and ripped the perspex half off its hinges, so he could get into Paco.

Ferris watched as he leaned into the cockpit and examined the boy's body.

"He's still breathing," the mechanic said when he ducked back out. He looked back up the runway at the approaching rapid intervention vehicles.

"Better wait for help."

Ferris couldn't follow all the Spanish but the paramedics argued about whether to go to an adult or children's ER and which they could get to faster.

An airport police cruiser arrived as this discussion was going on. Hector DeJesus and his partner got out.

"Listen," Hector said to the paramedics. "Just get moving. The paperwork can take care of itself."

"Easy for you to say –" One of the paramedics started truculently, but whatever expression he saw in Hector's eyes changed his mind and he said, "We could do with some extra red lights." Hector jerked a thumb over his shoulder at the police cruiser. "We're ready to roll when you are."

Hernandez, Hector's sergeant, took over the scene and Ferris spent a frustrating afternoon in interview rooms. The airport police grilled him as if they believed he had done something wrong.

At about two p.m., Hector DeJesus came in and greeted Ferris by name and the atmosphere changed. Hernandez grudgingly wrapped up the proceeding with a last mention of whether the Cub had been locked.

"It's not looking good for Paco," Hector told Ferris outside on the concourse. "I'm going to drop in later when I finish up here, you're welcome to come along."

CHAPTER 26

"I'm sorry but I cannot allow the gentleman inside," the ward sister said in English. For Ferris's benefit he presumed. "Only authorised personnel and next of kin are permitted, and it's stretching it for you, officer."

DeJesus looked at a Ferris with a grimace. "Rules," he said with disgust.

"What about the next of kin?" Ferris asked.

DeJesus shrugged. "Sorry to say, these kids run wild. I don't know if Paco has any family apart from his gang. Maybe his mother is too poor or too strung out to look after him. The city police are following up on it but I wouldn't hold out much hope."

"Well in that case, maybe this will help." Ferris pulled out his credit card. It was after all for emergencies and this was a true emergency.

DeJesus's eyes widened. "That's pretty generous of you Tony, considering the boy stole your airplane and wrecked it."

"He didn't mean to wreck it," Ferris said. "And besides, he's only a boy." The front-desk receptionist was going off duty but was happy enough to take Ferris's credit card details.

They went back up to the ward, and DeJesus went back to talk to the sister again.

The conversation was again in English and Ferris sensed that this formality kept it from getting heated. "No, he can't stay here," The sister repeated.

"That's ridiculous!" DeJesus exploded. "He just paid the kid's bill, didn't he?" DeJesus looked quite formidable. Ferris wondered after all if he was the country policeman or just a cuddly exterior like a grizzly bear. But the staff nurse was on her home turf and wasn't giving an inch.

"That's as may be officer but the regulations are the regulations and all the managers are gone home and I don't make the rules, I just follow them."

DeJesus hitched up his belt and cleared his throat. "I'm sorry, Tony. We can maybe fix something in the morning, but for now you have to leave when I do."

He sat with DeJesus in the corridor for about an hour, and then a doctor came and talked to the ward sister and she pointed them out.

The doctor came over and nodded to them. "It's good that somebody cares," he said. He took off his glasses and squeezed the bridge of his nose and blinked. "I'm sorry, it's been a long day. We are short-staffed at the moment. If you were family, I would be more gentle." He paused and stared into space. "Not that you ever get used to it. Not that you would ever want to get used to it."

"It's okay doctor," Ferris said. "There is nothing wrong in being human."

"I don't hold out much hope," the doctor said. "We've stabilised his condition for now, but the injuries are massive. He'll perhaps make it to the morning with the ventilator but after that, I don't know."

When the doctor had gone, DeJesus shifted in his seat. "Look, Tony – I gotta go home. My wife will be wondering where the hell I am. I rang her earlier but she will be expecting me, and I want to say goodnight to my own kids. Especially after this."

"That's okay Hector," Ferris said, touched. "You head on." DeJesus shifted in his seat again. "You can't stay here. Regulations. You're not next of kin so they can't allow you. I know it's bullshit bureaucracy and all when you paid for the kid's bill, but that's the way it is." Ferris hesitated.

"There's nothing more you can do," DeJesus said.

"I know," Ferris said. "Okay, Hector. Let's go." He nodded to the nurse as they went out.

Two stocky Latin men were coming up the stairs. For a moment Ferris couldn't place them. But then with a surge of dismay he recognised them as the two DEA agents he'd run into at his own crash.

"Well lookee, what the cat dragged in," said one. They both stopped on the steps and smiled in an unfriendly manner. "Just coming off duty we heard about your latest adventure and just couldn't stay away. Don't you wonder how you could be so accident prone? We do. Has it occurred to you that one of your coke-running buddies might have fixed your plane for you, eh?"

"Of course not. I have no 'coke running buddies', as you put it."

"Huh. So you say. Maybe you're right, maybe you're too dumb to see it. Maybe you looked funny at one of the bad guys."

"That's ridiculous," Ferris said. "Paco crashed because he's a child and couldn't handle the plane."

"What's ridiculous is you telling tales out of school, Homes."

"I'm not Holmes. You know my name is Ferris."

"He serious?" The agent appealed to his colleague with pantomime surprise.

"I think he's serious," the partner said, the perfect straight man. "And he is a foreigner."

"Jeez," said the agent. "Maybe you lived under a rock last ten years. Homes is short for home-boy, dumb-ass. As in if we like, we own you. You can complain to Perez or the OPR Board all you want, but if we want, your ass is ours. Perez is a career brown-nose. All he wants is to serve out his time here with his big overseas allowances and get back home to Springfield, VA to golf on up the greasy pole. He avoids trouble like the plague."

"That was a lovely speech, Agent Oliviera."

"No, I'm Rodriguez, he's Oliviera. What's with you – can't you tell Latinos apart?"

"I can't tell Feds apart."

"I'm so hurt. We're not just federal agents, we're special. So why don't you like us Ferris?"

"Why don't you like me? You tried to feed me some runway at gunpoint. What's to like about that?"

"Let's go Tony," DeJesus said watchfully. He started down the steps again.

Rodriguez reluctantly stood aside. "Heads up, dipshit. Your plane didn't just fall out of the air. The accident investigators already ruled out metal fatigue, at least in the normal sense. They're running tests overnight. But already they think some sick son of a bitch sabotaged it. Few enough people round here would do that just for giggles. You should have a long hard think about it, Homes. And remember who the enemy are and who are the ones trying to uphold the law."

DeJesus grabbed Ferris by the arm. Ferris wasn't aware he'd moved into attack mode.

"Easy, Tony," he said. "He has a badge and you don't."

"He can take off the badge," Ferris said.

Rodriguez threw a punch which grazed Ferris's cheek.

"Why you –" DeJesus said.

"Whatsamatter you, *shitil*?" Rodriguez said. "Which side you on?" The blood drained out of DeJesus's face and his hand went to the hilt of his nightstick.

"You'd better get out of here before she calls security," he panted hoarsely and nodded down to where receptionist watched them from below.

"Is that supposed to be a threat?" Rodriguez said. "Balls to you and your hospital rentacops."

"I heard they got issued with tasers last month," DeJesus said.

"I doubt that," Rodriguez said. But with less assurance.

"Ease up, man," Oliviera said. "You're way out of line here." Oliviera dragged Rodriguez away up the stairs.

"You're right, Hector," Ferris said loudly. He put his hand on DeJesus's wrist. "He's not worth scrapping with. I'll just go to their disciplinary board. And complain again."

At Ferris's insistence, DeJesus dropped him off at a bus stop on the route to the Sheraton.

He had one last piece of advice before he drove away. "Don't mix it with these guys Tony. They're a law unto themselves. It's different for me, I have the whole San Juan P.D. to watch my back."

CHAPTER 27

Ferris felt his skin crawl to the tick of the cooling engine metal.

At first, the surgeons gave Paco a one in three chance of surviving. How they put the number so high was beyond Ferris. When they turned off the ventilator, Paco died of a crushed spleen and liver, a punctured lung, and a severe build-up of fluid on the brain.

It took nineteen hours, and Ferris sat up for all of it, blaming himself. As Paco never regained consciousness, Ferris supposed that he had really died at the crash, even if the doctors said differently.

No parents or other relations came forward to claim Paco and DeJesus persuaded Ferris to allow the city to bury the boy. "He's gone, Tony," DeJesus said. "You did your best. Save your money and let him go."

Ferris booked a seat on the next Harvey Air flight, to bring back the vaccines and test results. After that simple task, he had too much time on his hands and things slid out of control.

The next two days went by in a haze of beach drinks and unhappy divorced women.

DeJesus found Ferris drinking by the pool in the last light. He looked even more formidable out of uniform. "Just dropped by on my way home."

He declined the offer of a drink.

"Just a quick heads up, Tony. You know I've been at the airport a long stretch of years so I know people, some who might talk to me easier than to DEA heads. But you've got to keep this under your hat."

Ferris nodded encouragingly. "It goes no further."

"The FAA investigators think somebody put boron carbide powder in your engine."

"What?" Ferris frowned in disbelief. "So Oliviera was right, it was sabotaged. But why?" DeJesus lowered his voice. "Hell of it is, I've never heard of boron carbide, sounds like something to clean your drains. It's used in magnetic levitation trains. And the techs tell me the OSS used it against the Nazis."

"I know all that." Ferris sat back and shook his head. "Hector, I wasn't bluffing those DEA morons. It must be a mistake. I can't think of any reason the CIA or anyone else would want to mess up my engine."

"I believe you," DeJesus said. "But it's one hell of a mistake. The investigating officers will probably want a chat, but as I'm not involved I'd say get the heck out of Dodge until they find the perp."

"I'm flying back to St. Marc tomorrow," Ferris said.

"Good," DeJesus said. "They'll go through the CCTV, but we're dealing with a cool customer here. If we're lucky all we get is a still of some guy wearing a boiler suit and a baseball cap who looks like a million other guys."

He headed off after urging Ferris to stay alert.

***

On Saturday morning before Ferris went to the airport, a detective Martinez came to see him. Ferris presumed he was keen and working his weekend on the case.

He mentioned the carbide powder to see what Ferris's reaction was. Ferris didn't bother pretending to be surprised and said the DEA had told him his plane had been sabotaged, which didn't please the detective. As expected, he also showed Ferris a print of a CCTV screen-grab but the image was too murky to tell much beyond what DeJesus had predicted, a foreshortened man in overalls and a baseball hat. So anonymous under the peak it wasn't even possible to tell if he was Caucasian or Latino.

At eleven a.m. on Saturday he went to catch the new OutAir service. There were six other passengers, a tourist couple in their thirties with two children of about eight and ten, and Quintero and Braun. Ferris felt uneasy although he didn't know why. They nodded to him politely and sat at the back of the cabin, Braun got papers out of his briefcase and worked on them for the flight, and Quintero put on Walkman headphones and hid behind a Spanish language newspaper – Ferris guessed he was a nervous flier.

Ferris chatted with the tourist family, recommended two beauty spots to visit on St. Marc, and in less than forty minutes they were on the approach. Ferris took note that even though the Cessna was slow compared to the Navajo, it put the Super Cub in a bad light and he had to concede that Davern was right. With a jolt he remembered the crash and realised that the whole discussion was academic. Now it was the Bonanza or bust.

CHAPTER 28

Some weekends there was cricket practice on Saturday, and Ferris went along to check the parade grounds, more to while away the time to sundown than for any other reason.

Amos was trimming a border with a machete and chewing tobacco.

"Police say it's too dangerous for cricket. Especially for the wild kids. Trouble over the hill." Amos pointed inland with his machete. "It's been a week since poor Shareen been killed. People say there should be an arrest to show how the police doing their job."

"What do you think?" Ferris said.

Amos spat a stream of tobacco under the bush discreetly.

"I'm no policeman but they need to do something quick. Money is short this year and it's damn hot and folks are hungry and quick to anger.

Some people say, Mr Schroeder them cut his hand, now them grow bolder, them kill a kid." Ferris gestured helplessly. "That's a big jump. From a mugging to murdering a child."

"Maybe so," Amos said. "Hatred, that's a moving target and no stopping to consider. They say the Haitians, they come here and they very sure of their rights but not their responsibilities. There, nine million of them, they say, we open the gates and we get drowned in them and their criminal ways. Just look at them, they say, them been independent forever and them still can't do nothing right. If them think this a land of opportunity maybe them shoulda gone to the States instead. Them live down to their reputation, them." Amos ran the nail of his thumb along the blade of the machete, testing the edge. "That's what folk saying." Ferris felt a chill of despair. Perhaps he had been naïve to expect the island to be untouched. Aziz was right damn him, bad things happened to good people. He walked on to the bistro.

The bistro was lightly patronised, but a live band were playing relaxed calypso influenced tunes. The members of the card club were not to be seen. Ferris hadn't come to drink but he knew from his consumption of the last few days that he could hold a fair amount of liquor. Angelique served him warily.

He was getting into his stride, when Davern came in and stood across from him. "They say 'Misery drinks alone'."

Ferris grinned humourlessly. "I thought it was 'Misery loves company'."

"In that case I will join you."

"Surely. That's why I'm here. I could just drink rum on the yacht."

"Sorry to hear about the plane, and the boy. It's a terrible thing, the death of a child."

"It's ugly," Ferris said. "The police think somebody put boron carbide powder in the engine, just enough to wreck it. If I'd been flying, I could have got her down safely. That's the worse part of it. I think maybe someone was sending me a warning."

Davern wrinkled his brow. "Why would anyone do that? It makes no sense."

"That's what I told them, it must have been meant for another plane, or some random act of a lunatic." Something moved in Davern's eyes and Ferris said, "What is it?"

"I know somebody in the FAA in DC, I'll phone and see what they can find out. But you mustn't blame yourself, Tony. And you certainly won't find the answer in a bottle."

"Who the hell are you to tell me how to live my life? I've had enough amateur psychology for one night. Talk about the damn national debt, I like it better when you're being a banker."

Over the sound of the band, there was the distant but unmistakable crack of a gun shot. Davern looked enquiringly at Ferris. "Fireworks? It's not independence day."

Not everyone in the bistro noticed although a few fell silent and listened. When the firing was not repeated, the uneasy lull passed as people resumed their conversations. Davern made up for his faux pas by telling funny stories of helping with government cut-backs in various countries. Over the next thirty minutes, Ferris thought he heard faint detonations, but nothing as clear as the first. Davern didn't pay the noises any heed.

Sergeant Aziz stepped into the front doorway and Celine went forward to talk to him. Behind them, Ferris saw the fat Constable Gombs carrying a shotgun over his shoulder. A hush fell over the bistro, but after a brief discussion the police left and conversation surged again.

The next time Angelique hurried past, Davern touched her on the wrist and asked her what was the matter.

"Not here," Angelique said with a half smile. "But there is a riot over the hill. The sergeant says there is no danger here but there might be a curfew if the trouble doesn't stop."

"Sounds serious," Davern said. "Just as well we're only a few yards from the hotel. Although I still have the car."

Then, about ten minutes later, a tannoy announcement cut through the hubbub, and almost everyone turned to look at the door. "This is a police announcement. Due to a severe outbreak of disorder, a curfew has been declared. All persons, irrespective of position or nationality, are advised to clear the streets by midnight precisely. Any infringement will result in immediate arrest. Further instructions will be announced by radio and public announcement if the disturbances continue. This is a police announcement ..."

Throughout the bistro, people muttered discontentedly as the tannoy speaker faded away along the street outside. The patrons Ferris could see stirred nervously. A few already stood up and gathered their belongings to leave. "This will spoil a few holidays," he said.

"Come on," Davern said quietly, "I'll run you down to the marina in my Toyota." Ferris shrugged and rose and followed Davern out into the car park.

As they drove off, an open police Land Cruiser turned into the street and drove past. In the back stood half a dozen military police armed with slung rifles, perspex shields and three foot long batons.

"Things are getting uglier still," Ferris said, when the truck had gone.

Davern gave a low whistle and shook his head. "I'm afraid so. This looks bad, Tony." He stopped the car at the marina barrier. "I will talk to my contact in the FAA tonight and based on what he says I'll bring you up to date in the morning. Is it okay with you if I drop down, say at eight thirty, and pick you up on my way to the airfield? We can talk then?"

"Sure," Ferris said, puzzled. "Why not talk now?"

Davern's smile was a gleam in the light cast by the marina sodium arcs. "Because I might be wrong. See you tomorrow Tony."

As Ferris walked the pontoons he heard several distant shots. The noises echoed across the bay, unpleasantly clear in the hot night air.

He unlocked the cockpit of the *Trinidad*. Behind him a woman said, "Hello the ship. Permission to come aboard?"

"Permission granted," Ferris said and looked around to see Marcie stepping onto the pontoon from the stern of her own boat.

She wore a loose kaftan over a bikini top and cut-off jeans.

"Hi," she said with a wan smile. "I –"

A report bounced off the hotel and echoed back from the quay walls. Marcie flinched. "I know it sounds silly, but could you check my boat for security? If I felt like locking myself in for the night?"

"Of course," Ferris said. "But I'm not a security advisor or a police officer. And there are two officers outside the hotel."

"I didn't like the policemen. The fat one and the skinny sergeant. I didn't trust them. I'd rather trust you."

"All the other police are fine men," Ferris said.

"Whatever. I didn't meet all the other police," Marcie said. "It's eighty-two degrees and I feel cold."

She folded her arms across her chest and hugged herself, emphasising her cleavage.

"Alright," Ferris said hoarsely, "Let's have a look."

"You don't you have a gun?" Ferris asked as she showed him over the deck. She had all the hatches and windows locked down.

"No, I always thought a can of mace would be enough. Now I'm not so sure." She looked at him hopefully. "Do you have one?"

"No, I never thought I'd need one. I could wave a flare gun at people in an emergency. Usually there's no trouble, this is the first time that ..."

"That a woman got killed?"

"She was barely a girl," Ferris said.

"But they used her like a woman," Marcie said.

Ferris said nothing and she led him below deck. Country rock played low out of a stereo system. The interior of the yacht felt much roomier than the *Trinidad* despite only being slightly larger. It was stuffy and hot but smelled of varnished timber and oranges and a tiny memory of perfume. He went through the motions of checking the hatches from the inside. Apart from the cockpit doors everything was sealed. The interior of the yacht was spotlessly tidy as he would have expected for a single-hander. He came to the galley and the galley table crowded with bottles of mixers and alcohol. The stereo system was worked cunningly into an alcove above the food locker. Like the boat, it was old but top of the range. Ferris cringed when he recognised the track playing as "Margaritaville". He absently moved one bottle of rum.

Marcie laughed bitterly. "I stocked up, but I didn't feel like another party after hearing about the girl. And now I don't want to be alone. How crazy is that?"

Ferris smiled. "It's not crazy at all. Mind if I fix myself a drink?"

"I'll do it," she said, "You go on checking."

She moved past him to get glasses and unnecessarily brushed her butt across his hips.

Ferris reached up and tested the galley sky-light. It was solid. "To be honest, I'm out of ideas." he said, "If you can bear the heat, then you could just lock yourself in and turn up the stereo."

"We could try that," she said seriously, mixing drinks into two tall glasses.

She pushed some buttons on the stereo and the music changed to "A pirate looks at forty".

"No sir no-how," Marcie frowned. She pushed again and the tune changed to "It's Five O'Clock Somewhere".

"Better." She increased the volume.

She handed him a glass. "Come back into the saloon. I'm frightened." Ferris followed her into the saloon. "You don't strike me as somebody who'd be afraid of anything, sailing single-handed." She looked him straight in the eye and said, "The sea doesn't scare me. I wouldn't go out alone in a force ten gale, but I wouldn't be afraid to ride one out at anchor in a good harbour. But people on a night like this, that does scare me." She turned at the table and toasted him. "To safety." She put her glass on the table and walked halfway up the cockpit steps and slid the hatch shut and snapped the catches.

"Do you think this would hold?" she said, still standing on the steps.

Ferris went up the steps and she stood aside slightly but he was very aware of her proximity. He pushed at the hatch and it didn't budge. "Um well that seems secure enough," he said, distracted as she pushed in front of him.

Ferris felt a singing in his ears as she put her arms around his neck and pressed her hard body against him and she kissed him.

"Mmmm," Ferris said around a mouthful of tongue.

He took his arms down and she took his hands and placed them on her buttocks.

Ferris broke away and retreated gingerly down the steps.

Marcie looked at him with an unfocussed look in her eyes and whisked her kaftan off over her head and threw it aside.

Ferris retreated backwards as she came down the steps after him.

"I need you," said Marcie and then she reached back and unclipped her bikini top.

Ferris bumped his head against the bulkhead and tripped back onto a bench.

***

When she got her breath back, Marcie laughed shakily. "Wow, that was lively." Sweat ran down between her breasts.

"We forgot to turn up the music," Ferris said.

"You're still mad at the Latin miss though," Marcie said.

Ferris flushed. "I'm sorry if –"

Marcie laughed again. "Don't worry, it adds a certain edge." Ferris felt annoyance stirring at the thought of Juanita. Marcie felt it too and said, "Whoa, there Tiger. Turn me over, I'm done on this side."

CHAPTER 29

The noises in the night had petered out and Ferris dozed uneasily, tangled up in Marcie who held on tight even asleep. Daylight woke Ferris. The humidity was stifling even though Marcie had relented and opened the side-lights.

Ferris carefully unwound from Marcie's arms and edged out of the bunk.

She stirred and sat up. "Thanks for being here."

"My pleasure," Ferris said with no irony. "You might want to lock up after me."

"Probably not. It's always a lot safer in the light of day. Witnesses." Ferris pulled on his trousers. "All the more reason to cover up."

"Jerk," Marcie said. She pulled the blanket up to her neck. "Ferris, I don't know if I like it here so much any more. Maybe I'll pull out... and search for another peaceful island."

***

Ferris felt tired and washed out from the alcohol and the exertion and he headed for an early shower. When he got back to the *Trinidad* he changed and turned on the radio to catch the end of the news while he searched for some breakfast. "... After the unrest yesterday, the police have announced restrictions on freedom of movement. The centre and north ends of the town are to be out of bounds to all except residents, and travel across the island will only be permitted to persons issued with special passes. OPEC has announced—"

He decided that Davern wouldn't be restricted, so he was waiting at the entrance when the rental Toyota turned in. Davern glared disapprovingly at Ferris as he climbed into the car. "You look awful."

"It was a noisy night," Ferris said. "With the riots and every-thing."

"Which explains the bites on your neck. Really, Tony, you'll catch something nasty if you go on that way."

Ferris grinned at him. "I was just comforting a lonely single-handed yachtswoman, and surely it's better than drinking." Davern snorted and muttered something about as well as drinking but none of his business, anyway.

"So how the hell do we get to the airfield?" Davern said more audibly. "If the town is closed to traffic."

He drove off, but after only a hundred yards, they came up on a detachment of police at a barrier under the direction of Sergeant Colbert.

"We have orders to close the road sir," the sergeant told Davern. "And not to leave any unauthorised persons through."

Davern pointed to the government sticker on his windshield.

"That's not exactly the authorisation the Super had in mind, sir. I haven't heard of any trouble this morning, but it's still not safe to go this way."

"The exact route isn't important," Davern said, "but I want to catch the flight to Puerto Rico at eleven."

Colbert looked doubtful. "Perhaps Mr Ferris knows the old logging road, if you go out past the petrol station. It joins the road to the airport about two miles out if you don't mind a longer drive. And it goes nowhere near the shanties."

"That sounds ideal," Davern said briskly. "Shall we go, Tony?" Colbert considered, and with an unhappy grin, he stepped back and waved them through.

"Damn, Bill, you're glib. You should be in politics," Ferris said. Davern snorted. "I already am."

"So what did your FAA friend have to say for himself?" Ferris asked. "That is why I'm along for the ride."

"I had to wait for a call back. Your information was the best. They confirmed that your plane was sabotaged, that it was boron carbide powder and that the police had no leads apart from a lousy CCTV grab."

Davern drove deftly along a street of old warehouses and cut around the base of the hill.

"I know all this already Bill," Ferris said. "Hardly worth getting me up early for."

Davern shrugged. "Now I want to get down to brass tacks. I also checked in with my contacts in Interpol and Homeland Security. They said nothing definite, but there are new players on the scene who play rough."

"Now you're sounding like Jimmy Chen. The Superintendent didn't have much time for his line of melodrama."

"Jimmy got spooked by shady characters fetching up on the island. But bad things happened. Shareen murdered, and your plane sabotaged. I don't believe in that level of coincidence."

"And I don't see a connection," Ferris said. "You want to take a left here." Davern took the turn. "You should stall Schroeder."

"I'm still holding out for the Bonanza, remember? And I'm only his Plan B."

"Garcia is a cowboy. The FAA will ground the Goose. Then Schroeder will need you."

"What is this Bill? You were all in favour of me helping Vic as a sideline."

"And now I'm saying I don't think that's such a good idea."

"I can't stall him," Ferris protested. "He has a deadline and government penalties if he delivers late. What's got into you Bill?"

CHAPTER 30

Ferris noticed suddenly that oily smoke was rising over the roofs ahead of them. Davern noticed too, and his voice became a little vague as he watched the sky ahead. "I can't go into details, Tony –"

The car rounded the bend onto an intersection, and Davern broke off and braked to a halt. People thronged the road ahead. Beyond them, the petrol station burned fiercely. A ragged howl came from the mob, and they surged towards the car, brandishing cudgels and machetes.

"Shit," Davern said and twisted in his seat as he put the car into reverse. A rock bounced off the windscreen, leaving a white impact scar. The mob howled again, and Davern said, "Jesus wept," and jammed on the brakes.

Ferris looked around to see another mass of people push a delivery van out onto the road behind them, blocking their escape. "There's a revolver under the seat," Davern said calmly. "If worst comes, the lever on the back of the butt is a grip safety. All you do is press the lever with the ball of your thumb, hold the gun normally, point and pull the trigger. Double action only. Got that?"

"Yeah," Ferris said hoarsely, his throat dry. Davern's matter-of-fact acceptance of the situation disturbed him more than the threat of the mob. "Hold tight," Davern said and reversed the car slowly trying to butt his way through the crowd.

The mob howled derisively, and bottles and stones rained on the car. The two parts of the mob converged.

"Lock your door," Davern ordered.

The mob pressed in on the car, and some of them rattled the door handles while the rest jeered and beat on the hood and roof with their hands and sticks. They rocked the car, trying to use the momentum from the soft springs to unstick the wheels from the road. Davern kept the car moving, and the power of reverse gear slowly pushed the crowd aside. With a collective disappointed groan, they seemed content to rap at the car with their hands or weapons.

A thick-set man pushed his way through the crowd. Unlike the others, he had his face partly hidden behind a scarf.

He shouted in fast dialect, and the mob surged forward, and Ferris felt the car tilt, as the rear wheels lifted off the ground. The engine whined as the rear wheels spun uselessly in the air.

"This is it," Davern said, and reached under his seat and when he sat up, he put the revolver in under the dash.

Then the windscreen exploded inwards as the mob attacked the glass. Ferris grabbed at the door handle as the car rolled over, and he held on as the car turned over onto its roof, then rolled over again onto its wheels.

The crowd howled in glee and surged at the car again. The window on Ferris's side shattered, and as he ducked and brushed off the broken glass, a huge grinning black man reached his arm in and tried to open the door from the inside to neutralise the child lock. Without even thinking, Ferris drew his fist back and drove it into the man's nose, feeling cartilage crack and seeing blood squirt out under his hand.

The man withdrew his hand as if he had been burnt, and staggered back, drawing frustrated howls from the mob. But the car was being attacked from both sides, and Ferris glimpsed a man wrench open the rear door on the driver's side, while Davern struggled grimly with two men who simultaneously tried to strangle him, the revolver lying forgotten under the foot pedals. Davern's door jerked open, and they were dragging him out, kicking savagely. One of his assailants fell to a swift karate chop to the throat, but then the crowd swallowed him up, and Ferris saw clubs rising and falling viciously. His own door snatched open, and he dived under the steering column and grabbed the revolver, and twisted quickly to show his attackers the gun. Even in their glazed, feral thirst for blood, he could see the will to survive assert itself briefly, as they drew back momentarily, but Ferris realised in despair that he could not use the gun, because they were caught up in the rage of blood and didn't really know what they were doing. One of those nearest to him seemed to realise this, and broke the spell with an inarticulate yell, lunged at the gun.

Ferris desperately raked the barrel across his face, but the mob were screaming for the kill again, and they closed in and Ferris could see machetes wink in the sun. He fired the revolver twice, into the roof of the car, and the crowd broke and ran instinctively.

As the crowd opened, Ferris saw Davern lying only a yard from the car, and he took his chance and got out, still brandishing the revolver, and grabbed the leg of Davern's trousers and dragged him one-handed back to the car. The mob were closing in again, cautiously but menacingly, growing bold when they saw that no one had been killed. As Ferris bent and used both hands to lift Davern into the car, they rushed forward again. This time, the sound of the gun only caused them to flinch and duck a little, and Ferris felt his guts turn to water as he waited to die. The mob, screaming exultantly at their invulnerability, rushed the car and turned it over again.

Deeper than the screams Ferris heard the rumble of a heavy truck, and the howls became yells of alarm. The myriad legs outside the overturned windows shifted and retreated and milled, and mixed with booted feet and combat fatigue trouser ends, and the howl of the mob faded to the sharp bark of orders and the crack of riot sticks.

A few of the rioters fell into Ferris's view, and then he lowered himself gingerly to the ceiling and looked out. The street cleared fast, as the rioters ran pell-mell, harried by a detachment of police, who were cutting little groups and individuals from the crowd, like sheep-dogs at a herd. The terrible knot in his stomach loosened a little, and he forced himself to look at Davern's battered body for the first time.

CHAPTER 31

Ferris hadn't felt the cuts, and there was no pain until he winced under an antiseptic swab at the hospital.

"Mr Ferris," the surgery nurse tutted as she dug broken glass out of his palms. "You're turning into our albatross. You came in along with three fractured skulls and your friend Mr Davern is the worst."

"Will he be okay?"

"It's pretty bad. Dr Sanders is going to induce a coma."

"I'd like to talk to Dr Sanders," Ferris said.

The nurse smiled thinly. "So would I, but I hear there are dozens of casualties from the riots coming in. Best for you to go home. You can't do anything, so you'll only be in the way."

She tucked the end of the bandage, safety-pinned it and pointed to the exit. "Next patient, please."

Ferris sat out in the lobby waiting for news. Superintendent Legett stalked in and his face went blank when Ferris stood up.

"I haven't time to talk to you now, Ferris." His voice was a whip-lash of anger.

"Sir –"

"In fact, I'm still trying to decide whether to have you arrested. If you want to do something useful, go make a statement at HQ. Colbert won't be pleased to see you but maybe Aziz will. You can walk easily and I hope you won't stumble upon any disturbances on the way."

With that, he turned on his heel and marched to the desk.

***

Sergeant Colbert wouldn't look Ferris in the eye. His face was grey with exhaustion.

"I'll try for Aziz," Colbert said. "But he's busy. It's a madhouse here."

Aziz looked annoyed when he came down. "Are you insane as well as stupid Ferris? We have people handcuffed to every non-moveable piece of furniture. Processing them will take days. I have no time to listen to your misadventures."

"Maybe you could get your miniature tape recorder?"

"Alright," Aziz grimaced. "Nothing like when the mind is fresh. But make it snappy. Gombs, bring F- Mr Ferris upstairs please."

Gombs dawdled up the stairs but even at his leisurely pace Ferris was sweating after one flight.

The corridor above sweltered and smelled of crowded bodies. The overflow from the cells of boys chained together on benches. Some had the same blank shining eyes from the riot. But the racket they made cut off instantly when they saw Gombs.

"In here, Mr Ferris," Gombs said and walked towards an office.

Ferris stopped in his tracks. Lincoln was chained on the end of a bench, with a big bloody weal on the side of his head.

"Lincoln," Ferris said in disbelief."What are you doing here?" The disappearance of Gombs into the office emboldened the boys and some of them were not actually handcuffed and they jumped up and started capering and scuffling. "Word up conchie? Conchie Joe," some of the locals said. "Blanc, blanc, blanc," chanted back some Haitian kids. It was like a slap in the face when Ferris recognised Sony Dubois and two of the other smaller Haitian boys from cricket sitting across from Lincoln.

Lincoln turned and tried to stand up. "Shut up, don't you say that to Mr Tony, you know better than to talk trash like that."

A tall Haitian youth sitting on the opposite bench lunged forward and punched Lincoln on his already open wound. Blood splattered the linoleum.

The corridor became a bedlam of shouts and scuffles. Ferris stepped forward to shield Lincoln. Gombs, grim-faced shoved the Haitian youth back onto the other bench and two of the younger boys tried to grab his baton and pistol. Gombs cuffed one of the boys with an open but huge hand and the boy flew sideways.

"No!" Ferris yelled and lurched forward raising his bandaged hands.

"Stop it!" Aziz bellowed. He was unarmed but there was a ferocity his voice and the youths stopped shouting. They lowered their eyes and sat down as he walked up the corridor.

"I turn my back for ten minutes ... I wanted to let you all go. But oh no. You want to get locked up? Fine. I thought maybe you were too young but it seems I made a mistake. I can lock you up with the grown men, it's your choice. You know I'm not joking."

Three more officers appeared and a near silence fell. Aziz paused when he saw Lincoln holding his free hand to his bleeding face. "Gombs get this boy a bandage for Christsake. He should be in hospital. The rest of you, split them up. Half downstairs. And sharp, I want my police station back."

He unlocked Lincoln from the bench and led him into the office. Ferris followed.

"Try not to bleed all over my floor. I know you're Rolle's apprentice. I also know you are keen on a sports scholarship." Aziz pulled a box of tissues out of a desk drawer, and handed a wad to Lincoln. "We can talk another time. In the meantime, maybe Mr Ferris here will tell you how visas work, and why you can't get one if you have a criminal record. Wait downstairs." He waved Lincoln out.

Gombs knocked, and came in carrying a green first aid box. "Colbert says Mr Enright is at the desk. And he's not happy."

"Oh just what we need, a lawyer," Aziz said in disgust. "I'll be right down." He pulled out the micro-recorder, then threw it back in the drawer. "Ferris, we haven't got time for this. Come back at three to give your statement. Don't talk to anyone about it in the meantime. For now, could you make sure the boy gets medical help."

***

Lincoln waited patiently at the desk. He had a sticking plaster on his forehead and he looked better although dried blood stained the collar of his t-shirt.

Marlon Enright pounced on Aziz. "Sergeant Aziz, this is an outrage. You can't keep children in conditions like these."

Aziz nodded wearily. "I completely agree, Mr Enright, and I'm working on it. Lincoln, you're free to go with Mr Ferris."

Enright nodded to Ferris and turned back to Colbert and Aziz.

Ferris ushered Lincoln out onto the street. After about ten steps Lincoln paused. "I'm sorry Mr Tony, for those boys and for what happened earlier. I guess – folks got carried away. I know I didn't, nobody was supposed to get hurt, it was just a protest."

Ferris still had a sick hollow feeling in his stomach, because the burly masked man had moved a lot like Rolle.

"Lincoln how did you get mixed up in this?"

"A fella can make a mistake Mr Tony. Be influenced by people who ought to know better. The others, they think it's just a game. That's all I'm saying."

Ferris looked at him and realised that Lincoln was almost in tears. He forgot that Linc was only a boy. He raised his injured hands in a surrender gesture. "Hey, I'm not giving you a hard time Linc, that's been done."

"What did Aziz mean about needing a visa, Mr Tony?" Lincoln's eyes were a little haunted. "Was he threatening me?"

"I hope not, Linc," Ferris said evasively. "He just likes to talk tough." Ferris stopped and looked at Lincoln dabbing the cut on his forehead. "Is that still bleeding?"

"It's drying up." Lincoln straightened his shoulders. "The cut is nothing Mr Tony. I've been hit harder by the weights in the gym. I don't feel like going to the hospital, I don't need any bandages."

"If you're sure," Ferris said. He walked with Lincoln part of the way. The streets were back to normal, life went on.

"I'll just go home," Lincoln said. Ferris was glad to turn back, he wasn't sure what would happen if they went to the garage and Rolle made jokes.

***

When he got back to the marina, the blue forty-foot *Grainuaile* was gone. He felt glad for Marcie, although he could have done with her company and her drinks cabinet.

He tried sanding the hull for a time. Reaction set in so he had a nip of tequila and kept going but at two he felt too restless and swam ten lengths in the hotel pool. Still restless, he phoned the hospital. The nurse sounded tired and irritable. "I'm afraid we don't give out information about patients to journalists."

"I'm not a journalist, this is Tony Ferris."

"Oh." Her voice softened slightly then hardened with suspicion again. "We aren't giving any information over the phone. You'll have to call in person, Mr Ferris." She hung up before he could protest any further.

CHAPTER 32

When Ferris arrived at the hospital the only besieging journalist was Jimmy Chen.

"Hey Tony, sorry to hear you're mixed up in this. And about Mr Davern."

"Seriously Jimmy, you're staking out the hospital?"

"They chased us away from police HQ," Chen said and smiled. "This may be my big break. They told the television people to stay away from the hospital too."

"The police said not to talk to anyone," Ferris said.

"Of course they did," Chen said. "Care to comment on shots being fired in Davern's car?"

"No," Ferris said. "That's exactly the kind of thing I don't need the police to warn me about." Chen smiled again. "Fair enough. But you could talk to me, Tony. I am the news around here, you can trust me. You could get your side of the story across and be old news when it all blows up."

"I'll think about it, Jimmy. Thanks for the heads up."

Ferris went into reception and was delighted to see Doc Hank coming the other way. He looked exhausted.

"Hi Tony, I'm just stepping out for a smoking break. I don't smoke, but the doctors who do seem to get more time off."

Hank stopped and stared at Ferris. "Are you sure you didn't hit your head, Tony? You're sweating a lot. Any symptoms of concussion?"

"No, really," Ferris said, bemused. "I'm fine –"

"Damn, I can never switch off. Never have a card partner as a patient," Hank said in self-disgust. "Maybe I really should take up smoking. Take my mind off the job."

"How is he?" Ferris said, unable to keep up small talk.

Hank exhaled slowly. "Nothing much to report, his condition is stable, and no change expected soon. But he's a very tough bird, and very fit for his age."

Hank stiffened and said, "Oh crap, here we go again." Ferris turned to follow his gaze. Doc Hank went forward to greet the minister for internal affairs, Mr James, and the US honorary consul, as they came into the reception.

From behind them, Superintendent Legett's voice cracked like a whip. "No comment. I don't want to be on Miami television, Chen. And neither would you, if you have any sense."

Legett pushed through the glass doors with an angry gesture, his mouth in a thin line.

His expression turned even grimmer when he saw Ferris. He gestured with his swagger stick. "Back again, Ferris? You were treated this afternoon."

"Bill is a friend. I came to see how he is."

Legett looked away for a moment and then back at Ferris suddenly, the whites of his eyes startling against his skin.

"Well it's a bit late for a show of concern. Do you realise what you and he did, in your recklessness?" Legett said tightly. "For years, the government has built the image that St. Marc is a nice place for rich people to live, a safe haven from their muggers and taxmen and insurance salesmen. And the little trouble we had, we could handle. But today, all that changed. Two dead, and Davern in a coma. Two white men attacked, one of them an IMF adviser, why would anyone risk their lives visiting such a place, when even a high American official cannot be protected? Chen filed a report with his agency in Miami and the story has been picked up by the television news stations. The newsmen will come here like vultures."

"We didn't ask to be attacked," Ferris said listlessly, responding mostly by reflex.

Legett tapped the brim of his cap with his swagger stick. "True. And the situation had a few tiny points to salvage it. We've rounded up some of the ringleaders of the unrest, and with Mr Davern's mishap the consequences have come home to the people and wiser counsels have prevailed."

"I'll be on my way then," Ferris said. "Unless you wanted to tell me that as I have no plane now, I've no future. That I might as well be Haitian."

Legett looked at him without expression. "I see. So all this ... concern is ultimately about your work permit? I don't see any need to worry on that score. Your business relations with the government may be – shall we say, a little strained, but still amicable enough. When you can tear yourself away from your Davern intensive care vigil and stop feeling sorry for yourself, you might consider how lucky you are to be alive. I advise you to take a short vacation and set about rebuilding your business. I'm sure you're quite capable of it."

Ferris flinched, stung by Legett's callousness. "You're a cold, heartless bastard, did anyone ever tell you that?"

Legett stared him down in silence. "I am the biggest bastard on the island, Mr Ferris," he said quietly. "I went to all the right schools in England, learned as the butt of the master race of bastards. I am indifferent to your opinion, but be aware that I am leaving your self-respect, if you want to take it with you when you leave."

CHAPTER 33

Smarting, Ferris decided to head to the bistro directly from the hospital although it was early. There was no tannoy truck, but as he approached the bistro, an army truck jolted to a halt across a nearby side-street and blocked it with a rush of brakes. Policemen vaulted from the back of the truck and ran down the side-street. Ferris hurried into the bistro. A tense Pierre greeted him at the door.

"Snap raid," Pierre said of the police truck. "They have been at it all afternoon, got the bit between their teeth, I think the phrase is. What happened to your hands?"

Ferris told him and asked not to have it broadcast. "Poor Mr Davern," Pierre said. "And the people who were killed! All because of the food price increases, and they put them down again right away."

Ferris deliberately chose a back table with only one chair, but he had barely started on his drink when Rolle appeared and spun a chair from another table over and sat opposite him. "Bey, I hear you be havin' misadventures," he said genially, brandishing a cigar.

"*I* didn't get arrested."

Rolle arranged his face into an expression of concern. "I don't know what the hell Lincoln was thinking."

"Like he said, maybe he got led astray by people who should have known better," Ferris said.

Rolle waved at his own smoke. "Hey, the boy got ideals. All that volunteering to coach cricket and stuff. Maybe he wanted to make peace between the factions."

"Well it didn't do him much good at the cop shop, the little bastards tried to thump him good."

"Yeah well. Boys are like monkeys, hierarchies and such shit,"

Rolle said virtuously.

"So you have no idea why he got mixed up in the riot?" Ferris looked Rolle in the eye unblinkingly and Rolle took several puffs on the cigar. "I can't think of anybody 'cept that Dubois kid," Rolle said at last.

"Oh, I can," Ferris said.

Rolle took the cigar out of his mouth and examined the head minutely.

"What did Aziz have to say?" he said absently.

"Oh don't worry, I didn't tell him anything,"

"Damn Tone, do I look worried? You spent a lot of time at the cop shop today is what I heard, that's all I'm saying. Concerned like on your behalf that the poe-leece harassing you. Anyt'ing I could help with?"

"Oh please, give me a break. The island's dodgy mechanic who has a feud with the police sergeant wants to help me out with my law enforcement problems. Nice. Doesn't it bother you that your apprentice got arrested during the work day?"

"Boy had the afternoon off. Have his own life an' I ain't his Daddy by no stretch."

"So Lincoln spent his time off playing peace corps while you slaved over a cold engine?"

"Hey, I might be the island's answer to Hen-tree Ford but those jalopies don't fix themselves. I spent the day under a 1976 Ford TransAm belong to one of those fool Brunkard cousins – and a lot of thanks I'll get for that oily sauna – it'll be: 'bin five days cuzzint, and yow ain't finish yet'"

"Any police visit?"

"Oh yeah, that fat low-fence Gombs come by. Sticks his tongue out while he's writing alibis, that one."

Ferris's resentment, simmering under the application of spirits, boiled over.

"I don't see why you're so smug. Legett is arresting everyone he dislikes today. Somebody says the word, and you might get caught up in the net."

Rolle wagged his finger reprovingly. "You're on edge, kiddo. Otherwise you wouldn't say such nasty things to your bestest buddy, Rolle."

Ferris felt tired and reckless. "I'm having a quiet drink. Buzz off before I flatten your face." Rolle nearly dropped his cigar in a paroxysm of laughter, "Bravo, my friend," he said between coughs. "You never disappoint." He left nimbly enough when Ferris made to rise.

Angelique looked concerned when she looked in to replenish his glass. "You must not push him too far," she said.

"Just pushing back," Ferris said sullenly.

"Men," Angelique snorted and wiped down the table. "And you are drinking too much." It was true, Ferris decided, in a fit of self-disgust. He couldn't spend the rest of his life watching the world through an inch of rum.

Especially when it was like throwing petrol on a fire. He set his glass down, and resisted the urge to dash it against the wall.

"Alright," he said, "I'll have a soda water, please." Angelique looked at him in surprise.

"This is the first drink of the rest of my evening." He drank the soda water in one gulp, grimacing at the insipid sour taste, and banged the glass down heartily. "God that was bad, gimme another."

Angelique chuckled. "Ferris, you're incorrigible."

CHAPTER 34

Ferris stretched out the second tonic water and ordered some food. The quinine in the drink really was sour? And he realised just why the old boys put gin in it. Still, the mosquitoes would hate him.

Soon after dark, the card club regulars trickled in.

Chris sauntered in and shortly after him, Doc Hank and Jimmy Chen arrived within a minute of each other. Ferris joined them in the card room. On the way, he met Rolle's gaze and nodded politely.

Rolle sidled in after Ferris and looked at him quizzically for a moment but didn't break the flow of the conversation.

"I tried to see Bill, but it was family only," Chris said and turned to Doc Hank. "Damn doc, what's come over the hospital? It's gone security-conscious all of a sudden."

"Hey don't look at me, I'm not in admin. That's Jimmy's doing," Doc says. "Apparently, his articles on the riots have been syndicated and the government don't like it."

Jimmy laughed uneasily. Nobody was looking at the cards any more.

"Not exactly catching the kind of break I was looking for," he said. "Also, annoying the prime minister is never a good career move and writing about bad things happening to people I know isn't comfortable."

"Don't worry about it Jimmy," Doc Hank said. "We just play the hand we're dealt. We didn't expect any tricky surgery up at the hospital either."

"Does Bill have family?"

"Yes," Hank said unexpectedly. "He has a brother who is retired in Orlando."

"So no sign of Vic," Chris said. "I haven't seen him for a couple of days. He must not want to hang around with us younger guys." This got a laugh. "I think Vic's gone to Florida," Jimmy said.

"Is that so?" Chris said. "He hasn't looked well lately." Doc Hank shot him a glance that Ferris couldn't interpret but said nothing.

"I thought he looked younger and fitter," Ferris said. "Lost some weight." Doc Hank suddenly seemed very interested in examining his cards.

"That's true also," Chris said diplomatically.

The conversation took an unexpected turn to Mexican netball, of which Rolle seemed a well-informed enthusiast.

"Any news on leasing the Bonanza?" Chris asked Ferris.

"I'm starting to get impatient about the Bonanza. You got the second Ag-cat much easier."

"The second Ag-cat was more of a loan and profit share. Guy who was supposed to help me fell through. Probably flying the snow patrol and pulling down the big bucks if somebody hasn't let air into the back of his head. See, there are always easier ways to make money. Now farmers are learning to fly their own applications – cutting out the middle man, the ultimate 21st century DIY. Anyway no jobs came in and my leg mended faster than expected so that wasn't a biggie."

"But in the meantime I don't see what harm it would do to try out for the crop dusting," Ferris said. "I need to get back in the saddle."

"Aerial application," Chris corrected. "We don't officially call it crop dusting any more. Day after tomorrow, a rush job on Pig Island. It's your last chance this season, I'm pulling out next week. June to November I get the heck out of Dodge and let the hurricanes do their thing, it's the low season for me. Keep the plane under cover until the fall in SJ, safest place for it."

"Where do you go for the summer?"

Chris tapped his nose. "Acapulco. No, I do some stuff that maybe wouldn't stand up to examination, elsewhere in the world, and come back for more spraying next growing season."

"The stories are true then," Ferris said.

"Some. There are plenty of legal ways of making lots of cash – I could end up getting shot down legally by one side or the other. Still, it's a paying job and anybody who knew me ten years ago would be surprised I am still alive." He gave his characteristic choked laugh. "Anyway come to the boat tomorrow. Give you a real taste of the job. See what back-breaking thankless work it is and make up your mind from that."

"Also, everybody keeps telling me it would be useful to disappear for a couple of days." Ferris said.

Making sure that Jimmy was distracted, he outlined his DEA troubles to Chris.

Chris sat very still. "Do many people know about this?"

"Around here, the police and the government, Bill, and Vic. And you."

Chris shook his head. "I dunno Tony, you need to work on your diplomacy skills. I know it's the fighter jock spirit, but you can't beat city hall and all that."

"I don't like being hounded," Ferris said tightly. "And I'm not afraid of a few reporters."

"Ah but, Tony. Back-room government types are. They will do anything to make it go away. Especially in a laid-back place like St. Marc, the first time people feel the glare of a halogen lamp they lose their heads completely. So yeah, maybe a trip off the island is wise. The newsies are vultures but they have the attention span of goldfish. They will be bored and maybe gone by the time we get back. You can go over in the boat, go missing at exactly the right time."

Chris shoved the unplayed cards back towards the centre of the table and stood up.

"Well gents, it's been a blast. Early start for me and I need my beauty sleep. See you tomorrow, Tony."

CHAPTER 35

Two Seven to control – traffic on runway!

The nightmares weren't so bad but he didn't sleep very much with the humidity and in the morning, Ferris felt drained by the time he walked back to police HQ.

The station was much quieter. Aziz ushered him up to the office again, and turned on the recorder and took notes as they went.

"Why were you going to the airfield again? Davern I can understand."

"He wanted to talk about business. We never got round to it," Ferris said, almost truthfully.

Aziz grunted. "Continue."

When Ferris got to the shooting, Aziz interrupted again. "Oh yes. That reminds me, since when did you have a gun?"

"I didn't. It was under the seat of the car."

"So was it Davern's?"

"I don't know. But he told me where it was."

"How very mysterious," Aziz said smoothly. "What would a financial adviser want with a gun?"

"I thought maybe you gave it to him," Ferris said, not caring what he said.

"No, it's a bit fancy for us." Aziz held up a cellophane bag with the Airweight in it. "Apparently we should use paper bags again, plastic is forensically unsound. But I doubt Colbert got the memo. This it?"

"Yes."

"Good. It's got Davern's finger-prints on it and presumably yours."

"Do you want to finger-print me too?"

"The Super is really down on you, it's the end of the world or at least tourism. Reckless endangerment and all that."

"Yes. He told me himself last night."

"To be honest, the powers that be just want this to go away. You know how politicians get. Bad for St. Marc's tourist image. No one really cares if a few native girls have their throats slit," Aziz said bitterly. "Even a little rioting, people would understand, the natives are restless."

Ferris feared he going to get the same lecture again. "Do you want my fingerprints or not?"

"No need," Aziz said. "We're just going through the motions. Unofficially speaking of course. Go on, please."

When Ferris had finished, Aziz looked back at his notes. "This burly man, he sounds like a ring-leader. Would you recognize him again?"

"I didn't mention any burly man."

Aziz looked at him. "Yeah, but pretty much everyone else did. You shot in the air and the mob panicked and started to run away but the ring-leaders put them back in line again."

Ferris shrugged and lied. "I was busy trying to not break my neck, remember. Nobody stood out. A lot of them had their faces covered, like I said."

Aziz pulled his lip thoughtfully. "Best look at the mug-shot book, anyway."

Ferris dutifully leafed through the file of photographs, and Aziz unerringly flicked back to pages with suitably well-built men and none of the men looked much like the burly man from the riot.

"Rolle has an alibi," Aziz said.

"He's not in your book either," Ferris said.

"Not that I'd try to put ideas into your head," Aziz added.

"Thanks, I appreciate it," Ferris said. The irony seemed lost on Aziz. He tucked the pen and note-book in his pocket and stood up.

"Well, that's it for now. I understand you were talking to the DEA again, after your plane got stolen?"

"They talked to me," Ferris said. "I'm not sure what business it was of theirs. There was no suggestion of a drugs connection."

"True," Aziz said. "But in the game of making friends and influencing people, you lose out big time there."

"Do I look bothered," Ferris said. "Are we done?"

"Sure," Aziz said. "I'll have it typed up as usual." He looked at

Ferris steadily. "Notice how this has become usual?"

When Ferris got back to the hotel, Benny the night clerk gave him a slip for a missed phone call. A C Peterson had left a number fifteen minutes earlier. The name didn't mean anything to him right away but he decided to ring back despite the hour.

"Carla Peterson," a female voice said. "That you, Ferris?"

"Oh hi, Carla," Ferris was nonplussed. "I thought it was the lease company."

"You gave me your business card, remember?"

"How could I forget?" Ferris said. He remembered how good she looked in cut-off Capris, it lifted his mood. "Is this a business or social call?"

"Kind of public service karma I suppose. Guy I'm dating is a researcher at one of the news stations here. I didn't see the harm in it at the time, so when the news came in over the wires the other day I recognised Jimmy Chen's byline and your name and told him about our little fender-bender.

He dug around and next thing he had some bozo from the D-uh . . . narcotics interdiction let's just say . . . on the phone doing what the government types call a negative briefing – what the rest of us call a hatchet job – on you."

"Jesus," Ferris said.

"Yeah. But it was too obviously a libel to do anything of the sort. But my guy kind of glommed on to the Jonah angle."

"Jonah angle?"

"Jonah, like all the crashes that happen to you."

"Oh, that."

"Yeah. So it's kind of a heads up, if you want to be famous for your bad luck, hang around for the next shuttle from Miami and if not, a handy vacation might be wise.

"Thanks Carla, I owe you. I think."

"Whatever. And from one camera to another, tell Jimmy to watch his back too, he's swimming in shark infested waters."

Ferris felt elation replaced by hollowness as he put the phone back.

Ferris came to a decision. He rang the offices of the Courier. "You've just caught him," Mariah the receptionist said cheerfully.

"Hi Tony," Chen sounded breathless. "I'm just heading out."

"Is it true," Ferris asked. "Camera crews from Miami?"

"Yes. Well one anyway, the charter is due on the half hour.

That's what we're rushing for."

"But why, Jimmy?"

"You know the way the local guys are. They just re-broadcast, they're not a real television station. The government still practically owns the station, they just read out the news the police write for them. If Arnaud and his crew are here to harm the island, then they won't like publicity. To protect the island for the likes of Arnaud, we've got to make a splash, and this is the only way I can see right now."

"So I should get out of Dodge like Chris suggested?" Chen hesitated. "Gosh I'm sorry Tony, but maybe yeah. A couple of days crop dusting might be just the ticket."

"Aerial application," Ferris said absently. "Were you going to tell me?"

"If they asked about you, yes. Look Tony, I gotta go."

"Carla Peterson said to say hi and to watch your ass."

"What –"

Ferris hung up with a certain satisfaction.

CHAPTER 36

Ferris put the receiver down again, and it rang as he turned away. He looked over at Betty the receptionist and she nodded back at him. He picked up the phone again. "Tony Ferris speaking?"

"Hi Mr Ferris, Darius Olympiakos here. I just had a chat with a Special Agent Rodriguez from the DEA. I don't know what you're up to, but he said you had two crashes in the last two months and was dropping hints about having my plane impounded. I'm sorry, but I can't take the risk of losing that plane – being impounded by the Federal authorities would certainly not be covered by my insurance."

"But," Ferris said. "He's just a badge with a grudge. It's mostly slander. They have nothing on me ... "

"I'm sorry," Olympiakos repeated. "He has a real badge. You seem like a stand-up guy but I can't afford to have the DEA all over my business."

"I'll sue him," Ferris said. But he was speaking to a dial tone.

"Those DEA motherf-" Ferris slammed the phone back onto the hook. His hands shook and he clenched his fist. He realised he was in public view and restrained himself from punching the wall. He turned around but people looked away or down. "Thanks Betty," he said quietly as he went past the desk, and nodded to Charles.

He strode out of the hotel and into the baking soggy heat of the day and he could feel the blood pounding in his ears. He walked around to the pool and stripped off without ceremony and dived in the pool. As usual the impact of the water had some shock effect but very little cooling effect. He started with butterfly stroke and slapped out viciously with his feet at the edge of the pool at the end of each length and after ten lengths dropped into a crawl for another ten lengths and by the end of that his upper body was aching and he no longer felt like solving his problems by hitting something or somebody.

So the Doctor Killer was out of the question for now, but he had other alternatives. But he'd better check.

Marlon Enright's receptionist took one look at his set expression and went into Enright's private office without a word.

"I can see why you're upset," Enright said, and pursed his lips. "It's also why we have lawyers, Darius really shouldn't have gone to you direct. Is this DEA guy really scary?"

"Yes, to some people maybe," Ferris said grimly.

Enright sighed. "I'll reach out to his attorney. As far as I'm concerned we are still negotiating.

And Vic is due back tomorrow, maybe he can throw some charisma in the mix. I really wanted to keep this light-touch, friendly agreement between small operators, but Darius's attorneys have been dragging their feet. We can get scary too, if we need."

He rose and shook Ferris's hand. "Don't give up on it yet Tony, I'll keep you posted."

Ferris went back to the yacht via the marina gate rather than the hotel.

His bicycle, which should have been leaning against one of the huts, was gone.

So the crime wave sweeping the island had reached the marina. He hadn't even bothered to buy a lock for it, so safe had things seemed.

It was a little early, and normally he didn't like drinking on an empty stomach, but he took a stroll down to the rum store before going about the *Trinidad*.

A grey motor cruiser had berthed next to the *Trinidad*. A toned blonde woman in a halter top and cutoffs gave him a cheery 'hi' and Ferris managed a truculent reply before going below deck.

He turned on the radio, but the newsreader said something about the police being called to fresh unrest in the shanties.

Ferris snapped off the radio and reached for a glass. It was smudged but what the hell.

Fresh unrest? Was that even a thing, was there stale unrest? It was incredible to think that only a few days before that he had been happy and prosperous and independent, and getting slowly but surely better off, and living on a beautiful island paradise. And now everything had gone down the toilet and was dragging him down with it.

He re-tuned the radio, hunted past all the Latin ones, to a Florida country and western station. When "Margaritaville" got played it felt appropriate. Although the woman who had broken his heart was far from being a Mexican cutie, and it had been a long time.

With the money left, he could drink himself to death. It seemed a restful way to go.

The sun moved around the port holes, at some stage the rum bottle had slipped out of his hand. He felt around under the bunk for the bottle, and when he found it, it was empty. There was something left undone.

CHAPTER 37

He decided another trip to the rum store would do.

"Hey, Tony, where are you off to, buddy?"

He looked around at Chris, trailed by two muscular black men dressed in off-yellow coveralls tied at the waist by the sleeves.

He remembered.

"Sorry Chris, the trip slipped my mind. I've been drowning my sorrows," Ferris said.

"You sure took your time drowning them," Chris said.

"They were big sorrows," Ferris said.

"Have you changed your mind about the application trip?"

"No, just got distracted. Island is gone to the dogs," Ferris said by way of explanation. "I just decided to give up and beat the stampede."

Chris smiled at him quizzically, then dug into his pocket, found a quarter, and handed it to Ferris. "Go take a shower Tony, and sober up. By the time you've got your head together we should be ready for the second trip to the island before dark. This is Seth and Marcus," Chris indicated his two helpers, who bobbed their heads politely. "They do the heavy lifting, but there will be plenty of toil to spare. Nothing like back-breaking labour to restore a man's sense of purpose. You'll be glad you came."

Ferris gave a tiny grin, at that. He looked blearily at the quarter in his hand and waved a vague salute. "Anything you say, Chris."

When he had used to coin fed shower on the marina, Ferris felt a bit better, and grateful to Chris for snapping him out of his trough. He went back to the *Trinidad*, changed, and shaved himself in a tiny cracked mirror on deck. He even had a cheery wave for the blonde on the cruiser, and he smiled wearily at her disdain, and remembered how sullen he had been before.

Chris was waiting for him, hands on hips, like a Hollywood air ace. He grinned at Ferris as he came rather stiffly down the pontoons to the ferry. "You ready to join this hard-assed band, Tony? An intrepid flying gardener? We fly at dawn, literally. At least I do. I don't want to get caught in the bloody thermals. And the rest of you need to get everything in place for the morning. Francis here will take you over, and on the other side, Seth is in charge of arrangements. Theoretically John Marsh the plantation manager is in charge, but he won't be there until tomorrow."

Ferris looked rather dubiously at Francis the Ferryman. He was the cheapest rental boatman around, but his boat was a death trap. It was an old net-fishing skiff of about 20 feet long with a low cabin and a large outboard motor which looked slightly newer than the rest of the boat. It sat low in the water with the load of Chris's fuel and spray drums and other equipment, and this was the smaller load for the second trip. He was relieved to see at least a couple of life belts hanging in the cab, although the orange had faded to almost white on the seams.

He climbed in over the eighteen inch freeboard of gunwhale and sat gingerly on the stern sheet thwart. The four of them were crammed onto it, Francis in the middle holding the tiller and the others trying to stay out the way when he swung it around to steer.

The boat waddled out of the harbour gamely enough, and Ferris was surprised that the chop in the open sea was mild. The odd wave slopped aboard, but they were never in danger of being swamped.

Francis spoke with such a thick accent he made Amos sound like a radio announcer. Fortunately he was a man of few words and Marcus could interpret for him.

"Be there in about three hours," Marcus offered.

Ferris grimaced. He feared sea-sickness, but the calmness of the sea reassured him, and apart for the occasional whiff of the exhaust nothing seemed to set him off.

But he was concerned about the daylight time they would have at the other end. At this time of the year, the sun went down about eighteen forty-five in the evening and came up again at oh five thirty-five in the morning with very little variation. So they would have at most four hours to work before it got too dark to see.

Francis had an earthenware pot between his feet, which he lifted one-handed and swigged from time to time. Eventually he offered it around companionably. Sailors were fond of rum, and it probably staved off seasickness. Ferris politely took a swig when offered and tried not to think of the drool that came along with the drink.

Marcus became even more talkative as they drew away from land.

The contrast in personalities was striking.

Marcus "named for the island" couldn't stop talking, and Seth, named out of the Bible Ferris presumed, didn't volunteer much. Seth was a silent man with slate grey eyes and a brick red face, while Marcus incessantly told stories and jokes, often boring ones which he laughed at himself. The laughter reminded Ferris of Rolle, though not the intelligence. He presumed Seth had the sense to keep his mouth shut which immediately made him a more intelligent man. But the four of them got along well enough, as the rum flowed and shortened the crossing.

They raised Pig Island after nearly three hours as predicted. It would take Chris about six minutes in the Ag-Cat. Ferris wondered why Chris bothered with the boat. They puttered slowly along the coast line, watching the plantation rising steeply inland from the sea. Pig was much smaller and exposed than St. Marc and the leaves and branches of the trees leaned permanently to the west, even though the day was quite still. Prevailing winds in the islands probably coming from the east.

It was a good navigation aid for small boat sailors and airmen alike.

The island looked deserted. The boat came around into a natural cove with a rough jetty and a hut but nobody came out as they puttered noisily up.

"Where is everybody?" Ferris asked.

Marcus smiled. "It's okay here, nobody lives on Pig Island all year round. Maybe they're up in the fields or maybe they come tomorrow to see the spraying."

Francis switched off and hung a painter over the jetty bollard and they started to unload.

After the battering of the engine for so long, Pig Island was very peaceful.

CHAPTER 38

Francis had a wiry strength belying his thin form and did more than his share manhandling the drums ashore.

Ferris found himself panting, he was the only one seeming worse for the rum.

The islanders always seemed to work at a leisurely pace and it was the first time he had to do sustained lifting in the tropical heat and found that he struggled to maintain this lackadaisical rhythm. He did notice they had bottles of water which they drank far more often than the rum.

The four of them emptied the boat in a surprisingly few minutes, and Francis shoved off with a last wave.

Seth squinted up at the sun. "We got maybe two hour," he said. He wasn't even out of breath. "Best put our backs in it." He seized a barrel and started to roll it inshore. Marcus followed.

Ferris brought up the rear. The path they followed rose up through the plantations.

After five minutes they stopped for a breather and Ferris was well behind. He wedged his barrel and clambered up to Seth.

"Bad for the ticker to keep going," Seth said.

"Where's the airstrip?"

Seth gestured inland. "Up the hill."

"Why?" Ferris asked, gasping.

"Mr Chris says," Seth shrugged. "He land the airplane uphill, that way save fuel."

"Jesus," Ferris said in horrified fascination. "I can't wait to see that."

The working airstrip was a mere cleared stretch in the highland brush, running straight up the hill between avenues of guavas on one side and scrub on the other. Ferris estimated it at about sixty feet wide and five hundred feet long, a tight squeak even in an Ag-Cat.

Seth stopped at the base of the strip. A small terrace had been levelled on the beaten dirt, supported by wooden sleepers and littered with spraying equipment, twenty five gallon drums of fuel and spraying fluid, a tattered deck-chair and an electric pump.

"We can leave the drums here, bring the rest of the way in the morning." By the time the sun set, Ferris's back was on fire from the exertion. He hadn't really done labouring since he was a teenager and his body protested with every move.

Seth called a halt just before dark, and incredibly, he and Marcus passed around the rum again. Ferris declined and could barely crawl to his bedding before falling into exhausted sleep. He dreamed less of traffic on runway.

Dawn arrived abruptly in a shattering roar. Chris jolted them awake by flying past zooming the Ag-Cat so that the Wasp Junior roared and blared like a dive bomber.

Ferris groaned and rolled over. Sleeping hadn't made his muscles any more comfortable, and he ached in places he'd forgotten existed.

"Breakfass?" Marcus said hopefully.

Seth scowled at them both. "We move the drums uphill, then we eat." Marcus sighed and pulled his boots on without further protest.

As they trekked up the trail, they could hear and occasionally see the Ag-cat doing runs further along the island, the rising sun glinting on the undersides of the aircraft.

The lower boundary of the plantation was a stand of tall black trees which acted a windbreak to protect the fruit bushes from the sea breezes but were a navigation hazard to the aircraft. Each seaward run, the Ag-cat disappeared in the dip, the engine sound muffled and reappeared again as it zoomed up over the trees, into a port side wing-over, skidded around and vanished back into the dip. On inland runs, the plane would vanish and reappear on the brow of the hill doing a less dramatic starboard wing-over.

Chris had flown over with a full load of fuel and pesticide to have a head start. Ferris had expected caution due to the hilly terrain but Chris flew fast and low.

Chris landed for the first time after ten minutes

"It's pretty much an emergency, if the flies are sprayed now it should save the fruit. Nobody much likes using Fenthion any more. But it's a classic illustration of the productive power of the airplane. It would take days to spray by hand and the fruit would be spoiled. By then the little bastards will have eaten into all of it."

The caribfly aka *Anastrepha suspensa*. Nasty bastards. I like a bit of infestation to market my work but the little vermin are too successful. If they are too successful then my clients go out of business."

Chris looked at the rising sun uneasily.

"It's around five hundred acres last time they measured, I can do that in under four hours. We'll try to keep it fast, won't be much time for conversation.

I'll probably take a relief break and stretch my legs and that will be it."

Chris held up a hand. "Mask and gloves, Marcus," he said. "You don't want to end up like this." He pointed to his face.

Marcus grinned and laughed. "And I don't mean white," Chris said.

"I getcha boss," Marcus said amiably and went and put on the mask and gloves. "Dam hot though."

"Better sweat than Death," Ferris said and Marcus laughed again.

"Seriously Tony," Chris said. "It's not just the bugs it kills. Anybody gets splashed with that stuff, wash it off with water immediately." He pointed at two large plastic water drums.

Ferris found it hard to watch the plane – Chris was actually a careful flier, not as showy as it would seem to the uninitiated. When the plane was full at the start of the run, he flew more conservatively and got more aerobatic only when he had more control.

When the novelty wore off, Ferris lent a hand to rolling more barrels up to the runway. It took them the full hour and a half to roll the barrels up.

CHAPTER 39

The work entered a strange rhythm, in which Ferris appreciated the strength of Seth and Marcus. Every ten minutes the Ag-Cat would make its hair- raising uphill landing, taxi down to the barrels and Chris would step out of the cockpit while Seth and Marcus emptied ten drums into the hopper. They used a funnel and steady arms and were much faster than any electric pump Ferris had seen. And every fifth landing, while they were doing that, Ferris would top up the fuel tank from the other much smaller row of avgas drums, using the electric pump. He was usually finished after the other pair.

At first Ferris wondered why Chris didn't lend a hand if there was such urgency even allowing for the risk of being poisoned by the chemicals ... but as the morning went on he realised that even a much younger and fitter man couldn't help out without becoming hopelessly exhausted. The pilot had to sit there and rest, the flying was so intense.

Around the two hour mark, John Marsh the plantation manager turned up, accompanied by an assistant. Chris landed for a break and they had time to catch their breath and finally eat.

Chris handed Marsh a chart with the day's spraying plan and how much he had done. The discussion was technical, Ferris caught snatches: "... since it's pesticide ... big droplets ... five hundred microns ... Won't drift more than seven feet ... Twelve feet above the bushes ... ninety mph."

Marsh and his assistant went off, and reappeared an hour later with some small containers, looking satisfied. He gave Chris a thumbs up the next time he landed, then went away again.

Ferris watched Chris fly along the contours he sprayed swathes of the avenues of trees slight onshore breeze early in day he started inland and worked out towards the sea to get an even application and make sure he didn't fly through his own spray.

The morning passed in a whirl. There was only one scare when Seth spilled half a gallon of pesticide on himself. At Chris's insistence work stopped until Seth stripped naked and they hosed him down. He worked the rest of the morning, disgruntled and dressed only in an improvised loin cloth made of Chris's scarf.

Everybody looked increasingly exhausted as the work told on them, Chris went from looking drawn to aged and gaunt.

Ferris helped Chris out of the cockpit when he finally called it a day. His arms and legs shook from exhaustion, he could barely stand or walk.

"Glad to be shot of it. For some reason I hate this island. Gives me the creeps." He sank down on the dirt. "Funny. I've spent nearly four hours sitting and now that I can move I'm not able to.

"I'll have to wait for Marsh to come back with the last of the test containers to confirm the spray coverage is complete. In the meantime the hopper is empty but there is a quarter tank of fuel left. If you want to take a couple of runs along the island at tree top to get a feel for it," he told Ferris. "As a thank you for tagging along and seeing what a miserable day-job this is for a man approaching retirement age."

Ferris looked doubtfully at the short strip. "You fly at about twelve feet?"

"Above the canopy," Chris said. "No drift that way and it's the economics. The Air Tractors have a fifty-nine foot mono wing and they can get a thirty-eight foot spray boom with no chance of wing-tip vortices or other hydrodynamic weirdness so they can go thirty miles an hour faster.

I'm sure if I did the math I'd find I should just buy an Air Tractor, but I'm a stubborn old buzzard. But yeah, ten to fifteen feet about the canopy at ninety is about right. It'll be a walk in the park, Tony. Just like your Tornado days."

"I was an interceptor pilot, not ground attack." They used to call the GR's mud movers.

"Oh yeah, I keep forgetting, " Chris said. "Multirole combat aircraft."

When he had run the Ag-Cat up to the top of the short runway and turned to face downhill, Ferris suddenly regretted coming. Time to see if the light loading and the biplane wings gave the lift he needed.

He pushed the throttle open all the way, and soon the wheels bumped along the dirt, and the tail lifted off, and the bumps became bounces as the Ag-Cat struggled against gravity, and the topped trees at the end of the runway rushed in to meet him. Hoping he had the speed and power, Ferris pulled back on the stick, and the Ag-Cat gently slid up and over the trees.

Ferris felt the joy to fly a slow plane again, the light wing loading made it easy to handle. He climbed away and flew along the coast line for a while to judge the height of the contours against the altimeter.

As soon as he turned inland, the Ag-cat suffered a subtle buffeting as it hit the heat rising from the island.

Cautiously Ferris throttled back and lost altitude. The shadow of the Ag-cat raced along the hillside, huge and hopping over the fruit trees. He brought the plane down until he seemed to be flying almost among the crops.

Even though the cockpit of the Ag-Cat was set high, and he forced himself to keep his gaze fixed a good distance ahead, it seemed as if the ground was rushing up to destroy him. It should have felt much the same as a landing, but it wasn't.

A quick glance at the altimeter confirmed he was at least fifty feet about the ground but his hands started to shake.

He gained height and breathed for a while, then tried again.

He didn't go anywhere near ninety mph, but even so the shaking didn't stop.

He took the plane back up to a thousand feet, and felt himself relax. Landing back uphill was a nightmare but he put the Ag-Cat down without disgracing himself. He went through the post-flight shutdown very methodically. When he pushed back the canopy and got out, he felt in control.

"Well," Chris said. He was sitting in the nominal shade of the deck chair. "How did you like it?" Ferris swallowed. "I –" he started to sit down then unbalanced and sat down suddenly as his legs didn't take his weight. "I couldn't. The ground ..." He rubbed a hand over his face. "I'm not cut out for it."

"Maybe you're just the wrong kind of crazy, Tony," Chris said awkwardly, and patted him on the shoulder.

Ferris rubbed his eyes. "I'm sorry. Nothing I do works out ..." he trailed off. "Anytime I shut my eyes I keep seeing Paco. What's wrong with me?"

"Come on Tony, get a grip," Chris said, uncomfortably.

"Christ I haven't had a drink since last night," Ferris said and laughed shakily. "Maybe that's it. Withdrawal symptoms."

"It doesn't make it any easier to say so, but life goes on," Chris said.

They sat in silence after that. Seth had washed his clothes in the sea and they had dried, and he was dressed normally again, although with salt stains. Marcus and Seth rolled the empty barrels back down to the pier. Ferris watched them listlessly, the hollow booming of the empty barrels bouncing down the hillside like a deranged slow drum solo.

Marsh came back, satisfied that the spray had reached all the trees.

Chris stood and said, "I'll be going, need to hose down the plane when I get back. Wasn't just Seth got splashed with corrosive organothiophosphates. Take Vic's job, Tony. You need to keep yourself busy."

Ferris nodded. He sat and listened to the Ag-Cat until the sound faded completely and merged into the clattering diesel sound of the ferry approaching. Then he got up and rolled a few barrels down the hill to keep Seth and Marcus company. It was a lot less demanding but going downhill still made the muscles creak.

Francis puttered up, Seth brought down the electric pump and they piled as many barrels onto the skiff as could be tied on, and then they motored back to St. Marc.

Marcus joked again, mostly about Seth in his salt-water streaked shorts, but Seth took it in good spirits. The jug of rum did the rounds, much lighter like the boat. And although it warmed Ferris's belly, it didn't take away the empty feeling he had. Gradually he tuned out the conversation and didn't really notice how the others let him be, Francis nodding a warning to Marcus when a remark fell flat. Was he no longer capable of flying as a pilot?

But what else could he do? He had never been anything else. He had never wanted to be anything else, so long as he could remember. Flying was his trade, his art, his religion. He knew no other. What did old pilots do? Chris wasn't exactly a good example of how to get old gracefully.

CHAPTER 40

Francis dropped Ferris off at the end of the marina pontoons and puttered off to drop Seth and Marcus down at the fisherman's dock.

Ferris waved after the drum piled high skiff. When it was gone he hesitated for a moment.

Get back on the horse. Or drink more rum.

Ferris shook his head from side to side like a cow waving off flies.

He walked stiffly up the pontoons to shore. He was really going to be sore for days.

The blonde woman was dancing around to loud music on the deck of the motor cruiser. The Rolling Stones were back in the charts. Again.

As Ferris passed, the blonde leaned over the handrail and saluted him with a cocktail glass. "Party tonight, sailor," she said.

"If I don't have work tomorrow," Ferris smiled back.

"Open every night," she shot after him.

He hesitated at the foot of the gangway of the *Trinidad*. He had been going for more rum when Chris had turned up.

Ferris felt a yearning for a woman and a lot of drink. But he sighed and went up to the hotel. Maybe there would be a progress report from Enright, damn the man for sounding more upbeat than the situation warranted.

Charles, the concierge, waved at him as he came into the lobby, and handed him an envelope. Ferris tore it open, it said "Marlon told me about your situation. Call up any time, Vic."

When he rang at the Schroeder villa, the door was opened by Mrs Kun. Ferris hadn't spoken to her before.

"Is V- Mr Schroeder home?"

She looked at him impassively. "I go see," she said and closed the door.

There was a long pause and Ferris began to think he had mis-communicated. He raised his hand to press the door bell button again when Kun opened the door.

"Vic around?"

Kun's eyes slid away from Ferris. "Mr Schroeder not want to be disturbed. Mr Schroeder, he not home to visitor, very sorry."

"He left me a message asking me to come up here. Anytime." Ferris insisted. "Is something wrong, Kun?"

Kun looked back at the direct question but would not hold his gaze. "Not want to be disturbed ... I say you called. You leave now please, come back later maybe. Good day, Mr Ferris." He closed the door again before Ferris could protest. Ferris felt something was badly wrong. Kun was not the sort of person to not hold your gaze. He was too impassive to ever show social discomfort. Could it have been worry and sadness.

Still Ferris felt needled. He had hardly trekked all the way up the sweaty hill with a sore back and legs to be denied.

Schroeder was fond of the beach, despite his expensive pool.

Ferris strode around the side of the house and took the path down to the beach. The false horizon feature around the pool meant he could go unobserved. There was a jetty for the sea-plane but only a small motorboat was moored at present. And Schroeder's Veep beach buggy was parked at the shore end. But there were no signs of life nearby. The beach front for maybe four hundred yards was owned by the new country club. About a hundred yards down, a man and a dog were wading ankle-deep in the surf.

Ferris made good time along the beach, the sand was firm underfoot. Up close he could see it was Schroeder with Puppy. Schroeder was absently skimming a stick into the surf and Puppy was retrieving it. Neither of them noticed him.

"Hey Vic," Ferris shouted at him, over the sound of the waves. The dog looked towards him, and Schroeder turned round. His expression cycled through a flurry of emotions.

"Damn it to hell, I told Kun I wasn't to be disturbed. What is it with this island and privacy?" And then he recognised Ferris and changed his expression and a smile wiped away the other emotions. "Oh, hello Tony."

"I wasn't in the mood to listen to hints from Kun – is that his real name?" Schroeder smiled affectionately. "You mustn't mind Kun. And it's his given name. 'Oh' is the family name. He didn't want his wife to be known as Mrs Oh. So I call them Kun and Mrs Kun. We go way back, to when I started in the container business in Vietnam. Kun was a QM with the South Korean army. He's like a second brother to me." A cloud passed over his face. "What can I do for you Tony?"

"I got your message," Ferris said. "To call up."

"Oh yeah," Schroeder had the grace to look put out for a moment.

"Yeah, I got some news from Miami, and I came down here to ... think. Other things slipped my mind."

"I'm sorry to intrude," Ferris said awkwardly.

"No worries," Schroeder said, mastering himself with obvious difficulty.

"I was sorry to hear about your lease falling through. I've told Marlon to use my name to try and persuade Olympiakos but if the DEA have spooked him ... it could be back to square one."

Schroeder carried what looked like a torch with a flattened handle and no glass at the bulb end. If he didn't know any better it looked like a gun.

"A torch in the daytime, Vic?"

Schroeder looked down at his hand as if he had forgotten the torch. "Oh that? It's useless junk." He bounced it in his hand for a moment. "Useless," he repeated and turned back to the sea and threw it in a good overhand motion. It spun in the air and glinted in the sun it before it fell into the waves. Puppy ran into the surf but lost concentration and after swimming in a circle waded ashore and shook himself.

"I know it's a set-back," Schroeder resumed. "But in the meantime, the telecoms shipment is delayed and the Goose is still in San Juan being inspected. Could you catch the Harvey Air shuttle tomorrow and collect that Beech 18 for me?"

"Are you sure you want that Vic?"

Schroeder grimaced. "Time is money. You know about those penalty clauses.

"But dang if Hollis isn't the strangest salesman ever, went out of his way to assure me the plane is a lemon. But Tony, I really want to get that mobile network up. So, yes, I am sure."

"I don't know Vic, I haven't had much luck with planes lately."

Schroeder nodded emphatically. "Yeah, I hear you. A bad streak. Poor Shareen, just tried to give her a foot on the first rung – you don't think Luis . . . " His voice trailed off, and then he shook himself just as the dog had.

"Just now, everyone I help gets hurt – but in the end everything passes, and you get yourself back together, Tony."

"I suppose," Ferris said dubiously. "It doesn't have anything to do with Arnaud, does it?"

"No. For now, it's just ferrying the plane over." Schroeder nodded again. "Work. There is always more stuff to get down, things to make better. Making a difference." Schroeder rummaged in his pocket. "Here, I want you to be more mobile." He held out a car key.

"It bothers me to say so but it's no longer safe here and we might as well all admit it. You cycling through the shanties, well, it's just foolishness. Take the keys of the Veep." He held up a hand. "Don't say anything now."

"Alright Vic, my bicycle is missing," Ferris said. "So thank you."

"Take the Veep for a few days, at least until things settle down. It'll make me feel easier in my mind."

"What the hell, Vic! Why should you feel responsible?" Schroeder shrugged. "Damned if I know, but it would make me feel better."

"Okay Vic, thanks again."

Schroeder nodded, and picked up a stick Puppy had dropped in front of him, and threw it into the waves. Ferris took this as the end of the conversation and went back to the jetty. He shrugged and got into the Veep and started the engine.

He looked along the beach. Schroeder and the dog were forlorn figures in the distance – the surf was getting up, a long reach of the wind from the Cape Verdes, presage of a storm.

CHAPTER 41

Ferris groaned. Luis Munoz Marin International wilted in a blistering seventy-five Fahrenheit, the sun bouncing off the tarmacked surface of the small aircraft park. Alcohol was oozing from every pore and his sunglasses weren't doing a great job of cutting down the glare. The blonde, Faun, mixed strong daiquiris and showed an Houdini-like ability of slipping out of his grasp and back into the thick of the party. It had seemed like fun at the time, but now it didn't feel worthwhile.

Nielsen had given him a thumbs up getting off the shuttle, and he had been saved a stiff walk by an old truck guy who must have seen his misery.

Ferris stood for a moment examining the Beech 18 parked outside the OutAir hangar.

It had the bulge of a spar strap under the wings and the high sheen of regular polishing. Hollis was of the old school of fighter pilots, clean low drag surfaces and all that.

"Ferris, you son of a bitch!" He barely had time to react before the huge black man grabbed him in a bear hug.

"I'm pleased to see you too Hollis," Ferris said, when he disentangled himself.

"Always a pleasure to see an old drinking buddy unexpected," Hollis said. "On the phone, a name without a face – never does it for me, but seeing you here it all came back in a piece. Tony Ferris, last of the dog-fighters."

"You were the last of the dog-fighters, duking it out with cannon fire," Ferris said. Rubbing his arm. "I shot down a Serbian MIG with a missile."

"Through a cloud of stealth fighters and F15s. Don't sell yourself short man, that was some achievement."

"But Phantoms were before your time, right?"

"Just missed them," Ferris said.

"Sad," Hollis shook his head. "Not the greatest plane ever, but compared to some of the other stuff . . . if you ever saw the Saber dance you thanked all the gods for the Phantom. It would be good to know somebody who flew them later."

"Nostalgia," he clapped Ferris on the shoulder. "Glory days as Springsteen says.

Damn it's good to see you son, I can be my own self around you, not have to be uppity Mr Hollis the way folks seem to want me to be. Hell even my father wasn't Mr Hollis. I tell them to call me Matt, but behind my back I bet the call me 'mister'. Means I have to pretend to have dignity or something. Act like the boss."

"The burdens of command," Ferris said with a grin.

"Yeah well," Hollis said. "But down to business." He indicated the Beech 18. "That's her. She shines on the outside but is worn-out on the inside."

"And a gremlin in the port engine, you said," Ferris prompted.

Hollis grimaced. "I'm not superstitious, but this one . . . We stripped it down, one cylinder at a time . . . can't figure it, it's like one of those squeaks in a car that the garage never manage to get at.. Maybe it was a Friday afternoon engine. Half a mind to send it back to Pratt & Whitney, they must still have a workshop to have the engine x-rayed."

"But it passed all the safety checks?" Ferris asked.

"With flying colours," Hollis said, "It can fly a thousand miles without a hitch and then the damn engine won't turn except by hand. I've sat it on the apron a while. But I could afford it. I have the uncanny situation of having more planes than pilots to fly them. As you know, that never happens. I can't say I'm happy about letting her go out," Hollis said. "There was an advisory a couple of years back about engine fires. Never seen it on a baby Wasp, seen a couple on the Doubles at air-shows, B29s and the like, amateurs – probably flooded the engine and burnt off the excess fuel as it vented out. You remember the Gooney last year that the nose burned right off?"

"Yeah. Hydraulic fire wasn't it?"

"So they said. They never did get to the bottom of it. Everyone got off safe but it would have been a different story in the air and not on taxiing. That's why I'm leery of sending one of these old ladies out unchaperoned."

He led Ferris aboard the Beech, and as Hollis warned, the worn paintwork on the cabin made it look very dilapidated. The seats had been re-upholstered and the instruments had been updated but even this new aircraft smell didn't dispel the background air of ancientness.

Hollis saw the dubious expression on Ferris's face, and said, "All the mod-cons. Full suite of Bendix-King, Flight Director, NavCom and Transponder. All that's missing is one of them there new-fangled GPS. And you could see she's had the central spar strap reinforcement done."

"Yes I saw it. Well she's been well cared for, and doesn't look like she's been to the wars but she's an old bird."

"Full disclosure is the name of the game," Hollis said cheerfully. "I'm not going to try to sell you a lemon."

"Well, it is the back-up plane," Ferris said, remembering the huge gash in the hull of the Turbo Goose.

"Escape," Hollis said. "Cargo doors can be pinned as an Airstair, in the cockpit starboard side there's an out-size window you should be able to get out of if you're trapped up front, and starboard side just forward and opposite of the main doors is another small emergency door."

Hollis brought him in the office and showed him the documentation and as expected it all checked out. Then they went back out and rotated the screws by hand with the help of a mechanic who stayed to keep watch while Hollis and Ferris got back on board the Beech and ran up the engines. Both started flawlessly.

"See?" Hollis bellowed over the engines. "Sings sweet as a bird. And yet I never relax."

"I'll take her with the warning," Ferris said. "From what I understand it might only be a three hour round trip, here and back."

"Nothing might happen," Hollis said.

"Right," Ferris said. But do you trust the mechanics thoroughness or a pilot's instinct, Ferris wondered.

"As an old jet jock like myself, I know you won't get offended if I give you a few pointers. These old round motors ain't nothing like anything else, and each an individual. As you can see this model IAS reads in miles per hour, others are knots."

"One seventy to two ten cruising speed?"

Hollis grinned. "So it says in the manual. If you set the manifolds to thirty-two and sit her at one fifty-five, this old gal here will fly forever, thirty gallons an hour tops. She could probably go well over the twelve hundred miles range. Very handy if you don't have a deadline."

Hollis had filed a flight plan, and so there was no reason to dawdle when they had got up to date.

When Ferris got into the pilot's seat, and got used to the heat, his discomfort fell away. The hangover symptoms receded and his doubts evaporated.

It was a warm up for Ferris, to get his mind back into working with manifold pressures and all the other arcana of radial engines. The Beech 18 was very definitely an ancestor of the King Air, but there was no mistaking that it was made from the technology of an earlier era, very solid and magnificently well made, but lacking most modern conveniences that came with a turboprop and requiring much more respect. But the old magic started to flow for Ferris, and he took her out and endured the broiling of waiting on the apron fully familiarising himself with the eccentric instrument layout, the locking tail-wheel, and having to look over the nose.

As Hollis advised he kept the speed down and the Beech behaved impeccably for the one hour and twenty minute flight.

The flight was a joy, and all was right with the world, except he wondered why Schroeder had ordered full tanks.

CHAPTER 42

When Ferris landed the Beech 18 back on St. Marc, it dominated the deserted airfield. Tuffy the dog came out of the shade to look at whatever had the unfamiliar engines, and panted back out of sight. Wally Brunkard came to the doorway and mopped himself with his handkerchief. Ferris signed a long form, which he presumed would be used to soak Schroeder for landing fees.

Ferris locked the Beech and looked around doubtfully. Supposedly there was a night watchman for the airfield but he had never seen one and with the rioting lately he felt the plane was vulnerable. And he missed his Super Cub.

He shrugged it off and drove into the town in the Veep, leaving Wally to lock up.

His first stop was at the hospital. Davern had come out of his coma, and his brother had come to visit and spoken to him. He was very weak but out of danger and asleep.

Then Ferris drove up to the Schroeder villa.

Kun showed him into Schroeder's study. The chaos of the builders was completely gone.

Schroeder was pacing the room talking on his sat-phone, while Luis Garcia sat at the desk, shuffling through a sheaf of papers spread on a maritime map of the Antilles.

"I'll call you back when I have a solution," Schroeder said and hung up. "Bad news Tony, the ship carrying the cellphone equipment has run aground on Wilson's Cay."

Ferris shook his head. "They're weeks behind and now they run aground? This is turning into a nightmare."

"It's in the Turks & Caicos," Garcia said helpfully and pointed at the map. "I looked it up."

"What the hell Vic, that's over six hundred miles away," Ferris said.

"Six hundred and twenty," Garcia said with a grin. "Easy trip in the Goose."

"Goddamn it," Schroeder said in frustration. "I'm don't trust the Goose to go island hopping. It's still leaking."

"Hey Mr Schroeder, no fair," Garcia said. "I have to defend the old dame's honour. Water gets in anyway even at the best of times." Schroeder went over to the map. "The good news is that Flat Cay is right beside Wilson's Cay, and it has a runway."

"Yes, but from the nineteen fifties," Ferris remembered. "Destroyed by a hurricane, wasn't it?"

"It was back in the news three years ago," Schroeder said. "It was going to be billionaire hideaway, they cleared the ground and then ran out of money. The old airstrip could still be used, right?"

"Do you realise what abandoned means, Vic? It's not like St. Marc where the airfield has been kept clear down the years. We're talking a desert island here, gone back to scrub fifty years and the waves probably took away the surface decades ago. Landing nearly four tons of aircraft on an unapproved strip at eighty miles an hour? One big tree root and we're stuffed."

Schroeder shrugged. "Same for the Goose with underwater obstructions," he looked at Garcia meaningfully.

"Hey, I have 30/20 vision," Garcia said. "For real. But if I had Tony along as a second pair of trained pilots' eyes, I could be very sure of landing in clear water."

"Landing the Goose on water is far safer than taking a chance on a strip cleared by some cowboy developers," Ferris said forcefully. He looked at the documents he'd moved off the map. Some were fax paper.

"Luis asked me to get the weights and dimensions of the cargo," Schroeder said, following his gaze. "You could have a quick look in case we need to do the same for the Beech."

"Manifests," Garcia said. He vacated his chair. "I did a loading plan. The stuff you want is marked in red."

Ferris sat and shuffled through the papers. Ministry permits, customs declarations, and inspection reports, all listing the same cargo, "GSM base-station equipment." The relevant manifest had marks against seven boxes, six boxes of one hundred and thirty pounds and one of one hundred and twenty pounds, the six boxes were small and the final one was five feet long. As an exercise,

Ferris visualised the interior of the Beech 18, and saw not too much of a challenge to arranging a balanced load. It would probably end up tail-heavy but he could trim the plane to counteract that. It was a small load for a Beech 18. He noticed that the small boxes were much heavier for their dimensions than he would have expected, and the large one much lighter.

Schroeder cleared his throat. "You'll ah be taking another couple of passengers." Ferris was nonplussed. Garcia was a perfectly competent pilot ... the far end would have strong arms and backs needed to hump the heavier boxes, but sending anyone else was over-kill and micromanagement. It was Garcia's call as pilot, but Ferris couldn't help saying, "Is that necessary?"

He looked at Schroeder quizzically.

Schroeder coughed. "Dry throat," he apologised. "All this phone talk. Luis, you know your way to the kitchen. Go ask Kun to get us some beers, will ya?"

"Sure thing Mr Schroeder," Garcia said and jingled out in his cowboy boots.

"Juanita Cardénas has to go," Schroeder said firmly, when the door shut behind Garcia. "And Arnaud."

"Oh Come on Vic! You know I don't like that woman, and you know why." Schroeder wrinkled his nose. "Lighten up Tony, it's about getting the job done. I really want this job to go smoothly. I want to be able to say yes, I made a lot of money but then I invested in things that would last – the new hospital wing, and the mobile phone network. I don't know what hold Juanita has over Arnaud but she worked with these people from Telefónica and that seems to be a key part of the deal. And you know these things are all about relationships. It seems like a shit deal to me, but it's the only one on the table that fits the time frame, you can't just drop into the nearest Radio Shack and buy the base stations for a cellular network." And what happened to making Mizz Cardénas go away, Ferris thought, but out loud he said, "And what about Arnaud? Why another one hundred and eighty pounds of deadweight?"

"The Goose is a big plane. It's a good idea to send somebody of Arnaud's stature. Whether it's the freighter or the shipping company, somebody is screwing the pooch. I'd go myself to light a fire under them, only ... I have a lot to do here."

"You don't really need me to go, Vic – come on, Garcia is a

good pilot."

Schroeder grimaced. "Is he? I don't trust Garcia any more. Those the scratches on his face ..." He trailed off irrelevantly. "Since he hit that log, I mean," he added more coherently. "I'd be happier if you went along. You can babysit his navigation and all that stuff. I know that the Goose is a hard plane to fly, maybe just having somebody a bit older along will keep him steady." Ferris felt his determination wilt. Schroeder was so resolved to go through, and he couldn't care less what objections Ferris raised.

"I dunno Vic, I don't trust Arnaud, and that tattooed guy gives me the creeps." Schroeder gestured as if waving added power to his words.

"Just this once Tony. As a favour to me, and it's not just about me. Truly. I'll explain it to you after ... I know you think Arnaud is a shady character, but that's all taken care of, I can handle that."

"Chris says never shit on your own door step," Ferris said.

Schroeder nodded vigorously. "And he's right. He's right. It's just, the timing. This deal has to go through and it has to be from here, and now, and I don't like it any more than you do. Trust me, I can make this right. Hang in there."

Schroeder was so animated, Ferris wondered if he was entirely sane.

On the other side maybe he, Ferris was making too big a deal about Arnaud. Schroeder was paying the bills after all.

A knock on the door, and Garcia entered and held the door open for a disapproving Kun, carrying a tray of beers.

"Sure, Vic." Ferris said.

"That's settled then." Schroeder beamed and saluted him with a beer. "ASAP," he added. "I can phone and fax through VFR flight plan right? Just give me the details when you're ready."

Ferris realised that he had lost the initiative, and was back taking orders.

CHAPTER 43

And so they were back in the air less than two hours later.

Ferris didn't have time to pay much attention to the passengers. Getting aboard, Arnaud was affable as ever, and Juanita looked at Ferris expressionlessly. She had her hair tied back in a ponytail so severe, it stretched her olive skin tight across the bones of her face.

Garcia good-naturedly insisted they don their life jackets. "I only intend one water landing, but better safe than sorry. Just remember to wait till your outside to inflate them, okay?"

Ferris sat into the copilot seat and surveyed the instrument panels with awe. "Sheesh. None of these old ladies have anything like a standard layout do they?" To be fair, the Turbo Goose had some mod-cons not seen on the Beech 18, but it had the same yoke-style steering wheels for both pilots.

"Tell me about it," Garcia said ruefully. He seemed to know his way around the controls naturally, but Ferris reminded himself that this was the guy who had bent the Turbo Goose. He enjoyed the novelty of being an extra pair of trained hands though.

Garcia took the plane up to eight thousand feet, and with the exchanges with San Juan ATC done and the plane flying on course using the surprising modern auto-pilot, he had time to chat. Mostly he seemed to want to bemoan the lack of cutting-edge night spots on St. Marc, but Ferris found that amusing enough.

Arnaud popped his head forward between the pilot seats. "Excuse me captain, it is permissible to remove the seat belts, yes?"

"Slightly more risks than a larger aircraft, but no danger with today's forecast, Commander," Garcia said.

Arnaud made a face. "Please. Arnaud, if Robert is too informal for you. The flight is long, perhaps three hours each way?"

Garcia looked down at the faxed weather report. "At this altitude we should have a tail wind of maybe fifteen knots, we'll be there in under three hours. I might push a bit harder because we need to get back in daylight. Coming back I will have to fly slower, to save fuel and also we will be fighting against the same wind, which will blow us off course. So most likely under three hours on the outward leg and nearly three and a quarter on the return."

"Very well, we have plenty of time to catch up on our paperwork then," Arnaud said.

"Say Mr Arnaud," Garcia said. "You were in Mexico for some years, did you follow the leagues down there?"

Arnaud smiled. "Of necessity, Luis. Some of the biggest names in the various *Ligas* and their clubs were clients. When your protegé's safety is affected by their performance on the field, you take a keen interest, I assure you."

The discussion degenerated into Latino versus Anglo players and they lost Ferris, who barely kept up with the cricket news, although he admired the speed of baseball play.

The flight passed without incident, navigation was not particularly challenging, although it was an almost empty part of the Caribbean with the major archipelago of the Virgins, Puerto Rico and then Hispaniola receding to the port, the taller mountains remained visible.

Garcia got his position confirmed by ATC whenever he got handover to the next control zone, and politely handed his calculations to Ferris for a second opinion. They were all perfectly competent, Ferris remained mystified about why Schroeder had sent him along.

The flight was unexciting. Garcia invited Ferris to take over for a stretch, "to give the autopilot a break." Despite the archaic layout, the plane flew nicely, the type was infamous for its water handling rather than having any flying vices.

After two and a half hours the Turks & Caicos appeared as a cloud bank and then a smudge on the horizon, and then separated into individual islands.

Wilson's Cay was easy to find, with the ship towering over it. The two cays lay very close together, and were tiny, separated by perhaps fifty yards of water.

Garcia flew a circuit of the two cays at about four hundred feet, the freighter rode high in the shallows, the turquoise water and white sand sparking off the rusted hull of the ship.

A darker blue stretch of water showed that the ship had wandered off the channel on a dog leg.

"Incomprehensible," Arnaud said disapprovingly, poking his head forward again to look out the windshield. "All that empty ocean and they drive onto the only coral reef for kilometres."

"They probably made a short cut between the islands and ran aground that way," Garcia said.

A large red and green ensign of Portugal fluttered from the stern of the tramp freighter. Ferris took note of the wind direction. The ship didn't look much, rust streaks leaking from the anchor chain and from the pump outlets along the side.

"MV Porto Praia, Madeira" Garcia called out, confirming his sharp eye sight.

Flat Cay was indeed flat, but no more so than Wilson's. It looked to be only a half square mile in size, and the outline of the airstrip stood out, running all the way down the long axis of the little island.

A small motor tender lay hauled up on the beach. Some ant-like figures were carrying boxes up the shore.

"Those are our guys, I'm guessing," Garcia said. "Keep an eye out for a natural ramp, Tony." Garcia flew over the island once, losing height gradually. The shore-line looked clear and level.

Oddly enough despite the scrub dotting the island, Ferris had none of the sense of impending crash as had flying the Agcat over the hillsides. Here, the flat low terrain reassured him. It blurred past at ninety miles per hour even with the flaps down, detail lost in the speed.

"This is where you earn your keep, Tony," Garcia said cheerfully. "We don't want to hit no stinking logs today. Eagle eyes peeled."

Garcia brought the Turbo Goose around and did a pass at about fifty feet, over a dark blue stretch of water paralleling the shore. The water looked clear of obstructions.

"Anything?" Garcia asked.

"Nothing but maybe back the other way," Ferris said. Just to be sure, Garcia brought the Goose round in a gentle turn, and went back. This time the lowering sun picked out slight shadows of the waves.

"Seems clear," Garcia said. "Going in early and slow." He

brought her round again, lined up, and said, "Seat belts please everybody. Tony, this will be a miserable back-seat driver experience for you."

"Once we don't go for a swim, I'm good," Ferris said.

"Such confidence," Garcia said, and brought her down.

Ferris held his breath. All the Grumman flying boats were known for 'porpoising', but after the first touch of the keel on the water, Garcia used a deft hand and never let the plane get away from him, throttling back at just the right moment so that the Goose settled into the water and lost way with a pleasant deceleration.

True to his word, Garcia had come down early and they motored placidly along like an over-powered motor boat to the stretch where the men and boat were waiting.

Garcia lowered the wheels and gently rolled the Goose out of the water and onto dry land.

He grinned at Ferris. "Never know how it's going to turn out, but that one was sweet. Everyone okay?"

"That was invigorating," Arnaud said.

"I'll remember to charge extra next time," Garcia said gravely. "Wait till you experience the water take-off."

Garcia taxied up onto level ground above the water line. When he was thirty feet away from where the small group of men waited by a small pile of crates, he braked to a stop and killed the engines completely. "Better safe than sorry," Garcia said in an aside to Ferris. "I need a fast turnaround, but I also do not want a clueless sailor to walk into the blades."

CHAPTER 44

"I will talk to these men," Juanita said imperiously as Ferris helped Garcia swing open the cargo hatch.

Juanita barely waited for them to run out the ladder to ground level before stepping down backwards.

She was again wearing the linen suit that made her look dumpy, and Ferris looked in askance at her, but Arnaud nodded encouragingly.

Six men stood waiting. Two heavyset Latin men in baggy clothes, and four scrawny sailors stripped to the waist who looked like Asians. The two Latinos glowered when they saw Arnaud coming forward but smiled when they saw Juanita. She embraced them both and chattered and then introduced Arnaud.

"Friendly looking dudes," Garcia said. The sailors looked on, with bored expressions. One of the Latinos spoke sharply and gestured to the plane, and the sailors picked up a small crate each with much straining and staggered towards the plane.

The first sailor struggled coming up the steps and grunted as he slammed the crate any old where through the hatch, ignoring Ferris's instruction.

"Easy easy," one of the Latinos yelled, striding over, he continued in a weird mixture of English. Portuguese and Spanish. "That stuff breaks."

"It's very heavy," the sailor said sulkily.

The other three clunked their boxes onto the plane with a little less violence under the glare of the two Latinos, and went back for the rest of the boxes.

All the crates were blond wood, unpainted, with
"Handle with care
Electronic equipment"

"FRAGILE"

"Alcatel"

"Made in Spain"

stencilled in English and Spanish on them. Ferris insisted on moving the smaller boxes himself, and their disproportionate weight for their size reminded him of nothing so much as ammunition boxes.

Ferris wrestled with the boxes a moment.

"Leave it," Garcia said. "We'll get the big crate towards the tail first."

Ferris looked around at the freighter towering over Wilson's Cay. The ship looked even more rundown from ground level. It didn't look lopsided, the only indication of trouble was how it rode high in the water at the front, but wasn't moving with the waves. A knot of dark figures stood on the bridge facing towards Flat Cay. The sun glinted on lenses and Ferris felt the urge to wave cheerily.

"How are you going to get your ship off?" Ferris asked the second scowling Latino.

The man shrugged and spat. "Tug due tomorrow," he said without interest.

He glared back at the approaching sailors. "Don't drop the big box!" Ferris stopped trying to make conversation.

It took a multi-lingual argument with much arm waving to get the crates stowed to Garcia's satisfaction, and the Latinos were very solicitous of the large crate. Finally Ferris and Garcia secured the load with webbing belts. The Latinos shooed the sailors away towards the boat.

Ferris let Arnaud and Juanita squeeze past the load and up to their seats while he and Garcia walked around the Goose for a quick check. Satisfied that all was well, Garcia started up the turbines and taxied back into the water. Garcia dropped the floats and jacked up the wheels.

"Hold on tight," Garcia said, "This could be hairy." The engines wound up with a race-car whine and the Goose built up speed quickly but without and jolting or sudden moves. At relatively low speed tremendous plumes of water splashed up as far as the high wings.

Then the plane got up on the step of the keel and the splashing was much reduced, but now they were hurtling along at ninety miles per hour. "I'm keeping the nose down," Garcia mumbled on the intercom.

"I know it looks like we're going by water, and a couple of small waves would be nice to get her unstuck, but I'm not letting her get away from me."

Almost as soon as the words were said, the Turbo Goose whined into the air and Garcia retracted the wingtip floats and the plane responded immediately. Garcia sighed in relief, but apart from a quick grin to Ferris, he kept busy trimming the plane for flight.

The banshee wail of the turbo-props moderated slightly. "A bit noisy on take off isn't she?" Ferris asked.

Garcia shrugged. "Well, confession time, I might have thirty-twenty vision, but I love death-metal and listening to that dialled up to eleven I might not be the guy to ask about engine noise."

He brought the Turbo Goose round in a banking turn that took them back over Flat Cay, and as he did so, Ferris saw that one of the Latin men was standing with his back towards the plane. Most people, presented with the spectacle, couldn't resist watching a water take-off. Yet the Latino never looked around. It was as if he was standing guard.

CHAPTER 45

When he had the Goose at eight thousand, Garcia set the plane gently descending, but since they were now flying into a wind of fifteen to twenty m.p.h. he kept the airspeed up to the less economical cruising speed of two hundred m.p.h which burnt about twenty percent more fuel. He explained this to Ferris.

"I don't want to run out of fuel, but I also don't want to arrive for a night landing." St. Marc didn't stretch to runway lighting, even the old runway markings had long since flaked off in the sun and rain.

"Could you do me the favour of checking the cargo hasn't shifted or got loose? There isn't much room for that to happen but I'd like to be sure."

Ferris went back down the hull. The disproportionate weight of the smaller crates struck him again. He made sure all the straps were secure, and then went forward again.

Juanita looked up from a folder of papers as he passed. "Captain," she said.

"Mizz Cardénas," Ferris said gravely. It really was a pity he didn't like her.

"Any excitement?" he asked Garcia.

"Naw," Garcia said. "But she did get very tail-heavy when you were back there."

For a time, Garcia and Arnaud again bantered each other about whether Mexican league players were good enough to be bought into North American leagues. But eventually Arnaud went back to his briefcase and started worked on his papers.

To relieve the monotony, Garcia asked Ferris to double check his navigation and dead reckoning, and allowed him to do some of the course corrections. But it still left a lot of time to spend thinking about the cargo.

It seemed a very small consignment. Granted St. Marc was a small island, and Schroeder had insisted it was just the most essential equipment that needed to be rush delivered. Outside of military applications, Ferris didn't know much about telephony or even electronic equipment, but he had seen an upgraded telephone exchange, with the digital equipment sitting in tiny computer-sized boxes surrounded by the huge empty racks of the old switching equipment. True, the Foxhunter radar on the Tornado had been called Blue Circle to start with, a joke about the concrete blocks used as ballast when the real radar gear got delayed, but in the meantime electronic equipment had shrunk ridiculously.

And then there were the Latin toughs on Flat Cay with their concern for the crates. Did telephone equipment need such protection?

At least it couldn't be drugs, because they were going in the wrong direction, on the narcotics-money leg of the golden triangle.

St Pierre passed slowly by under the starboard wing, and they were flying across the strait between the islands, and Ferris saw tiny white slivers that were ocean-going yachts, their crews blissfully unaware of the plane passing overhead. The topographic detail of St. Marc began to stand out, and Ferris was relieved to see the new road intersecting their path, exactly where he expected it. Garcia levelled out, with the setting sun behind him, and eased down an invisible hill which ended at the start of the runway.

Schroeder's Dodge Ram was parked next to the Veep and Brunkard's jalopy outside the clubhouse.

As the Turbo Goose taxied, the Ram started up and drove out towards it. Two men stood in the bed who Ferris recognised as Seth and Marcus. He smiled grimly. They were going to earn their money again, even if it was only from the hatch of the Turbo Goose to the back of the Ram.

Garcia cut the engines.

"Nicely judged, Luis," Arnaud said, snapping his briefcase shut. "The sun is yet to set. The plane can be ready for tomorrow, eh bien?"

"I don't think Vic needs it tomorrow," Ferris said.

"I'll bring her down to the harbour empty and let her sit in the water overnight," Garcia interrupted hastily. "But it's looking pretty good, don't think we need the Beech 18 after all, Tony."

Arnaud's eyes narrowed. "Quite so. Well, thank you, and we must see to the unloading now I expect."

He and Juanita filed down past the crates and out the hatch which Garcia already had open.

"You made great time," Schroeder beamed at him as he stepped onto the ground. He and Wally Brunkard stood supervising. Seth and Marcus loaded the last of the small crates into the bed of the Ram and came back to the plane.

They smiled and nodded to Ferris and grabbed the big create. "Gently now," Schroeder said unnecessarily. Seth and Marcus made it look effortless, and the larger crate overflowed the cargo well of the Ram.

"If you guys just hold on to it, I'll ease up to the shed real gentle," Schroeder said.

"Sure thing, boss," Marcus said, and squeezing Brunkard, Arnaud and Juanita into the cab, off they went.

While Ferris was walking over, Seth and Marcus carried the last of crates into the shed. Damn but those two were strong and efficient. Wally Brunkard made a great show of locking the door as they came out. Ferris grinned, and wondered if Wally knew the secret rumour about the padlock.

Juanita intercepted him with a look of tight-lipped hostility.

"We do not need you here," she said. "Mr Brunkard has taken care of matters."

"And you're welcome too," Ferris said lightly, and stared pointedly at her chest. "I'd like to say hi to Mr Schroeder if that's alright with you." Something flashed in her eyes, and he almost flinched.

"Good work, Tony," Schroeder said, interrupting the tension.

"The flight was art and joy, Vic," Ferris said. "Even with Miss Positivity here along for the ride."

"No problems with the Goose?" Schroeder said uncertainly, looking from Ferris to an icy Juanita.

"Luis flew like an angel," Ferris said, "Nothing to criticise. Well Vic, you can stop worrying now that your rush delivery is here."

Schroeder looked strangely blank. "Why yes it is. Thanks Tony."

Ferris turned to Brunkard. "Mr Wally, is the clubhouse open?" Brunkard hesitated. "For you it is, Mr Tony. But first we should refuel your plane, yes?" Ferris turned to Schroeder. Schroeder looked as inscrutable as his man Kun.

"Get Wally to fill her up, Tony." He said. "Just in case. Some of the kit is being assembled in San Juan and is nearly ready."

"Okay Vic," Ferris said, baffled. "It's your money." Garcia volunteered to help refuel, but Ferris waved him away. Everyone else except Wally hitched a ride back with Schroeder.

Ferris and Brunkard watched the Turbo Goose take off empty. It was a lot less entertaining, although Ferris still found the high revs scream disturbing.

Wally Brunkard got flustered at the idea of refuelling such a large aircraft. He looked very relieved when it only took eighty gallons. Ferris bought himself and Brunkard a Bacardi and Coke each, and watched the sunset from the verandah, slowly sipping his drink.

CHAPTER 46

Ferris felt only slightly guilty about driving to the hospital with a rum inside him. The island's drink driving laws were somewhat outdated.

"Mr Davern should make a full recovery," the desk nurse said. "But he is still very weak and no visitors are allowed. He sleeps a lot."

Ferris thanked the nurse, and it was only when he left that he remembered that the last time he had phoned from the airfield he had been told to mind his own business. Things were getting back to normal.

On his way through the town, he thought he was being followed. It didn't register at first, but there was an unknown young black guy on a moped who kept on appearing, either ahead or beside him, at street corners and intersections with the same yellow and green Brasil soccer shirt and the same green bandana knotted around his throat. Ferris cheekily drove the Veep into the bistro car park and watched and waited, but saw no more of the moped or the Brasil t-shirt. He shrugged. Unlike the engine problem, just a coincidence.

He went into the bistro. Angelique smiled a greeting but she had a strained air, and Ferris was only slightly surprised when Rolle appeared at his elbow.

"Well lookee here," Rolle said genially. "How was the Turks?" Ferris felt the heat rise to his neck. "How do you even know where I was?" Rolle shook his head and grinned.

"You really have no idea do you? There is three types of people in the world, the people who make things happen. And the two types who wonder what just happened. I think you're in group two."

"What do you want, anyway," Ferris asked tightly.

Rolle raised a reproachful eyebrow. "Nothin', just shooting the breeze with a buddy. We still tight, yeah? Although that kind of tone might give me cause to think different."

Ferris controlled his temper with difficulty. Rolle could probably slit his throat in the blink of an eye, and anyway, it would be wise to listen. "Alright, what the hell are you implying."

Rolle produced one of his inevitable cigars. "I think you know very well what I mean. I told you to watch your back, not to trust certain people, all that jazz. But no, you wouldn't listen to your uncle Bob, and now you're wondering."

"I'm not," Ferris said, without conviction.

Rolle grinned at him. "Things all add up do they? Nothing that only sorta makes sense until you think about it hard, like a bad alibi? I sort of like you, Tone, but there's none so blind as those that don't want to see. You make a fool outta yourself because you can't stay away from the flying business. I hope you collected your fee in advance."

Ferris shifted uncomfortably. "I have no idea what you're on about," he said.

Rolle made a disgusted gesture. "Said my piece. On your own head be it."

"You're damn right it is," Ferris said trenchantly. "It always has been. And I don't need people like you and Legett telling me what to do with my life." Ferris waited for Rolle to reply, and was a bit put out when he merely said "Oh yeah," and left.

Ferris brooded on what Rolle had said, and decided the man was just messing with his head, he was a practical joker of epic proportions and it was just Ferris's turn to be the butt of the joke. After all, apart from the man on the moped he only had vague suspicions. It could all be paranoia or post-traumatic stress of some sort.

He remembered the blonde and her open cruiser party invitation and brightened up. He finished his drink.

To Angelique, he said, "And now I think I'll visit an understanding sailor, if you don't mind." She grinned back at him. "Why should I mind, Ferris? Maybe she's not my type."

Ferris was still laughing as he drove back to the marina. He got no sense of being followed this time.

CHAPTER 47

If Schroeder hadn't lent Ferris the Veep, he would have enjoyed himself at the party.

The big grey motor cruiser was called "Sans Souci", and he should have been without a worry. He had done his work for the day, and everyone was happy and he could relax. The crowd swarmed all over the cruiser and spilled over onto the dock. Ferris had a fixed grin and a double-gibson, and he listened to the willowy blonde, Faun who claimed to be a corporate lawyer and spoke animatedly of wind-surfing. Ferris fancied her in an absent-minded way, but he kept thinking of overly heavy packing crates.

If Arnaud was in to anything illegal, then he, Ferris, was an accessory to the crime, no matter how he looked at it. In that case, the best way to get around it was to expose the illegality. If government officials such as Mr Wally were involved, it was doubly dangerous, but doubly creditable to blow the whole thing wide open. If he wanted to be a citizen of St. Marc, he had to be public-spirited. Legett could hardly do anything without proper suspicion, but as a person with access to the airfield and a vehicle – it always came back to that, no matter how often he went over it in his mind, Ferris had to go to the airfield and see what was in the crates. The shed might be guarded, he had no excuse to be there, but he could deal with that when he got there.

Faun was puzzled, and the next time somebody interrupted her, Ferris excused himself to go to the head, and slipped off the boat unnoticed. Looking back as he went up the pontoon, he marvelled at the number of people on the cruiser, and the noise they were making.

At the airfield the night was warm and soggy. Ferris had hoped being inland would make a difference but the island was too small to have a variation in humidity.

There had been no sign of the young man on the moped, and Ferris was glad. The drive was interminable in the dark with no street lighting out of the town, the lamps on the Veep being largely ornamental.

He switched off the lights and engine at the turnoff for the airfield and coasted the rest of the way, enjoying the silence after the sewing machine clatter of the Volkswagen engine.

The Veep sighed gently as he braked it to a halt just short of the clubhouse.

Ferris picked up the torch and screwdriver he had taken from the toolbox and got out.

The moon came out from behind clouds, which Ferris hadn't noticed. The weather was getting worse. The flatness of the airfield in the moonlight made it seem that anything that moved would be seen, unless in the cover of the deep shadows by the buildings.

Ferris stood still for what seemed like a very long time, listening to the night, and straining his eyes to see if there was anyone on the airfield.

The lack of noise was a little eerie, as if the tree frogs and crickets were also holding their breath. Ferris told himself that he was being jittery. Nobody lived within a mile of the airfield, the fields were given over to crops with no houses.

There was no sign of Tuffy, or any other life form. He decided that there was no one, but walked over to the shed as quietly as possible, and stopped every now and again to listen and search the darkness.

He reached the customs shed without encountering anyone, but by then he was breathing shallowly and bathed in sweat.

He stepped to the door, and tried the handle.

He rattled it unthinkingly for a moment, then realised the noise he was making, and again stood silently and listened, conscious mostly of the beating of his heart.

He turned on the torch and placed it lens up under the ground below the padlock.

He knelt and studied the padlock in the torch light. He had never paid it much attention before, just smiled at the joke about Brunkard's simple-minded trust in a faulty lock.

The door was like the door of a shipping container. The lock itself was attached at an awkward angle, but after some tinkering he got purchase on the shackle. He jiggled the shackle, varying the angle and pressure of which he pressed down on it with the screwdriver. He felt the click as the lock gave.

After a long moment, he grunted and inhaled, aware that absurdly he had held his breath again in the concentrated moment of jiggling the lock.

He unhooked the padlock, swung open the handle, picked up the torch and pushed open the door.

CHAPTER 48

Ferris shone the torch around the shed briefly, and resisted the temptation to turn on the lights.

A workbench stood against the inside wall, littered with non-Customs tools including a crowbar.

Despite having no windows, the shed didn't feel any cooler than outside. And it smelled peculiarly of over-ripe fruit, saw-dust and mould.

He shone the lamp in a slow arc, and found the crates.

The crates looked untouched, no new customs seals or anything of the sort, but also no sign of how to open them in a way that would not be noticed.

He was too wary to turn on the lights, but the narrow beam of the torch hardly gave enough light to make out which parts of the crates were the lids. He picked the crowbar off the bench.

He hit his first snag. He hadn't paid attention to the construction of the crates on the plane, more their weight and size and it hadn't sunk in that the large crate was made with screws rather than nails and levering off a couple of planks without causing noticeable damage was not really an option. The number of screws securing the lid was myriad and although the screw driver had a pump ratchet action, it would be a long job.

So first he turned to one of the smaller crates, which were more crudely constructed. Faced with the enormity of what he was doing, Ferris hesitated, the blood pounding in his chest and ears, and the sweat dripping off him. He swallowed the lump in his throat, and sat the torch down carefully. One edge of the crate bottom seemed to be nailed on a little roughly, so Ferris tried to lever the nails on that plank, and they straightened a little, and lifted out when he levered with the flat-edged head of the crowbar.

He repeated the process at the other end of the plank, and then tried to lever the plank out. The wood started to tear under the blade of the crowbar, so he switched to loosening the second plank. This was nailed in with greater skill, and took longer. Ferris paused frequently to wipe the sweat out of his eyes, and to look at his watch. For some reason, he felt short of breath. The second plank finally lifted off with a long creak, and Ferris froze again, but then rushed on in a frenzy, levering the two planks out without regard to noise or damage.

Then he dropped the crow-bar, and shone the torch into the four inch wide gap. There was slightly smaller crate inside. He saw elaborate stencilling of this-way-up icons and more "Alcatel" markings but Ferris was not deceived. It was a US Army ammunition shipping crate, of the size designed to hold two M2A1 ammunition boxes. He was so sure he tapped the two planks back into position without looking any further.

Ferris got the screwdriver and went back to the large crate. He pumped it as hard as he could and although his hand ached so much that he had to switch hands, he got the screws off one of the short sides, and levered off the panel it off. Inside was a block of styrofoam packing, and he levered that out to reveal a large steel box inside, painted camouflage green, with yellow stencilled writing on it. He could make out some Cyrillic lettering, 9К34 Стрела-3. For a moment it made no sense and then he had sick feeling in the pit of his stomach when he recognised the serial number for a Strela 3 anti-aircraft missile.

So Arnaud was some kind of weapons runner. How much did Schroeder know? Ferris felt sick as he looked at the missile container. Ferris started to screw the side panel back into position, but he felt a draught, and the lights came on.

"You can keep right on fixing the crate," Braun said.

Ferris looked around, feeling his knees turn to water. Quintero was pointing a pistol at Ferris's stomach. In his big hand, it was as solid as he was, unwavering, like it was part of him.

Ferris didn't know which one of them to be more afraid of. He wished he was elsewhere.

He wished he hadn't left the party that evening. He could be entertaining the willowy Faun, if he had minded his own business.

"I can see from your expression that you are putting the screws back not taking them out, unfortunately." Braun added.

Ferris's stomach felt very hollow, and the sick empty feeling went all the way to his throat, and his skin crawled as he waited for the first bullet.

"Well, go on," Braun said impatiently. "We don't want anyone else to see in there, do we?" Ferris nodded dumbly. Still crouched over the crate, he put back the rest of the screws.

He gestured to the doorway, and Ferris followed him numbly, Quintero bringing up the rear.

"What about the jeep?" Quintero asked.

"It's safe enough here," Braun said. He walked off, not even looking back to see if Ferris followed. Ferris saw how he had been surprised, they had parked their car back near the turnoff from the main road, so that the engine noise hadn't carried. Quintero gestured Ferris into the rear passenger side seat, and settled himself before Braun got in to drive.

They passed no traffic on the road to the town, and the streets were deserted.

To Ferris's surprise, Braun drove past the hotel and up the hill to Schroeder's house.

CHAPTER 49

Despite it being 3 a.m, The Schroeder mansion was lit up like the White House.

A sullen Kun opened the door when Braun rang. His eyes flickered when he saw Ferris and Quintero's gun, but he gave no other sign of reaction.

Braun rather ostentatiously locked the front door from the inside and ushered Kun and Ferris ahead of him down the corridor to Schroeder's study.

Schroeder, Arnaud and Juanita stood at the table. Schroeder looked up irritably and whatever he was about to say to Kun froze on his lips along with a look of dismay.

Juanita folded her arms in an I-told-you-so attitude.

"Ah Mr Ferris," said Arnaud. "I wondered if we would have trouble with you."

"Oh Tony, I told you I could handle things." In the artificial light, Schroeder looked terrible. The study had expensive natural light lamps but the harsh shadows picked out his gauntness, a flushed edge to his cheekbones, how his cheeks were hollow. It made him look what he really was, a sick man struggling to cope with a situation he couldn't control.

"It seems to be working out alright Vic," Ferris said.

"We found the captain re-assembling the ah ... system crate," Braun said obliquely.

"How unfortunate," Arnaud said flatly. "But a crisis is an opportunity, no? Now the pretence is over, perhaps you can be persuaded, Captain Ferris?"

"What do you say, Tony?" There was an anxious appeal in Schroeder's voice and in his expression.

Arnaud inclined his head. "How do you say, you have set the

cat among the pigeons, but as far as I am concerned, nothing about our arrangement needs to change. Mr Ferris is the cat but need not have the fatal curiosity. All he need do is give his word as a gentleman not to divulge what he has seen and we can proceed as before."

"You didn't tell him about the weapons, before," Braun pointed out.

Arnaud nodded. "Of course – because Mr Ferris wouldn't have agreed, and maybe won't agree now."

"I didn't think you were a melon farmer," Ferris said to Arnaud. "Too much soldier in you and you don't try to hide it."

Arnaud smiled appreciatively. "Once I tried to run a shop, and then a garage and petrol station and then an agricultural repair business. Each of them failed. If at first you don't succeed, you are trying the wrong thing – life was telling me that I am not Cincinattus and that Peace was not my business."

"I saw the weapons container," Ferris said calmly. "And not just weapons, anti-aircraft missiles – why would you want to sell such things – the only people who don't have them are rebels."

There was a pause for just too long and Juanita looked Ferris in the eye and said "I don't think that will work, commandant. Mr Ferris is a man of principle."

"What you are doing is illegal," Ferris said.

Schroeder groaned. "Tony –"

"No my friend, not just illegal, but audacious." Arnaud smiled. "And why not? For the money and satisfying the curiosity of a military man. As I said, peace is not my profession. For a large, no, an obscene sum of money. The little Brazilian trainer aircraft are a huge nuisance to our clients. A cartel, you might say, of interested parties got together to offer a bounty to anyone who could provide weapons to shoot down this – Embraear Tucano, yes?

As for my professional interest, I am sure the military use counter-measures and we can doubtless gather valuable informa-tion for future reference."

Arnaud paused when he saw Ferris's stony expression.

"I see you are not persuaded," said Arnaud regretfully. "It would have been nice to have two pilots, but plans can be changed. Garcia can fly, since his hydroplane is now again operational and it has the range."

"No he can't," Schroeder objected. "How do you know he'll say yes." By way of reply, Arnaud pressed the buzzer on Schroeder's desk and the door opened and Garcia swaggered in.

"Howdy Tony. Sorry Mr Schroeder, but the commandant made me a better offer."

Garcia lifted the left side of his mouth in a crooked grin, looking more like a cowboy than ever.

"Very good," Arnaud said. "In that case we no longer require the services of Captain Ferris."

Ferris saw Schroeder's expression and the look that flicked between Arnaud and Braun and suddenly his stomach tightened as he realised that the debate with Schroeder had not been about Garcia's merits as a flier but about Ferris getting out alive.

CHAPTER 50

Schroeder looked very pale. "Well I suppose there is no more to be said." He looked at the window. "It sounds like the wind is getting up. If we're using the Turbo Goose, maybe you should go check the moorings."

"It's okay," Garcia said carelessly. "She's on the beach, pegged down well above the high-tide line."

"I'd be happier if Kun checked anyway," Schroeder said earnestly.

Arnaud shrugged. "A wise precaution. Quintero, accompany Mr Kun." Ferris thought a fleeting look passed between the two older men, but before Quintero closed the door, Schroeder drew back his attention.

"Luis, do you need Tony to check your figures?" He unrolled a map as he spoke, and weight down the end with a plastic tube.

"No need, it's almost exactly the same distance," Garcia said airily. "Just flying south-west instead of north-west, same prevailing winds, the only question is whether the storm they're forecasting develops into a hurricane ... "

He went over to point it out on the map. Arnaud joined Schroeder also.

Ferris watched in horrified fascination. The plastic tube holding down the map was the same heavy duty plastic torch with something wrong with it, that Schroeder has thrown into the sea the other day.

In a very natural move, Schroeder took the torch away so that Garcia could lay his finger on the map.

Then he reversed it and pointed it at Garcia and pressed his thumb on the button. A flash came from the empty torch face and a deafening clatter filled the room and the front of Garcia's shirt fluttered.

Garcia said "Uh," and grabbed at his chest. He swayed and blood seeped through his shirt and he fell sideways. Juanita screamed.

It seemed a whole second passed before Braun pulled a pistol out, and Schroeder clicked uselessly on his torch-gun as Braun brought his gun to bear.

Braun fired four times and Schroeder staggered backwards, dropping the torch.

"Cease firing," Arnaud yelled, but Braun swung his gun around to Ferris, looking for further threats, but Ferris had his hands up.

"You idiot, you nearly shot me," Arnaud said indignantly. He had a gun out as well, aimed at Schroeder, who lay on the floor wheezing. "Don't shoot the pilot."

"*Pardon, patron*," said Braun. "It was an instinctive reaction."

"No matter," said Arnaud. "Check Garcia."

Braun knelt beside Garcia, who lay on his face, very still. Braun felt for a pulse and shook his head. "*Mort.*"

"Search Ferris." Arnaud said, and went over and patted down Schroeder. "*Tiens*, Vic, what possessed you?" He picked up the torch-gun and examined it briefly. "I have heard of this but not seen it." Satisfied it was safe, he tossed it into a corner.

When Braun had searched Ferris, Arnaud said, "Secure the house. I don't want the servants to raise the alarm."

He pointed his gun at Ferris as Braun went out. Juanita had unfrozen and had pulled a pistol from her handbag.

"Well, Mr Ferris," Arnaud said philosophically. "It looks like we have need of your services after all, and this time I will be telling you, not asking you."

Muffled in the distance, Two shots rang out.

Arnaud swore under his breath, but stood patiently at the table, tapping his foot, an officer to the last.

Schroeder moved one of his feet and coughed feebly.

"Vic?" Ferris asked Arnaud.

"No hope, I'm afraid, help him if you wish, but make no sudden movements."

Schroeder's shirt front was a mass of spreading bloodstain, and the carpet under him was darkening as well. He opened his eyes when Ferris pulled the shirt aside to see the wounds better.

"Sorry kid," Schroeder said feebly. Ferris pulled a cushion off one of the chairs but it was a forlorn attempt. Schroeder grunted and coughed wetly again as Ferris tried to apply pressure.

"No good Mikey," he said. Ferris wondered if he meant Mike his long-dead brother. "But don't worry I'm so hopped up on pain killers I can barely feel a thing. So sad about the girl, so very sad. Somebody had to stop him you know ... "

He shrank away before Ferris's eyes. "For God's sake, get an ambulance," Ferris appealed to Arnaud.

"Out of the question," Arnaud said.

Schroeder whispered, and Ferris had to lean in close. "I never wanted you in this deep, Mike. Couldn't have a second pilot. Too much risk. I shouldn't have asked you. Tell Chad I'm sorry I was a bad father. I was never there for him."

He coughed again and convulsed and Ferris jerked away from the blood. He sat back on his heels in despair.

Quintero bustled in, the left side of his face a mass of running blood.

"Well?" Arnaud said.

"The old woman must have got behind me. I saw something at the last moment and fired, I held onto my gun but I was stunned for a few seconds and when I got back to my senses there was no sign of the valet or the woman. Braun went outside, but he told me to lock up."

"He has men outside," Arnaud said.

The doorbell rang, and Quintero went out to check it.

Braun rushed in moments later. "*Patron*, we have a problem. The seaplane has rolled into the sea and is sinking. And the house is on fire!"

CHAPTER 51

"Without Garcia, the aircraft is of no consequence," Arnaud said. "Your men did not stop the servants?"

"No," Braun said. "They escaped."

Arnaud looked at his watch. "No matter. In fact, the fire may cause a certain amount of confusion. The boat is ready?"

"Yes, patron," Braun said.

Arnaud looked at Juanita. "There is just about enough time to drive to the airfield and load the aircraft before dawn. I will stay here to make a diversion."

Juanita looked stonily at Ferris. "What about Ferris?" Arnaud smiled. "I think he will do what he is told. Won't you, Captain?"

A spray of sparks showered off the eve of the roof at the side of the house as they drove off, and highlighted the smoke of the fire.

As before, Quintero sat in the back with Ferris while Braun drove, Juanita in the front clutching her briefcase.

At the bottom of the hill, a police cruiser passed going the other way. "It begins," Braun muttered. But he continued to drive normally.

Dawn was a very pale sliver on the horizon when their rental car pulled up beside the Veep.

Braun looked around at Ferris. "We will need you to help with the load, Captain. Miss Cardenas will cover you so please don't try to run away. We need you alive but she can always shoot you in the leg which would stop you from running and be a nuisance for flying, I imagine. And if that is not enough deterrent, Quintero is very good at hurting people."

Quintero nodded and slitted his eyes. It should have been ridiculous but it wasn't.

"Okay," Ferris said hoarsely, "You've made your point."

It took the two cars to carry the crates out to the plane, because Braun wanted to do only one trip.

They loaded the plane by headlights, but by the time the load was tied down securely, it was bright enough to see inside the fuselage without them.

"It is bright enough to fly now?" Braun said, it wasn't really a question.

"I have to do the preflight checks," Ferris said. "Are we going back to Flat Cay?" Braun smiled. "I am not going anywhere, Captain Ferris."

"We are going to Colombia, Captain." Juanita opened her briefcase and shoved papers at him. At a glance, Ferris could make out a hand-written flight plan and a faxed meteorological forecast.

"Garcia had a map also. You will see it in the air."

With Quintero and Braun trailing him watchfully, Ferris walked around the aircraft, checking through the preflight check ups, seeing that the tail planes and fins were free, the ailerons and flaps, and the tyres still inflated.

Ferris looked at the sky. The storm building up was more than a thousand miles out, halfway across the Atlantic, but a weather system could move a vast distance in a few hours. The sky was reasonably clear, though not the usual way when it was good flying weather. It was almost like back in Europe, you thought in terms of weather rather than seasons. There was bad weather on the way alright, and not too far away. They might even have to fly through it.

He reached up and started to pull on the port propeller.

"What are you doing?" Juanita demanded. She looked like she was going to pull a gun again.

"Rotating manually," Ferris grunted. "To prevent hydraulic lock."

"How long will this take?" Braun asked impatiently.

"Nine full rotations," Ferris puffed. "Thirty seconds each." Braun and Quintero went to the starboard propeller and cranked the blades. They finished before him, but he was glad of the help. He was sweating already. The dawn was only four degrees cooler than the rest of the day.

Ferris stood back, satisfied.

"Ready to go now?" Juanita said.

"Yes," Ferris said. As he spoke out of the corner of his eye he caught movement beyond the airfield perimeter. He looked around, and saw a truck bouncing along through the scrub, and he recognised the direction as being from the plantation track off the main road. The truck was dark green, and he could make out men riding in the back, being jolted about by the motion of the truck.

A tannoy-boosted voice echoed across the airfield. "This is the police. Stay where you are. Raise your arms above your heads and do not move."

CHAPTER 52

Quintero swore in Spanish, and Juanita pulled a MAC-10 machine-pistol from her briefcase.

"Allow me, mademoiselle," Braun said politely, holding out his Beretta. "I can draw them away from you. This will be safer on the aircraft."

Juanita reluctantly took the Beretta and racked the slide expertly.

Braun pulled out the magazine of the MAC-10 and made a face. "Nine millimetre short. Oh well. *Bonne chance.*"

In an explosion of movement, Braun jumped into the rental car and reversed away, and Quintero backed the Veep away and vaulted out without switching off.

"What are you waiting for, Ferris," Juanita screamed. "Start the engines, damn you. And get us out of here!"

Ferris secured the cargo doors and with Quintero on his heels, Ferris went to the cockpit, and started to run up the engines.

As the starters whined into life, he heard the tannoy voice again, distinct, unhurried and precise.

"This is the police. Do not attempt to resist. Lay down your weapons, and shut down all engines. This is your last warning."

The truck reached the edge of the airfield, and men were jumping from the back and fanning out into a line.

The starboard engine caught, and Ferris no longer heard the tannoy. Juanita came up and Quintero gave up his seat to her.

As the port engine caught and the propeller moved, flames splattered out of the cowling flaps. Ferris lowered his hand to the throttle lever. "No," she levelled the Beretta at Ferris. "We must take off. Now."

His hand hovered over the fire extinguisher switch, Ferris

shrugged mentally. You could never tell with the old radials, sometimes the prop wash and the action of the engine could put out a start-up fire. Then again the whole engine could go up in a fireball and burn off the wing.

Ferris looked at the port engine cowling anxiously. He increased the rpm and the plane vibrated and a ring of black smoke gushed back from the exhaust pipes and dispersed in the prop wash. The flames vanished.

"Taxi towards the runway." There was a crackle of small-arms fire from the direction of the gate, out of cycle with the roar of the engines. He pushed the throttle forward gently, and the Beech began to roll forward slowly. Instinctively, he leaned forward to check to the starboard, and saw a second truck racing to cut off their path.

"We'll never make it to the runway," Ferris said grimly.

Juanita pushed the gun against his ear. "Then take off across the field."

"No," Ferris said, remembering the first day at San Juan, where it all began. "We'd never make it. We'll be killed. It's too short." Juanita bared her teeth. "Quintero, show Ferris that I'm not joking." Quintero leaned between the seats and tapped Ferris on the knuckles of his right hand with the sights of his pistol. Pain shot up Ferris's arm.

"You bitch," he said bitterly.

"It is your choice," Juanita said. "You can die now, for certain, when I shoot you, or you can maybe survive, if you try to take off."

Ferris saw the look in her eyes, and he knew he had no real choice. He opened up the throttles and the Beech picked up speed. It hurtled along, but the two trucks were still outpacing it and converging at a point long before the point where the Beech would attain take-off speed.

Ferris opened the throttles wide, and the twin Wasps bellowed and the Beech slowly outpaced the trucks, although they were now blocking his path.

At the last moment he throttled back. A shot smashed through the perspex panel of the window beside him, and he was deafened, his skin stung by the powder. Through the buzzing in his ears, he heard Juanita say, "Take off or die, Ferris."

Ferris flinched, but concentrated on his task. He unlocked the tailwheel, and throttled back the port engine abruptly. The Beech staggered, and, then recovered, and swung around to face the way it had come.

He was confident the two trucks would take a few seconds to understand his reverse of direction, so he equalised the throttles and pointed the Beech across the grass parallel to the runway. He estimated some calculations in his head. It wasn't ideal but he had maybe sixteen hundred feet before the boundary of the field, which should be just about enough if he got the airspeed.

He pushed the throttles into the red and the Beech leapt forward. Someone else had been calculating too, because a third truck, a blue one, swerved onto the airfield attempting cut him off again.

However this driver was too keen and mis-timed his interception and turned into the path of the Beech too soon. Ferris put down fifteen degrees of flaps. He concentrated on the essentials, a clear path to take-off, keeping ahead of the truck, reaching take-off speed and gaining enough ground to get it.

The treeline of the plantations went from distant to alarmingly close.

The tail of the Beech lifted hesitantly, bumped back, lifted again, and stayed in the air.

Ferris pulled the stick fully back, and the Beech lurched up, banged down on the main wheels again, bounced wildly. He fought the controls, and the tail stayed up, and the Beech bounced into the air again, and he stopped fighting the torque to the port and let the plane drift slightly, gaining them some yards.

They flew at ninety miles per hour straight at the trees. Ferris snapped at the undercarriage lever, and the Beech wobbled as the wheels came up. Because of the fire he didn't trust the engines and he went for speed and not height. He remembered in time to press the brakes, as the still spinning wheels slammed home and vibrated the plane. He pulled back on the stick again, as the undercarriage doors clunked shut, and the Beech soared, crazily, sucking him back in his seat, pulling his stomach out through the floor.

The tree tops fell out of the windscreen, and he felt the bite of the blades and before the controls could slacken as the plane neared a stall, he levelled out quickly. They were high enough to clear the trees.

"Jesus Mary and Joseph, Holy Mother be praised," Juanita

breathed, and she no longer pointed the gun at him. He throttled back to cruising speed, and settled the Beech into a gentle climb. The port engine sounded rough again, and the temperature was climbing. But for the moment, Ferris couldn't care. For now he was happy to be alive.

CHAPTER 53

His seat was awash with sweat. Ferris looked at Juanita blankly, then touched the bullet hole in the side window. "What the hell was that about?"

Juanita stared at him. "You needed to be encouraged."

"I accept your apology," Ferris said.

For some moments, Juanita chattered excitedly at Quintero about their escape, relieved and overjoyed. He was taciturn as ever. Then, Juanita stood up. "Quintero, you know what to do?"

Quintero sat into the right seat and pulled out a Leatherman. He selected a thick blade and stuck it into the join between console and the transponder face panel.

"What are you doing?" Ferris asked in horror.

"Sorry Captain, but we are better off with any identification. And we do not trust you."

Quintero levered with the blade on all four sides of the transponder casing until something splintered. He pushed, got purchase and dragged the whole assembly out of the dash. He selected a pliers and cut the wires. He then repeated the process with the Navcom radio.

Then he nodded and stood up with the two casings.

Juanita sat back in. "It is time to look at the maps again, Captain, to be sure you understand what we are doing. You know There is a USAF AWACS base in Ecuador, yes?"

"At Manta, yes."

"We do not wish to attract the attention of their interdiction radar. So we have a flight plan filed for Aruba. No one will be alarmed when we do not radio in, they will assume a fault. There is no reason for the authorities in St. Marc to find out about our flight and even if they communicate with Aruba in the next three hours, what can they do, send a coastguard helicopter?"

Juanita opened her briefcase and handed Ferris the flight chart and a sheet of scribbled notes.

"We will fly at five thousand feet, like a normal passenger aircraft. Assume a direct course to Aruba. A course of 231.20 degrees and a heading of 226 to account for windspeed."

Ferris noted the pencilled course to Aruba, where the course turned East South East and cut across the top of Colombia, towards the city of Barranquilla but then stopped short of a river delta.

"This is insane," he said. "Barranquilla is over nine hundred miles. That's over five hours. You saw the fire, we shouldn't attempt a long flight with a faulty engine. The most sensible thing to do is fly to San Juan and get the engine checked out."

Juanita curled her lip. "And the first thing that would happen is that the police would arrest us. I think not. This plane can fly on one engine, yes?"

"Yes but the reason they have two is that the second one keeps working if the first one fails. Now we only have one reliable engine."

"Bah," Juanita said. "I know about this, this is the plane that never quite works but never breaks. We will keep on, there is nothing to discuss."

"Jesus woman," Ferris said. "Talking to you is a waste of breath. Nothing went in, did it?"

"Listen, Ferris. You're a shit-hot pilot, okay?"

"I wouldn't use that phrase but I'm pretty good, yes."

"Well then, you know what to do to make it work properly. I've been up all night so I'm going to sleep now, wake me when we get to Aruba."

Ferris swallowed his ire. "I have to recalculate the figures. Garcia worked it for the Turbo Goose."

"Garcia is dead," Juanita said coldly. She pointed to a splash of blood on the map.

Ferris paused, he hadn't noticed it. "Anyway. The heading will change, this is a slower plane."

"Whatever," Juanita said. "It's cold. You got no blankets on this thing?" She loosened her seat belt and shifted around, looking for a more comfortable position.

"One more thing," Juanita said, and held open the briefcase to show him the butt of the Beretta. "If you have any ideas about flying the wrong direction, both I and Quintero understand compass courses."

CHAPTER 54

Ferris set the autopilot and examined the chart and notes.

The sun rose in a lovely golden glow, despite the cloud banks. The beauty of the moment passed without comment. Juanita dozed with her chin twisted onto her shoulder and clutched her arms around her briefcase.

Ferris didn't want to think ill of the dead but Garcia was an arrogant idiot. A flight to Aruba was six hundred miles of dead-reckoning across empty ocean. With no waypoints and without being able to communicate with ATC the margin for navigation error was huge. With a strengthening easterly from the storm system forecast at twenty five miles per hour and rising, the plane could drift west and if the sun went in you could easily fly on until reaching Nicaragua, Panama or until the plane ran out of fuel. When he checked Garcia's calculations he grudgingly had to admit they were sound, except they didn't take into account the possible increase in wind speed. He re-did the course correction for the slower cruising speed of the Beech. Ferris decided to bring the cruising speed up to lessen the drift. It would burn thirty percent more fuel but it lessened the time without a visual indication of their location. He added another degree to the heading for luck. If he over-corrected they would make landfall over the Venezuelan coast.

Ferris was so engrossed in his calculations that he forgot Quintero was sitting behind him and he started when Quintero stuck his head forward and spoke. With a glance at the sleeping Juanita, Quintero said, barely audible above the engines, "The commandant said that you are an officer and a man of honour. And so I feel I should speak to you for the señorita. In this matter Señorita Cardénas is my commanding officer and her word is law. She is a woman of high standing and her principals are people of most impeccable. Because she has slighted you, maybe you feel your honour has been insulted. Some say that your people no longer think as we do, but I think all men are the same. Your pride has been hurted and to defend your honour you might feel that the señorita has to be slighted also. And that to revenge yourself on her you will do foolish things. And that is why I must say to you that the commandant is very serious and has given me the strictest commands to carry out her wishes to the letter. That is why I say this to you so that you know that I am completely serious.

"I understand fully, Quintero," Ferris said, coldly.

St Croix and the rest of the US Virgin Islands slid out of view far to the starboard and Sint Eustatius and St Kitts & St Nevis fell behind in the distance to the port. And there was nothing but open sea and sky ahead.

Ferris rechecked his figures. Ahead, he could see a cloud layer at about twelve hundred feet. If it continued he would have to rely on raising the coast to get a fix.

The sun coming around over his left shoulder as the morning wore on was a reassuring indication that he was staying on track.

Over time the twin Wasp Juniors took on a hypnotic hum, the engines were beautifully tuned and synchronised despite what Hollis had said, and the port engine made no more off-key sounds.

The Beech 18 was famous as a stable flier, trimmed properly it could pretty much fly itself and stay on course even without an autopilot, so as long as the engines held up he didn't have to worry about that aspect.

He tried to relax and enjoy the flight, but he couldn't. It was impossible to ignore the abnormality of the flight. He was a prisoner, and also attempting a long crossing with an untrusted engine. He kept an eye on the time and speed and adjusted the course dutifully at each of the waypoints he had scribbled on the map. The course corrections and calculations absorbed him, but in between, he fretted.

Normally when Ferris flew, the world stood still, and he became absorbed in the here and now. But this time, he remained on edge, thanks to Quintero's little speech.

The cloud layer below broke up as they flew beyond the reach of the storm system and the sky cleared.

In just under three hours the cloud cover of the Venezuelan

coast became visible, and not long after he could make out the coastal foothills.

Ferris kept an eye on the fuel flow needle. He hadn't flown the plane enough to trust the fuel gauge. He flicked through the selector for wing tanks, and they were all showing near empty.

Juanita stirred. She sat up straight as she saw the fuel gauge.

"You fool! You have run out of fuel," she said in a panicky tone.

"No I haven't, the gauge is ..." Ferris said reasonably.

"Liar! Always you lie, you pig." She lunged at him and whipped the Beretta back and forth across Ferris's face. He jerked his head back but the second swipe, raked his skin, drew blood. Ferris grabbed at the pistol blindly and caught the barrel.

Quintero's hand closed over his before he could take it away from Juanita, and the three of them froze.

"Let go of the pistol and explain please, Captain," Quintero said.

Juanita scowled and sat back when Ferris let go of the pistol.

Struggling to sound calm, he flicked the fuel gauge selector around. "See? There is only one gauge. The rear wing tanks are empty, the front wing tanks are low and the nose tank is full. Are you happy now?"

"Tell me exactly when you make landfall at Aruba. I will give you further instructions," Juanita said.

Ferris wiped the blood off his eye-brow.

It was pleasant enough at five thousand feet, and by allowing the plane to virtually fly itself, with only small adjustments, Ferris had little to do but check the instruments and listen to the engines, but he still found that his muscles ached with tension, and the sweat was beginning to soak through his clothes.

CHAPTER 55

Rather than slump into a daze of reaction and inactivity, Ferris kept his attention external. It took a few more minutes before he identified their location to his satisfaction. They were coming up to the east of Bonaire, with the other Dutch islands Curaçao and Aruba and beyond them the Gulf of Venezuela and Maracaibo Lagoon to the west. He adjusted the course to line up for Aruba. He allowed himself a moment of pride for a job well done. He throttled back slightly to conserve fuel, they were ten minutes ahead of his calculations.

Soon they approached Aruba.

"Aruba landfall in two minutes," Ferris said.

Juanita looked at another sheet she had taken from her brief-case.

"Now I have instructions: descend to nine hundred metres and fly a course of two hundred and fifty degrees for three hundred and eighty kilometres, then tell me when we have reached that point."

"That's another hour and a half," Ferris objected, doing the conversion in his head. "If it's much further than that you are going to really want to pistol-whip me." He pencilled in the course. "And the Sierra Nevadas are fifty seven hundred metres, we will be flying lower than that."

Juanita glared at him. "We will fly just inland of the coast, we will not go to the mountains," was all she said.

Ferris shrugged and adjusted to the new course.

After another twenty minutes with the coast tantalisingly out of reach on the port, the Beech crossed over the top north-east-most point of Colombia, and flew over a burnt lowland scrubland that was almost a desert. Ferris presumed that flying over land was deliberate to confuse the radar signature but he was puzzled, the north-east coast was an area known for some guerrilla activity but was mostly under government control, unlike the Pacific coast and the western highlands.

Over an hour's flying the burnt, flat land changed character, it became greener and more hilly.

Ferris constantly scanned the sky. The air force bombed unauthorised strips and had taken to shooting down mysterious aircraft with no radios. But mostly he was exercising caution. They flew past few signs of human civilization, no large towns and only the occasional road or small river.

They drew nearer to the mountains, and passed several sizeable towns. "Three hundred and eighty kilometres coming up in one minute," Ferris said. They had just passed a large town and what looked like a huge open-cast mine.

"Look for a river mouth five kilometres after that," Juanita said.

It took less than two minutes to cover the distance, and Ferris identified the river on the map immediately, a small sandy delta with a sandbar across the mouth, and wondered at the pointless secrecy.

"Fly two kilometres inland to where the river bends and then descend to three hundred metres and then begin to circle anti-clockwise," Juanita read. "Circle five times."

Ferris could see the point without even needing the map and flew inland.

The land rose further inland but it was almost flat here where the river slowed down and turned back on itself like a giant worm.

The banks of the river were heavily wooded. As he circled, Ferris spotted a large stone building on a cleared stretch on the bank of the river, and a couple of small roads that looked like logging tracks but nothing that resembled a landing strip.

He throttled back. "Well? We have maybe an hour's fuel left if I husband it."

"Wait," Juanita said. She clenched her hand around the butt of the pistol but said no more.

On the fourth circuit, a jeep he had not seen drove out from behind the stone building and stopped at the edge of the woods. With a flurry of activity, and group of men jumped off the jeep.

Ferris couldn't watch as he brought the Beech around again, and this time magically an avenue was opening up in the trees.

One of the forest paths transformed into a wide strip as groups of men pushed back loose foliage.

"Now you have to land as quickly as possible," Juanita said briskly.

"How long is it?" Ferris asked.

"Four hundred and fifty metres."

Ferris grimaced as he converted to feet. You could land a Beech 18 in twelve hundred and fifty feet which left two hundred and some feet to spare but it didn't really leave much to chance.

He came around again, and satisfied himself that the cleared stretch was nearly twice the width of the wingspan. Then he lined up and came across the river very low. He allowed the Beech to overshoot any sand, because he didn't want to risk overturning, and put the plane down hard on the start of the dirt section. He landed the plane and let it run on two wheels, and kept the starboard lever slightly more open as he throttled back and touched the brakes as soon as the tail wheel took. The Beech slid to a halt in a cloud of dust. Sure enough there were two hundred feet to spare before the trees.

Quintero leaned forward between the seats. "I am a bad passenger, but you are a good pilot, Captain. It has been an honour."

Ferris said nothing, and the others showed no inclination to move.

"Taxi to the end of the runway. There will be space enough to turn around," Juanita said.

Ferris gingerly rolled the Beech forward, and was surprised to see that the start of the forest was actually another area covered in camouflage netting. After unlocking the tail-wheel he turned the plane using the throttles. Facing back, he killed the engines. He watched the strip disappearing as groups of men, some of them wearing combat fatigues, pulled netting across the strip and other groups behind them hoisted the netting up on poles. It looked utterly unconvincing from ground level but had worked from the air.

Then a jeep came along the runway, winding between the groups of men, and stopped near the Beech. Juanita jabbed Ferris with the Beretta, and he got up wearily and followed Quintero down the fuselage, past the crates. Quintero helped Ferris open the cargo doors. The cabin of the Beech had already warmed a lot since landing and the instant the door opened and the heat outside hit him like a blast from a furnace. Sweat started out of him from unsuspected pores.

Juanita jumped down and embraced the leader of the group from the jeep.

He was tall and lanky with a Fidel beard and wore a Breton cap with an eight pointed star.

The leader stepped back with a beaming smile as Quintero and Ferris stepped down.

He spoke in such a chatter of rapid Spanish that Ferris only caught parts of it.

"A pity. I was hoping to meet the incomparable Commandante Arnaud," the leader said.

"We had to leave in a hurry and some plans got changed," Quintero replied.

"No matter," the leader said. "It is still an honour to meet one of his men." He looked at Ferris. "We lost our pilot," Juanita said carefully.

"Captain Ferris is a reluctant participant."

The leader's features became less friendly as he listened.

"We can discuss it later," he said. "First I want to see the cargo, and not have to pinch myself." He ducked through the cargo door and said, "The big box? I can't believe it. Now we can do something that will make them pay attention." A knot of men had formed around the plane, laughing and chatting.

"Hey you guys, lend a hand," the leader said. "Careful now." They piled the jeep high with the crates. The leader still grinning, sat into the driving seat. "Roberto," he said, "Refuel the aircraft and lock up the pilot. But get him a bandage and no rough stuff. I'll talk to him later." A large sullen man in camouflage fatigues tapped Ferris on the shoulder. "You heard the chief, let's move it." Ferris looked up at the engine nacelles as they walked past. The light under the camouflage nets was not great, but apart from some scorch marks behind the cowling flaps on the port side, he could see no evidence of the fire, and against the plant smells and hot engine smells, he could detect a faint whiff of burnt aluminium, but it was no more than if somebody threw a beer can in a beach bonfire.

"There's no need to look worried," Roberto said in English. "If El Murillo was angry, you would run along behind the jeep tied to the axle. Don't let the smile fool you."

CHAPTER 56

Ferris looked at the stone building as they walked closer.

It had to be over a century old, built of a mix of stone blocks and concrete with a derrick made of girders near one side. Ferris guessed it was a mill for crushing rocks for a mine. It looked abandoned many years, the derrick was rusted, the paint peeling.

Also not visible from the air were a row of low houses which the jungle had almost taken back. But the buildings were in good condition, the roofs still on, and it looked as if the guerrillas had had their camp there for a long time.

The other guerrillas had finished re-erecting the camouflage nets and were trailing back to the camp.

They wore a narrow selection of para-military fatigues and denim, and although some of them carried rifles they looked like a group of back-packers with a liking for military surplus.

A concrete hut stood under the derrick, probably an old tool shed, and Roberto hustled Ferris into it.

At the doorway, Roberto said, "Take a good sniff. Smell the fear. This is where we keep the prisoners. We don't keep them long, and if they don't agree to join us, we shoot them, so enjoy the thoughts of your predecessors. If you do get out of the hut, the plane is guarded and the woods are booby-trapped. If you don't kill yourself on a land-mine, you will get your head cut off by some savage who likes your watch."

He shoved Ferris, and as Ferris stumbled into the hut, the door slammed shut behind him, cutting out the light. He heard the bolt go home, and stood indecisively in the semi-darkness. He hadn't had a good look from the doorway, and by the smell of the place, sitting on the floor might not be such a good idea.

Ferris looked around as his eyes adjusted to the gloom. The

crack of light around the door edges spoiled his night vision without revealing much in the room.

People had been very scared in here. There was a trapped smell, a foetid odour of excrement and urine, vomit and stale sweat, all mingled in a choking record of despair.

Ferris tried not to breathe too deeply, convinced that the air was thick with germs. The sleepy buzz of flies seemed to confirm this.

He sat anyway and sweated and tried not to think. He caught himself checking his watch frequently, the fluorescent markings on the dial the only thing he could make out in the gloom. It was a nice touch, leaving him his watch, as if they had forgotten to rob him, as he wasn't dead yet.

Then again, maybe Roberto wanted him to know how slowly time passed in this situation.

But after a few minutes he realised how very tired he was after a night of no sleep and he decided to risk a lumpy mattress in a corner and lay down and slept.

***

The sound of the bolt being drawn and the door flung back woke Ferris.

He blinked at the sudden sunlight, the rush of cold air of a mere thirty degrees centigrade. "You're a cool one," Roberto said, sounding disappointed. "El Murillo worried that the heat was getting to you."

Ferris glanced at his watch, two hours had passed and he didn't feel much refreshed.

Roberto and a side-kick shoved him across the compound to one of the adobe houses. Normally, Ferris would have stopped and told them to lay off, but he was too relieved to be out in the relative cool of the sun to put up a fight.

El Murillo, the man in the Breton cap, sat behind a battered desk in a dilapidated office.

He was polishing a rifle. He turned and leaned it against the wall. "Mauser seven millimetre," he said. "The Germans always make beautiful guns, don't you think? But the Russians make even more beautiful missiles."

CHAPTER 57

He smiled like a kindly young uncle. "Do sit down, Señor Ferris. I am Murillo. I'm in two minds about you. Juanita says you are a liability, but Mr Quintero tells me his chief hoped to persuade you to work for him, and not at gunpoint. But this very strange murder by Señor Schroeder," Murillo shook his head. "That was an act of madness, I can't account for it. He has ... was very supportive of us over the last couple of years, he brought commandant Arnaud into this whole matter in the first place, I cannot understand at all what happened. I was very sorry for it.

It was a misfortune that the other pilot was killed but I hear he was not a steady man. Of course, it is the reckless men we attract. A more steady man such as yourself, you might be hard to persuade but once you are sold as they say, you would stay sold?"

Ferris was acutely aware of Roberto standing behind him, and he knew that it was all hogwash. But he asked with genuine curiosity, "Why do you think you can persuade me if Schroeder couldn't?"

A woman in combats came in and placed a tray on the table. She didn't speak, and Murillo didn't continue until she had left, with only a sideways glance at Ferris.

The smell of coconut and chicken reminded Ferris that he hadn't eaten for even longer than he slept.

Murillo looked at him quizzically and then pushed a bowl of chicken and rice across the table.

"Perhaps you will join me in eating?"

Roberto snorted, but Ferris saw the hard look in El Murillo's eyes. "That will be all, Roberto," he said, and the big man shambled out, muttering.

"I think a man performs better if he sees a reward at the end,"

Murillo said.

The chicken and coconut smelled delicious to Ferris, after the foul hole he had been cooped up in. He ate in silence and efficiency.

Murillo finished his meal with every sign of relish, then put the bowl down with a sigh.

"You think we are FARC," he said, when Ferris paused in eating.

"Or something like them," Ferris said.

"There you are wrong," Murillo said triumphantly. "We fight against them. The government couldn't govern and called on everyone to stand with them, and now that they think they have power within their grasp again they don't need their friends any longer. But we find the power in our grasp that they seek, no? We have tasted freedom and have a right to defend ourselves."

"Absolutely," Ferris said. "The only problem being, most of your enemies don't have aircraft and a big part of the shipment is anti aircraft missiles"

"You could have mixed up our baggage perhaps?" Murillo asked.

"No mistake," Ferris said firmly through a mouthful of food.

Murillo gave a bellow of laughter and clapped his hands. "Ah it's true, sadly. We had a country once and may have again. But now we are wild men and control our own destiny against all comers. Now you know we are not really rebels, will you reconsider?"

"Well, my boats are burnt. I can hardly go back to St. Marc, I'm probably wanted for questioning for murder along with whatever Arnaud did."

"Yes I see your point, you probably need to disappear. We could make it worth your while. We can always use more pilots."

"Especially with Garcia dead," Ferris couldn't help saying. "I've got nothing left to lose. What are you offering?"

"You could live in Nicaragua," Murillo said. "We have friends there, and the US don't hunt us there, they leave us be if we stay away from the cocaine."

"And do you stay away from cocaine?"

Murillo looked haunted. "It is difficult, Mr Ferris. The end justifies the means, and our freedom is bought with our blood and force of arms, backed up with money. But we found another high value cargo which is less repugnant. We can offer a commission and your hands will be clean, of the drugs trade at least."

He looked brightly at Ferris, who was regretfully finishing the stew. "Would you like some more?" he asked courteously.

"No thank you," Ferris said equally politely. "I'm sure you have barely enough to go round. I suppose it's hard to get food here."

Murillo nodded appreciatively. "The people understand the struggle, and they help as much as they can, but sadly, they have little to spare. The irony that we must cause greater suffering to end the suffering." He looked so mournful and earnest that Ferris almost laughed in his face. But the knowledge that some unfortunate could have been beaten within an inch of death to extract the makings of the stew soured the food inside him.

"So you have a return cargo and no pilot," Ferris said.

"I hope I do have a pilot," Murillo smiled charmingly. "The only uncertainty is how to change our plans as it is not safe to go back to St. Marc. I should have more information by tomorrow about that. In the meantime, the aircraft is refuelled and there is nothing more for you to do. What do you say, Captain?"

"I don't have much of a choice, now do I?" Ferris said ironically. "I accept your offer, five percent of the value of the cargo."

"Let us say, three percent of the value of each cargo successfully delivered. This time, it is only a small sample, but next time, when we know we can trust Arnaud, we will send more, so your commission will go up, considerably."

"Fair enough," Ferris said, finding it hard to keep any conviction in his voice.

Murillo's smile threatened to split his face. "This is excellent. We have a deal. I think we should celebrate."

He pulled open a drawer in the desk and pulled out a bottle of rum, and some not too clean glasses.

"It disinfects itself," he said apologetically, rubbing his thumb inside the glass.

Roberto came back in, and took a glass and saluted them glumly. Ferris felt immediately better as the rum went down.

"Juanita does not understand the proverb, the honey gets the bees not the vinegar. It would have been a shame to shoot you, an educated man with skills."

El Murillo tossed back the rest of his rum, and nodded pleasantly. "I regret having to lock you up again, but we have to be careful. Roberto will take you to another room now, where you can rest. I trust you will find it better than your last quarters."

CHAPTER 58

Roberto led Ferris to the large mill building. They passed some of the guerrillas talking loudly as they opened crates and took out the munitions boxes inside them.

Ferris braced himself when Roberto swung open the door of a room. It looked cool and clean, with a simple iron bedstead with a wafer thin mattress and a grey blanket.

"This is the luxury suite," Roberto said. "It actually stays bearable in here. I do hope the chief isn't going soft. Juanita really doesn't trust you."

"And you trust opinion her more than his?" Ferris challenged. Maybe the rum lit a fire in his belly. He knew it was no time for butting heads but he couldn't help himself.

"I'll be watching you," Roberto said, and locked the door.

There was no window. Ferris looked around the room hopefully for a moment, and saw no possible means of escape. Then the light went out.

He settled down on the bed, and stared at the fading element of bare bulb on the ceiling.

He wondered absently where they got the fuel to run the electricity generator.

He could hear the hum of the generator, close at hand. It was like the faint song of an aero engine. Lulled by the drone, he drifted back into an exhausted sleep.

A burst of automatic gunfire shattered his sleep. With his heart thumping, he stood and went to the door. He stood listening for a moment.

An assault rifle crackled again, and he heard a faint cheer and laughter, and a scatter of single shots. Ferris peered intently through the crack in the door jamb, but there was no movement.

He supposed that they were out playing with their new toys.

Ferris felt his way back to the bed and lay down and slept again. This time he dreamed of traffic on the runway, and woke sweating, his heart hammering, but not from real events.

The past was so vivid when he was asleep, why not face it awake? Ferris emptied his mind, and thought of the past. He remembered the day of his first solo flight, a cold morning with grey skies, when the dew had sparkled on the grass of the old aerodrome, and the bite in the air had been enough to make him glad of the sheepskin jacket that Jack Foster had lent him. He had been physically sick with excitement that morning, even having to go to the toilet the moment he arrived to the clubhouse. Jack had sensed his nerves, and had stood by the Tiger Moth while Ferris went through the pre-flight checks. When Ferris went to the cockpit and unlatched the little half door, Jack had said, "Just keep on as normal Tony, you know enough about it now." Ferris had nodded, and climbed into the cockpit. Once he had strapped himself in, the leaden ball in his stomach seemed to soften, as the old familiar smells of oil and leather and fabric cocooned him. Still, when Jack had stood in front of the nose to swing the propeller, Ferris had found his voice shrill and reedy when he called out the ignition sequence. But when the engine caught, he had felt all his nervousness melt away, leaving only a quivering of anticipation at being alone at last in an aeroplane. He had steered the Moth along the grass of the field, just holding her straight as he gently opened the throttle, and had lifted her off into the air as he passed the five bar gate, as Jack had taught him to do, and five seconds later, when he brought the Tiger Moth around in a climbing turn over the field, he had been a pilot.

Well, it had been downhill all the way after his solo flight.

He could fly much better now, but then, he could walk much better now than he had when he was two years old. It wasn't saying much.

How old and wise Jack Foster had seemed, all those years ago. A full man, a complete human being, self-assured and kind to others. Ferris realised with surprise that he was older now than Foster had been back then, and he still wasn't half the man Foster had been. Of course, at seventeen, he had probably romanticised old Jack a bit, ascribing him Biggles-like qualities, which he might not have had. And he supposed that a fellow put his instructor on a pedestal, the way he did with his first love. And that was Evelyn, a big West Country lass, innocent times indeed.

The vivid slow-motion replay of the Tornado turning into a tumbling fireball as Tommy Skelton flew into a Scottish mountain right ahead of him. It was the second time somebody in his flight had flown into the ground on a landing approach, and Ferris had been badly shaken. And soon after, he had allowed Jenny talk him into leaving the RAF. She had really got off on being an officer's wife, but they would have more time together and more money if he became an airline pilot. So she said. He might miss it, but it would be worth it, she said. What he didn't miss at all were the welts you got from the water-proof seals in the survival suits from sitting around wearing them twenty four hours a day when you were on standby to go out and nudge off the Tupolev Bears when they came on intruder missions.

It was worth it for Jenny alright, she got to spend his money and while he entertained stewardesses on long haul stop-overs, she entertained money-flashing gits like car salesmen and football managers.

One time she asked him to send her money for a termination. She had an excuse, her career, maybe they could try for a baby in another couple of years. Afterwards it didn't make sense. It felt as if she had been blackmailing him, especially as she had a nice new Volkswagen Golf GTI convertible next time he was home. He hadn't been around to see, he had never been around.

Reality caught up with them eventually – "Oh Jenny what were we thinking?" Ferris groaned.

Ferris shifted, his legs were cramped, and he shivered despite the heat. But it felt much more comfortable than what he had going on in his head.

The numbing boredom of being an airline pilot and the break-down of his marriage had led him to anaesthetise himself with drink.

He told himself that he wouldn't drink close to flight time, right up to the night the 737 had skidded off a wet runway in Heathrow on landing. Ferris still had a mild hangover, and even though no one had the presence of mind at the time to test him for drink or drugs, he admitted to himself that he was finished with airliners.

To make a complete break to allow a fresh start, he had gone as far away as possible, to the Americas, and worked back eastward until he had run across Frank Harvey, and had finally settled for the Caribbean and St. Marc.

And then the crash in San Juan. The upside-down Heron. God he hoped Murillo had more rum.

CHAPTER 59

The slam of the door crashing against the wall jolted Ferris back into the present, and he sat up to see Roberto standing in the doorway. "Come, the chief wants to talk to you again."

"Does he have news?" Ferris asked.

"Nobody tells me anything," Roberto said surlily.

The sun had set when they got outside, and Ferris looked at his watch and realised he had not adjusted for the time zone.

Murillo was eating when they got to his office, Quintero stood against the wall. "Please Mr Ferris, you would like some grilled pork? Please take some" Murillo wiped his fingers. "I wanted to let you both know the good news. I have no details, but I have heard from Commandant Arnaud that he wants you to fly back to St. Marc. It seems the commandant has reached out to the right people and that things at that end will alright." Murillo sighed. "It's always a disappointment when the authorities show a resistance to bribery. It shows an exaggerated sense of integrity. Still, better late than never."

"How soon will this happen?" Quintero asked.

"It already has," Murillo said. "I am waiting for a confirmation message, but you might be able to fly back tomorrow morning."

"That sounds very unlikely," Ferris said. "Automatic weapons were used. It's not like . . . " he was going to say "here" but thought better of it.

"You know what I know," Murillo said, spreading his hands.

"The Commandant is a genius at public relations," Quintero said impatiently. "If a way can be found to save the situation, he will find it."

Ferris fell silent and enjoyed the food. He was sorry somebody had lost their rather stringy pig to feed him, but it couldn't be helped.

Juanita came in. She and Ferris glared at each other, then she said to Murillo. "All is well. He suggests arriving at two pm tomorrow."

Murillo nodded. "You can just about beat the storm captain. The reports say it has sped up." He stood up. "You will probably want your charts to plan the flight back, I will send for them now." He handed Ferris a faxed meteorological report. "You can read Spanish? We couldn't get one in English." Ferris nodded. He wondered how they had got it.

With Murillo translating some of the more obscure technical terms, he pieced together the forecast. The storm was expected to stabilise and not develop into a full cyclone due to wind shear, but it was tracking north about 400 km off the Brazilian coast. It was moving west at about 50km per hour and the wind speeds were gusting up to 110 km per hour. Ferris worked the numbers in his head. The eye of storm was predicted to pass one hundred and fifty miles north of St. Marc which meant that if it shrank he could indeed beat it. But if it developed further then the second half the flight back could be a slog against a gale force headwind. Ferris decided a course to the north-east to intersect the vast length of Hispaniola was safe, it was four nearly five hundred miles but it was preferable to flying into the teeth of a gale for nine hundred miles and like the flight south, risk running out of fuel over an empty ocean.

"Can we get another report in the morning?" Ferris asked.

Murillo smiled. "I'm not a miracle worker, Mr Ferris. Getting fuel for the aircraft and that report exhausted our resources for now. You will have to make do."

"What fuel did you get?"

"Seven hundred litres of 100LL blue Avgas. That is correct, yes?" Murillo looked very pleased with himself.

"Well that's it for now Mr Ferris," he continued. "I will keep the charts here. You are free to go."

"Wait, you aren't going to lock me in?" In his surprise, Ferris looked at Juanita and saw surprise in her expression too.

"Certainly not," Murillo said. "You are our man now. And besides, where would you go? For now I must ask you stay away from the aircraft, and the missiles, but otherwise you are free to move about if you wish. Although for obvious reasons we don't have outside lights and use the generator as little as possible so life stops here after dark, like the old days. There is very little to do or see."

"Roberto, maybe you could get a chair for Mr Ferris to sit out on the verandah?"

"Sure chief," Roberto said after a long pause and went out muttering under his breath.

Ferris sat out on the verandah. The air was ever so slightly cooler, but the humidity was so high it was hard to tell. Roberto sat with him for a while, then decided he had better things to do and stamped off.

A murmur of voices from inside the house as Murillo continued his meeting with Quintero and Juanita, but no distinct words distracted him from the jungle noises. Crickets of some sort and tree frogs, Ferris guessed.

Ferris used the time alone to consider Schroeder's motivation. He still hadn't sorted out in his head what had happened at the Schroeder villa. But he guessed that Schroeder, who had known about the missile smuggling, had realised that two pilots was one too many especially when one of them was acting up. And had shot Garcia to save Ferris. And Schroeder suspected Garcia was the murderer of Shareen because he had no alibi for that night. And Davern's oblique hints pointed that way.

The realisation stirred something inside Ferris, and slowly, he began to think logically again. He would survive, so long as he behaved himself, and as long as they needed him to complete their transaction, or at least until they found another pilot. That meant that he had to listen carefully, and find out when his usefulness ran out. And get away before that happened.

CHAPTER 60

Scattered clouds marred the sky, but otherwise the bowl of the night was bright, certainly bright enough to walk in the open. The stars wavered and winked.

The meeting inside broke up. Quintero went by with a nod of "Captain," and Juanita ignored him.

Murillo came out carrying a small leather pouch and sat beside Ferris with a sigh. He took out a pipe and started to pack it with tobacco. He talked as he tamped down his tobacco. He was an educated man he said, a former university professor turned guerrilla. After a relative had been killed in a bombing by some narco-terrorist group – he would rather not be specific, his name was assumed – he had joined this right wing group. "I'm not a fanatic, Mr Ferris. Just a man who sees the world differently now. What is the phrase? A liberal is a conservative who has not been mugged yet? I used to believe in the rule of law, in a way I still do, but now I also respect the rule of the gun."

"As a former military man, I can hardly disagree," Ferris said.

"What is it between you and Juanita, the hostility is so ... extreme?"

"I'd rather not say," Ferris said.

"A point of honour then," Murillo said. Ferris could not see his expression in the starlight but he sounded sincere. "I am sorry for it. Especially as she must go back with you. Quintero would be an excellent chaperone but he is staying, we have made immediate use of his skills. I cannot really spare anyone else, but if you are to fight like cat and dog, I must send a neutral party. I will think on it."

They sat in a strangely companionable silence for a time. A jet flew past at altitude, the noise of the engines reaching them by some trick of acoustics, briefly overwhelming the songs of the night creatures, the navigation lights twinkling no brighter than the stars it was so far away.

Murillo rose and bid Ferris goodnight and went away.

Ferris sat on, listening to the frogs and crickets, or grasshoppers, he knew far more about the air force than the wildlife. He had slept enough during the day. But eventually he felt himself nodding off.

He got up and went back to the big mill building. He saw no sentries, but he knew they were there. The little room smelled of damp wool, but he found the smell pleasantly reminiscent of school-days camping excursions. He slept again, and dreamed of childhood escapades.

***

They came for him at five. It was Roberto and Juanita, and they looked just as friendly as ever. "Time for breakfast," Juanita said, as if she hated the idea of allowing him to eat. "We are going to leave at seven, so El Murillo wants us to get a move on."

They prodded him out into the morning. The sky out towards the sea had scattered cloud coverage, maybe at five thousand feet. Which wasn't an optimistic sign.

Ferris was already leery of going out again in an untested aircraft after a nine-hundred plus flight without having it investigated by certified mechanics but he knew now that a positive attitude was the best passport back to a place where the likelihood of getting shot in the back reduced to normal levels.

They went to Murillo's house again, and Murillo was already in his office. He waved at a large plate of empanadas and a pot of coffee and said "Help yourselves." Ferris thought the cook must be from the mountains, so much cooked food in the steaming heat.

To Ferris he said, "Captain Ferris, I hope you realise the government bomb all unapproved airstrips so we cannot move the camouflage until the last moment, and only if we are sure there are no aircraft in the area. So you will have to make your preparations, then we will clear the strip quickly."

Roberto drove Ferris to the plane in the jeep. Ferris was surprised to see that the camouflage netting and poles broke up the cleared ground rather than covering it completely, there was plenty of room for the jeep if driven carefully.

Ferris looked dubiously at the camouflage net strung like a hammock in the trees over the Beech 18.

"You've seen the plane before," Roberto said. "Get on, we have little time."

"Is that netting secure?" Ferris asked. "I don't want it sucked into the propellers."

"It's fine," Roberto said impatiently. "It stayed up yesterday didn't it?" He helped Ferris rotate the propellers, although he grumbled.

Getting aboard, Ferris saw a single crate standing unsecured on the floor surrounded by loose webbing ties.

"For God's sake," he said, "Get this thing off."

"No," Roberto said. "That's the cargo that is going back with you. No sense in wasting a good box, no?"

It was Ferris's turn to grumble, he tied down the small crate and tucked the webbing ties belts in out of the way.

Roberto sat in the jeep while Ferris went to run through the start-up checks.

As Murillo had promised, all the fuel tanks were full according to the gauges. He would have been happier to have seen the fuel, but beggars couldn't be choosers. Ferris ran through the checks, and ran up the two engines on idle to warm the oil.

The temperature gauges were just getting up to the right level when he saw Robert waving to get his attention.

Roberto made a cutting motion and Ferris shut down the engines and got off the plane. Roberto was listening to a walkie-talkie. He put down the walkie-talkie and looked doubtful. "Something is wrong. I have to get Juanita anyway. You'd better come back with me."

The rising sun touched the canopy and a steam of moisture rose from the trees as they drove back.

Murillo, Juanita and a knot of others stood outside the mill building, looking towards the sea.

When Roberto stopped the jeep and switched off, they could hear the sound of another piston-engined aircraft.

CHAPTER 61

Ferris recognised the distinctive tone of the Pratt and Whitney Twin Wasp motors, so he wasn't at all surprised when somebody said, "It's a Gooney Bird."

"Inside," Roberto said and pushed Ferris forward.

"No," Murillo said. "Tell Quintero to get the missiles ready."

"Holy Name," somebody said, "It's The Ghost." The Ghost was the local name for the AC-47 gunship.

"They cannot see the plane, the netting is good," Juanita said, as if in response to an unspoken question.

"Can't tell yet," Murillo muttered. "But get ready. Don't stand behind the missiles." Quintero came out of the mill, accompanied by another man carrying the bazooka-like missile launcher and the two other men followed, lugging the green-painted cases of spare missiles.

The plane resolved into a camouflaged Douglas AC-47. It flew past the mill quite slowly at about five hundred feet and climbed as it flew inland, and as it did, a cluster of bright lights detached from it and soared up in a separating cascade of flares. The engine noise reverberated off the hills beyond. Ferris was non-plussed.

Quintero planted his feet and adjusted the launcher on his shoulder. Then he threw himself flat.

A whine from behind grew into a burst of turbines and the whistle of falling ordinance and Ferris dropped to the ground also.

The ground shook, and the concussion felt like five hundred pound bombs.

Fragments hissed past Ferris and pieces of debris pattered down like rain.

Ferris looked up in time to see a pair of Embraer Tucanos rising above columns of smoke and dust from the explosions, shark-mouths painted on their noses.

He understood in a second. The AC-47 had identified the runway and radioed in the ground attack planes while acting as a decoy. He felt a sudden surge of concern and got to his feet. With the dust and smoke still hanging in the air it wasn't clear if the runway was damaged. Also, standing around in the open with a gunship about to make a strafing run was not going to be healthy. And the Tucanos might be coming back to give the runway another pasting.

The safest place to be right was the jungle, booby traps be damned.

"Jesus, fire the flaming missiles," Murillo shouted, as the Tucanos banked in the distance to avoid the hillside. Quintero was back on his feet, trying to an acquire a target.

"There's too much dust and the hills ..." Quintero started to say.

"Just do it," Murillo said dangerously. He had pulled a pistol.

"Listen – " Quintero said, but his assistant fumbled with his rocket launcher and fired. Ferris rolled out of the way before the back flashed and the missile roared out with a thunder clap as it went supersonic.

Roberto, in the process of standing up, was not so lucky and got the flash in his face and grabbed his eyes and screamed.

"I said don't stand behind the missiles. Get the fool away!" Murillo yelled.

Quintero gingerly fired a second launcher. The trails of the two missiles rose up, straight toward the Tucanos. The trails stayed true, but the two Tucanos separated and sprayed flares as they took evasive manoeuvrers. The missiles then veered off, one shot straight up and self-destructed. The second wandered off to the left, and then dropped in a snaking S into the forest.

"It's the hills," Quintero said. He was on his knees, carefully extracting one of the spare rockets from its case. "Chief, better get your people under cover. Next pass we'll hit them coming with the sea behind them."

"Alright, everybody inside the mill," Murillo said.

Ferris spotted the AC-47 again, arranging itself in a shallow banking turn which had the mill at the middle of its radius.

As everybody else ran toward the mill, Ferris tucked his head in and sprinted for the trees.

Somebody shouted after him, but Ferris didn't look back.

Over the throttled-back engines of the AC-47 tore the ripping nose of a mini-gun as the gunship opened fire.

Ferris threw himself down near the corner of Murillo's house.

He looked around and the wall of the mill disappeared behind a cluster of dust-strikes, and some of the running guerrillas pitched forward onto their faces.

Ferris crawled into the nominal shelter of Murillo's house and caught his breath. Then he sprinted for the trees, twenty yards away.

He kept running until he was well in cover, then stopped for breath.

He leaned against the bough of a low shrub, and looked back at the buildings.

He could hear but not see the circling AC-47. Dust filled the air. The mini-gun fired again, and Ferris retreated further into the trees.

When the gunship paused fire, he heard the lighter crackle of M-16s somewhere ahead in the woods. The sentries were burning off some of the extra ammo he had brought them.

The air force were probably softening up the base for an infantry assault, and the infantry had stumbled into Murillo's sentries.

Ferris checked the direction and then set off towards where he guessed the Beech 18 was. If it was in one piece.

CHAPTER 62

His blood ran cold as he heard the rustle of branches behind him. He turned, and saw Juanita coming towards him from the woods, the Beretta levelled at him, her face pale.

"Get back to the plane," she said. Ferris hesitated, but the way she jabbed the gun at him shut him up. He turned back and walked parallel to the clearing, his back crawling in anticipation of a bullet from Juanita, his jaw working in anticipation of the impending infantry assault.

For a few minutes he heard nothing untoward, only the drone of the circling gunship and its brief bursts of fire, and Juanita's footsteps behind him.

Then an M16 chattered unnervingly close and an M60 battered back at it and Ferris threw himself to the ground and rolled.

The machine gun bullets had their own sound, little explosions as they broke the sound barrier, and the air was full of kicked up dust and sonic reports and fluttering ricochets, and Ferris lay very still. The machine-gun switched to a more interesting target, and Ferris rolled quickly back to the bushes. After an age, when his move hadn't attracted fire, he crawled a bit further, then stood up. "Ferris!" The hoarse cry snapped his head around, and he saw Juanita, trying to stand up.

Her right shoulder and left thigh were large blotches of blood, and her twisted face was pleading. "Please ... help me," she gasped, trying to support herself with one arm and leg.

Ferris hesitated, almost going forward, and as he took a step forward, the ground around Juanita churned with spouts of dust, and she shuddered, splashes of blood jumping from her body, and her arm collapsed just as a bullet tore away most of her face. Ferris screamed in horror and ran. He ran heedlessly, pushing aside branches, ignoring the ones that scratched his face, anything to get away from the brutal monstrosity of exploding blood and bone. He fell heavily, tripped by a root, but the impact hardly shook him. He had the strength of ten men in his revulsion, he got up again and ran on blindly, cannoned off a tree, tripped on more roots, fell again, fought his way to his feet again, and ran again, all to get away, away, away.

When he finally came to his senses, Ferris was lying on the ground after another fall, completely spent, sobbing helplessly, his vision blurred by tears. Reaction hit him and he vomited violently, retching and rocking back and forth on his knees, feeling as if his guts were being burnt out of him. At last, he wept quietly, and he began to notice his surroundings. The sky was small dappled specks through a canopy of leaves. The trees grew tall around him well spaced, and there were few plants between. Gunfire echoed through the woods, distinct but strangely muffled. Ferris wondered how far he had run. It was all a blur. He looked at his watch but the face was smashed, and there was a bloody furrow along his wrist. He couldn't remember being hurt.

His watch was stopped at five past six. Probably only a couple of minutes had elapsed. He supposed he had fled roughly south-west, but he had no way of navigating, because the trees hid the sun.

He could still hear the AC-47 and oriented himself so that the engine noise was to his left.

Trying not to think of what he had seen, Ferris walked slowly back towards the gunfire. He paused every now and then to judge the direction, and after a while, he came to a small clearing, where a shaft of sunlight broke through a gap where some trees had toppled and leaned against their neighbours, and he found that he was walking roughly east.

The trees thinned and shrunk, and the under-brush grew thicker, and he smelled fire and dust and realised he was closing on the bombed airstrip.

An M60 fired uncomfortably close and Ferris threw himself into a bush, and waited. Feet pounded, and a small detachment of soldiers ran past, heading towards the sound of firing. Ferris considered. The M60 fired again, but further away, so he guessed he was now behind the military lines. They might not be watching too carefully, with the guerrillas neatly bottled up around the mill.

But then again, it was likely that anyone he bumped into would shoot first.

The sound of firing grew slowly louder, and then he saw that he was coming out of the trees into the strip cleared for the plane.

He stayed back in the trees and made his way as briskly as he could.

Then he caught sight of the Beech 18, looking untouched still virtually hidden by the netting, and no one near it.

Ferris stopped and surveyed the runway. In the unpredictable way of explosives, the bombs had knocked or burned most of the camouflage canopy and the supporting guy ropes and poles. Part of the camouflage netting was still on fire, the burning he had smelled. The bombs had also blown three craters, but from what he could see the runway was still intact. The nearest crater was the worst, it looked about three feet deep and twenty feet wide. With his eye Ferris measured the distance from the Beech and tried to calculate if there was enough runway left to allow a take off. It looked like it would be bumpy and he would have to follow the meander in the river to get over the trees at the far end.

Mind made up, he ran until he was under the wing of the Beech, and slumped against the wheel leg, his vision full of dancing white spots, bands of iron across his chest. He looked around, and no one had spotted him, yet.

Ferris sprinted around the plane, rushing through the pre-flight checks, wiggling the control surfaces to see they were free, checked there were no holes or breaks from bomb fragments and finally clambered in the door.

Only to find himself looking into the muzzle of a pistol. With Quintero, sweating, at the other end. Quintero's shirt was streaked with blood and the hair on the left side of his head stood out in blood clotted tufts.

"Oh shit," Ferris said tiredly. The pistol quivered slightly in Quintero's hand, but his voice was even. "Boy am I glad to see you, Captain Ferris. I thought the army had me. I think it's time we left. How about you?"

Ferris turned wearily and closed the door, and went up to the cockpit.

"Might as well get going," Quintero said conversationally. "I'd like to wait for Juanita and Roberto, but somehow I think they're probably dead already. You got any cigarettes?"

CHAPTER 63

Ferris switched on, and checked the instruments. Full fuel tanks, trimmed for take-off ... Inside the cabin, he couldn't hear the gunship.

"What are you waiting for?" Quintero asked loudly.

"That," Ferris said, as the AC-47 droned into sight.

The starters whined, and he fired up the engines. Ferris looked up as the port engine caught, and saw a squad of soldiers breaking out of the trees half-way down the runway. The engines had alerted them. The soldiers broke into a run towards the Beech. The starboard engine caught, and Ferris leaned on the brakes and worked the engines up toward red. The camouflage netting fluttered under the prop wash of the engines, and Ferris let the brakes go.

The Beech leapt forward. Ferris tried to use the engines to steer around the large crater but the plane bumped heavily as it climbed one rim. It rolled down without going in fully, and the cabin jolted, but the wings didn't hit the ground.

A number of bullets drew sparks as they skidded off the engine cowling, and one scoured a white line along the windscreen. He used the starboard throttle to swing the Beech around a second crater.

He kept an eye out for any debris that might wreck the under-carriage or puncture the tyres but they were now moving so fast that he could only cross his fingers. The Beech passed the spot he had seen the soldiers, but they must have ducked.

Ferris wasn't consciously aware of having timed the circuit of the gunship, but sure it enough it passed ahead and he was in its blind spot as it banked around, tracking the mill building.

Ferris opened the throttles all the way, the Beech surged forward, the end of the runway and the bank of the river approached at terrifying speed.

He didn't have much choice but to go through the last crater and hope the wheels of the Beech were separated widely enough to pass over the worst of it. The plane staggered, but then it recovered, and he felt the tail coming up on its own. The levelled stretch was running out rapidly. Ferris held the Beech down an instant longer, then pulled the stick back. The plane flashed over the sand of the river bank, the water a blur below the wing-tip. Ferris hoped that they had enough speed not to stall.

Ferris retracted the undercarriage, and glanced at the tail of the AC-47.

Time slowed down and the AC-47 seemed to hang in the air. The crew were concentrating on the port side as they strafed the mill.

Ferris held his breath.

The Beech passed well below and behind the tail of the AC-47, still invisible in the blind spot.

Ferris brought the Beech up to fifty feet above the canopy and risked a glance over his shoulder.

The AC-47 banked to the starboard, and he guessed that the pilot had broken off his attack run to confirm for himself that a plane had been seen. Ferris had no worries about a pursuit, the AC-47 had the same top speed as a Beech 18 so he could outrun it. But it was far more likely that the gunship would vector in the Tucanos, which were probably loitering on standby if they had finished their bombing runs.

Ferris climbed and banked towards the coast. He stayed below five hundred feet in the hope that he might stay off radar. It might also discourage jet fighters who would be wary of overshooting into the sea.

Another quick glance back, and he couldn't see the AC-47 against the hillsides. The coast fell away too, and the Beech was over open sea. The sea was disturbed, long wind blown white-capped rollers moving towards the shore. The waves would cause a lot of reflections on AWACS radar.

"Jesus, but you're the best, man," Quintero said enthusiastically. "Next stop St. Marc." It gave Ferris a terrible jolt, because he had almost forgotten Quintero in the excitement. "Yeah," he said. "Next stop St. Marc."

CHAPTER 64

Ferris saw that the cloud-base was at about five thousand feet and he started to climb. Hiding in the clouds seemed like the best short-term plan. He opened up the throttles and the Beech climbed, gratifyingly close to the twenty feet per second maximum. It guzzled fuel at over fifty gallons per hour at this speed, but for four minutes it was worth the expenditure.

The Beech 18 was passing through the two thousand foot mark when twin trails of tracer flickered past the nose. Ferris felt a surge of adrenalin and instinctively stamped on the left rudder pedal and hauled the Beech around.

Ferris levelled out as two Tucanos blasted past in a roar of turbines, buffeting the Beech.

"What the hell?" Quintero yelped in protest.

"That was a warning burst," Ferris said, "He didn't mean to hit us."

"I know that," Quintero said mulishly. "Where did they come from?" Ferris felt very tempted to drop the undercarriage and surrender, warnings shots indicated that law and order was re-asserting itself, no matter what was happening back on the ground at the mill.

But Quintero had a wild glint in his eye. The injury to his head had made him erratic.

So Ferris got the Beech climbing again. He kept an eye on the two Tucanos, flying en echelon. For a moment he thought they would attack head on, but instead they circled.

"We're not going back," Quintero said. It wasn't a question. He had his pistol out again. It looked like a Glock.

"No," Ferris said soothingly. "Two minutes and we can shake them in the clouds."

"Okay," Quintero nodded vehemently and sat back. "Good."

Ferris felt his long-ago fighter training clicking into action and had to restrain himself. In a King Air or any other prop-liner he would have been able to out-run the Tucanos. There were two ways to win a fighter combat when you had no weapons, you could out-run them, or you could stay out of the cone of fire until the fighter pilot got bored or ran out of fuel or ammunition.

The Tucano could reach two hundred and eighty miles per hour and could pull 7g. A new Beech 18 could reach two hundred and twenty five miles per hour and pull 2.5g. And even though this particular one had extra spar strap under the wing roots to help prevent metal fatigue, it was still over fifty years old and Ferris knew better than to try any aerobatics.

The Tucano was capable of out-flying the Beech 18. It could out-climb, and out turn, and probably out-dive the Beech 18 and about the only pure physical advantage was that the Beech was an old-style machine, riveted and built like a truck whereas the Tucano was a modern glue-and-carbon-fibre sort of plane and if he rammed one he would probably come off the better, but he wouldn't have taken any bets on being able to get home after. If they had trained in dog-fighting he might as well give up now because the speed difference was almost a perfect match for a vintage plane shoot-down. The Brazilian air force Tucanos had been shooting down drug runner planes for years which were much faster.

So the Beech 18 was just fast enough to be the perfect sitting duck. True, the Beech was solid, but a stream of Browning .50 calibre shells would tear it apart like a giant electric saw. And even one round in the fuel tanks could be catastrophic.

The only advantage was experience. The Tucano pilots were mud-movers. They would have trained and gained their combat experience in ground attack and mastering low-level flying. Even though they probably knew all the moves and theory of air combat, doing it for real was a different matter and even in a beat-up old transport an old fighter jock like Ferris might be able to frustrate them. The main danger was that one of them was a conversion down from a fighter squadron, or one of those natural instinctive fighter pilots who know there was more to it than getting into the six o'clock and hosing the other fellow with bullets.

CHAPTER 65

The blind spots on the Beech were huge. It hadn't been an issue until now but he guessed about one hundred and twenty degrees.

Ferris banked the plane, leaned to the left and craned his neck and he glimpsed a Tucano banking in behind, tracking the Beech and slowly easing into an attack position.

Ferris eased off the rudder and let the Beech enter a natural side-slip. He hoped that the Tucano pilot would be concentrating on the deflection and not notice the change of attitude of the controls of the Beech.

Sure enough the Tucano pilot instinctively fired when he reached the position where he expected the Beech to be in his sights. A short burst of tracer streaked well in front of the nose of the Beech. Ferris could feel the controls of the Beech getting mushy as she lost power from the side-slip and the stick shaker rattled briefly. He opened the throttles and threw the Beech into a starboard bank. With luck it looked like he was somehow able to predict where they would fire next, and take evasive action, as opposed to the fact that they were firing at the wrong patch of sky.

Both of the Tucanos whistled past as Ferris banked.

"Have you your seatbelt tied?" He asked Quintero.

"What?" Quintero's voice sounded slurred. "Yes, of course."

"Tighten it," Ferris said.

Ferris racked his brain, but couldn't remember if the Tucano had external gun pods with either Browning .50 or .308 calibre guns, with full belts they would have twelve to thirty seconds give or take of firing time, a lot of lead to stay out of.

He forced the Beech to climb again, the twenty feet per second now painfully slow as he watched the Tucanos use their turbo-props to zoom up, gain height and wing over. They came around much more aggressively and came head-on. One aircraft dropped back and separated a hundred yards. "Good lads," Ferris said. "You catch on quickly."

"What's that?" Quintero asked querulously.

"Hold on to your hat," Ferris said.

He banked slowly away, keeping the lead aircraft in sight over his right shoulder. He eased into another side-slip, pulling the throttles back and used both ailerons and rudder. The Beech 18 lost a lot of speed and height, yet the Tucano pilot still fell for it. He throttled back and tried to track the Beech but, fixated on the deflection, he fired well ahead of the Beech and overshot again.

"I'm not wearing a hat," Quintero said peevishly. "I got shot in the he– " Ferris regretted telling Quintero to strap in, what happened next would have taken him out of commission.

He glimpsed the second Tucano cutting him off from the left and hoped the cargo was securely fastened too. And the spar strap.

He banked, gave the Tucano a tempting target and then snapped the Beech over into a split S.

Quintero yelled in fear.

When the Beech came out into level flight, the two Tucanos were well out of position and above. He had lost about five hundred feet he couldn't afford and surrendered a huge height advantage to the Tucanos, but at least he was flying roughly eastwards.

His arms and legs started to ache, the controls were manual and surprisingly light in normal operation but for aerobatics it was too heavy and solid.

Ferris put the nose down and dived north-east, varying the pattern by running away so that the Tucano pilots didn't have too much time to think about what had just happened.

He pulled out at about one thousand feet, the Beech 18 had exceeded three hundred miles per hour which was enough strain to put the poor thing under. He banked to get a look at the Tucanos, they were still above, a couple of miles behind and two thousand feet higher, but closing and diving. He kept the throttles open. It would be interesting to see if they had figured out the side-slip yet.

The Tucanos levelled out and banked off to the south.

"What's happening?" Quintero asked. He was paying attention, but not processing it seemed. "Did you scare them off? That was some fancy flying, Captain."

"Orders," Ferris said. "Otherwise we'd be dead."

"Well man it feels good to be alive then," Quintero said. "Even with a sore head." Ferris felt flat, the Tucanos were gone but he was stuck with an unpredictable hi-jacker with a head wound.

"Let's just hope they don't think were important enough to send jets after," he said crushingly.

Ferris set the Beech back into a shallow climb and looked at the charts again. He had burnt about an hour's fuel in a couple of minutes, but there was no helping it. He would have to husband the remaining fuel against the headwinds. He needed to recalculate his navigation.

CHAPTER 66

Ferris flew low until he was sure that the territorial limit was far behind, then he climbed to five hundred feet below the cloud base and throttled back to one hundred and fifty-five and set a course north east.

The clouds broke up further away from the coast, their bases were lower and they didn't reach as tall.

In the normal course of events Ferris flew the Beech 18 at five thousand, but the weather report suggested strong winds of forty miles per hour at five thousand so he took it up to seven thousand. He also took the precaution of making the heading more easterly.

For about an hour, the Beech flew on peacefully. The clouds ahead remained scattered but many miles to the east Ferris could see enormous thunderheads piling up far into the stratosphere. That could be well over a hundred miles away but it was far nearer than anticipated.

It became clear that he had another problem apart from racing the storm. The Beech started to struggle above seven thousand feet and Ferris didn't want to burn even more fuel by climbing hard, but he coaxed it up to nine thousand. Without oxygen there wasn't much point, and the superchargers on the Beech didn't deliver much power above where they were now. But it gave the option of losing height when conditions deteriorated, when gaining height might be difficult. It planted the thought about hypoxia in his head though. In his long ago training, Ferris had been the champion of The Yellow Submarine, the RAF's hypobaric chamber, he had stayed conscious and lucid for longer and at greater simulated altitudes than anyone else.

Quintero derailed his train of thought.

"Captain, as you know, I lived and worked in Mexico City for many years." Quintero paused to catch his breath. "And so I am accustomed to altitude. But now I am short of breath and I think we are flying high enough. If we go any higher I must ask you to drop altitude."

Ferris shelved the idea. People suffering from hypoxia tended to become depressed and biddable, but with his head injury he seemed to have become unpredictable.

Quintero lapsed into a stupor for some time and then sat bolt upright clutching his pistol and looked suspiciously at the course and altitude.

"Braun thinks I'm a sadist," Quintero said suddenly. "It's true you can see the runways from outside the fence, where the plane spotters go. But I am a professional. There was no personal feeling. Perhaps you think that I enjoyed destroying your aircraft and killing the boy but really all I did was what the commandant ordered, he intended the boron carbide to render your engine inoperable so that you would work for Mr Schroeder, that was all. You understand this?"

Quintero seemed very anxious to make this clear. His eyes moved feverishly.

"Yes," Ferris said calmingly. "I understand what you are saying." Quintero subsided.

But a few minutes later he spoke again. Loudly but almost as if he was talking to himself.

"That is not to say I have not tortured prisoners and sometimes enjoyed it. I tell you this just as an illustration.

I have no reason to threaten you but as I cannot control the aircraft if you were to deceive me, I would wait until after landing. I would do it with a knife. It would be slow. I would slice off your manhood, and keep cutting until you beg me to kill you. That would be the best bit. But I have no quarrel with you."

Ferris looked at him, but Quintero had retreated into himself again.

And so it went for another hour, the weather slowly deteriorating and Quintero's mental state lurching from confused and disoriented to completely rational and back.

Ferris concentrated on flying, and kept his face blank so there was nothing for Quintero to read in his face if he looked up. Quintero was only one, he thought. The odds were even, if Ferris could distract him long enough to get rid of his gun. . .

The Beech flew on, and Ferris watched for his chance. Quintero sat dreamily holding his pistol, lulled by the deep hum of the engines.

CHAPTER 67

The sky grew cloudier. From small, broken isolated patches of white, the clouds gradually grew over the miles to fill all the horizon ahead in every direction.

The clouds darkened to grey, and towered up in huge column of cumulo-nimbus, genuine thunderheads. Ferris surreptitiously tightened his seat belt.

Quintero lolled in his seat, but his eyes flickered sideways when he sensed Ferris watching him.

"Make sure you're strapped in," Ferris said. "We are going to hit turbulence and there is no way around it."

Quintero sat up. "Please captain, you know I am a bad flier, is there no other way?"

"Not without a jet," Ferris said with a certain malicious satisfaction.

The sky darkened, and it was difficult to see anything in the cockpit, except the lighted instruments.

Five minutes after he had checked his course, they hit turbulence. It was as if the Beech hit a stone wall, and fell down the column of cold air like a stone.

The turbulence rocked and buffeted the Beech, and it soared and plummeted at terrifying speed. The plane again, as it hit the corresponding updraught on a warm thermal, and whizzed up like an elevator, faster even than its fall.

Quintero tightened his seatbelt angrily and waved the pistol at Ferris.

"You are doing this. Stop it now." Quintero shouted in Spanish, and retched, and the sour stench of vomit filled the cockpit.

Ferris flicked a glance at Quintero crouched over, getting sick on the floor. Ferris felt a malicious satisfaction, although he didn't like the smell.

The Beech flew on, battering its way through the disturbed air. Lightning flickered brilliantly ahead, and Ferris saw in the glare that the Beech flew down an aerial Grand Canyon, in a valley between massive walls of angry thunderheads. The rumble of thunder followed soon after the lightning, and they were flying right at it.

Ferris remembered the old flyer's trick, and lowered his seat.

He could barely see over the rim of the windscreen, but when the next flash of lightning came, the main glare passed him due to the protection of the dashboard.

The plane rattled tremendously. Ferris was caught off guard, but he glimpsed huge hailstones smash into the windshield, explode and bounce off in the slipstream.

The effect was mesmerising and Ferris forced himself to focus on the instruments. He had disengaged the auto-pilot and fought the storm manually. Ferris concentrated on the artificial horizon and compass for a while, and decided that they were being buffeted by cross winds, gusting severely and pushing the plane off course.

The hail abruptly turned into rain. The rain hit in sheets, blotting out the windscreen, robbing Ferris of what little view he had of the darkened sky. The rushing sound of the rain filled the cockpit. Water cascaded in through the bullet cracks in the windshield, forced in by the speed, and runnels of water rushed and scurried over the rim of the dash, down the side wall of the cabin. Ferris was soaked to the waist in a matter of minutes, and had to wipe the spray from his eyes more than once.

Quintero was sick again, and the sound would have made Ferris join him, if he was not so busy fighting the controls.

CHAPTER 68

Quintero slumped in his seat, like a bundle of old rags. Although he looked worn out, pale and bloody, his clothes drenched and stained with vomit, he had recovered and his eyes were alert.

The rough ride continued, and Ferris had no time to spare for thoughts of overpowering Quintero, as the fight to save the plane had priority.

Rain kept pouring in, and Ferris worried that some of the electrical circuits would be damaged by the invading water.

Rainwater and diluted vomit slopped around the floor, little wavelets scurrying across the floor each time the Beech hit an air pocket or banked. Ferris kept his feet out of the way.

The rain stopped as abruptly as it had begun.

The Beech butted on against the weather, and finally broke through the front of the storm. The cloud cover started to break up, visibility was probably less than ten miles but the Beech enjoyed a smoother ride.

As they flew into stiller air, Ferris put the plane on auto-pilot again.

The clouds broke up further and a solid heaped up bank of cloud about twenty miles ahead indicated land.

He flicked through the fuel indicators. It was still touch and go whether they would get to St. Marc without a refuelling stop, even if they made landfall where he intended.

Ferris automatically got out the chart and pencilled in his dead reckoning for the Dominican Republic.

As he drew his estimated position Quintero leaned forward in puzzlement, "Hey, that's the wrong map," he said suspiciously.

Ferris frowned. "I need distinctive landmarks to navigate by and get back to St. Marc along the coast, I'm aiming for Santo

Domingo, it has a large international airport with lots of traffic and radar, but that can't be helped. Look here, it's nothing to worry about." He offered the map across and dropped it onto the floor and it slid into one of the puddles at Quintero's feet.

"Damn," Ferris said irritably. "Get that for me, will you?" Quintero, tired and battered, lowered his pistol and leaned forward to retrieve the maps. As he bent down, Ferris unclipped his seatbelt, leaned over, and carefully punched Quintero behind the left ear. Quintero grunted, and would have fallen from his seat but for his seatbelt. Ferris hit him again, in the same place, and Quintero squirmed and tried to shield his head with his hands. Holding Quintero doubled over with one hand, Ferris hit him again with his fist. Quintero suddenly remembered the gun in his hand, but Ferris caught his wrist and twisted viciously. Quintero cursed, and his hand opened involuntarily, and the pistol clattered to the floor. Ferris rabbit-punched Quintero, and when he lolled stunned in the seat, Ferris undid Quintero's seatbelt and started to roll him onto the floor. But Quintero recovered suddenly, and jack-knifed around in the seat, catching Ferris across the thighs, and throwing him off balance back into his own seat. He realised suddenly that the advantage he had in size and weight was virtually meaningless, if Quintero could take a hammering like that and come back so fast. Well, old son, Ferris told himself, you've really gone and done it now; your only chance of getting out of it alive is to win.

CHAPTER 69

Before Ferris could even bring his hands up, Quintero leaped at him, swinging powerful punches to the body. Ferris warded off the worst of it, and raised his knee into Quintero's crotch. Quintero staggered back into the second row of seats, and Ferris followed him. Quintero caught his balance against the back of the third right seat, and butted Ferris under the chin as he came in for the kill. Ferris shook his head to clear the stars out, but Quintero was slamming punches to his unprotected head, rocking Ferris back on his heels. Like a desperate boxer, Ferris blindly reached out and grabbed Quintero to him in a clinch. He hugged Quintero hard and felt his back bowing under his hands. Quintero kneed Ferris in the groin, and again he butted Ferris full in the face. Ferris got his thigh in the way of the knee, but Quintero's forehead smashed into his nose and drew tears and blood. As Quintero brought his knee up again, Ferris twisted quickly and threw the off-balance Quintero against the wall of the cabin.

Quintero broke the impact with his arm, but his weight was on one leg and Ferris kicked him in the knee and Quintero's leg buckled under him and as he tried to recover, he turned his back. Ferris bore in and slammed his fists into Quintero's kidneys. Quintero screamed and arched his back against the side of the fuselage. Taking advantage of the respite, Ferris wiped his nose and blinked the tears from his eyes. Quintero leaned contorted against the bulkhead, so Ferris grabbed the shoulder of his shirt and started to shove him against the wall, swinging Quintero's body to hit his head against the side, but Quintero kicked back suddenly, catching Ferris in the testicles. Pain exploded outwards for Ferris so that he felt agony from knee to navel, and he sagged against the opposite seat. He forced himself up again, and saw Quintero pulling up his left trouser leg and reaching down for a pistol in his boot. Ferris saw the surprised look on Quintero's face as he flung himself forward, and he saw the pistol in Quintero's hand, coming up fast, and he knew he wouldn't reach him in time, so he grabbed the backs of the seats in front and behind, and used them to swing himself, and he threw his legs up in a scissors kick, as the gun came level, and then his left foot hit Quintero in the face, and then his right foot, with a sound like a double kick smacking a football. The pistol roared, the bullet tugged at the tail of Ferris's jacket. Quintero flopped backward, lifted off his knees by Ferris's right foot under his chin. Ferris almost fell on top of him. He rested briefly on the back of the seat over Quintero. There was blood trickling from the corner of Quintero's mouth.

The pain in his testicles hit Ferris again, and he doubled over and retched weakly on his knees.

Then he felt the tilt of the fuselage floor, and snatching the pistol from Quintero's limp hand, he rushed up to the cockpit. With all the weight shift of the fight, the Beech had tilted and was flying nose up, on the edge of a stall. Ferris corrected, and trimmed the Beech to fly nose heavy. He checked the sky for approaching aircraft, then unloaded the pistol, a Glock .380.

Ferris opened the windshield side panel and threw the pistol out. He double-checked the course, then went back to look at Quintero. The pulse in Quintero's wrist was disappointingly strong.

He searched Quintero and found in addition to the Leatherman, a dagger shoved down his right boot and a small holster in his left boot. Ferris got Quintero's belt and shoe laces and tied him up as securely as he could. Then he went back to the cargo deck and retrieved the excess webbing ties, and improvised a strait-jacket to further immobilize Quintero. Not that he expected him to wake up, but he was a tough customer.

He put the Leatherman in his pocket, then retrieved the other pistol, a larger Glock, from under the seats and went up front and threw the bigger pistol and the dagger out the side window.

Then he checked the plane was on course, and then, he went and quickly checked for damage. He found three bullet holes, all down the left side of the cabin. But the control lines seemed untouched. He limped awkwardly back to the cockpit, trying to ignore the pain in his abdomen. He strapped himself into the seat and brought the Beech down to three thousand feet to avoid airport traffic. He could imagine angry challenges from ATC, and considered briefly if he could repair the radio. Ferris felt very tired.

The Beech got near enough to land to make out the coastal features and he identified the bay ahead as Bahia de Neiba in the Dominican Republic, nearly fifty miles to the west of where he wanted to be. He hauled the plane around and set up a new heading eastwards, and went back and collected the radio and transponder from where Quintero had wedged them against one of the seats.

CHAPTER 70

Ferris spent some time with the radio, but Quintero had cut the wires too short to reattach it to power. So in the end he concentrated on navigation. It was easy enough to keep track of his position but flying almost head-on into the wind used up a lot of fuel. He very nearly diverted to San Juan, but the fuel lasted and after three hours he raised St. Marc on the horizon.

Ferris felt enormous relief. He was going home. He almost forgot his pain, and sat a little straighter in his seat, and brought the Beech around to line up on the runway. For the first time he had flown it, he felt the old instinctive skills taking over.

He risked a last glance over the back seats, where Quintero stirred feebly but looked secure.

Ferris wondered a little callously what the police would make of the prisoner. He could see the town now, and the airfield flattening out beyond it, and he dropped the Beech down gently to make the final approach, tidying up the flight path so that he would come right down the centre of the runway.

As the Beech's shadow crossed over the coastal road, Ferris jerked back in his seat, Quintero drawing a webbing belt in an iron grip on his throat. As his eyes met Quintero's, Ferris felt pain and incredulity. He doubted if Quintero knew that he was landing, or even cared. It was just a continuation of the earlier fight, with Quintero having the upper hand. With Quintero crushing his neck down onto the back of the seat, Ferris could only see Quintero's face, and the roof, and the sky above. He felt his face swell up with trapped blood, and he took his right hand from the control column, stiffened his fingers into two prongs, and stabbed upwards at Quintero's eyes. He gouged hard, grimacing at the soft moist feel of the eyes, and Quintero jerked back, releasing his grip, and clutched at his eyes. Ferris swung his forearm desperately, and Quintero swayed back off balance. Ferris glanced out the windows, and found the plane was crossing the start of the runway, nose high. He shoved the nose down, and slammed the Beech in a side-slip towards the ground, and then Quintero hit him two-handed on the back of the neck. Ferris felt his head lift off, and he lost control of his hands. The control yoke seemed to tilt away towards his left leg, all of its own accord. From very far away, Ferris watched the ground swing up to meet the left wing. With the engines racing and the propellers chopping into the ground the Beech jolted and cart-wheeled, so that the ground was on his left, then in front, then on the right, and the wings broke off, and the plane slammed over on its back and skidded upside down.

When the Beech finally slid to a halt, Ferris was hanging inverted, looking at the furrowed up grass outside the smashed windscreen. He hung dazed for a moment, then wriggled in a panic, when he heard the ticking of the shattered engines.

He grasped the base of the seat, and pulled his inverted body up so that his chest was held by the waistband of the seatbelt, his feet dangling close to the roof. Then he released the buckle, and fell heavily facing the back of the plane. Quintero stirred feebly in the aisle barring his path to the door, and Ferris didn't think he had enough time anyway. He squirmed on his hands and knees, struggling with the large starboard side window. It wouldn't open. He kicked at it with his heel and dragged it back enough to get a head and shoulder into the gap and squirmed and clawed his way out through ignoring the way the shards of broken Perspex cut him. All he could think of was fire. The engines were ticking away like a time bomb, and the stench of avgas from the nose tank was as strong as if he'd had a shower in it. He struggled to his feet, looked around wildly, and ran. He was twenty yards away when the whuff of igniting fuel made his hair stand on end, and he put his head down and ran harder, staggering as the hot blast hit him. He lost his balance, fell to his knees, and ran on until he fell and was too weak to get up again. He turned and looked back. The Beech was a torch, reddish orange flames and thick black smoke roiling and billowing into the air. Ferris raised his hands to protect his face from the glare and heat, and dragged himself away on his hands and feet.

Then he saw a pair of polished boots in the grass ahead of him, and two policemen helped him up. He recognized Sergeant Aziz and his dim side-kick. Supported by the policemen, Ferris looked back again.

"There was another man on the plane," he managed with difficulty, and coughed.

"He's surely dead by now, mister Ferris," the constable said comfortingly. "Nothing could survive that. I don't think he suffered, much," he added kindly.

"I hope the fucker felt every second," Ferris said viciously, surprising himself and the policemen. The fire faltered and died as suddenly as it had begun. The smoke drifted away, and there were just a few small flames flickering on the blackened wreckage. One wheel burned fiercely, molten rubber running down the axle-hub and dripping onto the remains of the overturned wing.

Aziz and the constable helped Ferris to their cruiser. Aziz got out a first aid kit, and seeing his expression, Ferris became aware of his injuries. His neck ached from being strangled, and his head and shoulders stung from gashes and burns. "We'll get you to the hospital," Aziz said encouragingly.

Ferris fainted when they sat him in the back.

CHAPTER 71

Ferris was in a trance all the way to the hospital, and only the agony of the cuts on his face being treated revived him, and things came back into focus.

Doc Hank looked at him bemused, a wad of spirit swab in his hand. "You really are making a habit of this, aren't you?" he asked.

Ferris glowered at him. "It's just a very small world, doc. And while you're at it, be gentle. I can't see it, but it feels wicked."

The doctor grinned at him. "You're going to need more stitches than a new dressing, Tony. Hold him, nurse."

Ferris winced under the onslaught, but his head was being held still gently, so he couldn't escape.

Ferris watched in growing alarm as Hank threaded a seemingly enormous piece of filament through the gadget he did his sewing with. "New suture device," Doc Hank said conversationally.

"I hope you've experimented on someone else," Ferris said.

"Of course," Hank said stiffly. "Patients tell me it makes the stitches less painful." Ferris surrendered gracefully. As he wielded his device, Hank said, "Did you know Vic is dead? And Garcia?"

Ferris started to nod, then realised he couldn't move his head. "Yes I knew that."

"I don't suppose it matters much now, Vic came to see me a couple of days back, he asked for painkillers, said he wanted a few days . . . I didn't realise he wasn't rational." Another stitch. "I heard you were hijacked."

"Yeah," Ferris said. "But I think the police would like to hear the story first."

"Rightly so," Doc Hank said, tying one set of stitches deftly. Ferris squirmed. "We had the first instalment yesterday. It was like after the shootout at the OK Corral. The hospital seemed to be full of bodies. But I suppose I shouldn't tell you about it. And now, they tell me that the fire service will bring in a burnt body. Why do all these people die around you, Tony?"

This at another painful point of the proceedings. Ferris knew Hank was just prattling to keep him occupied.

"Just a talent I have, I suppose. Couldn't you give me a local anaesthetic or something?"

Doc Hank looked shocked. "Certainly not. Your blood pressure is all over the place. Might do harm. Now shut up, I need your mouth closed ... there. All done. How's that?" He proudly held up a mirror like a barber, and Ferris saw that his face was criss-crossed with hideous slashes, which barely missed his eyes. "Christ," he said glumly, "I look like Frankenstein."

"You looked more like Dracula's breakfast when you came in," Doc Hank retorted primly. "And if I've done my job, you won't have many scars when the healing is done."

"A distinct improvement," the nurse added, over Ferris's shoulder. "A touch of character even." Ferris grinned crookedly at her. "Maybe we can talk about it some time, sister," he said wryly, and winked awkwardly. The nurse giggled, and Hank tutted disapprovingly. "Really, children. This won't do. Nurse, tell the constable that Mr. Ferris might be fit enough to talk to him in three hours."

"Yes, doctor." She paused at the door, and winked back at Ferris.

"Nothing wrong with your charisma, Tony," Hank said.

Ferris looked down to find his hands bandaged. Hank followed his gaze. "Three stitches to the left, the rest are scratches. I didn't have to bother the ones on your legs. A few sticking plasters."

"I'll live, at any rate. What's the prognosis?" Ferris said.

"You're pretty run down, but nothing a couple of days rest couldn't fix. All the burns and most of the cuts are superficial. I'd like to keep you here for observation for a few hours, make sure your head injury isn't more serious than it looks on first examination. But after that there's really no need for you to stay. By the way Tony, I could do without your further custom. I came here to treat the impoverished masses, not accident-prone airmen."

The nurse returned with an orderly pushing a wheelchair, and an embarrassed young police officer.

"What's this?" Hank, asked, displeased.

"Sorry sir," the constable said. "The super said I wasn't to let

Mr Ferris out of my sight." Hank muttered under his breath about zoos. "Alright, you can tag along, and sit outside the ward if you have to."

CHAPTER 72

Ferris was wheeled up to a ward and slept for a time.

Hank Sanders woke him with a cold stethoscope. "Sorry Tony, I can't put Legett off any further, he's downstairs and insists on interviewing you himself. I managed to put him off, but it must be police going home time."

Hank took his blood pressure. "Sound as a bell. Or rather as fit as could be expected in the circumstances. You really should rest in bed for a couple of days." The orderly brought a change of Ferris's own clothes. "The police thoughtfully brought you those," Hank said. "You might as well put the dressing gown on over them, and we'll bring you down in the wheelchair again, it might make Legett go easy on you. You do look terrible, from a non-medical viewpoint."

"Thanks Doc," Ferris said. "How is Bill Davern?" Hank raised an eyebrow. "I'm impressed you're able to keep track. He's conscious, able to eat and talk, and no, you can't visit him in your current state, maybe tomorrow or the day after when you are both fit." The orderly wheeled Ferris down to Hank Sanders's office, accompanied by the doctor and with the same police constable tagging along.

When they got to the office, the constable held the door open respectfully for Superintendent Legett. "You can go now, Smith," Legett said. The constable saluted and left.

"I'll leave you two alone," Hank said, and Legett nodded absently. "Thank you, doctor." He stared at Ferris intently when the door closed.

"Oh for God's sake," said Ferris wearily. "I'm very tired, Superintendent. Too tired for staring matches."

"Fine friends and business associates you have, Ferris," Legett said. "Automatic weapons at the airfield. I lost two men. And the gunmen got away."

"They were Schroeder's business associates," Ferris said doggedly.

"Oh yes, Schroeder," said Legett. "Another fine how-d'ye-do as they used to say in the old country. Strange goings on, couldn't locate the staff, half the Schroeder house burnt down – strange strong rooms. I think I misjudged Vic Schroeder. Not who he appeared to be at all, even allowing for how eccentric the rich can be. And a dead Guatemalan air force pilot who already died in a crash three years ago.

But they say we mustn't talk ill of the dead. Although I would have taken a much greater interest in Mr Schroeder when he was alive if I had even the slightest suspicion. His nephew has been advised not to talk to us by his lawyers. Do you also want to talk to your lawyers before giving a statement?"

"I'd rather get it over with and go home to my bunk," Ferris said.

"Very well, I will call in the stenographer."

Ferris told Legett everything he could bear to relate, leaving out the more painful bits, and keeping it short. When he got to the crash, Legett said, "That will do for now, we'll probably need more detail but it can wait until you have recovered. You know, I feel a sneaking admiration for you, Ferris. I'd like to think I would have acted more wisely than you, in the same position, but hardly any better."

Ferris couldn't resist saying, "Well then Jimmy was right about Arnaud and his gang."

"Yes, it seems Chen stumbled on an actual conspiracy," Legett said wryly. "And then he got to write some syndicated articles about The St. Marc Blood Bath, made the island sound like a cross between Washington DC and Beirut ... not that it was all roses. One of the constables killed was his second cousin."

"I'm sorry to hear it," Ferris said. "I didn't mean to sound flippant. I've seen a lot of deaths the last two days."

"As have we all," Legett said bleakly. "At any rate, you've cleared up a few things that were puzzling me. I'll get my driver to run you down to the marina." Legett held up Ferris's passport. "I'll be holding onto this. Don't try to leave the island without permission. I daresay your boat would sink in this weather if you tried."

"Why were they at the airfield?" Ferris said.

"Who?"

"Aziz and whatsisname."

"Gombs? We got an anonymous tip-off, straight to Aziz's direct line. Very mysterious." Something about that didn't sound right to Ferris but he was too tired to put his finger on it.

Ferris rubbed his hand over his face. The stitches were beginning to itch. "Alright, I'd like to go home now."

Legett smiled grimly. "Very well. In a couple of days I'll send someone to collect you. And I'll have someone keep an eye on you, just in case."

"By the way," Legett said, as he stood up. "Did you open the cargo door to get off the plane?"

"No," Ferris said, mystified.

"It was open when the fire died down. My men didn't see anyone else getting out, but the fire crew haven't been able to search at this stage, the plane is still too hot."

"I said before they don't have enough foam to fight aviation fires," Ferris said.

Legett shrugged. "Either way they didn't see a body."

"Quintero was definitely there, you can see what he did to my neck." Ferris said.

"I believe you, Ferris," Legett said with a sigh. "Perhaps he got off the plane too. I'd like to see some sign of him, dead or alive."

After he signed the statement, two policemen then drove Ferris to the marina.

When he got out of the police car at the gate of the marina, Ferris felt the wind blow hard against his cheek. Dusk was falling and the grey clouds of the storm were foreshadowed by the little flecks scudding across the sky. Little wavelets were rippling across the bay, first one way and then the next.

CHAPTER 73

The marina was almost deserted. All the pleasure cruise set had sailed away, fleeing the storm, and only the local and the foolhardy remained. Some workers were hammering nails into sheets of wood over the windows of one of the kiosks at the shore.

"Expecting bad weather," Ferris asked.

One of the men looked up, and stared at Ferris's battered face. "Yup," he said. "Wind up to eighty miles per hour, them say." He nodded at the Grand Hotel. "Smash all the windows, and all the damn fine boats too, maybe. You best pull your boat up on the shore mister, drop the mast and bury her up to the scuppers. Otherwise you could be mighty sorry."

Ferris nodded. "Thanks for the hint."

"My pleasure," the man said, "Good day to you."

"And you," Ferris said, strangely touched by the little exchange.

Apart from the unfortunates in the hospital, he had felt as if the world was full of evildoers, that a Quintero lurked in everyone. The practical matter-of fact advice of the worker had snapped him out of it. Not that he could follow the advice.

The *Trinidad* was much too large to haul out on his own, even if he felt up to it, and he couldn't afford the amount to pay a gang of men to do it for him. So the yacht would have to take her chances with the wind, and hope the narrow mouth of the bay would break any storm surge waves.

Ferris plodded wearily along the endless catwalk out to the *Trinidad*. Before getting aboard he tightened the mooring lines so that the yacht was snug against the fenders and pontoon. There would still be wave motion but the yacht was as close as was possible. Then he climbed aboard and felt drained.

He wondered should he maybe move the *Trinidad* inshore to a shallower berth, but he didn't want to leave the cabin once he was in. He was battered and weary, bone-deep, body and spirit, and he wanted a few days to himself, to repair. It would be a race to see if the storm or his recovery arrived first. But now, all he wanted was to sleep.

He threw himself on the bunk, listened to the wind. A heavy feeling crept over him, and he knew no more.

CHAPTER 74

Ferris awoke from a horrifying shapeless dream, and the wind was blowing harder. The sheets were clacking against the mast. It was daylight, but when he looked at the clock he realised that he had been asleep for fifteen hours. He felt a bit better, but still very, very tired.

He got up, rummaged around, and finally settled for a bar of chocolate and a can of soda water. As he ate, he looked out the porthole to the sea, and saw the rolling swell of low waves moving in the harbour.

The sky was low and grey. Ferris shivered, and sat on his bunk to finish his chocolate.

He noticed the motion of the *Trinidad*, rocking from side to side as the swell hit her on the beam. Out beyond the mouth of the bay, the sea was white and angry dark blue, waves breaking high, sending spray over the narrow reef at the mouth of the bay.

He closed one of the skylights, and left the other only open a crack, collected his spare blanket, stripped to his shorts, and climbed back into the bunk. He really knew he should have a shower, and do something about the boat, but a strange primeval withdrawal had come over him. Do it in the morning, he told himself, and to reinforce the resolve, he set the alarm for six, then he curled into a foetal position and pulled the blanket over his head, safe in a child's fortress. Safe, safe. The rocking of the boat lulled him away, remote from the wind, screaming outside, and he was safe, and sleepy, needing to rest.

When Ferris woke again, it was dark, and the clock glowed indistinctly, not strong enough to show the time. He wondered what had woken him, and supposed it must have been the rising wind and the rougher motion of the boat. The bilges had been disturbed too, and the smell of stale water wafted through the cabin. He listened to the wind briefly, then pulled his blanket over his ears and snuggled down again.

The same instant, it seemed, a light came on, and rough hands pulled him from his bunk, bouncing him on the floor. Ferris looked up in shock, and the cabin seemed to be full of men. Hard faced strangers. Braun stood behind them. Braun said, "Rise and shine, Captain, I must have words with you." Two men seized Ferris and lifted him back onto his bunk. He was too stunned to resist.

Braun leaned back against the table, and smiled thinly. "Now that we have your attention, Captain Ferris, perhaps you'd like to tell us about where you stashed the diamonds."

Ferris stared at him without understanding. "What do you mean, diamonds? The bloody plane burned, and your pal Quintero and the cocaine went up in smoke with it."

"Never mind about Quintero," Braun said callously. "The plane broke apart in the crash, and perhaps the package in the crate got thrown clear. Apparently the police found the crate, but it was empty. The only other person who knew it existed was you, so it follows you took the gems. They might even be hidden on this yacht."

"You're off your head," Ferris said. "I didn't take anything off the plane. Just look at me, you stupid bastard! I barely got out alive!"

Braun shook his head sadly. "Nice try Captain, but not credible. Will you tell us, or do we have to beat it out of you?"

"For God's sake," Ferris said, waving his hands wildly, "Can't you listen. I haven't got your bloody coke, or gems or whatever it is."

"Very well," Braun said. "You two interrogate the captain while I search." He pushed past the other two into the forward of the boat.

One man pinioned Ferris's arms behind him, and held him off balance. His bare feet slid on the polished wood deck. The first man moved around in front of Ferris and smirked. "Say, Cap, you look kinda stupid in your under-shorts." He laughed, and held up his right hand. "This is gonna hurt you a hell of a lot more than it hurts me, sport, cos all your poor stitches are gonna burst, and all these rings are gonna make pizza of your kisser." He twisted the rings on his fingers deliberately, so that Ferris got a good look.

His eyes moved, and Ferris tried to duck, but the blow crashed into his face, and he felt a suture split, and drops of his blood splattered the deck.

The man hit him in the solar plexus, and Ferris doubled over, gasping.

He stepped back and allowed Ferris catch his breath. He tutted. "Oh, my, oh my. Looking kind of nasty here now captain. Did you know they can't really fix up stitches that get burst? It'll be a pity if the boss finds the diamonds anyway and you get a ruined face for no reason. Another couple of rounds and you'll be paying for it on Saturday nights."

The man holding Ferris guffawed hilariously. "You really slay me, Clive," he said, and Clive scowled. "No names, you dummy." He grabbed Ferris by the hair and pulled his head up. "Anybody home, Cap?"

The other man laughed again, shaking so hard that his grip on Ferris's arms loosened. Crockery smashed on the floor of the forward cabin. "I dunno anything about diamonds," Ferris mumbled, spluttering blood. Clive's fist crashed into his face again, and this time it really hurt, the pain of the bursting stitches scalding Ferris's face.

Braun came back. He held up a burnt satchel. "Where are the gems, Captain Ferris? I have no time for your witty repartee."

CHAPTER 75

Clive grabbed Ferris by the hair again, and said, "Hey, Ferris, You ready to make your confession yet?" The thought of more pain was too much for Ferris, he screamed, and used his elbows on the man behind him, two jabs to the ribs, and as he sagged and let go, Ferris lifted another elbow to the face, and in the same movement, he lunged at Clive, and butted him in the face. Clive lurched back into Braun. Taken by surprise, Braun overbalanced and the edge of the bunk caught him behind the knees, so that he fell away and Ferris ran past him, instinctively making for the steps.

Braun shouted after him. Clive grappled with Ferris on the steps. The man's hands slipped as Ferris's naked torso gave him nothing to grip and Ferris struck desperately, and the Clive grunted, and Ferris broke free and pushed him back. Clive grabbed at his shoulder, but missed.

Ferris ran and vaulted over the skylight to the other side of the boat, as the other came up from the cabin. The man had a gun drawn, but he came out of the hatch too fast. His head struck the boom for the mainsail, and he staggered. Ferris grasped the guide rope of the rail, and swung himself out into the water. The impact made him gasp, and he took a mouthful of water as he went under, and he came up coughing and shaking his head, body tingling. A wave immediately slapped into his face as he took a breath. Over the wind, he heard one of the men say, "Don't shoot, asshole, keep it quiet."

Ferris looked up, and saw three figures looming above on the deck of the *Trinidad*. He struck out away from the boat, and a second voices said, "Asshole yourself, in this wind no one will hear."

Ferris took a deep breath, ducked his head under water, and

dived. He heard shots, muffled by the water, and felt the impact as small concussions against the water. He swam down and away as fast as he could, using a breast stroke, kept under until his lungs felt like bursting, then he let the air bleed out as slowly as he could. He tried to prolong the dive, but he couldn't hold back the rush. As the air exploded out of his lungs, he clawed up blindly for the surface. When he came out into the air, he tried to be quiet, but the splash and the panting of his lungs sounded like a pod of whales.

He looked around quickly as he trod water, trying to orient himself, and keep his face above the vicious little waves which swamped him. He found the *Trinidad*, and saw the figures lining the rail, searching the water. That made him duck back down, and let the waves wash over his face, because he was barely thirty feet away. He tried to submerge quietly, and swam away again. When he came up again, he felt it was safe to swim on the surface, and he struck out towards the shore.

The water was warmer than the air above so it was safe enough to stay in for hours. It was certainly safer than on the yacht. Ferris felt even more exhausted from the recent struggle. He trod water as his arms and legs tired of the unaccustomed motions. Finally he rested, holding onto a pontoon, and when he realised that he was clinging on to one of the walkways other than the one leading to the *Trinidad*, he pulled himself out of the water in stages, and lay aching shivering and dripping on the top, the hard edges of the wooden laths digging into his back. After a moment, he revived enough to stand up, and his first thought was clothes. He couldn't go back to the boat, and he had to get help, but first he wanted to get dry, and get dressed. But he knew instinctively that asking any stranger for help would be useless. They would just shy away from a blood-stained, wet and desperate man clad only in shorts, not wanting any trouble.

Ferris rose and padded to the nearest boat. It was locked, no lights showing, the sails lashed down hard. He climbed aboard, and hammered at the cabin door, but there was no reaction.

He did the same at the next boat, and then gave up and headed for land because Braun was sure to check all the walkways.

He picked out figures ahead and slipped back into the water and paddled up behind them.

As he got in close, he could make out two men, one wearing

a police uniform. A cigarette lighter flared and showed constable Gombs bend his head to put his cigarette into the flame of the lighter held by Arnaud.

"There was to be no shooting," the police officer said.

"Relax, constable." Arnaud said.

"If there are any complaints we will have to investigate."

"Don't worry, we will be gone by dawn."

Ferris paddled backward, all motion underwater, then took another huge inhalation and submerged again.

CHAPTER 76

He swam on around the ends of another couple of pontoons and climbed out of the water again, completely drained by now.

He ran clumsily along the catwalk, wincing at the scratching of the splintery wood on the soles of his feet. When he came to the place where the walkway joined the one from the *Trinidad*, he crouched beside one of the anchor piles, and looked up towards land, and saw no one. He looked back out the piers. He tensed as someone flickered past one of the walkway lights, coming from the direction of the *Trinidad*. Ferris lunged up and ran for the shore. The walkway boomed hollowly under his feet, strong even in the shrill scream of the wind. A gust of wind buffeted him, pushing him to one side, ruffling his hair, tugging his open cuts. He reached the concrete of the pier wall, and swung around to look back. He was standing in twilight where the weak low lights and the overhead neons of the pier left a gap, and as he looked back, he saw a group of men walking briskly towards land from the direction of *Trinidad*. Ferris looked around, and ran into the shadow of one of the kiosks.

He scurried along in a crouch, darting from kiosk to kiosk, until he was almost to the gateway of the marina. He studied the gateway for a moment, noting that the lights made the entrance bright and bare. He ran to the fence, and worked his way along in what shadow there was.

He walked away from the marina towards the road, and he looked back at the pontoons so much that he didn't realise until he was right up to the gates that there were vehicles parked outside them. He looked around but there were no shadows on the way to the gates. He had no choice but to just keep walking forward as normally as possible. There were two cars and a delivery van parked outside the gates of the marina, along the pavement.

They were all empty. He was relieved to see no sign of a police car, Gombs must be on foot patrol, alone.

Beyond the cars was a Dodge pick-up truck. It was Rolle's. There was a movement in the cab, and before Ferris could change direction or react, the door of the pick-up opened. "Hey Mr Tony," Lincoln said in a hoarse whisper. He poked his head out. He was the last person Ferris expected to see.

"Hey Linc," Ferris said. "What are you doing here, in the middle of the night?"

"Bob sent me to say he'd like a word." Lincoln looked uncomfortable. "He said it was very important." Ferris felt a sense of betrayal as well as fear and apprehension. "You mixed up in this too, Lincoln?"

Lincoln looked as frightened as Ferris felt. "Just get in the truck Mr Tony, You're in bad shape and we ain't got all night." It had been a rough couple of days. Ferris threw a hurried glance back towards the marina and climbed into the Ram.

"What's going on, Linc?"

"Mr Tony. If it's all the same with you, I'm going to take you to see Bob. It's all jammed up. But Bob will know what to do."

Lincoln drove off with his usual uncanny competence. He drove in silence, slowly and without fuss. The streets were deserted, and any house with shutters had them closed.

Up ahead Ferris saw the loom of headlight beams coming the other way around a bend.

"Better stay down, man," Lincoln said. Ferris ducked down below the level of the windows.

"Police," Lincoln said out of the side of his mouth.

Ferris crouched rigidly, his muscles aching with the strain. Lincoln drove on placidly.

"They're gone," he announced after a minute and Ferris sat up. He recognised the neighbourhood. Although he had never been there, he realised that Lincoln was making for Angelique's place.

Lincoln pulled up the Ram, and turned to him. "Ring at number three, Mr Tony."

"Look Lincoln –" Ferris began.

Lincoln interrupted. "I want to go to college Mr Tony, that's why I help out with the kids and why I'm scared of Sergeant Aziz and all the cops. You can't get a scholarship in the States if you don't have a visa and you can't get a visa if you have a criminal record. I may not know much but I know that much."

Ferris couldn't think of anything to say, but hesitated.

"You go on in Mr Tony. It's what he wants. I'll park the Ram round back and wait."

"Alright Lincoln," Ferris said at last. He climbed out of the Ram and crossed over to the house.

CHAPTER 77

Ferris rang the doorbell, and when there was no reply he thumped on the door.

The thud as his palms slammed into the door was considerable. Nothing happened, so after a moment to catch his breath, he hammered on the door again, and almost fell into the house when the door opened a crack as he used his shoulder to make a bigger noise.

"Oh, it's you." For a moment he didn't recognise the voice, but it was a man, not Angelique.

The door swung in to reveal Rolle standing in a hallway, stripped to the waist, a short automatic pistol in his fist.

"Looks like it's open house at Angie's place. Come on in, Tony," Rolle said lazily. "The more the merrier."

He unhooked the chain and leaned out and looked both ways and watched as the Ram disappeared around the side of the block. After that, he stood back and opened the door fully.

Ferris staggered as he went up the step. He leaned against the wall for a moment to recover, then pushed himself forward.

Rolle checked the street again and then locked the door behind him. He followed Ferris into the living room.

"Not looking so hot there, Tony boy. Somebody muggage you up good. Better come in and sit down before you fall down."

The room was dimly lit, and the air smelled of burnt cannabis.

Rolle turned up the light to show a pleasant and spacious room finished in white with a huge wide screen television and framed pictures of beach scenes. Palm tree patterned curtains covered the window. The furniture was fake cane, made of nylon with floral patterned cushions.

Angelique sprawled on the cane-effect sofa, holding a shot

glass, looking at the ceiling with a glazed expression. She was wearing a short night gown that wasn't covering her very successfully.

Ferris felt his heart twist in dismay.

"A tequila for our wet friend here," Rolle said. When she looked at them dully, he added, "You know who this is, Angie?"

"Hi Tony," she said in a listless voice. She lolled back again.

"You'll have to excuse our informality, we were about to watch Mexican Women's Junior League netball, gets us both in the mood. All those fit Latin girls, you don't know what you're missing."

"Girl, stir yourself and be useful. Get towels and bandage. The man dripping water and blood all over your nice rug."

"Awright," Angelique said in a far-away voice. She struggled to her feet and shuffled out of the room, smoothing down her night gown.

Ferris sagged into a cane chair. Despite the heat, he shivered involuntarily. The last fifteen minutes he had run totally on adrenalin. He was surprised to discover the chair was solid. The legs were a mixture of real cane and heavy steel tubing.

Rolle stood behind another.

"You seem surprised Tony. Well, I'm damned surprised to see you too. Or maybe you thought Angie could afford a place like this on waitress tips?"

"I've never been here before," said Ferris.

"I know it. Still got your nuts on, don't you?" said Rolle, "But just think, if you couldn't afford to live in this neighbourhood on a pilot's pay, how Angie gets by?"

Ferris said nothing.

"I thought you didn't like drugs," Ferris accused Rolle.

"Naw man, not for kids. But I gotta keep her company. The girl like Caribbean gold and Tequila. She not a good island girl, seeing we got our own drinks. But when she stoned she like to lick salt and lemon off the Rolle, know what I'm saying."

Rolle looked at Ferris in his shorts. "Well bey, you obviously left a party early, to judge by your state of dress. I got more clothes on than you, and I'm indoors, entertaining a lady. When we say around here 'shirt-tails' it means a fella have no pants, but look at you in your tighty-whiteys! Man, you really let yourself go. From fighter pilot to ageing fatty. Hee-ro to zee-roe."

"Look who's talking," Ferris retorted.

Rolle patted his pot belly. "Oh you know what they say, a big hammer to drive a mighty nail. All muscle baby!" He guffawed at his own joke. His bloodshot eyes glittered in the lamp light. He shook his head now.

"What happened to you man? You were a fighter pilot, a man on the top of the pile. What the hell happened to you?"

The question made Ferris nearly as uncomfortable as having a gun pointed at his navel. He had no answer so instead he asked, "Why did you send Linc?"

"I'm busy here man, you can see that. I wasn't at all sure you'd be in trouble. Otherwise I would of exerted my own self.

Besides, I send him to keep an eye on you, not bring you back. He suddenly all initiative or the boy playing a game of his own."

Before Ferris could query this, Angelique came back with towels and bandages. She handed Ferris a towel, bent over his face, and gently wiped the blood from his cuts.

The neckline of her gown sagged low under Ferris's nose, and he could see her body without any obstructing cloth, and despite his exhaustion and predicament, he felt aroused by the sight of her.

"You shouldn't have come here, Ferris," Angelique said in a very low voice. She sounded completely lucid. "You shame me."

Rolle caught his eye and grinned at him, and Ferris felt despair blot out any other feeling. He sat numbly as Angelique cut sticking plaster to size and fixed them on the cuts, and he smiled his gratitude as she backed away, her eyes large and no longer dopey. Rolle spun a chair back to front and straddled it, and folded his arms on the back-rest. The gun hung loosely in his hand, pointed at the floor.

"No," Rolle resumed. He was also now alert. "The boy playing a game of his own. I think they follow you here."

"Arnaud and Braun? You don't seem too worried." Rolle shrugged. "Out of the frying pan into the fire, or rather out of the cigar smuggling and into some profoundly serious shit. But no percents in crying over spilt milk." Angelique made to sit back on the sofa. "Where your head at girl?" Rolle said coldly. "Go get the man some clothes."

"You live here as well?" Ferris said.

"Of course I don't," Rolle said scornfully. "But I keep some clothes here, so that I lack for nothing on the occasions when I come here to surprise the lovely Angelique."

He turned and raised his voice. "And sandals for Tone here. Man, you got big feet for your size. Toes sticking out all over, makes me curious about your other attributes, you know what they say about foot size. Maybe I should be feeling inadequate here."

Angelique returned carrying clothes and a pair of sandals.

Rolle watched as Ferris tried on the selection of clothes. "Aye, the gang's all here," he said. "Lookit that girl fussing."

The jeans were too narrow in the legs and hips, but Ferris squeezed in with an effort. The t-shirt was loose, wide in the shoulders and too tight in the waist, but it served. He felt much better dressed. As Rolle had predicted, his toes curled over the front of the sandals. Rolle laughed at Ferris's appearance.

"You would never pass as me, Tony-oh" he said. "You're much too paunchy. So, what did Arnaud want?"

"He sent Braun. He seems to think I have a packet of diamonds from the plane. As to their coming here, I don't see why, how should they know?"

"Local knowledge man. He fly enough to buy it. You know who he have?"

"No," Ferris began, then he remembered. "They had a police-man helping them at the marina. Can't remember his name. Dim sort. Sergeant Aziz's side-kick."

"And I just bet you were going to ask me to ring for the cops."

CHAPTER 78

"Yes. No. Maybe," Ferris said.

"Tony, the way I see it, you're the fall guy. The police find the diamonds on the plane, you don't even know they exist, but they like to tie up loose ends, it's their training. So then they tell Frenchie-pants it must be you and he sends his people after you. The cops allow them just enough room to finish the job and then arrest or kill them all. It's not like they've shown much inclination to surrender up to now, and the cops will be well heeled next time."

"No way Legett would stand for that," Ferris said, horrified.

"Superintendent Boy Scout? Maybe so. But I know it's what I would do. A mysterious murder and some missing diamonds that might never have existed? Can't miss, and not all the poe-leece are such straight shooters."

"Where do you figure in all this?" Ferris said disbelievingly.

Rolle tapped his nose and winked irritatingly. "Tole you before, I have my own methods."

"I don't understand Arnaud," Ferris said. "Why risk staying here?"

"Oh yeah, he's a persistent cuss, your French friend. He's been sniffing around alright. Must have a lot of cred and cash sunk into this bullshit. Don't like the man, warned you about choosing your business associates."

"And you were right," Ferris said.

"So he the one who done the job on you? Yep, you all shoulda listen to your Uncle Bob, he know best."

Angelique folded back on to the sofa.

"Monsieur Arnaud seems like a nice gentleman," she said absently. They ignored her. She picked up her glass and lost her alertness.

"Tony, Tone, conchie Tone. Smoke reefer Conchie Tone?" Angelique crooned, and looked at Ferris over the rim of her glass. She giggled at her own joke.

Rolle laughed uneasily. "Ah that girl crack me up. Pay her no mind Tony, she got a mouth on her when she stoned, but tequila bring out the wild. And sometimes, she puts up a fight, but that gives it some spice." He laughed again.

Seeing the miserable look twist Angelique's face, Ferris started up, "You –"

Rolle raised the pistol warningly. "Relax yourself, Tone. No need to get excited now that you made yourself presentable."

Angelique jumped up grabbed at Rolle's arm pleadingly. "Please, don't –" without taking his eyes off Ferris, Rolle struck her across the face and she staggered back and fell to her knees.

"Stop it, why'd you hate everyone?"

"You man-hating little whore," Rolle said viciously. "You don't know what's good for you unless it's beat into you. You want me to wonder why you are so protective of our friend Tone, would you? You know how I am when I get jealous."

"Doan you ever relax man? Not even the weed settle you down." This time Rolle snarled and raised his free hand into a fist.

She shrank away from his raised hand, and he didn't even glance at her, looking all the time along the barrel of the gun at a point halfway between Ferris and Angelique. She started to cry, hiding her face in her hands.

"Stop it now," Rolle said sharply.

She obeyed immediately, and went back to the sofa.

Rolle turned and smiled humourlessly at Ferris. "See, you made us have one of our quarrels."

Ferris said, "For God's sake, why can't you just phone the police and get it over with? It's only one man."

Rolle laughed. "I always liked your way of thinking, Tony. I admire you for your courage but not for your lack of brains. Of course it's more than one man."

"So you are in on this!" Ferris said in disgust. "All that talk about crack-houses and keeping drugs out."

Rolle looked indignant. "You got drugs on the brain, Tony. You heard Jimmy – it's the new golden triangle – the guns come down from up north, in exchange for the illegal diamonds that come across from Africa in exchange for the cocaine that all those war-lords like to keep their soldiers hyped up on."

"So it's okay to send the drugs to Africa?"

"Hell man, those people gotta take care of their own selves. I'm not my brother's keeper and I sure as hell ain't gonna spend a thought on what happens with guns and drugs in New York or Sierra Leone or Colombia. And if somebody steals the diamonds, then it won't buy any more guns or drugs in Africa or any elsewhere – and besides what do you care, whitey?"

"People are right about you," Ferris said bitterly. "Vic warned me."

"Bah, Schroeder, and his great white father complex. I warned you about him, but oh no. He went off reservation didn't he? Anyway relax, it might never happen ... so stop worrying. I can keep you under wraps here, feed you tequila and premium contraband cigars and you can look at Angelique through her night gown. And you can enjoy a few hours out of harm's way, while Arnaud and his guys sweat it out looking for you and hopefully wear themselves out against our excellent police force. Now, relax, and try a cigar and a rum."

Rolle offered him a cigar. Ferris declined the cigar, but took the rum.

He felt just as empty as ever as the rum burned down his throat and warmed his belly.

Rolle said, "You know Tony, I be trueing what you say. On second thoughts, it might be safer for us to take a trip down to the cop shop at sun-up."

Ferris closed his eyes and breathed deeply, determined not to be toyed with.

"Why not now? Linc is out back with the Ram."

Rolle laughed. "So keen now. One, I don't know that I, or you, can trust Lincoln. Two, who knows who's on the night desk. I suspect it's not old man Colbert, who is the only one I would trust with my life. Well, I suppose you don't believe me. But there it be."

Ferris didn't believe for a moment that he could trust Rolle. Rolle was looking out for himself. And if he could not gain, he would be equally ruthless in cutting his losses, and Ferris felt that he might become a loss to be cut. Rolle chatted on again inconsequentially, as if there was nothing unusual in their situation, but held the pistol always ready in his hand.

Rolle smiled benevolently at him. "You're not enjoying the suspense, Tone. I am. But I don't like the way you're twitching in your seat, that hunted look, the way you keep twisting that towel in your hands. The nerves are contagious."

He sighed. "Keeping you here for your own good, not by force."

"Oh really?" Ferris said bitingly. "What's the pistol for then?"

"Home defence. Well okay, maybe a bit of force, but if you promise you won't try to leave before dawn we could all relax, some of us might even sneak a little private time? I'd believe you if you gave your word, because you're that strange sort of man, with a sense of honour."

Ferris stared at Rolle coldly. "I may not be that kind of man any longer. I could have changed, the things I've seen in the last two days. I spent years flying in an air force, and I only saw four people killed, all in accidents. Two days ago, I saw a dozen cut apart by machine guns. The world changed for me then."

Rolle studied him dubiously, and switched the pistol to his left hand, while he scratched his head. "Yeah war is hell, bro."

Curled up on the sofa, Angelique said, "For God's sake, do as he asks, Tony." Rolle looked at her sharply, and then laughed and looked back at Ferris. "The first sensible words I've heard her utter. What do you say?" Ferris considered. Rolle probably wasn't as out of it as he looked, and Ferris was in no shape to take him on, gun or no gun. "Fine, I'll stay here until six." Rolle beamed. "Angelique, some more tequila to celebrate Tony's good sense. Now we will really be able to relax. I wonder how Braun and his boys are getting on, looking for you?"

Ferris only half listened, as Rolle prattled on, then stiffened suddenly as he heard a car engine come along the street out front and then switch off. Rolle saw the movement of his eyes, and smiled. "More suspense so soon?"

The three of them listened.

The front door thundered under an urgent knocking, and Angelique gasped. Ferris clenched his fists, and glared at Rolle. Rolle smiled, a little tensely.

"I'll get the door," he said, and rose. He hesitated, removed the magazine from his pistol, and checked it. "Be right back. Don't go anywhere."

Then he nodded and went out into the hall. As soon as the

door closed behind him, Ferris was on his feet, ignoring the way Angelique looked at him pleadingly. He flattened himself against the wall by the window and tried to see the front door through a crack in the curtains. The pounding came again, and he heard Rolle say, "Alright, alright, I'm a-coming."

CHAPTER 79

He heard Rolle open the door on the chain. "Well lookit here if it isn't St. Marc's finest of the fine crime-busters."

"Very droll, Rolle," Sergeant Aziz said. "Can we come in?" Ferris sat back down.

Rolle came back in, followed by Aziz and the big constable. "Tweedle Gombs and Sergeant Azee," he announced, ostentatiously stuck the pistol into the back of his chinos and sank down into one of the armchairs.

"Sure men, make yourselves cosy," he said as Aziz and Gombs edged past Ferris into the living room.

"Well Tone, that must be a relief to you. Matter of fact you had me worried a bit, first time in my life I'm relieved to see the five-oh. Ha!" But he didn't look relieved at all.

"To what do we owe the honour sergeant? We were just talking about the police, but normally it takes a call to 911."

Aziz didn't answer immediately. Instead he took an exaggerated breath and fanned the air with his hand. "Oooh it frowsy in here. You smell that Gombs? Serious amounts of Caribbean gold circulating the air here."

"Yessir sergeant," said Gombs. As always, Ferris wondered if he was a bit simple. But he looked around the room alertly enough.

Sergeant Aziz and Gombs both wore rubber evidence gloves. "I hate these," said Aziz, gesturing. "Sweat like a bastard in them, nasty condensation as if we don't get enough of that."

Rolle raises his eye-brows. "What, you going to do a body search, man?"

"I wouldn't mind doing a cavity search on the girl." Angelique stirred on the sofa, showing a lot of breast. She bared her teeth at Aziz.

"So why'd you never offer the girl to me?" Aziz said, not taking his eyes off her.

"She a hard sell man, you know she not normal," Rolle said.

"Don't talk about me like I wasn't here," Angelique said suddenly. "I wouldn't let you touch me you were the last man on the island. What you are you can't eat!" She extended her middle finger at Aziz. "Pig and foreigner!"

"You no manners girl!" said Rolle. "Pay no attention to her, it's the weed talking."

"So, you see," Aziz said, mostly looking at Ferris. "That is the sort of talk I have to put up with. I'm a Christian, my people were Christians five hundred years before they came here to be among Christians but that's not the point. Why should a Muslim or anyone have to listen to that sort of talk? It was better before 9-11, but after that, it was towel-head this and rag-head that, people talking like that to my face even though I was a serviceman. So I came back to the island, I figured at least this is where I'm from, it wouldn't feel so bad."

Rolle said, "Ferris, you look constipated man – spit it out, whatever it is."

"That's him, the one with Arnaud at the marina earlier. He's in on it."

Rolle looked at him contemptuously. "Of course he is – I did give you a hint. You only figure that out now? Man, no offence, but you low-fence."

Aziz looked from one to the other.

"Tony here just getting up to speed on you being hand in glove with Commandant-ee Arnaud," Rolle said.

"Oh that?" Aziz said dismissively. "Appearances can be deceiving, Ferris. I'll explain later."

"I'd love to be a fly on the wall," Rolle said. "Make no mistake, Tony, he's in on it too. What good is a criminal conspiracy if you don't get a few cops in your pocket?"

Aziz gave Rolle a look of disdain. "If there's a conspiracy, you can be sure Rolle is in on it, as he probably just told you, running his big mouth off."

"But you hate each other," Ferris protested.

"Legett hates people," Aziz said. "I just do business with them." He turned back to Rolle.

"That gun licensed?" Aziz said.

"Surely is," Rolle said lazily. "All legit. And the Caribbean gold, quantity well within legal bounds for personal use. You think I'd let you in the door otherwise?"

"You could be bluffing, but I didn't come here for that," Aziz said indifferently. "I'm not here in an official capacity. You might say in a personal and illegal capacity. I came to ask about the diamonds."

CHAPTER 80

Rolle's face stayed completely blank.

"What diamonds?" Ferris said.

Aziz looked from one to the other and shook his head. "Ferris, you I believe. It makes sense."

"No clue what you're talking about Aziz," Rolle said carefully. "But, if you come to break down the door in the middle of the night to sell diamonds, it's the strangest visit ever. I ain't never been in the gems business. But I do know a little old jew-ler called Solly in Queens, who will buy anything you can bring him. No questions asked."

Aziz made an impatient gesture. "The diamonds Wally found out near the plane. The diamonds Mr Arnaud and Mr Braun are crazy to get back."

"Ah," Rolle said. He sat up straight in the armchair. He said nothing for a moment. "Is Wally gone to join the stiff toe gang?"

"No, Wally is almost family. I leaned on Wally in a quiet way, police style. I couldn't let them know. That Braun is a nasty piece of work."

Arnaud wasn't much better, Ferris thought, but he said nothing.

Rolle said, "Cousin Wally is weak. It runs in that side of the family. His grandpa also known as Brunkard the Drunkard. You can imagine how much drinking they have to do to get a name like that in this town."

"A corrupt policeman's work is never done," Aziz said. "Super-intendent Legett is off at the airport, with most of his men, they had a tip-off that there were diamonds hidden there. And most of the rest of the police are off on the west of the island, investigating a report of a disturbance involving gunfire. They will be going slowly and cautiously, be some time before they get back. So that left me and Constable Gombs to respond here."

Rolle said, "You hear that, Tone? The good sergeant saying he no longer on side of the angels." Aziz glanced at Ferris. "No man, Aziz is always looking out for number one. Aziz is always thinking of Aziz." Ferris didn't like the way the two men were looking at each other, the air was electric even though they were both empty-handed.

"We still have to discuss Ferris," Aziz added.

"Ferris is my guest. He stays here."

"Oh yeah, like it's your house," said Gombs.

"Who asked you, genius," Rolle retorted. "You should both leave now."

"So you let us in," Aziz said. "But since you don't own the place, you can't really ask us to leave. Technically." Angelique stirred on the sofa took a second to take this in. "I want you to leave too."

"Okay," Aziz said. "You heard the lady."

Gombs looked surprised when Aziz turned to him. "Take the car back to the station. Write up a fault report for the radio, say we couldn't get anything at all again. Say I went to investigate a suspected burglary. Don't check in at any of the phones on the way back."

"Are you sure?" said Gombs, looking from Ferris to Rolle.

"I'm sure." Aziz said sharply. "Cobb went home sick so Rogers is night dispatcher tonight. Take over the dispatch. If there are any reports of shots, stall them back at the station, if there are not, give Rogers the car and send him across the island to the Superintendent. Give him some bullshit errand. Anything comes through, let me know first and sit on it as long as you can without making anyone suspicious. Clements is the only other constable on duty. If he comes in the station keep him busy, send him to clean the toilets or something."

Aziz smiled.

"He won't like that," said Gombs, smiling back.

"God almighty, that was a joke, you simpleton. Do I have to think of everything myself? Alright, if you have to, send him to patrol the marina, it will be safe enough now. I've got things under control here. Bring me in the box from the car."

They sat in silence and faintly heard the hollow noise of the trunk of the car, then to Ferris's surprise, the rumble of the police cruiser engine starting. Nobody else noticed.

Rolle said to Aziz: "Always wondered, why you come back here man? You could have been a US citizen."

"And why did you come back?" Aziz said.

"Shit, you know why. Dishonourable discharge is why. I'm a criminal, they would have deported me if I stayed around. No place like home eh?"

"Something like that," Aziz said, showing his teeth.

"What," Rolle said, with a nasty grin, "And no respect for your war record here neither, hey?" Aziz turned to Ferris again.

"Rolle likes to jazz me about my war record. Yes, I was with the war graves people. I joined the Quartermaster Corps. I thought it would have some sort of career progression into the military police, but instead I ended up in Mortuary Affairs.

It was a valuable lesson. You know what the lesson is? You see enough dead people, you realise civilisation is a bullshit sham. We butchered them." Aziz said, looking at Ferris "You butchered them from your fancy jets."

"I was a fighter pilot, not a bomber pilot," Ferris objected.

"Whatever. Butchery. I've seen hell on earth. While you were up there in your jet, playing the worlds most expensive video game, thinking how unreal it all was, we were picking up the pieces. When you've seen what a 30-mil chain gun does to a truck and a platoon of soldiers you know there is no God, no right or wrong. Only today and being dead. Kindness exists surely but it's skin deep. Scratch a man, any man from any country and you find yourself a genocidal monster."

"That's a terrible thing to say," Ferris retorted.

"Is it? I know why you help teach the young lads how to play cricket – it's not to give something back or whatever you think it is. You're afraid and you want to hold back the darkness. See people being given a chance."

"What the flip this?" said Rolle. "Lower than I thought you could go man. Tired of you and your palaver. You get out of here, you hear now."

CHAPTER 81

Ferris didn't like the intense way Aziz was talking. The car outside drove off. Then the front door opened again.

Quintero came in. Bandages and yellow ointment covered half his face.

"Damn," said Aziz, "I do declare this place is a zoo. I thought I told Gombs to shut the door."

"I met him on his way out," Quintero said flatly. Part of his moustache was missing and he looked tired.

"Well mother sick," Rolle said and barked a laugh without humour. "I'm getting a bad wibe here. Either the smell of brimstone or Burning Man from our supposedly dead friend here."

Quintero handed a presentation box to Aziz, who opened the box and said, "You know, Ferris, your friend Schroeder had some messed up idea of a hobby. Did you know he was a major gun collector? Us neither. Part of the house didn't burn, fireproof strong-room full of weapons, most of them totally illegal."

Rolle stood up. "Don't let the door hit you in your parrot-ass on the way out, you hear? I'm not afraid of you."

"I know you're not, big man," said Aziz, "And you're looking at the wrong guy."

"Damn you to hell Aziz," Rolle said.

Aziz grinned at Rolle. His eyes glinted, suddenly animated. "I figured out where the diamonds are. Pretty slick, Rolle. When we finished searching you went back and put them where we already knew they weren't. Am I right or am I right?"

"You're crazy man. I wouldn't keep them here."

"Well that much I had guessed already. Anyway, don't want to gabbing on about them."

"Leave. Now." Rolle said it through his teeth, his fists clenched.

"Yeah, yeah," Aziz says still excited. "I'm nearly gone. Just want to show something to Ferris."

Aziz pulled a gun out of the box and held it up, looking at Ferris.

"At first I thought it was just a sawn-off .44 police Special, but there was something strange about the bullets. I had to look the damn thing up in a book, didn't know what to look for on the internet. I remembered Schroeder might have been in Vietnam and that's when I found out. It's a Smith & Wesson AAI Quiet Special Purpose Revolver, also known as a tunnel gun. Brilliantly untraceable. Fires tungsten pellets." As he spoke, Aziz put the gun back in the box and handed it to Quintero. Quintero took it, and Ferris suddenly noticed he also had surgical gloves on. He suddenly knew what would happen next. He wanted to shout at Rolle to get out.

Quintero pulled the revolver out of the box, and faced Rolle. Rolle reached around for the pistol in his back and ducked to the side.

Quintero fired. The shot sounded like a loud door slamming, less than a .22 but it was still deafening indoors. Rolle jerked and then looked down at the dots that had appeared on his t-shirt.

"Louder than I expected," Aziz said, dispassionately. "Still sub-sonic and no stopping power." Rolle lurched and finally got the pistol out. Quintero shot him twice more in the chest as he stumbled backward trying to bring up his pistol. Rolle dropped his pistol and fell on his back.

For a second Ferris froze and then Angelique screeched and threw her tequila in Aziz's face and lunged for his holster. "Damn, don't you, girl," said Aziz. He fended her off and blinked his eyes clear but she paid no attention and kept coming.

"Don't shoot the girl," Aziz said, but Quintero fired once more, and Angelique sprawled across Rolle.

Quintero turned towards Ferris, his finger tightened on the trigger. Ferris turned up his empty palms.

"Stop now," Aziz said, in such a hard voice Quintero lowered the revolver slightly.

"Ah. Shit." Aziz said tiredly, "Nobody listens round here."

"I don't understand," Quintero said stiffly.

"You'd never have made it as a real policeman," Aziz said scornfully.

"You've ruined the setup. I wanted a nice scene for forensics – powder residue and shots from the right angles, the whole ball of wax."

Quintero didn't relax. He still held the tunnel gun in his hand.

Aziz knelt next to Rolle and gently rolled Angelique aside. "Hold on, girl. Ferris get over here and help her."

"Quintero, stand out of the way," Aziz said as he placed the short pistol back in Rolle's hand. He wrapped Rolle's limp fingers around the butt of the pistol, then looked up.

Quintero edged sideways then brought the tunnel gun up in a panic when he saw that Aziz had drawn a bead on him. The hammer clicked on empty chambers.

"There were only four shells," Aziz said. "Count them." He brought up Rolle's pistol and shot Quintero four times, so fast that the shots rolled into each other. Quintero's eyes widened and he fell stiffly backwards. He bounced off the door and left a bloody mark as he dropped to the ground.

"Thought you'd got away with it, motherfucker?" Aziz said dispassionately. "That was for Shareen."

Then he adjusted Rolle's nerveless fingers around the pistol and fired another two shots into the wall above the door.

While he was looking away, Ferris hefted one of the chairs. He measured the distance in his head.

In two steps Ferris closed the distance and swung the chair and hit Aziz on the back of the neck.

The chair broke and Aziz checked his fall with his elbows, the gun skittered out of his grip. He grunted and shook his head to clear it. "Dammit Ferris can't you see I'm helping you."

Ferris re-adjusted his grip on the good remaining steel cored leg of the chair and hit Aziz again before the words registered. Aziz went down and Ferris was the only one standing.

CHAPTER 82

Ferris snatched up Rolle's pistol. He knew there were maybe a couple of rounds left, but he couldn't bring himself to turn it on Aziz. He put on the safety and stuck it in the pocket of his borrowed jeans.

Quintero was obviously dead, his eyes open and glassy and a spreading pool of blood on the tiles around him.

Rolle was lying on his back with his head turned to the side at an uncomfortable angle with his eyes shut but dead looking rather than sleeping.

Angelique was lying on her side, blood seeping from her shoulder. She moaned faintly. Ferris got the towel he had dropped and pressed it against Angelique's shoulder. She stirred and tried to move away from the pressure. "You hold it," Ferris said gently. "Where are there more bandages?"

"In the kitchen ... only sticking plasters," Angelique said faintly.

"I'll go get help," Ferris promised and stood up. Maybe Lincoln was still parked out back.

"Quintero, what's going on? *Qué está pasando*?" Somebody shouted from outside.

Ferris went quickly into the hallway, and had just opened the kitchen door when the front door slammed open. He looked back to see Braun and Clive. Clive held a pistol.

Without thinking, Ferris dropped on one knee and pulled out Rolle's pistol and fired at them. He missed and they ducked back. Ferris hit the light switch and plunged into the dark kitchen slamming the door behind him.

He flicked on the light, and looked around quickly.

"Hey, Ferris," Clive called outside, and fired. The kitchen door had two bolts, and Ferris slid them home.

The kitchen was full of cupboards ranged along the walls. It had windows on two sides, looking onto the alley.

As he reached the back door, he could see Rolle's pickup parked outside.

The door was locked and he couldn't see a key.

He struggled with the window catches, but saw that countless coats of paint had jammed them.

The kitchen door shook. "Hey, Ferris, come on out. We just want to know where you put the diamonds," Braun called through it.

"Come on out, or I'll shoot through the door," Clive threatened. "You got ten seconds." Ferris started pulling open cupboards at random. The second contained towels.

He wrapped a towel around his head and wound another around his hands and arms to the elbows.

As Clive said "Nine," Ferris ran at the alleyway window. He held his arms in front of his face, and shut his eyes at the last moment. His fists smashed through the glass, and pulled his feet up behind him to clear the window sill in a dive. The impact of the cobbled alleyway stunned him. He lay for a moment fighting the pain in his shoulder and back, then rolled over.

Shots rang out from the house, and he could hear the kitchen door being hammered again.

Ferris sat up and shook off the towels with a tinkle of glass. He got to his feet and ran for the Ram, his feet slapping on the cobbles, in Rolle's tight sandals.

The engine of the Ram started up, a deep rumble in the confines of the alleyway.

CHAPTER 83

The pick-up truck filled alleyway. Ferris jerked open the passenger door and piled in. "Jesus Mr Tony you give me a start, jumping through the window," Lincoln said.

"Let's get out of here, Lincoln," Ferris said urgently.

Lincoln shifted into gear and looked over his shoulder. "Hold on while I back-back," he said, and reversed.

A man came out of the side alleyway beside the house. He raised a pistol and Lincoln accelerated, the Ram's engine suddenly shrill.

Ferris reached for the gun in his pocket but it was gone, lost when he jumped through the window.

The man leaped to one side but the back of the truck caught him on the thigh and the momentum spun him off his feet and into the wall of the next house. Another man appeared as Lincoln got the truck into first gear and shot off forwards so suddenly that Ferris's head snapped back.

Ferris caught a fleeting glimpse of Braun's face blurring past.

A double report of two shots in quick succession rattled around the alleyway and Ferris ducked instinctively. A hole starred the safety glass of the wind-shield. He risked a look over the dash as the truck screeched onto the street and the back end swung out as Lincoln shifted it into third gear.

"Stay down Mr Tony," Lincoln said. The Ram fishtailed, barely missing a car parked in front of the house. There were no further shots and Ferris sat up fully.

"How come you waited, Linc?" he said.

Lincoln glanced across at him with a hunted look. "I got a conscience, Mr Tony. After I dropped you, I knew Aziz would come. I hung around. I still thought he was mostly doing his job, but after he sent Constable Gombs away, a car pull up with some bad-asses in it.

Then I had to stay. Rolle dead ain't he?" He sounded a bit slurred.

"Where are we going?" Ferris asked

"Outta town man. Bey, that fella was a good shot." When they passed a street lamp Ferris could see a dark glint spreading on the right shoulder of Lincoln's Hawaii shirt.

"Christ you're hit!" Ferris said. "Pull over."

"Nah nah I'm fine. We gotta keep going."

"Pull over before you faint or go into shock. Let me look at it."

Lincoln pulled over under a street lamp and he looked drawn as he pulled up the hand brake. "Man that hurt."

"Lean forward," Ferris said, and saw the glint of fresh blood seeping through Lincoln's shirt. There was a nasty tear over the shoulder blade but no exit wound. Ferris pulled off his t-shirt, and wadded it up.

He didn't want him to go into shock so he arranged the t-shirt over the wound and said to Lincoln, "Press down with your other hand and don't worry about the pain. I'll get you to the hospital."

"Don't feel like much," Lincoln said woozily. "Don't want no trouble, Mr Tony."

"Scootch over," Ferris ordered. He had to help Lincoln slide over to the passenger seat. Then he got out and went around to the driver's side. He couldn't hear much over the rumble of the Ram's engine but he saw no other cars. A very slight pale streak to the east promised the dawn.

Ferris turned his attention back to his driving.

He set a new speed record getting the truck to the hospital.

He threw the truck through the front gates of the hospital in a skidding turn. He spun the wheel to avoid a parked ambulance, and braked hard at the bottom of the steps. Lincoln slumped forward against the dashboard when he pulled to a halt.

Ferris exploded out the door, and ran up the steps.

People stared at him as he burst through the swing doors into the hospital. He had to duck to avoid a trolley, and almost stumbled over the feet of a row of patients sitting on a bench.

Ferris reached the enquiry desk. He propped himself up on the desk with his elbows. In the bright light he noticed blood running down his arms from glass cuts.

"I've got a sick boy outside. Lost lots of blood. He's been shot."

CHAPTER 84

"I must inform the police," said the nurse on the desk. Ferris didn't recognise her. The nurse didn't look much put out at having a shirtless bloodstained white guy shouting at her. Just another night at the emergency room.

"You can do that *later*," Ferris said. "He's not going anywhere. Right now he needs a doctor."

She made up her mind and pressed an intercom button and Ferris went back out to the pickup and half carried a sagging Lincoln into the lobby.

By then, Hank Sanders had arrived in a mixture of scrubs and combats, accompanied by two orderlies with a trolley.

Hank gaped at Ferris, "My God Tony – your face needs treatment right away."

"I'm alright," Ferris said impatiently. "See to Lincoln." After one look at Lincoln, Sanders shouted orders. Many hands lifted Lincoln on the trolley and rushed him into the emergency room.

Ferris was left facing the nurse on the desk. "You'd better ring for an ambulance to go to Angelique Gaillard's house. There are two more people suffering from gunshot wounds and yes, do also send the police."

"I don't know the address," the nurse said imperturbably, although she might have become paler.

"3 New Street, The Hill," Ferris said, to his own surprise. He didn't consciously know the address.

The nurse picked up a phone and spoke rapidly, relaying what he had said.

Ferris relaxed a little. He didn't care what Rolle had said, all hell would break loose now, the police couldn't ignore the trouble that had brewed up.

The doors of the emergency room opened and the nurse who had treated him before came out. Recognition dawned on her face. "Mr Ferris, you're bleeding all over our floor. Get in here at once."

She ushered him into a cubicle and as she did so, Ferris caught sight of his reflection, and it shocked him. His face was streaming blood.

The nurse dabbed the blood away from his face, and concentrated on staunching the flow from the gashes on his forearms. As she gently put on dressings Ferris felt the full searing pain of the cuts.

"This looks like glass, again," the nurse said accusingly "Window glass this time," Ferris said lamely. "It's different."

"Oh I can see it is," the nurse said gravely. She worked very efficiently and only a couple of minutes later Ferris was trussed up.

"You should probably wait to see the doctor," the surgery nurse said.

"Alright," Ferris said. "I want to know how Lincoln is too."

"Well you certainly can't sit out front in that state. You'll upset the other patients."

Ferris looked down. He hadn't noticed that Rolle's jeans were streaked with blood.

"Wait a minute," she said and went out. She was back almost immediately, carrying a green scrubs tunic. "You can borrow this for the moment."

Ferris put on the tunic and suddenly felt self-conscious of the blood stained jeans, but the nurse just said. "There, you won't cause a stampede now. Just don't pretend to be a doctor."

He went into the washroom and tried to wash the blood out of jeans and stopped when the worst of the redness rinsed out.

Ferris went to sit out in the waiting room and this time the duty nurse did raise an eyebrow at his appearance.

He sat down on a row away from the queue and looked out the window. Dawn had begun to lighten the sky. He felt the urgency of the adrenalin begin to fade.

He glanced out the window again, and a dark blue Toyota Camry swung in through the gates of the hospital. The parked ambulance blocked his view, but when the car pulled around to beside the Ram, the doors swung open, and he saw Braun leap out of the Toyota.

CHAPTER 85

His heart hammering, Ferris got up and went to the desk. "Is Mr Davern allowed visitors?" he said.

"It's the middle of the night, Mr Ferris. Not visiting hours." The nurse looked taken aback.

"I know that," Ferris said reasonably. "But is he well enough to visit later?"

"Yes, but he tires very quickly."

"His room is on the second floor isn't it?"

"No, the third," the nurse answered almost automatically. "But you'll have to ask a doctor first –"

"Thanks," Ferris said, and ran for the lifts.

"Mr Ferris, you can't go up, you're not authorised," the nurse shouted after him. "I'll call security!"

"And call the police too," Ferris yelled back.

Ferris reached the bank of lifts just in time to see one going up. The other two were already on the third floor. He decided not to wait. It was only three floors, after all, which meant a mere two sets of stairs.

As he ran to the stairs, he wondered why he wanted to see Davern. Perhaps it was because Davern seemed to be involved from the beginning, that he wanted him to do something now. The only other place to run was the police station, and with Braun and his thugs outside he didn't think he'd get that far. He almost fell on the first landing, and bent double, holding the rail, as nausea swept over him. The stairwell undulated and blurred before his eyes.

His breath came and went in vast shuddering gasps, and he forced himself upright and ran on up the stairs. He stopped on the second floor to recover slightly.

Ferris forgot to breathe all the length of the two flights to the third floor. Little lights were dancing in front of his eyes as he ran down the corridor, trying to remember which room was Davern's. The lifts were at the far end of the corridor from the stairs. The first door he tried was locked, the second was a changing room, with spare gowns and scrubs hanging all along the walls. The third room was occupied by an elderly unconscious patient fed by a yellow intravenous bottle. The fourth room was Davern's.

Davern was sitting in a wheel-chair at the foot of the bed as Ferris threw the door open, and he started. It took him a moment to recognize Ferris.

"Tony! My God, what's happened to you?"

Ferris swayed, breathing raggedly, wanting to be sick. "Bill, great to see you up and about."

Davern said, with a bit more edge, "What the hell is going on?"

Davern had recovered well. He looked pale and frail but the determined set to his face was reassuring.

"I have a bit of a situation. Arnaud's man Braun is after me, he thinks I have a batch of illegal diamonds belonging to him. He doesn't seem to care who gets hurt in getting them back. He shot Lincoln. And just now I saw Braun in the car park so I came upstairs. What the hell am I going to do?"

"Okay, Tony, calm down," Davern said, and stood up. "Does he know you're here?"

Ferris shrugged helplessly. "I don't know. He's seen Rolle's truck outside so he knows we're here. If he gets rough on the staff, I'm sure he can find out I came up to see you."

Davern nodded. "Okay, so we barricade ourselves in the room and telephone for the police." He pointed to the phone by his bed. "Just connected."

"No, no," Ferris said. "That's not enough. These buggers shoot through doors, they don't care what they hit."

Davern pursed his lips. "We'll have to take our chances. I'll phone the police. Look, there's a revolver in the bathroom down the hall. Same type as I had in the car, remember? It's in a recess behind the soap holder. You get it, while I phone. First though, let's get the bed against the door." Ferris pushed the bed over across the door alone, afraid of Davern's frailty. Davern had the phone in his hand, dialling. Ferris slipped out through the crack left between the door and the bed.

CHAPTER 86

The bathroom was at the far end of the corridor. As Ferris ran, he strained his ears. It might take some time for Braun to find Davern's room, but if he was desperate enough, he could get the floor and number quickly by force.

He guessed the correct door, and quickly scanned the bathroom for a soap holder. There was a bath, hidden behind a shower curtain, and a sink, and a toilet and a bidet. There was a porcelain shelf next to the bidet, but when he tugged at it, it wouldn't budge. He looked around again. Where the hell was the soap holder?

In desperation, he tore aside the shower curtain, and there, just above the rim of the bath, a plastic basket hung from an attachment on the wall. Ferris grabbed at the soap holder with the hands of desperation, and ripped it away bodily, but the plastic tore and he only held the holder, the wall support still stood. It was difficult to pull off the piece on the wall, because he could get no leverage, and at last he got his finger nails under the edge of the plastic and pulled gently, pushing his panic down. The plastic panel came out easily, pieces of grout crumbling and falling into the bath.

Behind the panel was a recess, and a neoprene bag filled it. Fingers trembling, Ferris pulled out the neoprene bag, feeling the weight and the hard metal inside. He resisted the impulse to rush back to Davern's room, and unwrapped the pistol.

It was a two-inch barrel .38, with a safety catch set in the butt, as Davern had said. There was a polythene sachet with maybe ten bullets, Ferris didn't bother to count. He pushed open the cylinder catch, and as the cylinder swung out, he saw that there were five bullets in the gun already. Ferris dropped the neoprene bag, and crammed the sachet of bullets into the pocket of Rolle's jeans, wincing at the lack of space, and the discomfort. Then he carefully pushed the snub snout of the revolver into the waistline of the jeans in the small of his back, keeping his fingers well away from the trigger. Then he pulled the tunic down over it.

He opened the door slowly. The sound of feet clattering up the stairs carried to him clearly along the corridor, and he ran into the hall, then changed his mind as he realised that they were at the top of the stairs and he plunged in the next door, and slammed it behind him. He leaned against the door for a moment, and he saw that he was back in the changing room.

The sound of a door being shouldered reverberated down the corridor.

"Open the door, Ferris, we know you're in there," Braun yelled above the pounding. "Open up, or we'll shoot the lock."

Ferris couldn't hear the reply, but he realised that he could only hide for a short while, before they discovered he was not with Davern, and then they would search each room along the floor, until they found him. He grabbed a pair of scrubs leggings and pulled them on over his jeans, then rummaged in some drawers, and found a surgical mask and cap.

He put them on also, and examined himself in the mirror. It looked very convincing, and the mask hid most of the bandages on his face. His arms he couldn't do anything about.

He took a deep breath, opened the door, and stepped out into the corridor.

All he had to do was walk five paces to the lift.

He felt his knees buckle as he turned onto the corridor, and the noise suddenly ceased.

Out of the corner of his eye he saw three men stand back from the door to watch him, a doctor in a green gown as he strode briskly to the lifts. Ferris was sweating. They were sure to recognize him, and only some desire to keep their scheme private kept them from attacking a doctor. He found it difficult to keep a calm pace, not to run, and he kept looking forward, lest eye contact trigger recognition. He was four steps from the lift. Three. Two. The lift was on the floor, the light glowing on the glass number three. He pressed the button.

Braun said, "Merde, it's Ferris!"

The doors slid open, and he plunged into the lift.

He heard them rush him, thinking they could get to him before he made it, but he slapped the ground floor button, and then the door close button. The doors guillotined shut in the face of the first of his pursuers.

CHAPTER 87

Ferris laughed in relief, then ducked, as bullets ripped through the top of the doors, as they fired down at the dropping lift.

Then the shooting stopped, as the indicator flashed onto the number two. Ferris sagged against the back of the lift. They would follow him down, using the stairs. The lift bumped to a halt, and the doors opened.

He tottered dazedly out, and stood swaying indecisively for a moment. He heard the heavy hammering of someone taking the steps two at a time. He tore off the cap and mask, and broke into a run. He didn't see an orderly pushing a trolley, and shouldered the man aside so that he fell onto the trolley, and elbowed his way through a group in excited conversation at the emergency desk. They shouted angrily at him, but he didn't even glance back, running for the doors.

Ferris blew the doors back onto their hinges as he burst out onto the steps. He took the steps in one leap, almost falling as he landed, going heavily on one knee. It was almost fully daylight, with no covering darkness to run into.

"Hold it," a man shouted, and Ferris looked around as he regained his feet.

Clive jogged around the back of the hospital, gun coming up. Ferris swerved, and vaulted over the bonnet of the Toyota, using his hands as a pivot halfway across. Then he hunched behind the Ram and ran for the gate.

He ran across the street, ducked behind a departing bus, and, in the cover of it, darted down an alley towards the old town.

The lane's surface was cobbled, and his sandalled feet twisted and slipped on the polished uneven stones. It was almost deserted, only a few of the early workers out preparing for the day.

Ferris had no plan, except to keep running and stay ahead of Braun and his crew.

He ran almost blindly, dodging obstructions and people, anything that would impede him.

Running downhill had its own momentum and if he had been running from life these last for fifteen years then now running felt like the right thing to do.

He turned again, into another narrow alley, and ran on until he came to a main street again. He stopped then, giving in to the lead weight in his legs, arms and shoulders and the dragging stitch in his right side. A haze clouded his peripheral vision, and he leaned against a wall, and panted. He looked back, saw nobody following him, and wondered if he escaped.

He sagged against the rough stone wall of an old warehouse for ten pounding beats of his heart, and he listened to the growing bustle in the street ahead. He decided that they wouldn't be foolish enough to try to take him in a busy street. He could hide himself in the crowd until he found a policeman. Sirens blared up ahead, and he forced himself into a run, and was just in time to see a patrol car and police truck rush past, on the main street, heading towards the hospital. Ferris straightened up and turned onto the street back towards the hospital. People turned to look at the unusual police activity, and Ferris merged with the crowd unnoticed. With the authorities now alerted, surely Arnaud's gang would give it up as a bad job and try to slip away quietly. He strode confidently through the sparse crowd until he saw a blue Toyota Camry pulled over to yield to the police vehicles blaring past. He cursed again.

It would be safer to go to the police headquarters by the back streets of the warehouse district where large cars couldn't fit, and less risk of running into Braun before he got there.

He forced himself to walk normally in the crowd, ignoring the curious stares at his scrubs and bandaged face and arms.

CHAPTER 88

He needed to ditch the scrubs leggings. The green colour stood out in the distance.

As soon as turned into the alley again, he pulled them off and wedged them behind a rubbish bin. He kept the tunic on, it would attract less attention than a bare torso.

Ferris broke into a trot and headed downhill along the cobbled alleyways, dropping towards the level of the police headquarters. However, he missed the most direct turning, and broke out onto the market street, which was thronged with people. It was less than ideal, but he let himself be carried along by the crowd, intending to work his way back up-hill towards the police headquarters.

As he started along the market street, he saw the head of a white man held high, trying to see over the heads of the crowd. He recognised Clive. Ferris turned away, hunched his shoulders and quickened his pace. Looking back, he saw Clive closer, and he knew that he could not reach the police station. It meant going up hill, and Clive easily pick him out of the crowd. Instead, Ferris hurried down hill, heading towards the harbour, and the police traffic kiosk at the bottom of the hill.

"I have him," Clive shouted, from thirty yards away. Ferris stepped off the pavement, and threaded his way through the scooters, buses and cars, to the other pavement, keeping low. He stopped for a moment, and counted as they ran out of the crowd and tried to cross at different points, drawing angry hoots and yells from the motorists. There were three of them. Ferris ran along the edge of the pavement, not caring about concealment any longer, dodging out onto the road where the crowd was too thick, heading down-hill towards the big intersection, where in daylight a policeman was always on traffic duty, in one of the little sentry box affairs. He would be armed. Ferris looked over his shoulder, as he dodged out past a stall on the pavement, and saw that the first of his pursuers was barely twenty feet behind. Even as he looked, the man stopped braced his legs, and raised his pistol. Ferris crouched and lunged through the crush of pedestrians at the nearest alleyway. The man fired, three shots in quick succession, and chips of stone flew off a wall and stung Ferris's face. A woman screamed, and from the corner of his eye, he saw someone fall. The sight urged Ferris into greater speed, and he passed into the alleyway as the man fired again. A ricochet screamed around the alleyway, but Ferris ran on wildly, throwing his body from one side of the alley to the other, to make a difficult target. His feet pounded painfully on the cobbles, and his lungs felt as if they would burst.

His breath came in short harsh gasps. He saw the alley open up in front of him, and realised he was running into the warehouses directly above the harbour. He noticed the high wind for the first time, as it buffeted him, almost throwing him off balance. He jinked as he came out of the alley, and ran toward the nearest warehouse. He heard the footsteps gaining on him, and a shout. At the same time came a loud report and a huge hammer hit his right arm, slamming him to the ground. He bounded up again, slipped and rolled, got his feet under him, and ran in the door of the warehouse. His arm was numb. He realised he had been shot.

He wondered why he didn't feel more pain. The warehouse was deserted, bales of copra stacked man-high in long rows. They were like little streets. Ferris ducked between two rows, and saw rough wooden stairs in the middle of the building.

He limped towards the wooden stairs. The door of the warehouse slammed shut, and a voice said, "He's got to be in here somewhere. There should be blood. I hit him, he went down like a rabbit."

Braun said, "Alright, spread out and find him."

CHAPTER 89

Ferris looked up at the stairs. The old warehouses were built very tall, and it looked a long way up the steps. He put his left hand across and felt his numb right shoulder. His palm came away greasy with blood. He looked down at the blood and felt faint. Then he saw a splash of blood on the floor behind him, and he put his left hand back up to stop the blood dripping down and leaving a trail. He sidled along, his back to the bales, and ducked between two stacks as one of the gunmen came and looked down the row.

Ferris crouched down and looked out carefully into the next row. No one in sight.

He carefully took his left hand from his shoulder and sprinkled some blood where he had just stood, then backed away in the opposite direction, into the other aisle. He listened as the man walked slowly down the aisle Ferris had been on, and looked around for a weapon. There were batons of wood everywhere, broken off the pallets that the bales stood on. He grabbed the thickest one he could see. It was about two feet long and an inch square. The man had stopped, and in the light of the windows high up the wall of the warehouse, Ferris saw the man's shadow on the space between the two stacks of bales, as he paused and studied the trail of blood spots. He heard the man suck his breath in, then the shadow's arms came up, and the man swung into the gap, and out the other side, facing the direction the blood led.

Ferris gripped the baton as firmly as he could, and swung his weight behind it. He hit the man across the left side of the head. The baton broke, and the man collapsed onto the bales of copra. Ferris ran towards the stairs. Silent in the sandals.

"Hey, Lewie," Braun called, "Get back up here. I want to ask him about the diamonds. We need him alive." A note of suspicion entered Braun's voice, "Hey Lewie, are you okay?"

Ferris put his head down and walked as fast as he could for the stairwell. The effort took him to his limit. Even jogging was beyond him now. Running feet echoed around the warehouse, as the gunmen converged. Ferris crouched in the shadow under the stairs, and when he was sure the piled bales of copra mats masked him, he started up the stairs quietly. Braun bent over Lewie below him. Clive was with him, he moved his head as scanned the warehouse. It hadn't occurred to him to look up yet.

"Jesus," Braun said. "He fell for some dumb trick. Out cold." A step creaked and Clive looked up and saw Ferris. "There he goes," Clive shouted, and fired at the stairs. Ferris tried to run again, urging his exhausted body on up the steps.

Splinters of wood and dust sprang in front of his face, and his right leg twitched and he staggered. But he shuffled on up, it was only a few more steps to the first floor. He wasn't going to make it to the second floor. Braun barked an order and Clive stopped shooting. Ferris could hear them rushing for the stairs. He reached the landing, and felt his trouser leg was wet. He looked down to see a large patch of blood on his right thigh, then saw the blood, bright red and trickling down from a tear in the leg of his jeans.

It was as if the air had been let out of him. He staggered, lunged at the doorway into an office, and the floor spun up and hit him in the face. Then it rocked viciously from one side to the other, and Ferris thought, this is it and I didn't feel a thing.

He could hear a hurt animal whine, and realised it was his own voice.

He heard them running up the stairs. I won't let them find me here, cowering like a dog, he thought savagely. He forced his left arm under his body and lifted himself off the floor and pushed with his good leg. His arm quivered from the strain, but he shoved himself across the office floor, and towards the far wall. For a moment he saw Juanita holding herself up on one arm and leg, her face pleading. Then he fell forward, turning his head to avoid the impact. Then he pushed his body over, so that he lay on his back, and he shoved again and lifted himself up into a sitting position against the wall. His lower back ached as metal dug into it, and he almost laughed. He twisted his good hip sideways and took the gun out of his belt, and put it on the floor. He could have stood them off any time before this, and now he remembered the revolver? That was a hoot. He tried to pull the bag of bullets from his pants pocket, but the effort was too much. He looked down at his right leg, and saw the red streak along the floor leading to it.

His leg jumped and quivered with shock, and even now he could not feel it. Blood still trickled out, bright red and shiny even in the weak bulb of the office. He was bleeding out before his own eyes. Ferris unbuckled the belt of his jeans one-handed and fumbled to get it under his injured leg.

He could hear them, moving around one flight of steps below, discussing something. He tightened the belt around his thigh as far as it would go, awkwardly twisted the leather into a knot, held by its own pressure. The rush of his life became a trickle. He sat back, exhausted. If he was going to die, he wouldn't make it easy for them. It was fitting, but so unfair, that he should meet his end at the hands of a bunch of bungling thugs, for the wrong reason. The perfect end to a futile life. But he might take one of them with him, if they were careless. But after what happened to Lewie, they would be very wary. It was bloody unfair. He picked up the revolver, now strangely heavy. But he could hold it in his left hand, and squeezed the safety catch in the back of the handle.

He waited. It seemed an age, and he worried that he would be too weak if they waited too long. Then at last he heard footsteps on the landing outside, and finally the top of a head appeared in the window of the office.

"Jesus H." Clive said. "There's blood everywhere." Awed, he stepped up another tread, and his head was in full view through the window, and Ferris aimed carefully and fired. The revolver was deafening in the enclosed space. The window starred, and the man ducked, and ran across the doorway with a yell of alarm. Ferris blinked, and fired again.

Ferris remembered some of his small arms training from the RAF, and aimed more carefully. He heard the man hit the first step of the next flight, and fired at where he thought the third step should be, firing blind through the board wall.

Something bumped on the stairs.

There was a long silence, except for the ringing in Ferris's ears.

"Where did he get a gun?" asked an aggrieved voice. Feet shifted on the stairs, and then a face popped up at the corner of the office window, and Ferris fired at a spot a foot below it, and the man fell out of sight with a gurgling scream, and Ferris had the satisfaction of seeing spots of blood speckle the glass, and trickle down, leaving pink streaks.

From a safe distance, Braun asked, "Can you hear me, Captain Ferris?"

"Yeah," Ferris yelled, "Come and get it, Braun." Then he remembered that he should conserve his strength, spin it out.

"Where are the diamonds, Captain," Braun said. "You know if you just tell me that, we'll leave you alone, right?"

Ferris laughed shrilly. "You stupid berk, Braun. Aziz figured out Rolle had the stuff all along. Maybe you should go to a séance, and ask him about it. Or maybe you come up here and I'll send you to hell after him."

Indistinct voices muttered below, and Ferris strained his ears as he heard feet shuffling and descending. He got tired of sitting and felt himself sliding down onto his elbow. It was so hard to hold the gun up, he wanted to go to sleep. Not die. But that was what sleep meant now. He wouldn't go easy, leave them come up without a fight, if he could take two, he could take more.

Vaguely, above the pounding in his head, he heard police sirens, getting louder.

It seemed as if the sirens cut off abruptly outside, but Ferris couldn't be sure. The room seemed to recede. The feeble light bulb was growing dimmer.

A voice on a loud hailer said, "This is the police, come out with your hands up. You have two minutes."

It was like high-altitude training. The vision went first, then the will. The hearing kept working. He had to concentrate, just to keep the gun in his hand from pointing at the floor.

A shot from below, and a burst of automatic gunfire. Then a heavier weapon, firing bursts, one every few seconds. After a lull, glass broke and gas stung his lungs and face, and Ferris coughed weakly. He heard running steps, and a voice shouted "Police, halt or I fire," and Ferris yelled "No," which came out as a whisper, and he squeezed his finger on the trigger and nothing happened.

Ferris heard the revolver drop to the floor, and booted feet pounded on the stairs, and he could just make out his left hand, open and resting on his lap. He stared at it without interest or surprise. The gun was no good without bullets anyway. He felt himself slipping away into a warm darkness, barely interrupted when a man in combats sprang through the doorway in a crouch and levelled a rifle at him. Ferris smiled and let the darkness take him.

CHAPTER 90

Ferris had a dream that he was being carried on a stretcher, that he was in an ambulance, that guys in green smocks and masks and caps were peering at him under bright lights. A disjointed dream where everybody was gripped by an urgency Ferris didn't share, he wanted to rest. He even dreamt that Hank Sanders was bending over him, speaking very earnestly. "Hang on in there Tony," he said. "We're with you all the way. Don't give up. Keep holding on kid."

The bods in the green fancy dress kept gabbling about forceps and sutures, and blood transfusions and haemorrhages, and vital signs being stable. And then they got all frenzied, and one guy with grey hair sticking out under his cap pounded Ferris on the chest with both his hands, "Come on Tony, you can do it, yeah, atta boy."

But Ferris had a lot of sleep to catch up on, it was important to repair, he had been through a lot, what did they want? Then, after a while, the blokes in green seemed to calm down, and were quite pleased, and let him alone.

After that, his dreams were normal, and when he opened his eyes he saw Doctor Hank sitting beside the hospital bed, smiling at him cheerfully. "Welcome back to the land of the living," Hank said.

"It got rocky there for a while, the blood loss from the severed artery was so bad Mr Richardson thought we would have to take your leg off. Then you looked like you were going to do a full Rip van Winkel on us. Did you hear us talking to you?"

Ferris eyed him ironically. "I should say. You interrupted one great dream."

Hank Sanders grinned at him cheerfully. "I'm sure you'll thank us for it, some day. After all, you can die any other time you like."

Ferris felt a sudden sinking of guilt at forgetting. "What about Angie – Angelique?" he asked, his throat suddenly dry. Hank said gently, "She's dead, Tony. I'm sorry. It didn't look like a serious wound but she ex – bled to death before help arrived."

"That bastard Quintero," Ferris said dully.

"Quintero's dead," Hank said. "And Bob Rolle. And Braun, and two other men. It got intense."

"And Sergeant Aziz?" Ferris asked.

"Was he injured? He seems to have disappeared, nobody has seen him." Ferris said nothing.

"Anyway," Hank said uncomfortably. He looked critically at Ferris's face. "Your cuts are beginning to heal up very nicely. And most of them may not even leave a noticeable scar. You may need a tad of grafting and plastic in some areas, but I wouldn't worry about it now."

"We'll see," Ferris said non-committally, and slept again, with a heavy heart.

The next time he awoke, Hank came to see him again.

"The government are leaning on the hospital administration. Apparently the police are in two minds as to whether to throw the book at you.

"I've made a very good case that you are not fit to be inter-viewed formally, but Superintendent Legett insists on seeing you as soon as possible. So I have been overruled. Just a quick chat, no notes to be taken.

We'll have Marlon in the room for a formal interview. I'll take Jimmy's line on that one."

Superintendent Legett sat and listened without comment while Ferris talked through the events of the fatal morning.

"Of course you can't know for sure," Legett said when Ferris finished.

Ferris felt as if the air had been taken out of his lungs. "Excuse me?" Legett smoothed his jacket absent-mindedly and continued to look Ferris in the eye.

"Sergeant Aziz was undercover investigating a gun-running and narcotics ring," Legett said.

"He was not undercover, he was in uniform," Ferris said furi-ously. "And he just didn't give a damn."

"What you said shows you that Aziz was a policeman to the

last. He wasn't going to let Quintero get away."

"You have you no proof of that," Ferris said coldly.

"Well now that you have mentioned it, we can retrieve DNA material from Quintero and match it against the evidence from the girl's body. I'm not defending him, just putting a less bleak construction on what happened."

"But you can't be serious," Ferris said.

"As usual the politicians want it to go away and so they are trying to portray the whole thing as a falling out between various overseas criminals, which covers it well enough. They are willing to accept that you acted in self-defence and let the whole matter slide if they can come up with a convincing public relations angle.

Aziz has disappeared, as far as anyone knows he is just a policeman under cover who has gone missing.

Any allegations that he acted as a vigilante or in collusion with criminals would damage the reputation of the police force."

"And you want to protect the reputation of the police," Ferris said.

"Any new revelations would mean re-opening the investigation and re-examining everything, including the ballistics of the gun with your fingerprints on it," Legett said. "Nobody wants that, think it over."

"So it's just my word," Ferris said bitterly.

Legget leaned forward and patted him on his good shoulder. "Ferris, you are overwrought from serious burn injuries and are suffering from morbid thoughts. I've probably over-stayed. I'll leave you get more rest."

Legett rose and left and Ferris stared at the door in outrage and disappointment.

The ward sister took one look at him and took his blood pressure. "I'm sorry Mr Ferris, that was too soon. Do you think a sedative would help?"

Ferris was about to say no but changed his mind.

CHAPTER 91

He was calm the following day when Davern was wheeled in to see him.

"Just a visit, to give you the news," Davern said. "An ironic symmetry, me visiting you, after what happened."

"You're still not better?" Ferris asked.

"Some minor brain damage. The doctors tell me I have a very good chance of total recovery of movement. But I have to go back home for the therapy. I thought you'd like to know, Frank Harvey is here, and wants to see you."

"Friends in time of need, eh?" Ferris said.

Davern looked severe. "Maybe so. He has paid the fine for his bribery attempt. He is willing to give you your old job back if you want it."

"Christ Almighty," Ferris said thickly, "I don't believe this is happening."

"You're in the limelight again, Tony," Davern said, "And everyone wants a piece of the action. Even the government. But the important thing is that they trust you not to blow it."

"Not that again," Ferris said. "Bill, what the hell happened with Vic? You knew something about it didn't you?"

"No Tony, I knew something was up and I feared for the consequences but I had nothing to go on. I would have gone to the authorities if I knew how crazy it would get."

"You're not with the CIA then?" Ferris felt deflated.

Davern grinned. "Don't believe everything you read about the IMF. No, I have some contacts in the State Department, they talked to some people and the rest was an educated guess from the information available and a life-time of dealing with bureaucracy."

He stopped smiling. "And then there was the letter. Vic left a letter with Marlon Enright with the melodramatic instruction that it be sent to me only in the event of his death."

"Good grief," Ferris said.

"It's a long confession, but I'll give you the Cliff Notes version. Vic and Kun had some connection with the CIA going back all the way to the Vietnam War and the CIA occasionally got them to do little jobs, sometimes it was just business contracts that naturally came their way in the shipping and construction businesses."

"So Kun isn't just a house-boy?" Ferris interrupted.

"Seems he helped run the companies. He disappeared too, and Mrs Kun.

Anyway Uncle Sam wanted peace in Colombia after 9/11 and some groups the CIA supported just weren't willing to play ball. And they were trying to source anti-aircraft missiles. So some genius came up with a half-baked scheme of sabotaging missiles and letting them out on the market to see where the trail led. The whole thing seems to have been a scam to lure this Commandante Murillo out of the mountains to where the Colombian army could capture him.

Schroeder was working on it for a year, reeling in Colonel Arnaud and putting himself near the end of the supply chain. The trouble is, Vic was then diagnosed with late stage of cancer, he had treatment but it was too advanced and the doctors told him he had maybe weeks to live. At that stage he was probably not rational and it looks like he wanted to go through with the missile deal no matter what."

"I don't know," Ferris said. "He seemed to have doubts towards the end."

"Not enough of them," Davern said tartly. "God help him, if there is a God." They were silent for a moment. "Did he say in the letter why he shot Garcia?" Davern looked at him with interest. "Did he? No, there was some rambling about he suspected Garcia of murdering Shareen but that was just wild speculation. Perhaps it was enough in his state of mind."

"I suppose," Ferris said, dissatisfied. "Arnaud got away."

"He did," Davern said. "No doubt to somewhere with no extradition treaties. People like him are survivors, and unfortunately, our leaders like to use them to pretend they have clean hands. So he lives to poison another day. But you never know, sometimes they over-stretch themselves."

322

Reuters, Malabo, Equatorial Guinea
12:10AM GMT 10 Mar 2004

French mercenary Robert Arnaud was today sentenced to 31 years in prison for plotting to overthrow the government of Equatorial Guinea. The former French Foreign Legion major was sentenced after a trial last month during which it was claimed that a number of western governments knew about the coup plans.

THE END